GUNNING FOR THE GROOM

BY
DEBRA WEBB & REGAN BLACK

Printed and bound in Spain
by CPI, Barcelona

MILLS &
BOON

First Published in Great Britain 2016
By Mills & Boon, an imprint of HarperCollins*Publishers*
1 London Bridge Street, London, SE1 9GF

© 2016 Debra Webb

ISBN: 978-0-263-91898-4

46-0316

Debra Webb, born in Alabama, wrote her first story at age nine and her first romance at thirteen. It wasn't until she spent three years working for the military behind the Iron Curtain—and a five-year stint with NASA—that she realized her true calling. Since then the *USA TODAY* bestselling author has penned more than one hundred novels, including her internationally bestselling Colby Agency series.

Regan Black, a *USA TODAY* bestselling author, writes award-winning, action-packed novels featuring kick-butt heroines and the sexy heroes who fall in love with them. Raised in the Midwest and California, she and her family, along with their adopted greyhound, two arrogant cats and a quirky finch, reside in the South Carolina Lowcountry, where the rich blend of legend, romance and history fuels her imagination.

With many thanks to Kim, for your wealth of patience, love and priceless friendship!

Chapter One

Chicago, Illinois
Wednesday, April 6, 5:30 p.m.

Victoria Colby-Camp rose from her desk and turned to her beloved window. She watched the gentle spring rain falling upon the city she would always call home. Evening lights twinkled, reminding her that it was time to go home. *Home.* A smile tugged at her lips. How had she considered for even a moment that any other city on earth could take the place of Chicago?

The most wonderful years of her life, as well as the most painful ones, had played out here. Her son was here, as were her beautiful grandchildren. No matter how warm it was or how much sun south Texas had to offer, it would never be the Windy City.

Sensing Lucas's presence, she turned, her smile widening automatically. She had loved this man for so very long. Even when her first husband, James Colby, was alive, Lucas Camp had been her dearest friend. The two of them waited many years before allowing that life-long bond to bloom into a more intimate relationship. Their wedding day had been one of the happiest of her life—in part because that momentous occasion came almost at the same time that her son found his way back to her. Jim Colby had been missing for twenty years when he came back into her life. So many miracles had happened that year.

Victoria's life had come full circle now. Her family was safe and happy and she was back in the city she loved.

"You're ready to go?" she asked, when Lucas remained in the doorway.

"No hurry. I could stand here forever just looking at you."

"Lucas, you're too kind." Even after all these years as man and wife, she could feel her pulse react to his voice, as well as the compliment. "I'm ready."

Tomorrow was another day at the Colby Agency offices and she couldn't wait to see what it held.

Chapter Two

"Morning, Frankie!"

Francesca Leone, Frankie to everyone who knew her longer than a few minutes, smiled on her way to the office she shared with two other people. It wasn't much more than a converted storage space, but she didn't mind. She'd worked in tighter quarters during her time with the navy. Life in Georgia had been good to her. Landing this job as an analyst with the Savannah Police Department gave her a healthy, long overdue sense of renewed purpose.

The past eighteen months had been an arduous journey personally and professionally. An act of terrorism and the resulting injury had ended the navy career she'd loved. For too many months, her life had narrowed to a pinpoint focus on surviving the physical trials, only to be assaulted by the emotional upheaval that followed. She hadn't realized how much of her identity had been tied to her military service until it was gone. But here she'd found a fresh start and was building a strong new foundation, far from the looming shadow of her father's name and the constant worried gaze of her mother.

Feeling her back aching a bit from yesterday's extended run, she eased into the desk chair, setting her mug of tea to the left of her computer monitor and locking her purse in the bottom drawer. When her computer booted up, she wasted no time getting to work. A string of recent robberies crossed several precincts, and it was her job to find any connections to help the detectives create a list of suspect traits.

Although the work didn't rank as high in the elements of danger and thrill as her former SEAL team missions, she found tremendous fulfillment when her contributions helped close cases.

She was making notes on the similarities between thefts when her desk phone rang, and she picked it up. "Leone."

"Francesca Leone?"

She didn't recognize the quiet male voice on the other end of the line. "Yes." Pausing to glance around when someone called her by her proper name was a purely instinctive reaction. "How can I help you?"

"I worked with your dad on several operations," the man explained.

Her heart stuttered in her chest. It never seemed to beat properly when the topic of her dad came up. She bit her lip, refusing to deliver the coarse response on the tip of her tongue.

"I considered him a friend," the caller said into the prolonged silence.

And yet she noticed he didn't offer her a name. She wasn't an idiot. Since her father, General Frank Leone, had been accused and convicted of treason, no one claimed any kind of link to him. This couldn't be an old friend who'd lost touch or wanted to leave the general's daughter with a memorable photo.

Smelling a setup, she decided the caller must be a reporter sniffing out a new story angle. Unfortunately for him, there weren't any. It had been over a year since the verdict, and her review of every available shred of information had yet to yield any solid intel that could remove the terrible stain on her dad's career. "What do you want?"

"First, I'm sorry for your loss."

Her hand fisted around the receiver, but she didn't take the bait. Her father had killed himself ten months ago, shortly after the verdict came down. While she wasn't over it, she never let that weakness show—to strangers or friends.

"I just need a few minutes of your time," the caller said. "Your father trusted me with something you should have."

Curious now, she checked the urge to slam down the phone. "All right." A face-to-face chat was the fastest way to determine if there was anything legitimate about this guy. "And your name?"

"When we meet," he replied.

She'd anticipated that response. Odds were he wouldn't have given her a real name, anyway. "How will I know you?"

"I'll know *you.*"

Of course he would. Growing up on various army bases around the world with two parents who rated the highest possible security clearances, Frankie valued caution and understood paranoia. "Fine. Meet me at Bess's Diner in the historic district in an hour." That would give her plenty of time to drive by and get her head on straight.

Fifty minutes later she sat in her car, studying a man leaning against a bike rack in front of the diner across the street. Short, graying brown hair; late forties, early fifties maybe. Assuming he was the caller, she was pleased he didn't give off the hum of urgency she'd learned to expect from reporters. While nothing about him struck her as familiar, in her experience the best covert agents were comfortable hiding in plain sight. As she climbed out of her car, she inconspicuously snapped a couple of pictures with her phone. If the man really knew her dad, he'd know about her mother's work, and her own abbreviated career, as well.

Or maybe this wasn't the guy at all, she thought when he didn't react as she crossed to his side of the street. She didn't acknowledge him as she aimed for the diner door.

"Miss Leone." His voice proved she had a few instincts left. "Thanks for following through."

"Sure." She stopped, kept her stance easy and her hands loose at her sides while she waited for him to make the next move.

"Name's John," he said, extending a hand. "Your father was a good friend of mine."

John. She nearly asked if the last name was Smith or Doe. Not that it mattered. Anyone openly admitting to being General Leone's friend had bigger secrets than a name. She suddenly wished she had something more to go on than his pictures in case she needed to track him down after this meeting. His was one of those nondescript faces that would be hard to remember. This close, she could see that his eyes were brown, as well.

Straight nose. No scars. The kind of face that would blend in with the crowd.

They walked into the diner and found a booth. She noticed he took the side facing the door. If this guy didn't have covert operations training, he'd read all the right books. When the waitress approached, John ordered coffee and Frankie ordered hot tea with honey. She wasn't in the mood for anything, just wanted something to keep her hands busy while she listened to whatever John had to say.

"Your dad and I go way back," he said. "I count Frank and Sophia as my closest friends."

Frankie couldn't hide the unpleasant chill she felt at the mention of her mother's name. She hadn't spoken to the woman since her father's funeral. The once proud and strong Leone family had been fractured beyond any hope of reconciliation.

"You still on the outs with her?"

"Why does it matter?" Keeping things compartmentalized was practically a Leone genetic trait. Frankie's personal life didn't intersect with her professional life. She never discussed her parents with anyone. Clearly, this man knew the family dynamic, though the situation was fairly obvious. Her mother lived and worked in Seattle, while Frankie lived and worked here, as far away as possible. She still periodically checked for jobs in Key West, Florida. There were questions she knew she'd never get answered, so Frankie clung to the simple truth that distance preserved the peace.

"It doesn't." John leaned back as the coffee and tea arrived. When the waitress walked away, he continued. "Look, I know you were close to him and I know he was proud of your career."

"Thanks?" His well-informed statements didn't put her at ease. They only made her more uncomfortable. She stirred a spoonful of honey into her tea and went on the offensive, eager to hurry this along. "Any decent search of the internet could give you that much," she said. "When I was first attached to the SEAL team, they did a write-up in the local paper, got a glowing quote from him." She set the spoon aside. "Tell me why we're here."

The man's brown eyes were sharp as he studied her. "Because your father was a hero and someone turned him into a scapegoat."

Whatever his real name, she agreed with John on that much. Her biggest regret was that she hadn't been there for her dad during the ordeal. Injured or not, she resented that she'd never had a chance to tell him she believed he was innocent, or that she loved him despite the stones thrown from all sides. There hadn't been any tender farewell phone call or last words in a note. When her father made a decision, he followed through. He'd killed himself shortly after the guilty verdict, before she'd regained her ability to walk unassisted.

The memories of hearing the news swamped her and she raised her tea to her lips, the cup shaking slightly. Sophia, with no trace of emotion, had explained her husband's suicide and told Frankie what would come next regarding services, the will and estate, and the rest of it. In the days immediately following the tragedy, Frankie had tried to talk to her, hoping to make sense of the senseless. Her mother had been too wrapped up in the legalities and had quickly moved on as though a lifetime of marriage and family had meant nothing.

"He'd be happy to see you strong and healthy again."

John's quiet voice brought Frankie back to the present with an unpleasant jolt.

"I like to think so." She carefully placed the cup in the saucer.

"You've done well reestablishing yourself."

"Uh-huh." She toyed with the handle of her cup. "You said you had something for me?" She didn't want to talk about her father or her new life. Not with a therapist, not with a friend, and definitely not with a stranger.

"Yes." He reached into the pocket inside his sport coat and fished out a small gray envelope. "This matches a safe-deposit box in Tucson," he explained, his voice no more than a whisper. With one finger he pushed the envelope, which presumably held a key, halfway across the table. "No one mattered to your dad as much as you did. He can't tell you in his own words, but the answers you're after are there."

Answers. Frankie blinked away the rush of tears blurring her vision. She'd expected dog tags, or maybe her dad's class ring from West Point. Answers were a thousand times better. She hadn't been prepared for someone who believed her father had been railroaded, and wanted to help her ferret out the truth. She caught her trembling lower lip between her teeth and fought valiantly for composure. There would be time for emotions later. "How do you know what answers I'm after?" she asked, using his phrase. "Dad's case is closed." It was hard to believe this could be the break she needed to clear her father's name.

John left the envelope on the table, pulling his fingers back and drumming them on the rim of his coffee cup, watching her closely. "The case is officially closed, but it's nowhere near done for you. You take that and you'll have a chance to right a wrong."

She couldn't tear her eyes away from that slim gray envelope. "Why don't *you* do what's necessary with the information?"

He shook his head. "This is for family. I'm just the messenger."

Frankie sucked in a breath. He couldn't mean what those words implied. She'd learned that her mother's testimony had come into play during her father's trial, though Frankie had never understood why it hadn't helped. Sophia refused to discuss the matter, which left Frankie with more questions than answers at every turn.

"From where I'm sitting I'd say you got that stubbornness and tenacity from your dad," John said, urging her on in his quiet way.

Frankie covered the envelope with her hand, pulling it closer to her side of the table. Either she hadn't been as discreet as she should have been or John had the depth of access that went with the cloak-and-dagger routine. She thought of the inquiries she'd made after her father's funeral. All of them had turned into frustrating dead ends. Hope surged through her that this key would unlock the secrets about General Leone's final missions overseas.

She peered into the envelope before tucking it into her pocket. Taking it didn't mean she had to do anything about it. She studied John's inscrutable face. "How can I reach you?"

"You can't." His gaze moved systematically around the coffee shop. "My being here, even for a few hours, puts you in jeopardy. This has to be our only communication."

She gave a short nod as her mind reeled. This man was the first person who showed any sign of agreeing with her about her father's innocence.

John pulled out his wallet and tossed a ten-dollar bill onto the table. "You don't have to go and you don't have to be in a hurry," he said. "In fact, I recommend you take some time and think it through. What's inside the box isn't going anywhere."

She knew she had to go. She couldn't ignore this opportunity. A flight to Arizona was nothing in the bigger picture. Her family had imploded under the treason accusation. Knowing her father had died disgraced and alone, Frankie still felt an ache in her heart. If there was any information that would cast a light of truth into those dark final days and clear his name, she meant to find it. "I'll go." As soon as she could arrange a few days off work.

Getting to Tucson was the easy part of the equation. There was no way to tell what would come next until she'd seen the contents of the box for herself. After the last lead dried up a few months ago, she'd been less aggressive in her private inquiry, resigned that she might never learn who'd set up her dad. Cautiously pushing hope aside, she considered that this meeting and the trip to open a safe-deposit box could be nothing more than an elaborate ruse or distraction, though she didn't know who would gain by such a tactic.

"What you discover could make things worse," John warned.

"Thanks," she whispered, stunned by the dramatic shift her morning had taken. The key in its envelope felt like a stick of old dynamite in her pocket, shaky, volatile and ready to blow her life apart without any notice. "Unless you have more insight, I guess I'll figure that out when I get there."

"Whatever you decide, be careful." He slid to the edge of the booth. "The people who took down your dad have a long reach and violent habits."

She resisted the urge to try to enlist his help. He'd clearly done all he was going to do. "I can take care of myself." She'd trained hard to earn her place as a cultural liaison with the navy SEALs. Her well-honed skills and habit of excellence hadn't been affected by the back injury that wrecked her military career.

"I hope so." He stood up. "Your dad always wanted the best for you."

Frankie believed that was true. She watched her father's mysterious friend leave, disappointed when he walked out of view. She'd hoped to catch him getting into a car. Staring into the tea cooling in her cup, she weighed the pros and cons of each possible next step. Did the cons even matter? Every decision in life came with a price; every option held some risk.

Her gaze shifted to the window and the bustling activity on the street outside. She had a new career as a crime analyst. She enjoyed it. Her life was stable and she gained satisfaction in the work and being involved with the community. And she knew herself well enough to know that part of her fulfillment came from finding justice for victims.

The whole truth wouldn't bring her father back, but it could open the door for justice and potentially restore his reputation. He'd served honorably and deserved to be remembered for the way he'd protected national interests, as well as the soldiers under his command.

She pulled out her phone and researched flight options. By the time she got back to the office, she had her explanation ready and a realistic idea of the days off she would need to run down this lead.

Tucson, Arizona
Friday, April 8, 8:40 a.m.

FRANKIE CHECKED OUT of her hotel room and left the cool lobby for the warm sunshine of the Arizona springtime. Her boss had waved away her vague explanation of a family crisis and granted her time off through the end of next week. It helped that Frankie could do much of her work long-distance if necessary. She'd gotten on a plane last night. Waiting for morning had proved one of the hardest things she'd done in a while.

Hailing a cab, she gave the driver the bank address as her mind raced yet another lap around the same tired circuit that had plagued her since she left the diner yesterday. Every time she reviewed what she'd learned since her father's death, the timing of the charges and the sequence of events, she bumped smack into her mother's uncharacteristic behavior and apathy. Her mom was hiding something; Frankie just couldn't guess what or why. Hopefully, whatever her father had stashed in this safe-deposit box would take her a step closer to the truth.

Sophia, as a military analyst for the CIA, had the clearance access and professional connections to support the general's defense. At the very least, she should've given Frankie a better explanation for how things had spiraled out of control. Her injury and recovery weren't a reliable excuse any longer. Neither was the nonsense about Frankie's career being negatively impacted by her father's misdeeds.

He was *innocent*. Whatever had happened during those last few months in Afghanistan, Frankie knew her father hadn't betrayed his oath to his country, and she meant to prove it.

It was a relief when the cab stopped and she had to think about paying the fare. Taking her suitcase and the backpack serving as her laptop bag and purse, she headed inside the bank, then paused to look around. She didn't know why her dad had chosen this facility. They'd never lived on the nearby post, though she was sure both her parents had been here at one time or another, since Fort Huachuca was home to the Army Intelligence Center.

Frankie offered a polite smile as she showed her key and requested access to the safe-deposit box. Her palms were damp as she followed the teller toward the vault, the wheels of her suitcase rattling over the marble floor. When both keys had been inserted into the respective locks, the teller pulled out the slim drawer and walked toward a small alcove.

"Just draw the curtain back when you're done," she said. "And we'll replace the box for you."

"Got it. Thanks," Frankie said as the woman walked away.

She stared at the closed safe-deposit box on the table, her feet rooted in place. Now she had second thoughts. Her dad had left her something here, something he hadn't trusted to her mom's care. The truth of her father's downfall could very well be inside.

Frankie had come this far; she had to see it through. One step, then another, and she rested her trembling fingers on the cool metal box. John's warning echoed in her head. She believed with every beat of her heart that her father had been a scapegoat. Whoever had gone to those lengths to avoid the consequences obviously didn't want to be exposed.

If she looked inside, there would be no going back, no way to undo whatever she learned. Holding back or walking away—those weren't valid options, either. Not for Frankie.

"Don't have to like it, just have to do it." She whispered one of the favorite motivators from her SEAL training as she opened the box. She didn't have to act on it; she just had to know.

An envelope marked Top Secret was no surprise, though surely the evidence against her father should rate a higher clearance level. Under the envelope she found a flash drive, half a map and two passports. Slipping the drive into her pocket, she discovered both passports had her mother's picture beside different names and birth dates.

Assuming John had gathered the evidence in this box on her father's behalf, Frankie wondered how he'd gotten the passports away from her mom. Seduction or burglary? A small voice in her head suggested this field trip was a setup, and Frankie's temper flared in bitter denial. John was a wild card, definitely, but she would not leap to any conclusions until she'd exhausted every lead.

Frankie tamped down her frustration. The attention an outburst would bring was the last thing she needed here. She tucked the fake passports into her backpack and kept going.

A smaller envelope held her father's dog tags, and her heart stuttered in her chest. She looped the cool metal chain around her fingers. When she was little, her dad had often let her wear his tags when she played dress up with his boots and uniforms. If she'd had any doubts about John's claims, the dog tags dispelled them. With care, she poured the tags and chain back into the envelope and added it to her backpack. Only one item remained, a small jewelry box covered in worn black velvet.

Her fingers curled back into her palm. That box didn't belong here. Her father had kept it on top of his dresser in the bedroom. The ring inside came out only for official functions.

Frankie popped open the lid, praying she was wrong, that this was something else. It wasn't. She bit her lip, staring down at her father's class ring from West Point. Snapping the box shut, she pressed it close to her heart, as if somehow that would make everything that had gone wrong right again.

This ring was central to her image of her dad, of the honor, dedication and commitment he'd given to every endeavor. She opened the box again, smoothing her finger over the heavy gold band. All her life she'd watched him, captivated by the stories he told as he polished it for special occasions. She'd caught him once just holding it, dazed, when he returned from a deployment. Her mother had told her later that one of his classmates had died.

When had he stored it here and why? Frankie couldn't think of a single answer to either question.

"I'll figure it out, Dad. I promise," she murmured, sliding the ring box into a zippered inner pocket of the backpack.

Finally, she unwound the red string tying the large envelope closed and shook out the papers inside. After-action reports were on top. She skimmed each page, noting the details that weren't blacked out. The dates and locations matched what she already knew of General Leone's final months in Afghanistan.

She forgot everything else when she found the transcript of her mother's statement about his activities in Afghanistan. Icy dread tickled the nape of Frankie's neck and she steeled herself against the involuntary shiver. Sophia Leone had created a report that didn't support her husband at all. She'd tossed him under the proverbial bus.

What the hell? Her parents had *always* been a team. From Frankie's first memory they'd been affectionate and happy, devoted to each other. They'd embraced life, taught her everything she valued about being in love and being loving. They'd exemplified respect, support and drive as they went after their individual and mutual goals together.

How could Sophia turn on him?

Frankie blinked back a red haze of fury as she read the cold, sterile statements that tied her father to criminal actions. Fumed over the *implications* that he'd sabotaged missions for personal gain. The report did nothing to corroborate General Leone's account of critical operations. Good grief, in light of this statement, no other verdict than guilty had been possible.

Frankie pulled out the band holding her hair in a bun and worked her fingers over her scalp. At least she understood why her mother had refused to discuss any of this. Frankie wound her hair back up into place as she read the terrible statement again.

Two dates stood out to her, dates when she knew her father had been at the Bagram Airfield, when her mother stated he'd been in Kabul. She checked her watch, wishing she had time to boot up her computer and check the flash drive here. Now that she had a lead, she was eager to chase it down. With any luck the drive would have more details she could assess and pull into a cohesive case against her mother. No wonder her dad had killed himself. Someone had set him up so well with the treason charge that even his wife had turned on him.

"And I was useless," Frankie whispered to herself. During his trial she'd been stuck in a hospital bed while surgeons debated the best treatment for her spine injury.

She fisted the papers in her hands as something inside her shattered. John had warned her and he'd been right. Appalling as this was, the answers gave her a target. Sophia owed her more than another weak evasion. Frankie had asked her mother point-blank about the allegations and charges against her dad, and the answer had been to trust the legal process and keep believing in him.

Frankie had obediently complied and the process had failed her father. Along with a helpful boost from her mother, apparently. Even after the verdict, her mom had insisted things would work out, that her father wasn't done fighting. Now it was obvious those assurances had merely been more lies and platitudes to cover Sophia's part in the witch hunt.

Why? Who gained? Her mother had put the life in-
surance and other assets into a trust for Frankie, and
turned her attention to a new private security business
out in Seattle, Washington.

After stuffing the papers back into the envelope,
Frankie secured the tie, suddenly uncertain. Was it
safer to leave the evidence here or take it with her?

John had given her one key. Typically, safe-deposit
boxes were issued with two. He'd told her that his visit,
brief and cryptic as it was, put her at risk. She hadn't
done anything to hide her travel plans, so if someone
were watching, whoever it was could easily conclude
she'd been here. She decided to take everything and
create a new hiding place.

John must have gathered the legal and personal
items on her dad's orders. Frank would've known his
daughter would never buy in to the treason charges.
He wanted her to clear his name—Frankie felt it like
a flame deep in her heart. If he believed in her to do
that, why kill himself?

Confused and hurt, she couldn't quite see the next
step beyond leaving Arizona. Her gut instinct was to
fly out to Seattle and confront her mother. Just the
thought had Frankie braced for a battle. Showing up
in a fit of anger wouldn't help. Her mom was far too
composed, too deft at sliding around the truth for a
direct attack.

There was no way Frankie could do this until she
calmed down, planned it out. She needed to go through
the flash drive and it would be smart to get a second
opinion on the documents, just in case John was playing her.

She thought about the dog tags and the West Point

ring as she rubbed her knuckles across the scars and tight muscles at her back. If that was the case, she had to give him points for knowing his target.

"Think, Frankie." There were always options. Her military training had changed her way of thinking. As a SEAL she'd embraced the clever and creative strategies required for a small force to succeed when outnumbered by a larger, better equipped opponent.

She smiled as she made her decision. It was time to visit another friend of her father's. A friend, unlike John, she could be sure of, based on her personal experience. After the safe-deposit box went back into the vault, she booked herself on the next available flight to Chicago.

Victoria Colby-Camp could help her.

Chapter Three

Frankie had fond memories of visiting with "Aunt Victoria," though it was an honorary title. Somewhere in a box she had yet to unpack in Savannah, there was a framed photo of her with Victoria at a Fourth of July barbecue. When news of her father's suicide flooded the media, Victoria had been one of the few people who'd sent her a sympathy card.

The evidence of her mother's betrayal burned through her system as Frankie sat in Victoria's reception area. She wanted advice on how to proceed. Sophia couldn't be allowed to get away with this.

Frankie shifted in the chair. It was a nice enough piece of furniture, for someone who hadn't spent too many hours on airplanes recently. She needed to take a break to stretch and let her back recover, but she had no time to waste. All the physical therapy in the world couldn't change the simple fact that she wouldn't rest easy until this was over.

The receptionist stationed outside Victoria's office directed Frankie to the coffee service, and she had barely declined when Victoria opened her office door.

Frankie smiled. The woman still looked as regal as she remembered. Though her dark hair was now streaked with gray, Victoria remained beautiful.

"Frankie, what a pleasure to see you again." She crossed the room and gave her a warm hug. "It's been far too long. How are you feeling?"

"Fit as ever, though the navy docs didn't clear me for active duty."

"That's frustrating," Victoria said, guiding her into the office and closing the door behind them. "Have a seat and tell me how things are going. I hear you joined the Savannah Police Department."

Frankie smiled. "As an analyst," she replied, though she was sure Victoria knew that, as well. It would've been more surprising if Victoria hadn't checked into her background. "It's good work and I enjoy it."

"But not as exciting as your previous career."

"Few things are," Frankie agreed.

"Your message sounded quite urgent," Victoria said, concern in her eyes.

"It is. Thanks for seeing me."

Frankie had rehearsed the talking points on the flight and refined them in the cab. Now her stomach clenched. Maybe she should've taken more time to review the flash drive first. No, the statement alone was damaging enough to enlist Victoria's opinion and guidance. "I need some advice," she began.

Just start at the beginning and walk through it step by step, she coached herself. She was more convinced than ever that her mother had been part of the plan to railroad her father. What baffled her was why. And rushing straight to that conclusion without the backstory would get her nowhere. Victoria was her last chance.

"I'm glad you came to me," the older woman said, her voice soothing.

"You knew my parents well?"

She nodded. "I knew them both, long before they married."

"Did you follow their careers?"

"Not particularly. Mainly what they shared in Christmas cards or when your father made the news." Victoria reached for her cup of coffee. "For his successes."

Frankie rubbed her palms on her jeans, wishing she'd worn the one dress she'd packed for this trip. Her soft green sweater set felt too casual next to Victoria's polished style, and Frankie felt absolutely outclassed by the elegantly furnished office. Everything screamed experience and expertise. Which was why she was here. "I don't know who else to turn to," she admitted. "I found evidence that my mother lied to me about my father's case, and probably several other things, as well," she added, thinking of the passports.

Victoria set her coffee aside. "What sort of evidence?"

Frankie pulled the statement from the envelope in her backpack. Handing it over, she explained, "Sophia had a choice and she willingly contributed to his guilty verdict."

"Sophia?" Victoria echoed with an arching eyebrow. She studied Frankie over the top of the document. "You actually believe that."

"I've suspected it for some time," Frankie replied. "You're holding the proof."

Victoria picked up a pair of glasses and set them in place to read the statement. When she finished, she placed the papers gingerly on her desktop, as though they might explode. "How did you get this?"

"A friend of Dad's came to see me. He gave me a key to a safe-deposit box and warned me the contents could be dangerous. That document was one of several items inside."

"Go on."

"False passports with Sophia's picture, a flash drive with more information that connects her to my father's death, and other personal items from Dad."

"Did you recognize this friend?"

"No," Frankie admitted. She pulled out her phone and brought up the pictures she'd taken at the diner. "Do you? He told me he was close to my parents."

Victoria adjusted her glasses and carefully examined each photo. "I've never seen him. You should speak with your mother and verify your source and the accuracy of this statement."

"I have." Frankie swallowed her impatience. "Well, I haven't asked her about this man, but we've talked about Dad. Argued really. Her answers weren't clear or helpful. Or even honest, in light of all this."

"Frankie. You've been part of covert operations. It's a world of smoke and mirrors. You know reports rarely give the full picture of any situation."

"You won't help me get to the truth?"

Victoria sighed. "What are you asking me to do?"

Frankie wanted to get up and pace or scream, or otherwise release some of the frustration building inside her. Instead, she remained in the chair. "I have nightmares about my dad's downfall and death. He wasn't a traitor." She stopped and swallowed when her voice started to crack. "I can't believe it, not about the man I knew."

"Frankie—"

"I know I'm looking at this with a daughter's eyes. I talked with Sophia several times when he was accused and after they found him guilty. She was too composed through the whole mess. Never a tear or any sign of worry. What kind of wife doesn't worry when her husband is accused of treason?" Frankie paused, pulling on the tattered edges of her composure. Losing it would get her nowhere. "Sophia never gave me anything but the same tired reply—trust the process."

"It's sound advice."

"It didn't work." Frankie left out the irrelevant piece that trusting a legal process included zero comfort factor. "It was a self-serving answer," she argued. "Suicide isn't part of any fair or just process. How did he even manage that with the security team that must have been surrounding him?"

Frankie took a moment to compose herself. "Aunt Victoria, I have a new job, I'm making a new life, but I haven't moved on. Not really." She scooted to the edge of the chair. "I need the answers. I deserve to know what happened and who I can trust. There's no way I can move forward until I clear up the past."

"I understand how that feels," Victoria said, her words heavy with the wisdom of experience. "But leaping to conclusions will only hurt you. Others, too, most likely. I've known your mother a very long time. Her word should be enough for you."

"What word? She won't explain herself," Frankie

pressed, desperate for Victoria's help. "My father's been silenced. I want to understand what happened."

"You want revenge," Victoria stated bluntly. "Who will you target and what price will you pay?"

Frankie forced herself to calm down, taking a deep breath and releasing it slowly. "My dad isn't a traitor. Even dead, he doesn't deserve to bear that notoriety." She fidgeted in the chair, wishing again she could get up and pace. "Apparently the friend of his who found me yesterday is the only person who agrees with me."

"You don't know that." Victoria tapped the papers in front of her. "This statement doesn't prove your mother was complicit if there *was* a concerted effort to ruin your father. She had to make an accurate report. Her position and her integrity required it."

"It's *not* accurate. Dad was in Bagram when she stated he was in Kabul." Frankie hadn't felt so helpless since she'd woken in a hospital bed with no feeling in her legs. She needed an ally. Just as the candid support of the medical team had empowered her recovery, one trustworthy partner would make all the difference now.

Victoria's eyes lit with troubled interest. "How can you be sure?"

"Because I was there. I saw him." She nearly cheered when Victoria's brow furrowed as she reviewed the report again.

"Let me see the passports."

Frankie handed them over and endured the small eternity awaiting Victoria's response.

The older woman reached for her phone and pressed a button. "Ask Aidan to join us, please." She replaced the handset and met Frankie's gaze. "Aidan Abbot is one of my best investigators. No one's better with documents or ferreting through layers of security or fraud. He can tell us if the passports are fakes."

"How could they possibly be real?"

Victoria flipped through the pages. "Frankie, you know there are times when an established alias is necessary. Or all of this could be an elaborate setup to turn you against her."

"I've already been against her for months. We haven't spoken since his funeral." An event that had been postponed a full month so Frankie could attend. Too bad it hadn't made anything easier. The delay had only given her mother more time to pretend life with her spouse hadn't existed. The brutal lack of emotion had shocked Frankie. Still did. If Sophia so willingly cut out a husband, losing a daughter probably hadn't registered on her scale. Everything Frankie thought she knew about love and family had been turned upside down by a disaster someone had manufactured. Hurting, her blood beating cold in her veins, Frankie fixed her gaze on the window and the city glittering beyond it.

"Let's assume you're right," Victoria continued. "It would require serious planning and resources to systematically take down a man of your father's standing. To create evidence strong enough to ruin his career and push him to suicide without leaving a trail would be almost impossible these days."

A knock sounded on the door. Frankie turned to see it open and a man with thick, dark hair in need of a trim, and vivid, cobalt-blue eyes, enter.

"Aidan Abbot, Francesca Leone."

"A pleasure," he said, shaking her hand.

There was a trace of Ireland in his voice and it sent her pulse into some foolish feminine skipping. He probably got that all the time, she thought, irritated with her reaction. "Likewise," she replied.

"Francesca's a lovely name."

The way he said it made her want to sigh and forget why she'd come here. She cleared her throat. "Call me Frankie." She'd been named in honor of both her grandmother and father. Her full name had always felt too exotic. "Frankie" was a better fit for the tough and proud little girl who'd spent her life aspiring to be like her dad.

When he was seated, Victoria handed Aidan the passports. "Frankie has some concerns about these."

Frankie watched him examine them, involuntarily admiring his hands, as well as his attention to detail. More annoying was the difficulty she seemed to be having with the fact that he wore some appealing cologne that reminded her of the Pacific Coast on a clear, sunny day.

"One woman with two names implies that one of them is a fake," he said after a moment.

"Both are fakes," Frankie stated firmly.

Aidan arched a dark eyebrow, and his mouth quirked up at one corner. Frankie felt a warm tremor just under her skin. It was a relief when he turned that bold blue gaze toward his boss. "If there's no question, why call me?"

"There may be good reason those passports were issued. Would you mind taking a closer look into the names and any travel records?"

"Not at all." He tapped the closed passports against his knee. "How much time do I have?"

"A few hours at most," Victoria said, her eyes cool. "Frankie wants the information yesterday."

Frankie couldn't sit still a moment longer. Her back ached from the travel and the tension. She wanted the freedom and clarity of a quick run but settled for pacing the width of the office. The patience she'd relied on in the field and in her work didn't translate to this situation. "That's a start. Can you tell me what sort of legal action we can take?" She shoved her hands into her pockets.

"Why don't you give me what you have?" Victoria suggested. "Let my team investigate while you go back to Savannah. We're good, objective and fast. I'll call you as soon as we know something."

Frankie shook her head, her ponytail swinging. "I'm not sitting this one out." She'd been relegated to the sidelines too often since her injury. While she couldn't say she knew her parents better than anyone—the opposite appeared to be true—she wouldn't deal with this long-distance via secondhand reports. She wanted to see her mother's face when the truth finally came out.

"Then why did you come to me?"

She felt Aidan's gaze on her as Victoria waited for an answer. Frankie wished she could ask him to leave. She didn't want to share the ugly Leone family secrets with a stranger. "For support and guidance," she replied, keeping her gaze on Victoria. "I took vacation through next week. I'll go to Seattle and confront my mother about that statement while you investigate the passports and other documents. Won't that be enough time to know if we have a case against her?"

"Frankie—"

"I'll tell her I want to reconcile, to mend the rift," Frankie explained. "Hopefully, she'll buy it and open up. If that isn't enough, I'll ask for a job. Anything to lower her defenses."

Victoria glanced at Aidan. "Frankie's mother owns Leo Solutions, a security firm in Seattle."

"Cyber or personal?" Aidan inquired.

"Both, if I understand the setup," Frankie answered. "She and her business partner built it on the backs of their government careers." Regretting her burst of bitterness, she plowed on. "Once I'm out there, I thought I'd worm my way past her defenses. With your agency working this behind the scenes and me working on-site, I'm sure we can get to the truth quickly."

"Frankie." Victoria leaned back in her chair, her reading glasses in her hands. "Going out there with the intent to deceive your mother is a terrible risk."

Frankie paused, studying her. "I've worked undercover before." She couldn't afford to think of this as anything other than a mission. If her mother could ignore the bonds of family, so could she.

"That's not what I mean. Please, sit down."

Reluctantly, Frankie returned to her chair. She didn't want to endure a lecture on discretion or family unity in front of Aidan, but it seemed Victoria wasn't giving her a choice.

"Since I clearly can't stop you from going, I'm sending Aidan with you."

"Pardon me?" Having braced for the lecture, Frankie needed a moment to digest the actual statement. "That's not necessary." She shot a quick look in Aidan's direction. "Can't he research the passports and documents from here?"

"I want him on-site," Victoria said. "You shouldn't be out there alone."

"I'll keep you updated—" Frankie began.

"I know you will," she interrupted. "That isn't the point. I refuse to take any chances with your safety." She turned to her computer monitor, and her hands rattled on her keyboard for a moment. Then she met Frankie's gaze with a thoughtful expression. "Assuming your mother's statement is legitimate, your search will likely lead to someone better prepared to retaliate than offer up a confession."

Yes, Frankie was angry and she was hurt. That didn't make her a fool. "I've considered that and taken precautions." She didn't want or need a babysitter. The fewer witnesses to her family embarrassments, the better.

"Good," Victoria replied.

"You know I can protect myself."

"This isn't up for debate, Frankie. I've known you since you were a child. You'll give your mom a call and let her know you're coming out for a visit. We'll get Aidan an interview with your mother's company by Monday afternoon." She held up a hand when Frankie started to protest again. "I'm sure he'll be hired. As former Interpol, he knows his way around security and covert operations. Once the details are settled, the two of you can work together."

Call her mom? She wasn't a teenager caught smoking in the girls' room. Her mother wouldn't believe Frankie suddenly had an urge for mother-daughter bonding time, and Frankie wanted the element of surprise. "That's not—"

Victoria cut her off. "I *insist* that you have someone watching your back." Standing, she came around the desk and pulled Frankie to her feet for another hug. When she let go, her eyes were misty. "Legal debacles and strained relationships aside, try to focus on the things your parents did right. They gave you their love and affection through a wonderful childhood. Both of them raised a strong, independent woman."

Frankie did her best to muster a smile as the grief sliced through her. She'd questioned every nuance of her life lately, wondering what to believe about her parents and how that impacted her view of herself. Cornerstones of her upbringing seemed little more than loose theories in light of recent events. "I'll be careful," she repeated, not wanting to lie to Victoria.

"I hope your mother helps you find what you're after." The woman's smile was sad. "Would you like us to stay while you make the call?"

Frankie hesitated, but only for a moment. If this investigator would be trailing her around Seattle, he might as well get a taste of what he was in for. He'd be combing through her family's secrets soon enough.

AIDAN DID HIS best impersonation of an invisible man while Frankie spoke briefly with her mother. It was clear she wasn't happy about Victoria's insistence on the task, but his boss was difficult to outmaneuver. Her voice cool and her face pale, Frankie managed a polite exchange, excusing herself from the office the moment it was over.

"The woman's a spitfire," he observed, closing the door behind her. He admired her grit. Not to mention her lush sable hair, expressive dark eyes and that generous mouth. Even without the surname Leone tipping him off, her perfect posture implied a military background. Although with those cheekbones and long limbs, she could've passed as a model. If she wasn't a new client, he might have asked her out for a drink.

"I'm to get myself hired and then what?"

"Find a way to stay close to her. If the documents are real, she'll be a target as soon as the person pulling the strings learns she found them. I want you there. You're the best at unraveling knots like this one."

That was Victoria's way of saying she suspected fraud, his primary focus during his time with Interpol. "Do I report to you only?" The freedom and case variation were nice, though his favorite part of being a Colby investigator was the concise chain of command.

"Yes, please. I don't care for the way she was led to what she considers proof positive her mother willfully ended her father's career. The only thing I believe about the man who dropped this in her lap is that digging for the truth could get her hurt. Or worse."

"Yes, ma'am." Aidan waited for the other shoe to drop.

"General Leone was an excellent strategist," Victoria said, almost to herself. "Frankie takes after him. She's smart and highly skilled, but I'm afraid she's rejecting the most logical explanation. It's understandable under the circumstances. I'm sure you heard the temper and need for vengeance in her voice."

He bobbed his chin. "Hard to miss."

"Please tread lightly," Victoria continued. "As you meet Sophia Leone and work out the details with

Frankie, keep an open mind. You might be the only one who can."

"Of course." At least in this case he wasn't at the center of the storm battering the family. There was a great deal of comfort in that.

"I'll send you her file for review," Victoria said, leaning back against her desk. "The most pertinent fact is Frankie's service as a cultural liaison with the navy SEALs."

That gave Aidan pause. Though it was the only post women could fill on those operations, very few had the tenacity and fortitude to do so. "She looks a little young to have hit her twenty years already."

"She suffered a serious injury while her team was in a convoy that left her paralyzed for a time. Inconveniently, her recovery coincided with her father's problems. Surgery and months of rehab got her walking again, but the navy retired her for medical reasons."

That explained some of the anger, Aidan thought. He knew firsthand it was never easy to relinquish control when life dealt out an unexpected detour.

"She claims she's fit," Victoria added, "but I'm not entirely convinced."

"Duly noted," Aidan said. Healthy and able-bodied weren't the same as fit for service. If this case turned into a danger zone, he'd offer protection first and apologize for any insult later.

"Expect her to try to shake you."

He'd already reached the same assumption. "Do you think she'll blow my cover?"

"No. She wants the truth too much to take that chance. That doesn't mean she'll cooperate with you."

"She's not my first challenging case," he reminded his boss.

Victoria blessed him with an amused smile. "I was right to call you in on this one."

"I'll see her safely through whatever happens," he promised.

"Thank you. It's the least I owe her parents."

A firm knock sounded on the door and Victoria signaled for him to open it. He did, finding Frankie on the other side, her dark eyes sparking with impatience. She marched right past him to confront Victoria. "Your receptionist tells me she's booking us on a flight to Seattle tomorrow."

Aidan took a position that gave him the best view of the inevitable fireworks.

"That's right," Victoria said. "I'm not taking any chances, and you told me you didn't want to waste any more time."

"I need to go home first," Frankie replied. "I'll travel from there."

Victoria folded her arms across her chest. "Do you think your mother hasn't kept tabs on you? Traveling from Savannah gains you nothing. Sophia and I are friends. She might very well call me for advice about *you*. We've both had challenges with children."

Frankie didn't cooperate with the clear dismissal. "That's not it," she protested.

Victoria tapped her reading glasses against her palm. "Are you having second thoughts?"

Brick, meet wall, Aidan thought, watching the two women.

"No."

The internal battle Frankie was obviously waging dragged out for another long minute. She still didn't explain herself. Aidan caught Victoria's eye. "Frankie." He waited for her to turn his way. "Any gear you might want you can borrow from us. I'll show you the way."

Behind Frankie, he caught Victoria's relieved expression when the younger woman finally agreed, slinging her backpack over one shoulder and retrieving her suitcase. When they were alone in the elevator, he felt a modicum of tension ease. He asked what she expected to find in Seattle.

"I'm trying not to expect much of anything," she answered.

"That limits the potential disappointment." He'd walked through life a long while with that mind-set. "And the potential happiness."

She sighed, her hand flexing on the strap of her backpack. "I know I must sound like an overgrown toddler on the verge of a tantrum."

That wasn't what he saw at all. He saw a woman in pain, confused and wary. "I don't know enough about your situation to have an opinion."

She looked up at him and laughed, the startled, bright sound bouncing around the elevator car and spilling out as the doors parted. "Oh, you have an opinion," she said. "Maybe I'll ask for it later."

He didn't want to be fascinated by this new client with a huge chip on her shoulder, yet he couldn't quite stop himself. She exuded stubbornness, and he couldn't imagine what kind of strength required to overcome her injuries.

As an investigator, he was naturally curious about

all the things she hadn't said, but it certainly didn't help his concentration that she made such an art form out of walking.

Chapter Four

Aidan watched Frankie carefully choose a laptop and a cell phone to back up the devices she'd brought along. Together they decided on surveillance gear, both visual and audible, proving she understood the tech. He nearly laughed out loud, thinking he'd met the perfect woman. It was a relief that he couldn't act on the undercurrent of attraction teasing his senses. He was more than capable of working with beautiful women as partners and clients, and he'd sworn off ever bridging the gap between business and personal again.

As she examined some newer button cameras, he picked up a surveillance-signal jammer. When they moved toward the available weapons, he selected a 9 mm semiautomatic and a .22 revolver as backup, along with ammunition. Frankie shied away from all of them.

"No?" How was it possible an American with her background didn't carry a gun?

She shook her head, her pretty eyes clouded with something he couldn't quite label. "I prefer knives."

Knives? Was that some strange holdover from her navy days? "You brought knives? We're flying commercial."

"It'll be okay," she replied confidently. "I flew commercial to get here."

"Can I see them?"

She arched one dark eyebrow before consenting to rest her backpack on the table. "If you can find them." She stepped back, crossed her arms and waited.

He searched the main compartments, but other than her laptop, phone and a variety of other personal items, he found only her multipurpose tool and a digital camera no bigger than his palm. He patted every inch of the material, searching for a blade in a hidden pocket, until he finally admitted defeat.

With a shake of her head, she unzipped the main pocket once more and reached to the bottom. Then he heard the distinctive tear of a hook-and-loop pouch opening. A moment later, she revealed a black clip point, fixed-blade knife.

"That doesn't look like standard navy issue," he said.

She shrugged, a gleam of pride shining in her eyes. "It's what I carried when we deployed."

Any doubts he'd had about her military pedigree evaporated. "Won't do you much good in a gunfight," he pointed out.

With another hitch of her shoulders, she tucked it out of sight. "Haven't you heard? I'm not heading to a gunfight. I'm heading for a happy reunion with my mom."

She didn't sound the least bit happy.

"Why do you prefer a knife over a gun?" Aidan asked.

"It's easier to get through airport security. Easier to conceal no matter what I'm wearing. And I don't need a permit."

Considering the lethal-looking blade, he wasn't so sure he could agree with any of her reasons. "How *did* you get it through security?"

"The pocket is a double layer of ballistic fabric. Unless they know where to look and how to open it, it's invisible to a security scan."

"Nice trick," he admitted.

"How do you get the guns through?"

"Registrations and permits in checked baggage. The private investigator license helps, too," he added as he gathered up the gear. "How do you think your mom will react when you're on her doorstep?"

"I'm not sure." Frankie looked at a small button camera on the end of a pen. "At least we have gadgets and tools on our side. It feels like a spy movie set in here."

He laughed. He'd thought the same thing when he first arrived. "Victoria keeps us well equipped. She has a reputation as the best."

"That she does," Frankie said quietly. "You knew of it even at Interpol?"

"Yes." He could practically see the wheels turning inside her head. She'd been more than uncomfortable at the end of the meeting, pushing against Victoria's control of the investigation. He should've seen it earlier. Frankie had felt cornered and outnumbered, possibly even betrayed. She'd done what was necessary to get through it and out of the office, retreating but not relinquishing anything just yet. It made her a hazard—to both of them.

"You can trust her," he said, knowing he'd hit the mark when her gaze snapped to his. "And me, by extension."

"Sure." She looked around, studying everything but him. "Are we done here?"

"Pretty much." He checked his phone. "Flight reservations are booked. We're on a midmorning flight."

"Not the early one?" She reached for her own cell phone even as she leaned to look over his shoulder.

When she was this close, the ginger and clove scents of her hair teased his senses. He ignored the enticing aroma, the way it slid over and around him, in favor of keeping her talking. "Please tell me you're not a crack-of-dawn type of person," he said with exaggerated fear.

Her eyebrows puckered. "Why do you care? It's not as though we'll be living together." Then her mouth formed a perfect circle. "Oh. Victoria's orders?" She flicked those away with a twitch of her fingers. "Don't worry about playing bodyguard. I can handle myself. As long as we find time and space to check in regularly about the case, you won't have to follow me around."

It was far too early to throw himself on that conversational grenade. "Are you up for a review of the situation before we call it a night?"

"Sure." The tight curve of her lips hardly qualified as a smile. "It will give us more time on-site to scope out the area before we knock on her door."

He couldn't argue with Frankie's work ethic. "We can talk in the conference room."

"Great." Her smile carried little enthusiasm.

He wondered how her face and eyes might get in on the action if she ever smiled sincerely. Her outward calm didn't quite cover all the anger lurking underneath. He wanted a look at the evidence so he could gain some insight and perspective. Until he had a better grasp of the situation, her tension made him edgy, as well. Too bad he couldn't blame it all on mutual attraction, but that seemed to be entirely his problem. If she noticed him as anything other than an interloper, she hid it well.

"I'd like to learn all I can so I'm prepared to recon your happy reunion, and know the right words for my interview on Monday."

With a small nod, she trailed him to the elevator, her suitcase rolling along behind them. When the lift arrived, they stepped inside and he punched the button for the conference room. They decided on a pizza from a little place down the street, and he set about searching through what she knew and what she thought she knew about her mom.

An aerial view of Sophia's neighborhood and the surrounding blocks filled one of the computer monitors. "When you meet with your mother, I'll watch the house from right here," he said, pointing to a corner he'd highlighted.

"Are you worried I'll do something stupid?" Frankie gave him a long look.

He stared right back. "Are you planning on doing something stupid?"

She tilted her head to the side, stretching and massaging the long column of her neck. "Of course not."

Did she know she was irresistible? "Here." He stepped behind her. "Let me."

She shifted out of his reach. "No, thanks."

"No problem." He held his hands up in surrender. Though he was tempted to fib and tell her he was a certified massage therapist, he didn't want to give her any reason to doubt his word. In the short time they'd been acquainted, her trust issues were abundantly clear.

"It's just from the plane," she said defensively. "I tweaked it when I dozed off."

"It happens." He kept his smile easy, his stance casual. "If you change your mind, I've picked up a trick or two from my massage therapist sister." That was the truth.

"Rain check." Frankie looked back at the overhead images of the neighborhood. "If you're going to watch the first meeting, I assume you'll want me wired for sound, too?"

He was glad she'd been the one to suggest it. "If you agree, we could analyze the conversation afterward for any slips or stresses she makes."

"She won't slip up. Sophia Leone is too slick, too careful."

Aidan thought it was possible the apple hadn't fallen far from the Leone family tree. Frankie appeared to be an extremely cautious woman, as well. Whether it was nature or circumstance, he could honor that trait, respect it. He needed to earn her trust quickly, for everyone's benefit. "Once you're reunited, you'll have better personal access, and I can be looking for anything within the company records, associates or systems that implicate her or clear her of wrongdoing."

Frankie nodded, but he knew her mind was working overtime on something she wasn't ready to share. Leo Solutions had gone from idea to full-service business in a remarkably short time. That required significant capital, though Frankie blamed the instant growth on her mother's extensive connections. He'd withhold his opinion until he had more information.

He didn't discuss his reasons, simply made a list and kept digging. Sophia Leone's personal finances were remarkably transparent. She'd tucked the money from the general's death into a trust fund for their daughter. A fund Frankie refused to touch. Considering the salary Sophia drew from the company, she lived modestly and seemed to be socking away as much as possible into savings. This piqued his curiosity.

"Did you ever discuss your personal goals for after your service with your mom?"

"No," Frankie said, distracted by her study of her mother's neighborhood. "I was on active duty one day and retired the next. The transition time was filled with physical therapy." She zoomed out and moved the cursor to the Leo Solutions site. "Why did you leave Interpol?"

"Victoria made me a better offer." She had, in fact, saved more than his career when she invited him into the Colby Agency.

"Sounds like there's a story." Frankie shot him a sideways glance under her lashes.

That look landed like a punch to his gut, stealing his breath. "Isn't there always in our line of work?" If she wanted to hear it, he'd share a few of the more palatable details. He waited, relieved when she didn't ask.

Pushing herself out of her chair, she rolled her shoulders and then pressed her fists into her back. "I passed the physical," she said with a weary frown. "It's the new hardware in my spine the navy can't accept. You don't have to worry about me breaking on your watch."

"I wasn't thinking about that at all." He'd been thinking far less appropriate things about the gentle flare of her hips and the supple way she moved.

"You'd be the first."

"Will you tell me how you got hurt?" He needed to

find some common ground, a starting point they could build from. He had no intention of being the first of Victoria's investigators to go down in flames before a client left the building.

"It was an improvised explosive at the edge of a dirt track too vague and rutted to qualify as a road." Her voice was as quiet and still as a pond sheltered by a bank of fog. "They tell me I was tossed up in the air like a doll. It was the landing I screwed up."

He marveled that she could be almost meditative about such a life-altering event. The contrast between her distrust and temper over her father's demise and her serenity about her personal troubles intrigued him. His injuries had been emotional, though the alcohol required to silence his demons had taken a toll. "You don't remember it?"

"Not the explosion." She stacked her hands on top of her head. "I remember far too much of the recovery." She glanced up at the clock on the wall. "It's late. I really wish I could've gone home first."

He understood the subject was closed. For now. "What did you leave behind?"

"Clothes. I didn't pack for a week of socializing with my mom. She's always perfectly dressed for any moment. You'll see."

He wasn't buying that. What did he have to do to earn a peek into her real concerns? "You're not going to shake me," he said. "We're going from here to the hotel, to the airport. We're catching the flight into Seattle tomorrow. You can shop there if it becomes a problem."

She studied him, her big brown eyes impossible to read. "I don't want to shake you." Her gaze dropped to his lips. A long moment later, she glared at the computer as she shut it down. "Do I call a cab to get to the hotel or are you in charge of my every move?"

He grinned at her, noted her irritation. "We'll go together and call it team building."

"Team?" She snorted. "You'll be asking for a trade as soon as you meet Sophia Leone and get caught up on the fiasco that is my family."

Aidan didn't reply. Once he took a case, he stuck until it was closed. No matter what.

Saturday, April 9, 8:20 a.m.

AIDAN COUNTED IT a victory when they arrived at the airport on time and without further argument or conflict. When they were seated on the plane, he quickly changed his mind. The seats were too close, her body one temptation after another as she carefully situated herself and her belongings.

More than the fleeting, innocent touches of her arm or knee, the way her mind worked—swift and a little dark—compounded his problem. She was a *client* and deserved his best effort on the case. He had to find a way to ignore how she stirred him. More, he had to find a way to ignore the brief, assessing glances she'd been aiming his direction when she thought he wasn't looking.

They'd been at peak altitude for just over an hour when she shifted in her seat. "Aidan?"

Her hair was down today and as she pushed it behind her ear he caught that lovely scent again. "Yes?"

"I'm thinking we need to change up the plan."

He kept his expression neutral, though he couldn't

wait to hear what she'd been mulling over since last night. "How so?"

"If we go into Leo Solutions separately, the odds aren't in our favor. Either one of us could get tossed out if we're discovered. This may be my best chance to learn the truth. I can't afford to get pushed back to square one."

"You don't have much faith in me, do you?"

"It's not that." She twisted more, her knee bumping his. "We're walking into a security company. They're going to find out we were on the same plane, that we sat together."

"That won't be a problem," he said. The problem would be keeping his hands to himself if he didn't find some distance.

"It's too coincidental. We should go on the offensive."

He had a sudden image of Frankie charging ahead, leading a strike team, heedless of the American military rules about women in combat. "Dare I ask what you have in mind?"

She gave him a smile and it stunned him. No falsehood in this smile, no tension, just pure excitement. The expression lit her eyes and brought a hint of color to her cheeks. For a moment he was lost to anything but the gorgeous view.

"Rather than wait for them to confront us," she was saying, "why don't we just go in together?"

"We are going in together." Sitting together on the plane didn't have to be a big deal. For the case.

"No, together like a *couple*," she said, her dark eyes sparkling. "Let's tell Sophia we're engaged."

He stared at her, dumbfounded, while she hurried to explain.

"Hear me out. My mom's a big romantic. Always has been." Frankie's smile evaporated. "One more reason it baffles me that she tossed her soul mate under the bus," she added in a low voice. "If we show up and tell her we're engaged, we effectively distract her."

This was a bad idea. Horrible. "I don't—"

"I've thought it through," Frankie promised, cutting him off. "We'll tell her you applied to the company and when you got the interview on your own merit we decided to come out and surprise her with the whole truth. She'll eat it up."

"She'll see right through it," he argued.

"Not a chance. We'll tell her it's been a long-distance thing and we can't stand living apart anymore. This is perfect, trust me." Frankie nearly bounced in her seat.

His stomach pitched and rolled as if they were going through severe turbulence. "What about the living arrangements?"

"What about them? Being engaged gives us the perfect reason to talk to each other anytime we want through the workday or in the evenings. We won't need any excuses. It's a stronger plan all around."

It didn't feel that way to him. He had to convince her to drop it. "The plan was a hotel room for me and you in the house with your mom."

"Yeah…" Frankie shook her head, and the sable waves of her hair rippled. "No matter what we decide about this, I won't stay with her."

"It gives you tremendous access."

"Access or not, I can't do it." She tucked her hands between her thighs as if she were suddenly cold. "I've lived on my own too long. We'd be snapping at each other before I found out anything useful."

"We need to stick with the plan and cover Victoria arranged," he said, willing her to be reasonable. He couldn't be engaged. Not even for a case. "This kind of change should be approved." There, he'd found a point she couldn't argue with.

"What does it matter, if we get the job done?" Frankie countered. "This tactic simplifies everything."

Maybe for her. His fingers cramped into a fist, digging into his palm. This couldn't be happening. He wouldn't give in.

"Arriving engaged is the best answer," she said, patting his knee as if the topic was settled.

"No," he murmured, glancing around for anyone who might've caught their conversation. "I won't alter the op without approval."

She snorted. "Please. Victoria knows things change and investigators have to think on their feet. Let's make the most of it."

He shook his head and looked past her to the sky flying by the window. This was ridiculous.

"Is it such an impossible task to pretend to like me when we're in public?"

"Of course not," he replied. He was afraid how easy it would be to treat her as a fiancée. "It changes the dynamic. Significantly. Lying as part of a cover is one thing. Lying to each other is another."

"What do you mean?" Her dark eyebrows dipped into another sharp frown. "We'll be lying to the suspect, not to each other."

"Only in public," he said with a hefty dose of sarcasm. He hadn't missed how she'd termed her mother as a suspect. "Being engaged typically means affectionate displays and exhibiting a sense of closeness and trust." He leaned closer and she leaned away, proving his point.

"Are you afraid I'm going to forget it's for show and fall in love with you?" She rolled her eyes. "Please. I'm not prowling for a relationship, Aidan. Let's agree to do whatever it takes to get the job done efficiently."

He eased back into his seat, letting her believe she'd put him in his place. "Let me think it over." He flipped open his tablet and continued his study of the Leone family background.

"Just decide before we land," she whispered.

He didn't reply. Her need for control was likely a combination of her upbringing, her natural fiery personality and the career-ending injury. He couldn't blame her for that. He did, however, want to look at her "proposal" from all angles, especially from her mother's point of view.

He wasn't worried about his family finding out. In Ireland, they were all well away from any gossip, and the agency should be intercepting any queries. No, he was more concerned about how he'd feel playing Frankie's groom-to-be, even if only for a few days. He prided himself on being able to roll with the unexpected elements of his work. Surely there was a way to talk her out of this.

Eventually, he closed his tablet and reached over to take her hand.

"What are you doing?" She tugged, but he held on.

"Holding my fiancée's hand." This would be his ticket back to the sane side of this case.

"Oh." Her fingers relaxed a fraction. "You agree then that this is the best avenue to take?"

"I'm weighing the pros and cons."

Her brown eyes narrowed and her intelligent gaze turned suspicious. "I outlined the only pros that matter."

"To you."

"Aidan." She jerked her hand free of his. "What are you thinking?"

He grinned at the wariness in her eyes. She couldn't possibly want to play this out, not the way they needed to, to make it convincing. "I really don't think the fake engagement is the best way to go."

"Why not?" Lacing her fingers together, she balanced her hands on her slim thigh. Her brown eyes lit with a challenge and her foot began to tap. "Afraid you're not up to it?"

On the contrary. Faking an intimacy would be too easy with Frankie. His attraction for her was already cranked up and getting hotter by the minute. In other circumstances, with the slightest encouragement from her, he'd have made his move. When she gazed up at him, he could see flecks of gold in her brown eyes. He forced himself to take a mental step back rather than lean across the arm of the seat and crowd her personal space. "You're an only child, right?"

She nodded.

"If you show up on your mom's doorstep with a fiancé in tow, she's going to go ballistic with excitement."

"That's the *point*." Frankie waved off the idea that it was a bad thing. "I haven't spoken a word to her in months. The engagement diverts her suspicion about showing up now. What do you care if she gushes over you? It's a week, tops. More likely she'll be walking on eggshells, afraid to intrude in my personal life."

He wasn't nearly so sure. Sophia Leone didn't strike him as the selfish, remorseless woman Frankie thought she was. "I believe you're underestimating her," he pressed. Specifically, Sophia's love for and commitment to her only child. "Our original story is strong enough without the complication of a false engagement."

"Is there someone else?" Frankie demanded suddenly. "A girlfriend or wife who'd be offended by our plan?"

"Your plan," he corrected. "And no."

"Then discussion over."

"Not so fast." Leaning close, he caught that sweet scent of cloves and spices in her hair. "Are you prepared to play the part...*completely*?"

He watched her, relentlessly quelling his grin as her eyes went wide when his full meaning registered. It was gratifying to realize she wasn't immune to this electricity humming between them. He pulled himself together. The last thing he needed was to play with fire on a case Victoria had a personal interest in. He had to show Frankie this ploy was a mistake.

She moistened her lips. "Are you prepared?"

"Of course," he replied automatically. "I always go the distance in my investigations."

"And in other areas?"

"Are you flirting with me?"

She batted her eyes in an exaggerated move that made him laugh, until she closed the distance and pressed her lips to his. Warmth spread from that point of contact down his arms, sizzling in his fingertips. She pushed her hand into his hair and drew him closer for a full, sensual kiss that blasted through him like a flash grenade.

She was like a double shot of whiskey with a drop of

honey—all fire with a hint of sweetness. He changed the angle, tipping up her chin and taking control of the kiss. When her lips parted on a sigh, he slid his tongue across hers with bold strokes.

Belatedly he remembered the plane full of people and eased away. Her eyes were dazed, a mirror of his own, he was sure. "I think that will convince anyone." It sure as hell convinced him.

He prayed it would be enough to put an end to her irrational engagement idea.

Chapter Five

Frankie reached for the magazine, though she'd read it cover to cover already. It annoyed her no end that her hands shook. She could still taste the cola Aidan had chosen during the beverage service. The hint of crisp pine in his cologne tickled her nose and made her think of the rocky coast near Puget Sound.

Maybe he was right and pretending an engagement was the wrong move.

If that shocking kiss was any indication—even though she had started it—she'd have to be very careful. If they had to do much of that, it would be all too easy to believe the charade intended to knock down her mother's defenses.

Thoughts of her mom killed the lingering sizzle from the kiss. Sophia had boasted about keeping that spark of love and romance alive through thirty years of marriage. Obviously that had been one more lie on top of the heap. Her statement, all but convicting her husband, left no room for anything but the clear conclusion: Sophia's career had trumped love in the end. She must have turned against her husband to avoid the demolition of her career by association. How would her security business have succeeded if shadowed by General Leone's treason?

Distracting her mother was worth any personal discomfort to Frankie. The announcement that she and Aidan were engaged would give them a brief advantage, and Frankie planned to make the most of it.

She pressed her lips together, telling herself it was silly the way her heartbeat skipped when he touched her. It was true he could be her fantasy man come to life with his dark looks, quick smile and vivid blue eyes. And the accent? Dear God. Too bad this was absolutely the wrong time in her life. She had to find a way to deal with it if they were going to convince Sophia they were engaged.

Frankie had to remember her purpose, stay focused and keep the sexy man beside her at arm's length when they were alone. Hopefully it wasn't obvious to Aidan that the kiss had such a lasting effect on her.

Apparently, he'd finished protesting the change in their cover story. When they landed at the Sea-Tac Airport, he held her hand on the way to baggage claim and through the rental car line. Once they were on their way, even the new-car smell wasn't enough to distract her from Aidan's crisp, masculine scent. It seemed that one kiss had her locked in on him. She had to shake off this persistent feminine awareness of him. She couldn't allow anything to splinter her focus.

Knowing the city better than he did, she had offered to drive. Seattle was always bustling, and for the first time she was grateful for the snarl of traffic. It gave her more time to consider her approach. She tapped her fingers against the steering wheel while her mind surged into overdrive. She found her eagerness for the confrontation with her mother had faded, knowing she'd have a witness as cool and calm as Aidan.

"What about the ring?"

His question cut into her thoughts and she struggled to find the context. "Ring?" Frankie glanced at him. "What are you talking about?"

"If we're engaged, you should have a ring."

"That doesn't matter. Lots of engaged women go without a ring." She couldn't think of an example right now, but it had to be true. No way would she let him put a ring on her finger. "My mom's a romantic. She'll believe us if we tell her we were planning to shop for a ring together."

"I don't know."

"Trust me."

Aidan turned a bit in the seat, facing her. "I don't know you well enough to trust you."

That stung a little. "You have my file and we can cover the basics tonight," she protested. Why couldn't that be enough? She didn't need him cluttering the plan. "Just gloss over the details, get mushy once in a while when she's watching, and it will work out. We aren't going to be here that long."

"Uh-huh." His gaze returned to the congested roadway. "Why would I propose without a ring? I don't think that's something you'd tolerate."

"You just said you didn't know me."

"I said I didn't trust you. As for knowing you, I'm a quick study," he stated.

"Are you messing with me?" The freeway was at a full stop, so she gave him a long, hard look. The grin creased his face, ornery as hell and way too sexy. *Eyes on the road*, she ordered herself. "I don't wear jewelry."

"You're wearing earrings."

She thought of the small diamond studs in her ears. They'd been a gift from her father on her sixteenth birthday. She touched her ear with a fingertip, giving the simple, timeless setting a twirl. "These hardly count. I wore them to remind my navy buddies I was a girl."

"I have a hard time believing they'd forget that detail."

Frankie ignored what sounded like a compliment, her mind returning to the bigger problem of how best to greet her mom tomorrow.

Smiling would be the toughest part of this farce. Frankie had to find a way. A happy smile and sticking close enough to the truth that her mother wouldn't pinpoint the lies right away was the key to operational success. Oh, how the mighty had fallen. It hadn't been so long ago that the keys to a successful operation were preparation, attitude and the right equipment.

"We need to stop at a mall or something," Aidan said.

Frankie knew she needed better wardrobe options, but shopping was the last thing she wanted to add to their task list. "What did you forget?"

"Not for me, for your mom. It's rude to show up on someone's doorstep empty-handed," he said. "As your fiancé I should bring flowers to the first meeting."

She sighed, frustrated with his sudden commitment to her idea. "You're overthinking it." One of them had to keep this charade under control. "We'll grab a bouquet from a grocery store in the morning."

"I know you're angry with her, but I have standards. Flowers are friendly, polite and thoughtful."

"You didn't toss out this many objections on the plane," she said.

"I was processing the idea and we were in public."

"Right." She wasn't falling for that line. "You're an investigator. You process in real time."

"Not always. Indulge me and stop at the mall. I only need fifteen minutes."

"She doesn't need mall flowers."

"A future son-in-law showing up with cheap flowers is worse than no flowers. I can make you stop."

Frankie would like to see him try. "Would you just drop this, please?"

"No. This was your idea," he said. "Unless you'd rather go back to the original plan?"

"No." Catching on, she bit back the rant. She recognized a test when it smacked her in the face. Aidan had agreed to play this her way, and she wasn't letting him off the hook just because he was trying to annoy her. "We'll stop at the mall."

"I've found a couple of florists close to your house."

"Sophia's house," she corrected. The last family home Frankie knew had been the general's residence on the post. Sophia had moved quickly after the funeral to the more fashionable Queen Anne neighborhood. "I was an army brat. We moved to a new post every few years. And we're off topic again," she said through gritted teeth. "I'm at home in Savannah now." Sophia's address had stopped feeling like home when her father died.

Aidan mentioned two addresses and names of florist shops. "Which one is better?"

"I have no idea," Frankie said. "Just pick one."

He did and his phone started rattling off the directions for the altered route.

Following the prompts, they reached a sprawling shopping center less than an hour later. After parking in front of the flower shop, they got out of the car. As Frankie reached for the florist's door, she realized Aidan was headed to another store, two doors down. "This way," she called after him.

"We'll get there. Come here for a second."

What was he up to? She glanced at the hours posted on the door. "They close in half an hour."

"Then hurry," he said.

The sly expression on his handsome face challenged her and his quiet voice carried a clear command. Doing nothing to hide her irritation, she stalked over and realized he'd stopped in front of a jewelry store. "No." She crossed her arms. She was *not* going inside.

He leaned down and kissed her. That quick, brief kiss was enough to turn her knees to jelly.

"Yes," he countered. "We're going to do this right to be sure our cover holds up."

"You can't be serious." He couldn't possibly mean to buy her an engagement ring.

"I'm not a man who does things halfway," he said. "Your mother will pick up on that and wonder why I rushed to propose before I was prepared."

"This is *pretend*," Frankie whispered through gritted teeth.

"But it's supposed to look *real*," he retorted with an exasperating laugh. "When I propose to the right woman, I'll have a ring. We can't have Sophia thinking I'm flighty or unreliable. We want the woman to hire me, right?"

Frankie shook her head, wishing for a hole to open up and swallow her. It would solve so many problems. Her back was stiff, her legs aching from the flight. She needed to get to the hotel so she could stretch out the kinks. Seeing her mother while dealing with the undercurrent of pain would be a disadvantage. She'd already lost the element of surprise when Victoria insisted on that phone call. Frankie wouldn't give up more ground. "Fine." Better to give in and get back on track. "Solitaire, classic setting, no bells, whistles or wedding bands."

"Deal." He opened the door for her.

She didn't care for the amusement glinting in his deep blue eyes. "Are you charging it as a work expense?"

"Of course not," he replied, clearly offended.

She let him take her hand as they walked to the glass counter full of engagement settings. Her heart kicked against her rib cage and a familiar spike of pain shot down her leg. She pulled in a slow, deep breath to help unlock her seizing muscles, which were straining against the hardware that kept her pinned together. Frankie forced herself to match his longer stride, refusing to trip or lean on him. Sheer willpower carried her closer to the twinkling gems on display, when she wanted to be anywhere else.

She felt a trickle of sweat at the nape of her neck, under her hair. Aidan might have imagined proposing to a woman, but it wasn't a milestone Frankie had ever given much thought to. Her career had been at the forefront of her mind, and working in close quarters with men took a lot of the shine off the idea of choosing one man for a lifetime. Casual dates and having a good time with friends were enough for her, especially after watching her parents' relationship disintegrate. It would be a long time before commitment and permanence broke the top ten of her priority list.

While the injury had sent her career in a new direction, it had only emphasized the lack of potential for her personal life. At one time, Frankie had wanted that devoted partnership her parents had shared. Now that idyllic romance was clouded by secrets, lies and questions that might never get answered.

The last place she belonged was here, admiring the glitter and responsibility of diamond engagement rings. "You know what?" She patted Aidan's hand. "I'd like to be surprised, after all. You know what I like." She forced her lips into a bright smile. It felt as if her face would crack from the effort. "I know what kind of bouquet will win Mom over. I'll get the flowers while you handle this."

"That's a great idea, sweetheart," Aidan said smoothly. "Let's just get you sized first." His smile looked completely natural when he greeted the salesman. "I meet the future in-laws at brunch tomorrow," he said. "Can't leave any room for doubts or bad first impressions."

"You've landed a smart man," the salesman said.

Frankie swallowed and managed a shaky nod. The metal sizing rings jangled as the salesman slid one loop after another over the fourth finger of her left hand. Her stomach cramped. If she didn't get out of here soon, it was going to get ugly.

The salesman noted her ring size and she walked away as swiftly as possible without breaking into a sprint. A ring made all this too real, too extravagant. How did she keep getting outmaneuvered?

When they were done here, they were going to have

a conversation about the ground rules going forward. No more games. No more kisses. This was her problem and she was going to regain control of the operation.

AIDAN WATCHED HER LEAVE. More than a little concerned she'd take the car and leave him stranded, he'd palmed the key while she was struggling with whatever was going on behind those big brown eyes.

He'd been sure the idea of a ring would be enough to call her bluff on this engagement idea. Well, he'd just consider this practice, he decided, pointing out a few settings that he liked.

"She claims to want simple and classic," he explained to Ted, the salesman. Aidan answered questions about his budget and barely refrained from inquiring about the return policy. If her mother had the connections and skills Frankie and Victoria implied, she could send someone out to pester Ted about this sale. Aidan didn't want to give Frankie any reason to say this engagement nonsense had failed because of him.

She'd said no bells and whistles, and no wedding bands—obviously—but he didn't take the first glittering gem Ted showed him. Once he'd examined his favorites, he chose a three-quarter-carat princess cut on a flared band of white gold. It made the best statement. Classic, clean lines. The white gold matched the setting of her earrings. The stone was big enough without overpowering her slender, fine-boned hand.

He'd just completed the purchase and was waiting for the jeweler to adjust the sizing when the door chimed and Frankie returned, carrying an arrangement of some sort wrapped in tissue paper. The sweet fragrance filled the store. "They tell me these will pop and stay beautiful for days," she said, leaving as much distance as possible between the two of them.

He tried to decipher the scent to avoid sympathizing with her obvious discomfort. "Roses?"

"No." She shook her head, her nose wrinkling. "Lilies and tulips. Her favorites. She'll be wrapped around your finger in an instant."

"That's helpful," he said, rocking back on his heels. "Ted tells me your ring will be sized and polished shortly."

"Great." Her smile was brittle. "I'll, um, put these in the car."

"It can wait." Aidan stepped forward, crowding her just a bit. "I missed you." He brushed his lips to the corner of her mouth. "Did you miss me?"

She wanted to snarl at him, that was clear, but he was only playing the part that matched her idea. He needed her to go all in or bail out before they showed up on her mother's doorstep.

"I hardly know what to do with myself without you," she said, her voice far too sweet.

He laughed and took the flowers from her hands, setting the vase near the register. "Are you hungry?"

She shook her head again.

Aidan suspected pain and nerves were blocking her appetite. The faint brackets around her lush mouth and her stiff posture clued him in. If he thought she'd open up, he'd ask more questions about her recovery. She hid her injury well and he believed she was close to 100 percent. That didn't mean he couldn't be thoughtful or help her manage what must be challenging at times. He just had to do it in a way that didn't offend her.

Ted caught their attention as he returned with a

small, emerald-colored velvet box. "All set," he said, handing it to Aidan.

For such a tiny thing, it felt damned heavy in his hand. He studied Frankie's face as he popped open the lid, giving her a glimpse inside. "Will that do?"

Her eyes were huge as she looked at the ring, then up at him. "Aidan…"

He waited, but she didn't finish. "I think we hit the mark, Ted. Thanks." His fingers felt thick and sluggish as he pulled out the ring and nudged it gently onto Frankie's finger.

His breath backed up in his throat and he felt light-headed. Getting sick here would ruin the moment and he willed his stomach to stop churning. He'd vowed never to go through these motions again. Knowing it wasn't real didn't seem to help matters. He blinked away the hazy memories until he saw Frankie's hand, the new ring and nothing more.

She flared her fingers, her gaze locked on the ring, her lips parted in surprise. "Aidan, I… It looks so—"

He kissed her before she could finish and blow their cover. "I'm honored you said yes." He handed her the flowers and guided her quickly from the store.

At the car, he opened the passenger door for her. "I'll drive. You look a little shell-shocked."

He closed the door before she could answer, but the silence didn't last.

"What are you thinking?" she exclaimed as he backed out of the parking space.

"If it's too small, speak now and I'll exchange it," he said, his voice rough with the emotions he couldn't quite block out.

She swore. "You know it isn't. This is crazy, Aidan."

"Your idea or my cooperation?" What did he have to do to get her to drop this?

"Be serious," she snapped. "You can't just buy me a ring." She started to tug it off. "Go back to the store."

He pulled into the next available parking space. "Have you changed your mind about this approach?"

She glared at him, her hands tangled in her lap, the vase of flowers sitting at her feet. "No."

"Then it stays on." The command came out with more heat than he'd intended. "Think of it as the prop that will reinforce the story you want your mother to believe."

"You don't get a prop from a real jeweler."

"That's a matter of opinion." He set the navigation on his cell phone for the hotel they'd booked. "I suggest you get used to it. If your mother or anyone else catches you without it, you'll have bigger lies to weave." His second engagement was going far worse than the first one. At least this time around he knew it was temporary. Hopefully when he met her mother he'd have a better understanding of why Frankie insisted on this tactic.

"Fine." She drummed her palms on her knees. "It's just—"

"Find a complimentary word," he warned.

Aidan shook off the frustration and bad memories as they merged with the traffic. As the silence stretched he figured she couldn't find a compliment, or she was plotting her next strategic maneuver. Either way, he was grateful for the momentary truce. When he'd pulled to a stop under the hotel awning, he turned to her again. "Did you think to change our reservation to a single room?"

She sagged back into the seat. "No." She reached across the console, her hand soft on his arm, the diamond bright on her finger. "But let me handle this one, okay?"

Unsure whether that was wise, he brainstormed ways to mitigate the damage if she launched yet another surprise attack or kept the separate rooms.

Instinctively taking in the surroundings, Aidan logged every face and position of the other guests in the lobby. He'd reviewed everything Victoria had sent him last night when he was battling the typical new-case insomnia.

Sophia Leone co-owned a security company after her years as an analyst for the alphabet soup in Washington, DC. Her own daughter suspected her of abusing her position to eliminate her husband. To support the case, the Colby Agency hadn't bothered to hide their travel itinerary, and Frankie had told her mother she'd be arriving today. As the widow of a high-powered general, Sophia must have a vast network of friends from all over the globe. Aidan knew he and Frankie would be at a disadvantage in these early hours. It wasn't paranoia to suspect someone was on-site keeping watch.

Which guest was here as a favor to Sophia? Which one would report Frankie had arrived with a man acting like a boyfriend? Aidan put a mental tag on the two most likely candidates and then shifted most of his attention to Frankie as she checked in.

He was glad they planned to keep the initial mother-daughter reunion brief, so they'd have time to review the key players at Leo Solutions tonight. With any luck, his contact at Interpol would have more information on the passports Frankie had found.

"Adjoining rooms?" Frankie queried. "I was sure I booked a suite." She bumped Aidan's shoulder as she pulled out her phone. "How did I mix that up? Honey, do you have the confirmation I emailed you?"

Aidan pulled his phone from his pocket. "Let me take a look."

"We'll get it straightened out," the woman at the desk assured her.

"We just got engaged," Frankie explained, letting the diamond flash. "We're here to surprise the family." Her smile was as bright as the diamond. "I'm so excited." She rubbed her hand up and down his arm. "I probably clicked the wrong box by mistake."

Impressed—affected—by her performance, he cursed himself for asking her to commit to the role of excited fiancée. He should've just said no to the cover story change. She thought he was worried about her physically, when her emotional state concerned him more. Now he feared he'd fall for her if they kept this up. What a fool he was.

"Congratulations." The woman checking them in admired the ring before setting her fingers on the keyboard. "I do have a suite available. Let me just…" She tapped more keys. "That should do it." She glanced up and beamed at them. "I've adjusted the rate through the weekend." She programmed two key cards and tucked them into a small envelope, pushing it across the counter. With a map of the hotel, she pointed out their room and the basic amenities. "You'll be right here with an excellent view of the city," she said, circling what appeared to be a corner room. "Park wherever you like. The closest elevators are down the first corridor on your left." She pointed. "Do you need help with your luggage?"

"I'll manage," Aidan said. He wanted some privacy, and fast. He didn't want Frankie second-guessing or throwing him another curveball.

They made it up to the suite in one trip even with the flowers. Frankie walked inside and stopped short in the center of the room. "Holy cow. That view. We should get engaged more often."

The "we" gave him pause, though she was right to be thinking in teamwork terms. He blamed the strange twitch between his shoulder blades on the residual effect of sliding that ring onto her finger. Stepping up beside her, he enjoyed the floor-to-ceiling corner window that gave them a panoramic view of Seattle's west side. "You have a beautiful hometown."

"That's overstating it."

Her reflexive disagreement made him feel better somehow. "Did you ever live in a place that felt like a hometown?"

She turned away from the windows to set the vase of wrapped flowers on the tall dresser next to the television. "We moved a lot, obviously. Wherever we lived, there were certain items that went in specific places. Little things like the key rack near the door, a family portrait in the dining room. My mom's theory was those details made the transitions easier."

He followed as she rolled her suitcase into the bedroom. "Did it work?"

She looked over her shoulder, a mix of nostalgia and sorrow clouding her eyes. "Yes."

Should he point out the mixed messages she gave him about her mother? It was as if she described two different women: one a devoted wife and mother, possibly a hopeless romantic, and the other a sharp mind capable of wreaking havoc on the world at large.

A fresh awareness, and a desperate ache to fix everything for Frankie, filled him. Had he learned nothing from his mistakes? He was an investigator, end of story. He had to remember that, had to keep his focus on the facts, for her safety and his.

He backed toward the door. "I'm going to check on the leads I was working on those passports."

"Fine," she said, not looking at him. "I'll, um, work out a few things in here."

"Is an hour enough time?"

The only sign of tension was the little catch in her breathing. "That works for me."

Chapter Six

Frankie let Aidan drive to her mother's new house in Queen Anne while she held the flowers. Periodically she stretched her hands to relieve the tension that mounted with every passing block. After some restorative yoga in the hotel room, she felt better, stronger and ready to calmly face whatever came next. Though it hadn't done any good last time, a tiny part of her still wanted to charge in and blast her mother with an all-out attack.

Unfortunately, unless she used the condemning statement Sophia had signed, Frankie didn't have anything else confirmed enough to ask about. Aidan hadn't turned up any concrete information on the passports. The best he could tell, they'd never been used, despite the stamps inside. So why had they been in the safe-deposit box? Frankie reminded herself things were moving forward, intelligently if not quickly. For the first time since getting kicked out of the navy, she didn't feel alone.

She slid a glance at her undercover groom as they neared her mother's home, wondering what kind of reception to expect. Would it be stilted and weird or warm and happy? Her last conversation with her mom, in the cemetery at her father's grave, had been tense and ugly. Grief-stricken, she'd tossed out accusations and hammered Sophia with questions she wouldn't answer. Frankie prepared for an awkward encounter, though Sophia would surely pour on the charm with Aidan around.

Sunlight caught on the engagement ring. The fragrant scent of lilies filled the car. Frankie was showing up at her mother's house with a fiancé and a bouquet of flowers. Her emotions swung from one extreme to the other with every heartbeat as Aidan pulled to a stop in front of the house. The struggle had her waffling between the idea that going to Victoria had been smart, and the possibility that it had been foolish. Frankie needed investigative support to get justice and clear her father's name. No, she needed only one honest answer. It reminded her of being caught in an undertow. She could see the sunlight, knew where she needed to go, while an unseen force dragged her out to sea.

She looked up at the tidy Craftsman house with trimmed hedges lining the walkway and steps up to the porch, which was framed with flower boxes on the railing. The ironwork table and chairs had decorated patios or porches in various homes where they'd lived around the world for as long as Frankie could remember. How many quiet moments had her parents shared at that table over the years? What did it mean that her mother still had those pieces?

"This makes no sense."

"Which part?" Aidan studied her closely. "Your mom hasn't seen the ring or me. There's still time for the original game plan."

"The engagement is the only piece of this puzzle I

trust to work as expected." Frankie stared at the table and chairs.

"Is that an attempt to scare me off?"

"No." Her heavy sigh rippled across the tissue covering the flowers. She pushed the bouquet into his hands. "We're on, my darling fiancé. Let's make it count."

They climbed out of the car and Aidan locked the doors with the key fob. "Play nice," he murmured, brushing a kiss to her cheek as they walked up to the porch. "I've got your back."

She wanted to roll her eyes. He had no idea what he was walking into, though she was ridiculously grateful he was with her.

Her mother must've been watching from a window. The front door flew open the moment they topped the stairs. Sophia hovered in the doorway, her hands clutched over her heart.

"Frankie," she breathed. "Oh, thank heaven. You're home." She drew her into a crushing hug.

Frankie patted her mother's shoulders, biting back the snide observation that a house she'd never seen couldn't be home. There would be time for barbs like that later. Indulging her petty streak now would undermine the ultimate goal: to get the truth out of Sophia.

"Mom," Frankie said, escaping the embrace. "This is Aidan Abbot."

Aidan extended the vase of flowers. "It's a pleasure to meet you, Ms. Leone."

Sophia's eyes, shining with unshed tears, darted from Frankie to Aidan and back again. "Come in, come in. Any friend of Frankie's—"

"Fiancé," Frankie clarified. "We started as friends, though." She imagined whoever she married—if she married—would have to be a friend first. She held up her hand to show off the ring and sell the lie. Sophia's eyes widened and her lips parted, but she couldn't seem to speak. When they got back to the hotel, Frankie would admit to Aidan that he had been right about the ring making all the difference.

"Oh, come in! Come in here and tell me everything." Sophia gripped Frankie's hand for a closer inspection. Looking to Aidan, she said, "You have excellent taste."

"I thought it suited her." A smug grin crossed his face as they followed Sophia inside. "Frankie wouldn't have taken my proposal seriously without it."

Sophia beamed at her. "That's my girl," she said with pride.

Clearly Aidan planned to gloat over this when they were alone. At least Frankie could revel in being right about her mother's mushy romantic side. Thoughts of who'd trumped whom faded as her eyes landed on the family portrait hanging in a place of honor over the sideboard in the dining room. She stopped short, staring.

Sophia paused, as well. "You seem surprised," she said after a moment.

"Look at you." Aidan gave her hand a squeeze as he admired the portrait. "You're so happy."

Frankie would argue as soon as she got over the shock. Had Sophia put this here when she'd moved in, or had she dug it out of storage just for the visit today?

"That was painted when we were in Germany," Sophia explained to Aidan. "Frankie was seven. The local artist worked from a snapshot…"

Frankie stopped listening. Her mind had traveled back to those idyllic days when everything in her world had made sense. Her father had been a respected leader, her mother outgoing and friendly and involved with the community. Frankie had had a normal life and her body had cooperated every day. She hadn't known what real deception was, had no concept of scandal. Granted, she'd been seven and generally oblivious of anything beyond school and her young friends.

"You and Dad went to Austria for your anniversary that year," she said wistfully.

"That's right." Sophia cleared her throat. "How do you remember that?"

"I got to have a sleepover with Elise Stafford while you were gone."

"You two were always getting into trouble."

"That sounds like a story I need to hear," Aidan said, raising Frankie's hand to his lips and kissing her knuckles. "Who's going to tell me?"

Frankie let her mother do the honors. She was too busy analyzing why the pieces and collections they'd gathered to maintain that sense of home were displayed here.

She'd expected a woman capable of throwing her husband to the wolves would have purged all the reminders or shipped them to her daughter. It wasn't as if Frankie had given her time to prepare for the visit, either. Hardly twenty-four hours had passed since she reached out from Victoria Colby's office.

Sophia, relaxed and in her element as hostess, offered them water or lemonade and shared a few of Frankie's childhood highlights with Aidan as if there'd never been any strife between them. Frankie wanted to snap and claw; she wanted to demand the truth. The words nearly tumbled free—*to hell with patience, charades, proper channels and procedures*. She had only one question: *Hey, Mom, why'd you set up Dad?*

Except it would backfire. Her mother's stoic mask would slam into place and they'd be no closer to the source of information Frankie was sure they'd find somewhere inside Leo Solutions. Better to follow her mother's example, appearing to be one thing while carrying on as something else entirely in the shadows.

"Frankie?" Aidan bumped her knee with his.

"Pardon?" She forced her lips into a smile.

"Your mom asked about your back," he said, giving her hand another squeeze.

"Oh. It's fine." She hurried to elaborate when Sophia's face fell. "I'm running again."

"Oh, Frankie, that's wonderful. I know that was an important goal."

Her mother knew damn good and well the most important goal had been resuming active duty with the navy. Frankie smiled through the stinging bitterness of failure. "It feels good," she said, playing nice. "I'll be able to dance at my wedding, too." Though her father wouldn't be there to walk her down the aisle, she added silently.

"I can't wait!" Sophia leaned forward. "Tell me how you met."

Here came another undertow. Frankie gripped Aidan's hand in both of hers, hoping he'd get the hint and dive in. They'd come up with a loose cover story, but she couldn't seem to get it started.

"We met on a case she was working for the Savannah PD," he began. The way he told the story, she could see it in her mind. He made it sound as though he found her interesting and likable. Quite a feat, since she'd forced him into this engagement ruse. The man was excellent undercover and she owed him big for this. By the time he finished, she almost believed how much they loved each other, right down to an all-too-real startling rush of affection for him that soothed her nerves.

"Your daughter amazes me at every turn," Aidan said, raising their joined hands to his lips once more. "I can't tell you how happy I am that she agreed to marry me."

"This is wonderful," Sophia gushed, right on cue. "What do you have in mind so far?"

"In mind?" Frankie jerked her gaze from Aidan to her mother.

"For the wedding." Sophia laced her fingers together, bouncing a little in her seat. "We need to start planning."

A bear trap locked around her ankle would be more comfortable. "I, um…" Frankie cleared the tight ball of dread out of her throat. Her mother was supposed to be enchanted by the romance, distracted by a future son-in-law. She was supposed to respect Frankie's space, not swoop in with talk of wedding plans. "I'm still adjusting to being engaged. The rest can wait."

For the right guy and preferably for a time when she wasn't consumed with clearing her father's name.

"We wanted to tell you first," Aidan added smoothly.

Sophia's delighted smile only grew brighter with every word Aidan uttered. "How did your parents react?"

"Well, they're in Ireland," Aidan explained. "They sounded happy enough when I called."

Sophia's smile retreated as concern filled her eyes. "You haven't met them?"

"Not yet," Frankie said, improvising. She hadn't considered this wrinkle. "I look forward to it." She glanced at Aidan, deciding his family must be wonderful based on him: smart and confident and wrapped in that sexy chiseled exterior.

Chiseled? Good grief, the game she'd started was fooling her. She tugged her hand free of his and pushed herself to her feet. Pretending to be relaxed and in love was making her jittery.

"Are you okay? Can I get you something?"

"I'm fine, Mom," she said too quickly. "It was just a long flight." *Play nice. Stay calm.* She walked toward the kitchen island and refilled her glass from the water pitcher Sophia had set out. "I tried to nap, but the hotel mattress was lumpy."

"The girl could star in a modern *Princess and the Pea*," Sophia told Aidan.

"I've noticed she likes things a certain way." His eyes gleamed with amusement. "And I like making her happy."

"We doted on her," Sophia admitted. "Siblings might have helped, but it never worked out."

"What?" This was the first Frankie had ever heard about siblings. "You tried to have more kids?"

"There's no need to be offended now," her mother said with a sad smile. "Your father and I wanted a big family and we had high hopes, considering how quickly I got pregnant with you. But I never carried another baby past twelve weeks."

How could the woman blurt out a personal confession in front of a stranger and yet not be honest with her own daughter about her husband's trial and suicide? Frankie shot Aidan a helpless glance. "I never knew."

"It doesn't matter to me." His kind smile loosened the knot twisting in her gut. Whoever he eventually married would be a lucky woman, on the receiving end of that kind of attention. "Our future is sure to have plenty of ups and downs."

Truer words, she thought, her head still spinning with Sophia's latest revelation. Maybe she suspected Frankie's motives for showing up now, and this was her own form of diversion.

"By the time you were old enough to understand, we'd stopped trying." Sophia was everything calm and open. "It was something I meant to discuss with you woman to woman, but we never found the time."

"I get it." Frankie gulped her water. "Aidan's right." She couldn't meet his gaze. "I'm sure we'll have plenty of issues to work through along our way."

"You're ahead of the game knowing that's part of married life," Sophia agreed. "The doctors never suggested it was hereditary."

First wedding talk and now kids? Frankie wanted the world to slow down so she could step off for a few minutes. It was too domestic and too strange, considering their last conversation and the resulting estrangement. "We'll cross that bridge when we get there, Mom." She would *not* discuss reproduction in front of Aidan.

"Of course." Sophia came to the counter and refilled her water glass, as well. "Why don't you two check out of the hotel and move in here?"

Frankie choked, coughed. "No. No, thanks." She couldn't play the adoring fiancée role 24/7. "Mom, really, we're fine at the hotel."

"I understand." Sophia made an examination of the ice in her glass. "How long will you be in town?"

Crap, Frankie was blowing the happy-daughter-here-for-a-fresh-start routine.

"That depends." Aidan stepped up, his warm smile the epitome of devoted groom as he smoothed over her gaffe. "Since I met your daughter, it's been clear how important family is to her. One reason we haven't given the wedding much thought is that she wants to share that process with you."

"Is that true?"

Frankie could only nod at the impending train wreck.

"I'm not one to waste time," Aidan continued. "I lit a fire of sorts under my future bride. I sent résumés to several companies, including Leo Solutions, in hopes of landing a job right away."

When he wrapped his arm around Frankie's shoulders, it felt so…normal.

"Frankie took leave from the Savannah PD," he went on, "so we could spend some time out here and see how it goes."

"Then you *must* stay here," Sophia insisted. "There's plenty of room. I'll find places for you both within the company. Think of it as a test drive. No obligation." She hesitated, hope shining in her eyes. "Or if you find the work suits you, we can make it permanent. It's what your father and I wanted all along."

"Mom." Just the mention of her father set her teeth on edge. "Your home—"

"Will always have room for you."

"Thank you, Sophia." Aidan stepped into the breach

once more. "That's generous and we appreciate it, of course."

Frankie rubbed the scar her mother knew about on her hip, the one still shedding bits of dirt from that wretched road. "I keep weird hours with the physical therapy and early-morning workouts. Besides, we're used to being alone."

Sophia's cheeks turned pink. "I do understand. Why don't we get you set up in a corporate apartment? At least until you decide if you're staying."

Frankie was about to turn that down, too, when she heard Aidan accepting it with enthusiasm. "A corporate apartment? That's not an imposition?"

"Not at all. I'm happy to do it. They're fully furnished, have a scheduled housekeeping service and provide great access to markets and entertainment downtown. The interns love the location."

"Great. Thanks." Frankie almost meant it.

Sophia glanced at her watch. "I'm supposed to check in at the office to review a client proposal before dinner. Why don't we all head over? You can meet my business partner, Paul Sterling, and we can discuss possible posts for each of you."

Frankie couldn't get out of the house fast enough. She didn't try to convince herself it was all about the case and getting a look inside Leo Solutions. If her mother had been so determined to eliminate her dad, why did she keep so many reminders of the life they'd shared? The contradiction seemed like an unsolvable puzzle.

Or it would have if she'd been here alone. Few things seemed impossible as she walked hand in hand with the man pretending to be in love with her. The realization didn't make her particularly happy, but that analysis would have to wait for another day.

"Your mom seems genuinely happy to see you again," Aidan said, sliding into the driver's seat. He knew the opposite was true for Frankie and he wanted to give her space to vent whatever she was feeling, before round two.

Her lips thinned. "It would be nice if I could take anything she says at face value."

Aidan appreciated her quiet insistence that they follow her mother to the Leo Solutions headquarters rather than riding with her. Frankie had held up like a champ, sticking with the safe topics, but she clearly needed a breather. "How are you doing?" He ignored the way her hands fisted in her lap.

"I'm fine. Thanks to your quick thinking. You're amazing at the undercover routine."

The unexpected compliment sounded sincere. "Thanks. It got a little dicey here and there."

"Did the wedding talk upset you?"

Yes. "Not too bad." Talk of kids had been worse. He concentrated on relaxing his grip on the steering wheel. A year ago fatherhood had been one of those murky, inevitable points in his future. Now he'd written it off as something he wasn't qualified to think about. "You made it sound as though she'd ask for DNA and blood samples."

"She might yet," Frankie replied, her gaze firmly on Sophia's car ahead of them. "It's probably part of the new-hire process."

"Well, I think we're doing great."

"You can't be sure," she countered.

"I am sure. You were right about the engagement tactic." Her ego needed a boost and her mind needed the distraction. "She's in love with the idea of you being in love." He waited, surprised when Frankie didn't give him an I-told-you-so. "I saw the way you sized up her place. Planning to break in?"

"No," she said, her brief laugh tinged with exhaustion. "I was just startled by how many things sitting around were from our previous homes." She scowled.

"You weren't thinking about floor safes and security systems?"

"Only a little." She twisted the diamond ring on her finger. "Do you think she did the painting and other stuff just to impress me?"

"I doubt it." He wasn't sure Frankie wanted his opinion right now. From his vantage point, Sophia was fully devoted to repairing her relationship with her daughter.

"Nice work buying your way in to a highly competitive job for the small investment of an engagement ring."

"Small investment?" He faked indignation. "I would've gotten the job, anyway. Interviewers love me." Though he was teasing, he felt her focus on him and he struggled not to fidget under that steady examination.

"I bet they do," she said. "The flowers were a nice touch."

Another compliment. It gave him hope for surviving the situation. "It pleases me that you're pleased." He flashed her a grin.

She gave him one of those scoffing snorts. "Do you think her partner, Paul, will start us in the mail room?"

"She's surely discussing the options with him already. She's been on the phone since she pulled out of the driveway."

"I noticed." Frankie's hands tensed up again. "What sort of position does she think you're qualified for?"

"I can hardly say. I'm former Interpol. The agency loaded my résumé with fitness and combat training expertise. Self-defense, hand-to-hand, various firearms."

"Nice."

He felt his chest swell that she was impressed. "And you?"

"At the end of the day, I'm an analyst like my mom." She didn't sound happy about the comparison. "You're far more than that," he said automatically.

Frankie shrugged one shoulder. "She could fit me in as a trainer, but she won't. I don't think she'll ever let go of how weak I was right after those early surgeries."

Surgeries, plural? He wanted her to volunteer more information about her injury and recovery so he could avoid an invasion of her medical privacy. "You look perfectly fit to me."

"Is that a sincere compliment?" She was staring at him again.

"Yes." He shot her a smile. "Did you think the things I said in front of your mother weren't sincere?"

"No other conclusion." Frankie didn't sound the least perturbed. "You don't know me."

Every word he'd said in front of her mom, he believed. Unfortunately, he couldn't give Frankie an answer she'd accept, so he changed the subject. "What do you know about Paul Sterling?"

"Only what we looked at last night." She shifted in

the seat. "Did you get the impression there's a personal connection?"

"I hope not." Anything personal between Paul and Sophia threw a wrench into his assessment of the investigation. Bad enough he might have to anticipate how Sophia would rank her relationship with her daughter amid her commitments to the company. A lover only increased the twists exponentially, not to mention how Frankie would react. The last thing she needed was more pain. "We'll know soon enough," he said, taking the last turn into an industrial park near the airport.

They followed Sophia past the security guard at the gate and parked in a space behind the one reserved with her name on it. He caught Frankie's hand before she could get out of the car. "You're doing great," he said, his gaze locked with hers. "And you're not alone."

She shocked him with a quick kiss on his lips and a hot smile. "Game on."

Knowing this was all show for her mother, Aidan felt frustrated that his immediate reaction had nothing to do with the case. The kick in his pulse, the flash of heat under his skin were all about the woman. He watched her stride up to join her mom and wondered if his attraction was as one-sided as it felt.

"Paul's waiting for us in my office," Sophia announced.

Another warning that the man's purpose went beyond business.

Like Frankie, Aidan was cataloging every detail as they walked into the lobby. The information placard showed Leo Solutions had offices listed on the top two floors and one lower level of the seven-story building, with other companies scattered in between. The place was quiet, the furnishings expensive and understated. A tall vase exploding with fresh flowers spanned the space between the banks of elevators. He imagined clients felt safe and reassured doing business here.

"Do you always work on Saturdays?" he asked, when the three of them stepped into an elevator.

"Not always," Sophia replied. "We have a new client we're courting." Her eyes sparkled as her gaze danced between the two of them.

Aidan took Frankie's hand in his, a casual gesture of affection that Sophia noticed.

"Paul pulled your résumé, Aidan. I know some people might see it as favoritism, but I'm glad you told me you'd applied." She held the door open when they reached her floor. "Welcome to Leo Solutions."

Frankie's fingers tightened around his hand. He gave them a reassuring squeeze.

"We have offices on this floor and the next floor up. And a fully equipped gym and training space on the first sublevel."

"Is there anywhere in Seattle that doesn't have a great view?" Aidan asked as they strolled by a bank of windows.

"The views, the weather and the recreational variety were the things we enjoyed most as a family. Right, Frankie?"

"I remember."

"I just couldn't see planting the business anywhere else. Your father and I even looked at this building together."

"Really?"

"Really." Sophia's reply was a whispered echo, her gaze locked on the view beyond the wide windows running the length of the far wall. "Let's not keep Paul waiting. He's eager to meet you both."

Aidan hoped she wasn't putting words into her business partner's mouth. He hadn't been able to get through the company finances or the partnership agreement, so he didn't know if Paul would see Frankie as a threat or an asset. Although Sophia's warm welcome gave him the impression Frankie, as her only family, would be a beneficiary at the very least, it was too soon to know for sure.

Sophia led them down a hallway framed by cubicles on one side and small offices on the other. Her office suite was preceded by a receptionist's desk and double doors, currently standing open. Paul, seeing them, walked over from the seating area near the corner window. He smiled as Sophia made the introductions, but Aidan didn't feel any warmth in the expression.

"It's good to meet you," Paul said to Frankie as they settled into the seating area. "You mean the world to your mother. She's missed you." He took a seat at one end of a long couch and Sophia sat next to him.

Mentally, Aidan swore. There was a romantic liaison between the business partners. As he and Frankie took the chairs opposite the older couple, he noticed the way she eased her body into hers. That cautious transition from standing to sitting was the only allowance he'd seen her make for her injury. He wasn't about to jeopardize any progress he'd made by mentioning it to her.

"Sophia tells me we need to find positions within Leo Solutions." Paul cocked an eyebrow at Aidan. "For both of you."

"Only if it's convenient," he answered. "I'm happy to look for work elsewhere."

"Nonsense. You'll be family soon." Sophia's sharp gaze slid to her partner. "Aidan has the background and qualities we prefer."

He gave Paul his best easygoing smile. "I don't intend to force my way in."

Paul tapped the closed tablet balanced on the arm of the couch. "I'd flagged your résumé for an interview before Sophia called."

Aidan pretended to believe him.

"We didn't come out to insert ourselves into your business," Frankie interjected quietly as she reached for Aidan's hand. "I'm sure you know things were rough between Mom and me, but when Aidan proposed, I knew I wanted to tell her in person."

"She's willing to stay, Paul," Sophia said, her voice catching. "You know we could use her skills."

He nodded. "Would you rather work a desk or be in the field? I'm sure Sophia's told you we have three divisions offering cyber security, property security and personal protection solutions."

"A desk," Frankie replied, avoiding her mother's gaze.

Aidan saw the tension fall from Sophia's shoulders. It was such a typical, caring, maternal reaction. If he'd suffered Frankie's injuries, his mother would do the same thing. He'd reviewed the bulk of what Frankie labeled as evidence against her mother and he didn't have enough to verify the documentation as real. Still, he wasn't seeing any of the cold animosity Frankie insisted lurked under Sophia's reserved and polished surface.

"Based on your record with the navy and the Savannah Police Department, we can add you as an analyst."

Aidan listened as intently as Frankie while Paul outlined the details of the position.

"You'd be working closely with me, as well," Sophia added.

Aidan was sure that was a mistake, but Frankie managed a smile. "Sounds good."

"My only concern," Paul continued, holding up a hand, "is your status at the Savannah PD. Your supervisor isn't aware you're job hunting. He believes you're out here on extended leave."

If she was going to falter and blow their cover, this would be the moment. "I told him I needed some personal time," Frankie said. "And I agreed to continue consulting on cases as needed." She looked hard at Sophia. "I wasn't sure how things would go here."

"That's perfectly understandable," her mother said.

"Is it?" Paul countered. "We're in the midst of a major client pitch. I'd like to know the team is focused on that primary goal."

Frankie scooted to the edge of her chair. "I'll call in and give my notice on Monday. I'll do it now if you'd prefer."

Aidan watched as a wealth of information passed, unspoken, between the older couple. "Frankie and I don't mean to put you in a tough position," he said. "We have other options in the area and we can always just call this a vacation."

"This is *home*." Sophia pressed her lips together. "At least I want it to be." Her tender, pleading gaze moved to Frankie. "Give us six months. Please."

Frankie looked to Paul. "Will that work for you?"

He agreed with a nod. "Now, Aidan." His salt-and-pepper eyebrows dipped low. "We have a vacancy in the training division for our personal security team. You'd be overseeing everything from hand-to-hand combat to weapons proficiency."

"Sounds good."

"You're not afraid of paperwork, are you?"

"Not at all."

"Are you willing to venture into the field occasionally to help with planning and assessment?"

"Of course."

Paul stood and extended his hand. "Then welcome to Leo Solutions. We'll get the paperwork sorted on Monday."

The older man was friendly enough, appearing open and content with the new arrivals. Aidan had yet to pinpoint what bothered him about Sophia's business partner. Polite, not quite slick, Paul seemed to be hiding a cold, hard center. The man ran a security company; suspicions went with the job. Maybe he had painted himself as the protector here, of Sophia and the firm. Considering how and when the business had launched, it made some sense. It would've made more sense if Sophia exhibited any sign of weakness.

Like mother, like daughter, Aidan thought, knowing he'd never dare say so in front of Frankie.

Paul turned toward Sophia. "In the meantime, I'm sure you have plenty of catching up in mind."

"I do." She was as delighted as any adoring mother to have her child home, within arm's reach. "We'll start with a company tour, and then I'll take them over to the apartment," she said, leaning close to kiss Paul's cheek. "I'll be back soon to finish that proposal."

Chapter Seven

Sunday, April 10, 12:45 p.m.

Frankie's gaze moved from her empty suitcase to the nearly empty closet in the bedroom of the corporate apartment leased by Leo Solutions. She was wearing the only dress she'd thought to pack, a last-minute item she'd tossed in. Her half of the closet held two pairs of jeans, an assortment of shirts, one pair of khaki slacks and only two pairs of shoes in addition to her runners.

"Problem?" Aidan paused just behind her. "We can always go shopping or have a friend send you whatever you forgot."

"That's not it." She shoved her suitcase into the closet and closed the door. "I guess we're all moved in."

Her limited wardrobe was the least of her troubles. Currently at the top of her list of problems was the *one* bedroom apartment. They'd had more space— possibly more privacy—at the hotel suite. Aidan had made a valid argument when she tried to back out again: they had to make it look as if they were meeting Sophia halfway.

As they were wrapping up brunch, Sophia had invited them once more to stay at the house. Again

Frankie refused. Though she'd appreciated Aidan's diplomatic backup, she wasn't as enamored with his small touches, his chivalrous manners and the occasional chaste kiss.

Sophia, however, was overjoyed with every gesture that affirmed Frankie and Aidan were happy together. Unfortunately, while he played the doting-fiancé role like an expert, she struggled against an urge to skitter away. Or worse, burrow into him.

She had to focus, to stay angry with Sophia, but she was losing her grip on that bitter edge. Sophia had always been vibrant and outgoing, and being drenched in her mother's warmth made something deep inside Frankie long for the way things once were. The life she'd worked toward, dreamed of and enjoyed so fleetingly had been ripped apart and scattered.

Her family would never be the same, and not just because the Leones numbered two now instead of three. Frankie believed her mother bore the blame. She'd come all this way to prove it.

Except they weren't finding anything conclusive. She knew Aidan wasn't working against her, precisely. It just didn't feel as though he was working *with* her. Her mother's passports were bogus and he kept casting doubts over the source of the statement and documentation on the flash drive.

Now they were living together in an apartment that might very well be bugged. They couldn't speak freely and couldn't jam a signal without blowing their cover. They would go to the office each day and come back here. The engagement was working, giving them a reason to be together, yet Frankie felt trapped by her own scheme. She finally understood what he'd said on the plane about lying to each other in public.

"I didn't think this through," she said, just in case the bugs were live. "Six months will be an exercise in restraint." She sneered at the closet. "At least we'll have the company gear for work." Bags of Leo Solutions shirts and workout gear had been lined up on the corner of the furnished sofa when they walked in.

"Why don't we head out and see about stocking the kitchen?" he suggested.

"Great idea." She grabbed her purse, her smallest knife tucked inside. While they were out they'd have a chance to talk freely. Of course, that also gave their opponent time to search the apartment. On missions like this one, Frankie knew every choice came with a calculated risk.

It made her feel marginally better when Aidan planted a wireless camera to catch anyone who might enter the apartment. When they were clear of the building, she caught him watching for a tail, because she was doing it, too. "We're a pair," she said with a short laugh.

"A good pair." He took her hand and drew her close to his side, playing his role to perfection once more.

"You don't have to fawn over me all the time."

He only grinned. "Relax. I know you're not big on public displays of affection."

"I'm affectionate," she argued.

He laughed as they crossed the street. "Sure you are. Just keep following my lead."

His assessment gave her pause. "Do you think my mom suspects we're pretending?" That could put an end to her best chance to know the truth.

"No, she's seeing what we want her to see right now."

"Why do I feel slimy?" The moment the words were out, Frankie regretted them. Aidan tensed, just a subtle flex of muscle in his arm, and she chattered to cover the gaffe. "I know this approach was my idea. I stand by it," she insisted. "You said yourself it's working. She's distracted by wedding brain. We'll be able to get what we came for before she knows what happened."

"At this rate you'll be telling her you're pregnant by Friday," he said, his voice cool.

Frankie considered and dismissed the idea as too soon. "The corporate apartment can work for us, too."

"How? You think the doorman knows something?"

"No." Her patience had stretched thin during brunch, but she couldn't let it snap. Aidan was her only ally. She needed him to see the real Sophia under the social sophistication and perfect-mother image. "We'll uncover the truth."

They walked down the block toward the waterfront, admiring the blend of historic and new architecture spiking up around them. Aidan asked her questions about the city and she answered, trying to decide if this was part of the cover. A pleasant breeze toyed with the hem of her skirt. "Are you pleased or disappointed we don't have a tail?" she asked, getting the conversation back to safe ground.

"Pleased," he replied. "She trusts us. Paul might pose the bigger problem."

"Paul's reserved, that's all." Thinking about Sophia's business partner, Frankie couldn't help making a comparison. "He's the polar opposite of my father. Do you think she went for the quiet and serious type this time on purpose?"

"I think she partnered with the man who gave Leo Solutions the best chance to succeed. He and your parents go way back."

"Don't remind me." Aidan had found the connection last night and pieced together the trail. Frankie had been more than a little alarmed by the discovery. Not to mention the kiss her mother had deposited on the man's cheek.

"She wasn't having an affair, Frankie."

"You sound so sure." She reached back and pressed a point on her back, above her hip. Keeping pace with his longer stride created a good ache as her muscles loosened up.

"I am. I've been systematically working through your mother's history."

They'd divided the searches for the purpose of efficiency and objectivity. Everything Frankie found on Sophia only made her cranky, which stalled the progress. So she dug into the general's last months in Afghanistan while Aidan investigated her mom.

"Are you working present to past?" If so, it left her exposed as he learned of her mother's trips to hospitals and spine injury rehab centers to help Frankie recover. She pushed down the swell of embarrassment. Of all the people involved in this mess, she had the fewest secrets.

"A little of both, actually."

She could tell he had more to say, a new question or accusation about her lousy approach on this case. "Spit it out. I can take it."

He stopped to admire a display in a gallery window,

draping his arm around her shoulders. They were just a couple out for a walk on a fine Sunday. Though she wanted to sink into the comfort he offered, it was too risky. She couldn't afford to mirror her mother's mistake and get distracted by Aidan's false romance.

"You realize your mom took hits from all sides, nearly all at once."

Frankie caught her scowling reflection in the glass. She nudged him on down the street. "What do you mean?"

"Charges against the general were filed only a few days after you were injured. He was arrested. You were undergoing surgery."

"And?"

"That's a lot for anyone to handle. You were medicated before the surgery. Sedated for nearly two days after. Do you understand she never left your side?"

Frankie had no memory of the day before the IED or those immediately following. She'd learned the facts from her doctors and the survivors from her team. She had only a hazy recollection of Sophia being nearby in those early days.

"You're implying my mom chose me over my dad."

"I'm not implying. I'm saying it outright."

Frankie glanced around for a distraction, uncomfortable with the way her heart cramped at his words. "Another way might be to say she was already distancing herself from his problems."

Aidan sighed. "You told Victoria you tried to have a civilized conversation with your mom about your father's case."

"A complete disaster," Frankie admitted. People were bustling around them now as they strolled by vendors in Pike Place Market. The produce was bright and the scents of greens and fruits mingled with flowers and seafood and the close waterfront. She knew they'd have to return with something or eat out again, but neither of them moved to make purchases.

"Why?"

Frankie wondered how best to explain it, wondered more why she felt so compelled to make him understand this wasn't merely a vindictive witch hunt. "The last time Mom and I talked about my dad was at his funeral. I admit there's no such thing as rational during a time like that. I needed to understand why she hadn't been more vocal about his innocence."

"Did it ever occur to you he might've been guilty?"

"Absolutely not." To believe that went against everything she knew about her dad's character and integrity. She didn't care if that skewed her perspective.

"Frankie." Aidan took her hand and guided her past buckets of bright, happy snapdragons that mocked the misery inside her. "We've picked up some company. We need to start shopping while we talk."

She blinked, momentarily startled by the instruction. A quick glance and she thought she'd pegged one. "The guy across the street with the paper?"

Aidan nodded. "And one on our six." He chose a dozen snapdragons and pulled out his wallet. "Is there a vase at the apartment?" His movements gave them time to assess the men tailing them.

"If not, we'll improvise." She pushed her mouth into a smile to match his and felt that feminine flutter grow. If her mother would just come clean, none of this would be necessary and Frankie wouldn't be stuck knowing the best romance of her life was a complete fraud.

He handed her the flowers so he could pull out his phone. They looked at it together, just another couple consulting an electronic list as they checked the camera in the apartment. "Clear," he said, for her ears only. "Fieldwork can be such fun."

It made her laugh. "We can't let this take six months."

"You think it will be such a hardship to live with me?"

Not at all. The thought scared her. "I'd ask for hazard pay," she teased to lighten her mood. "I meant being this close to my mom. I'll crack if I have to play nice that long."

They strolled up and down aisles of vegetables, making choices and planning meals. Learning what tastes they had in common and where they differed. It was ridiculously real.

"Frankie, I'm begging you to be patient here," he said, standing too close while she selected fresh greens. "If you want the truth, you have to look at things objectively."

"You seem determined to repair a broken family. That isn't why we're here."

He was quiet as they started back up the hill to their building. The silence suited her, if only because he was right. She did have tunnel vision about Sophia. It would've been bad enough if her father had lived and been forced out of the army. She couldn't imagine the betrayal that drove him to suicide.

"When I asked her, point-blank, over my dad's grave, she said it was her fault."

Aidan stopped short and people flowed around

them on the sidewalk. "That's a big detail to keep to yourself."

Frankie could just imagine what Victoria would think when he sent that in. "Would it change anything?" She shifted her hold on the grocery bags. "Sophia wouldn't explain and she refused to cooperate with anyone who could clear his name. I walked away and didn't speak to her again until yesterday."

"Give me those," Aidan said, taking the produce bags from her hands. "Did you consider that she was speaking figuratively?"

"That's the real question, isn't it?" Frankie picked up the pace, knowing he'd drop the subject when they reached the apartment. "I can't let her get away with it. When Dad's friend showed up, when he gave me the key, I made a choice to follow through, no matter what hell I discover on the way."

"I don't think it's that simple."

Frankie jerked open the building door with a harsh laugh. The strained sound bounced around the marble lobby. "Of course it isn't simple. Families and weddings never are," she added, just in case the security guard was on her mother's payroll. "But we'll get through it."

In the elevator, he set the groceries down and took her hands in his. The move rattled her until she remembered the security camera high in the corner. "Promise me you won't make a decision about any detail unless we talk about it first."

She opened her mouth to agree, but he silenced her with a soft kiss. The fleeting touch left her lips tingling.

"Don't just say the words, Frankie. Mean them."

"You can make the same promise to me, right?"

He nodded. "We're in this together," he said as the elevator doors parted at their floor.

Together. The team concept had always been important to her. An only child and an army brat, she put serious value in that word. For years, it had been the Leone family taking on the world. Then it had been the navy and her SEAL team. She'd recognized and battled loneliness through the years. She hadn't realized how deep it went until this moment. It was nice to know she wouldn't have to face the inevitable ugliness to come alone.

She wasn't sure if the revelation was a good thing or if she'd only be more broken when she and Aidan went their separate ways.

AIDAN STOOD BACK as Frankie unlocked their door. He didn't like being tailed any more than he liked the secrets Frankie was keeping. At least whoever was having them followed had yet to order a search of the apartment. He didn't count on the privacy lasting much longer.

There was a rhythm to this kind of work, and he could sense something was about to give. He'd handled delicate cases before, played cat and mouse with some of Europe's worst offenders. This was an entirely different scenario.

As they put away the groceries and tossed around dinner ideas, he hoped they sounded like a normal, contented couple. Her mother believed it, which mattered more than how being this close, this affectionate with Frankie was driving him mad. Although Frankie followed his lead when he made romantic gestures, he was going to have to encourage her to reach for him once in a while. He didn't dwell on the potential mine-field of that thought.

He was relieved when she walked out to the bal-cony to take a call from Sophia. The line between his undercover role and his true feelings was blurring. He liked Frankie's spunk and admired her determination, even if he thought she was off target about her mom.

In Victoria's office, he'd seen a hurt, unhappy and angry woman. In Sophia's house, he'd watched the memories—good and bad—swamp her. Though he'd merely skimmed the surface of the classified morass that was the Leone family history, what he'd found confirmed that she'd been raised in a happy, stable home.

Frankie walked back in, tapping her phone against her palm. "Mom asked about setting a wedding date."

He smiled despite the chill slithering down his spine. "And?" Just because the gear hadn't picked up any ac-tive bugs didn't mean they could relax. If they were going to complete this investigation effectively, he might have to reserve a hotel room under an alternate name just so they could speak freely.

"And do you have a preference?" She slid onto the counter stool, watching him too closely.

Six weeks after never would be fine with him. "I thought girls spent most of their lives daydreaming about the perfect wedding."

"I'm a *woman*." Frankie crossed her arms and glared.

"I noticed." He came around the counter and grabbed her. "Anyone could be listening," he mur-mured at her ear, knowing that wasn't the point. Tip-ping up her chin, he planted a long kiss on her lips. For a moment she was shocked, her body stiff in his arms. Then she relaxed with a soft sigh that electrified his system. Her arms wound around his neck, and her fingers sifted through his hair. He forgot about the case as he slid his tongue between her lips and indulged in her warm, sensual taste. Need slammed through him, too tempting and far too convincing. He broke the kiss and smiled into her dazed eyes. "Name the date and time and you know I'll be there."

She slipped out of his reach, her face flushed and her lips plump from the kiss. "Mom suggested December. That gives us planning time."

He knew she was talking about the wedding as well as the case. How would a happy future groom reply? "You want to get married over the holidays?"

"There are lots of non-holiday days in December."

Was her irritation an act? Aidan glanced around the apartment. Although he was committed to the work, he didn't think anyone at the Colby Agency anticipated this assignment going for half a year. "Why not sooner?" he asked. The time crunch landed like a weight on his chest, making it impossible to get a breath.

"How soon can your family be here?"

His family. He knew she was teasing by the mischievous expression in her deep brown eyes. His eyes dropped to the ring on her hand. His gut clenched. Turning on his heel, he found a glass, filled it with cold water. Drink it or dump it on his head? He drank, buying time to think. Hashing over her past was part of the case. He wanted to keep his family, his mistakes to himself. Would Sophia respect his privacy or go snooping if he hedged on the family details? He knew the answer without asking.

He leaned back against the sink. "Does my family need to be here? I can call them after it's done. Send them a video of the ceremony. Live stream it."

"Aidan?"

The concern in Frankie's voice made him want to bolt. From the room and the case. Hell, from the planet. He struggled for control. "Tell her we'll look at the calendar," he said. "Tell her I'll reach out to my mom tonight." They both knew he wouldn't.

"Okay."

He had to trust the agency to field those calls properly, protecting their cover and shielding his parents from any unnecessary distress.

"We keep dancing around it, but if you think they won't like me, we can call this off. I don't want to come between you and your family."

"That's absurd." Hell, they'd probably love her under better circumstances. He stalked past her, wishing for something far stronger than the glass of water in his hand. He knew she was trying to stay in character. His problem was that she was suddenly so damned effective. Her eyes were his weakness. The woman needed his help whether she liked it or not, and he knew she didn't mean to hurt him.

"They'll adjust," he said. "They always do," he added under his breath, flopping down on the couch.

"To clarify, I'm not the one nagging." Frankie followed him, easing into the armchair. "If your parents aren't at your wedding, I think you'll regret it."

He could hardly tell her it wasn't any of her business, not here in a place likely wired for sound. "I'm familiar with the theory," he said. "We'll get it sorted out," he added, willing her to drop it.

"You haven't told them you proposed?"

Aidan stared at her, wondering if it was better to have this farcical conversation here, packed with double meanings she might not understand, or just take her out again and confess it all. They were likely under observation; they had to behave. He stayed on the couch, rolling the cool glass between his palms. "I haven't told them anything about you," he said quietly, testing her reaction. She would know that much was true. Whoever might be listening in would wonder why he'd lied to Sophia.

Frankie nodded. "All things considered, that's understandable."

A warning bell clanged through his head. "What?" He couldn't believe she'd diverted her relentless focus from her mother long enough to snoop through his past.

"As soon as you tell them you're seeing someone, that you're engaged, they'll pester you with questions. Being under my mom's microscope is enough pressure for us right now."

"I'm not going to crack."

"That's not what I'm saying." Frankie kicked off her shoes and tucked her bare feet up under her skirt. Reaching up, she pulled the clip holding her hair back and the silky dark waves tumbled over her shoulders.

He couldn't stop staring. The feminine, flowy dress and her loose hair softened the lean, tough woman. After his personal life had imploded, he'd never thought to be this emotionally intimate with anyone— personally or professionally. "Then be clear. I'm not in the mood for cryptic," he said, ignoring the irony.

She rolled her eyes. "I've seen it happen with friends. As soon as you let others into the relationship—just by saying you're involved with someone—it ups the expectations."

"You should expect more of me now that we're engaged." He tried to laugh it off.

"Stop growling like a bear." She came over, easing down beside him in that careful way she had. "I'm saying it's okay if you don't tell your parents anything until you're ready. We're not in any rush."

His pulse kicked as her ginger-and-clove scent washed over him. "But we'll keep lying to your mom when she's pressing for dates and plans?"

"I'll tell her to back off." Frankie picked up his hand and rested it on her knee as if they were really together. "You've gone the extra mile for me." She held up her left hand, flashing the ring and a wry smile. "It's my turn. Let's make a promise we won't let anyone else dictate what we want our life to look like."

Despite knowing the words were for a faceless listener, they soothed him. *She* soothed him. This was dangerous territory he'd entered and he couldn't see the exit. "I was engaged once before." It was too late to snatch the words back. Maybe if he opened up, she'd trust him a little more. "I never wanted to tell you."

Her dark eyebrows arched high, her eyes wide. "You don't have to tell me. It doesn't matter."

It mattered. Why hadn't he told her on the plane and avoided all this? He stroked his thumb along her ring finger, remembering another woman. "My family might not want to be around my wedding at all." She needed to hear the story just in case Leo Solutions got a peek behind the credentials the Colby Agency had created for him. "I met her through a friend," he began. "Call us foolish, but we went from introductions to engaged in about two seconds flat."

Frankie had the grace to blush.

"My family adored her. They were thrilled I was settling down, and thought being married would change my career goals."

"It didn't." She squeezed his hand, her eyes full of sympathy.

Between her upbringing and her career, she understood what he was saying despite what he left unsaid. It was a strange sensation. Though the case that killed his fiancée was officially closed and sealed, the guilt would follow him forever. "If we'd met while you were still in the navy, would we even be here now?"

"I doubt it," she said, her lips twitching into a wry grin. "My team never had much reason to be in Savannah."

At her joke, something like relief loosened the knot in his chest. Recognizing his honesty, she comprehended the concept of what had happened, as well as the lingering effects.

He might be able to play the part of a doting fiancé, but he'd never let another relationship get serious enough to put a woman at risk. "You've figured it out. She became a target." He kept his gaze on the window just past Frankie's shoulder. The memories assaulted him, anyway. "I couldn't save her. Our families were devastated by the loss. You know how it is. Hard words walk side by side with that kind of grief."

"Aidan. It's okay."

It wasn't. "Despite all that, I couldn't change who I am, what I'm good at."

"No one should ask you to change."

He couldn't stand the look on her face. Suddenly he wanted the sharp, tough Frankie, the woman impatiently searching for answers. He needed her to push him away. Instead, he pulled her body across his and kissed her, pouring all his frustration and desire into that sweet contact. Silently promising he wouldn't fail her as he'd failed others.

She didn't shove him away, but responded instantly, matching his urgency with her mouth and hands. He wrapped his arms tight around her, clinging until she was his only thought, his only awareness, his very breath. She knew his worst secret, his biggest failure, and she kissed him as if he was her hero.

Her head fell back and he feasted on the golden column of her throat. Her skin was so soft, with a trace of sweetness that was so at odds with her tough nature and determination.

"I love this dress," he said, slipping his hand under the hem to caress her knee, her firm thigh.

She trapped his hand with hers, stopping his progress. The move brought him back to his senses. He leaned away enough to enjoy the view of her stunning face. The personal and professional lines between them were more than blurred; they'd been obliterated. He forced himself to release her before he completely lost control. He'd never expected their performance, their *lies*, to get into his head this way. "I think I'll check out the gym." Awkwardly he pushed himself to his feet, left her there.

"I'll change and go with you."

He shook his head. "I'm okay. I'd like some space."

She sat up, smoothing her skirt, then her hair. "I'll work on dinner."

"Thanks." He shoved his hands into his pockets because he wanted to stay, to touch her and never quit. "I hope my past doesn't, um, change anything."

"Not a chance," she replied, busying herself with one of the throw pillows. "I'll come up with something so my mom doesn't pester you."

"You're a terrific fiancée." *In any context*, he thought. "I'll be back within the hour." He escaped to the bedroom and changed clothes, still reeling from that kiss. He left the apartment without risking another word. Taking her in his arms had nothing to do with possible spy devices and everything to do with the heat she stirred inside him. If he didn't stick with logic, if he didn't find his balance, the investigation could fall apart. Aidan had no idea what he'd do without the work and shelter of the Colby Agency.

What had possessed him to be so damned honest with her? If he'd told her that on the plane or in the jewelry store, she might have backed off the stupid engagement idea. Although, based on what he'd seen so far, she'd been right to take that angle. It gave her mother something happier to focus on than their difficult last meeting.

Aidan knew better than most how survival often hinged on finding a purpose beyond the tragedy. Her mother had done it, creating the business. Frankie had used the intention of clearing her dad's name to empower her full recovery. He knew how she felt. His dogged hunt for his fiancée's killer had been excused as a search for justice. Only the intervention of cooler heads had saved him from himself. He decided he was here not just as an investigator, but to be that same voice of reason for Frankie.

To follow Victoria's orders he had to stay close and protect Frankie from herself as much as her drive for answers. Surely he could find a way to do his job and keep his hands off her, at least when they were alone.

Chapter Eight

Frankie had never wanted a hotel room more than she did on Monday morning. In the hotel they didn't have to talk in code or maintain the act 24/7. It irritated her that they couldn't be sure of anything right now. That kiss never would've happened at the hotel, where they could be themselves. It had taken all her self-control to pretend that delicious, groping contact on the couch hadn't fazed her.

Already Aidan knew better than to try to talk with her before her first cup of tea in the morning. She needed quiet time to wake up. Time to adjust her back and her attitude before attacking the day.

When she wandered into the kitchen, he slid a cup of tea in front of her. He was working on a plate of eggs with slices of crisp bacon on the side. "Help yourself."

She shook her head as she sipped the hot brew. She'd never been able to eat first thing in the morning. By the time he finished his breakfast her nerves were frayed. Neither of them said much until they got to the car. It already felt like a long day and they hadn't reached the office.

"Nervous?" she asked as he started the engine. Being the new kids at the company would be interesting. How would the employees react to the prodigal daughter and her future husband?

"Not at all."

"How can you say that?"

"Toughest part for me was our conversation yesterday."

Every ounce of courage she possessed had been required to keep her mind off that subject. She couldn't dwell on what he'd told her or how she'd lost herself in his embrace afterward. It was too much. "I'm sorry. If—"

"No apologies," he said, interrupting her. "Your tactic is working and we'll have more freedom at the office."

"We hope." She twisted the ring on her finger again. "Sophia's waiting for me to bring it up."

"I disagree. She's waiting to hear you'll stay and be part of her life and company."

Frankie ignored the little voice in her head that said he was right. "I didn't think the company would be this extensive. I know we studied it, but during the tour it felt so much bigger in person."

"Should make for an interesting morning," he said. "We've both faced tougher tasks."

"I know." Even before he'd shared his personal tragedy, she'd checked on the public records of his time with Interpol. Aidan had been involved in closing several important cases. As much as she'd resented it, Victoria had provided the perfect investigator for this case. Frankie suspected she always did. "Thanks again for being here."

"Says the woman who wanted me to stay away."

"Don't gloat," she said as he parked the car in the space Sophia had assigned them. "Without you, I would've lost my composure a dozen times by now."

"So few?"

"I understand the need for discretion and secrets. I don't understand why she persistently lies to me. If we prove that she helped convict an innocent man, what kind of person does that make me? I'm her daughter."

"Whatever your mom has or *hasn't* done, her actions don't change anything about you, Frankie."

She paused, her hand on the door handle, and allowed his words to sink in. It was basic logic and only more evidence that she was letting her emotions and family memories cloud her view of the present. "No offense, but I want to get in there and catch her red-handed so we can go back to our regularly scheduled lives as soon as possible."

His blue eyes narrowed. "That's a dangerous bias during an investigation."

Frankie shrugged. "You're the investigator. I'm just a daughter searching for the truth." With that she picked up her purse and left the car.

"Hang on." Aidan quickly caught up with her. "We agreed to do this the right way."

"And we will," she replied, her gaze straight ahead. "When we can prove she set up my dad, I will see it through every step of the legal process." Frankie was determined to find facts her mother couldn't explain away. Facts, and the resulting anger, were easier to deal with than the big question hovering in the shadows: Why? Her every memory featured her parents as happy and affectionate. Loving, devoted to each other in their careers and at home. Had her entire up-bringing, her concept of love and relationships, been a web of deceit?

She pasted a smile on her face when she spotted her mother waiting for them at the information desk in the lobby. "Good morning!" Sophia embraced them both. "I thought I'd show you around before I turn you over to Human Resources."

Frankie started to remind her they'd had a tour on Saturday afternoon and had done the new-hire paper-work online, but Aidan spoke up first. "That's thought-ful, Sophia. Thanks."

It became immediately apparent her mother wanted to personally introduce them to everyone in the com-pany, if not the building. Frankie knew she'd forget names, but not the floor plans or office locations.

They were with HR through the morning, and by lunchtime Frankie was hoping for a hearty meal and some quiet. Instead, Paul and Sophia picked them up and led them to the building cafeteria. Once again Aidan carried the conversation while Frankie concen-trated on eating for the sole purpose of fueling up for the afternoon ahead.

"Frankie, your office is down the hall from mine," Sophia said as they wrapped up the meal.

"Office?" She hadn't expected that.

"I'll show you your space," Paul said to Aidan. "It doesn't have much of a view, but you'll be near the training facilities."

"Makes perfect sense," Aidan said.

Frankie's stomach churned. She had the distinct im-pression that neither she nor Aidan would be allowed to roam Leo Solutions unsupervised. Had her mother seen through their act?

"Tonight we can have dinner and you can fill us in on your first day over grilled salmon."

"That'll be great, Mom," she said, stifling her reluctance. More socializing meant more of Aidan's tempting touches. "Can we bring anything?"

"Not at all." With a winning smile for Paul, Sophia stood up and motioned for Frankie to follow.

Aidan didn't let her go without a soft kiss on her cheek. "Have a great day," he said with a wink.

"I'm so glad you're here," Sophia told her as they rode the elevator upstairs. "Your father and I wanted this to be a family business."

Frankie swallowed back the grief and temper, remembering Aidan's words of caution. "Do you miss him?" It sounded like a daughter question to her.

Sophia's eyes turned sad and the wistful smile was either genuine or well rehearsed. "He was a good father, a good man, Frankie. I'm so sorry you didn't get the closure you needed."

The elevator doors parted and not even Frankie wanted to push the topic with so many curious eyes and ears aimed their way.

"Here's your office," Sophia said, stopping halfway down the long corridor. She opened the door wide and gestured for her to walk in. "Feel free to order the supplies you need. You'll remember my office is at the end of the hall."

Frankie just stared at the space. The surface of the desk gleamed and the only items on it were a computer monitor and a notepad. Of course her mother would remember how much she detested clutter. "Thanks," she murmured.

"I didn't order a nameplate yet. I wasn't sure if you were going to use your nickname here. I assume you'll take Aidan's last name when you marry."

"Right," Frankie said, walking around the desk toward the luxurious chair. "You really went all out."

"I want you to love it here," Sophia admitted, pushing the door closed behind her. "I know how disappointed you were by the navy's decision. You are your father's daughter."

"You can say that, when you believe he committed treason?"

"I've been waiting for that." Sophia sighed, stepping a little closer. "Sweetheart, you have his drive and ambition. The charges and verdict are irrelevant. You need to let it go."

"How?" Frankie stopped herself just short of an angry rant, gripping the back of the chair. "He was disgraced, Mom. It haunts me."

"In the military it might have," she allowed. "It didn't haunt you in Savannah and it won't haunt you here."

"I'm not talking about career paths."

"I know." Sophia folded her arms and sighed. "If I had the answers, I'd share them."

Like the little girl she'd been, Frankie wanted to believe her. Wanted it so much she caught herself blinking away tears. She didn't trust her voice.

"Leo Solutions is built on a solid foundation," Sophia continued. "Yes, I had to shift the business plan after your father's problems, but we are stable. This company was his dream, our legacy to pass on to you."

Everything about her relaxed as her lips curved in a tentative smile. "And here you are at last."

Here she was, all right, Frankie thought. Ready to excavate any and all secrets and dirty laundry propping up this company.

"Take a seat," Sophia urged her. "When you log on you'll have access to our previous proposals as well as what we've pulled together for the current one. If you have any suggestions, let me know. We'll be having meetings all week to get this one just right."

"Okay." She wished she could take the office, the job and the warm welcome at face value. It scared her how much she missed the mother she'd known and looked up to as a kid.

"I'm counting on your analysis and insight." Sophia tucked her hair behind an ear and set her earring swaying.

Frankie recognized the nervous move. "Anything else?"

"You have full access to every detail of the company. I'll be honest—Paul was against that decision. I insisted. This company will be yours one day."

Hers? If Aidan had found that in his research, he'd kept it to himself. "Thanks, Mom." The highs and lows of the day were getting to Frankie and she sank into the chair. "I appreciate your faith in me." The lies between them were knee-deep by now.

When Sophia left, Frankie wasted no time logging on and getting to work on both the tasks her mother expected her to address and her real purpose for being here. By midafternoon, she had full comprehension of the company's roots, as well as a general feel for their largest clients in both cyber and personal security. She downplayed the sense of accomplishment that reminded her of her navy days. This position naturally ran to her strengths of gathering intel and organizing it quickly.

The new contract Paul had the entire company focused on was more than lucrative; it would establish Leo Solutions on a global scale. But something about the potential client felt familiar. Frankie used the gift of full access and dug deeper into previous proposals. As she researched, she had an excuse ready should anyone ask why she was poking around the legal side of Leo Solutions.

At last she stumbled on something Aidan needed to see: a photo of her mom, Paul and the man who was now on the board of directors for the potential client Paul was determined to sign. The picture had been taken in Iraq. Frankie vaguely remembered her mother taking that trip as part of a delegation while American troops were shifting responsibilities to local authorities.

"Thank God for electronic storage," Frankie murmured. The picture had been included in a media piece covering the Leo Solutions opening and its positive impact in the Seattle area.

It would require more research, and Aidan's expertise and contacts overseas to confirm, but this client could become more of a threat than a boon. One of the company's subsidiaries had been in the news last year for making charitable donations that wound up funding terrorism in the Middle East. Follow-up articles claimed the problem had been rectified and reparations made. Frankie couldn't shake the bad feeling.

Why push it? The influx of cash would never offset the blow to Leo Solutions' credibility if anyone found out they provided cutting-edge cyber security for this group. Her mother couldn't have overlooked this blatant connection. What were she and Paul up to?

Frankie took pictures of the images and documents with her phone to share with Aidan later. After she also downloaded the files to her flash drive, she headed downstairs to find him.

His office door was open and for a moment she just enjoyed the view of him working. Not even the drab company uniform toned down the lure he presented. Her lips warmed at the memory of his mouth claiming hers. She knocked before she lost her nerve and retreated back upstairs. "Got a minute?"

When he turned toward her, the furrow of concentration between his dark eyebrows faded. "For you I've got all the time in the world."

She wanted to tell him to stop it but wisely kept her mouth shut. "I might have a better view," she said, "but the furnishings are pretty much the same."

"Paul told me Sophia called in big favors with the office supply place to get us set up this morning."

"How are things down here?"

"You're just work, work, work. I don't know if I like it," he teased. "Come here and give me a kiss."

She rolled her eyes as she moved around to his side of the desk. "We should be setting a better example, Mr. Abbot."

"I'll wait to apologize until we get reprimanded, thank you." He caught her hand in his. "What did you need?"

It felt so close to normal she wanted to linger in the performance. "I found a recipe online." She pulled out her phone and showed him the pictures. "Maybe for tomorrow night, since we're going to Mom's tonight. What do you think?"

He scrolled through and when he looked up at her he was all smiles. "I think you could've emailed me."

"Well, I could have." Her tone was flirtatious. They both knew she couldn't risk leaving that kind of trail. His comment was for whoever was listening and potentially watching. She was getting used to their double-meaning conversations. "But then I would've missed your reaction."

"That has potential," he said. "Where'd you find it?"

"It was one of those email newsletters," she fibbed. "You could show a little more enthusiasm." Surely he understood the implication of what she'd found.

"I'll withhold judgment until I taste it."

He was reminding her not to jump to the obvious conclusion. Though this seemed crystal clear to her. "Fine."

He slid a hand over her thigh and she stopped the motion just before he reached one of the many scars. Recalling how she should react, she smiled and kissed his cheek. "We're at work," she said in a stage whisper as she escaped to the safe side of the desk.

"Can't wait until we're not." His eyes flashed with that attraction and awareness she couldn't deny. Her fingertips tingled as though she'd been playing with fire.

"I'll meet you at the car at five."

"I'd rather pick you up at your office and walk down together. I can carry your books if you have homework."

Shaking her head at his antics, Frankie returned to her office and the work her mother expected of her.

She couldn't afford to alienate anyone or squander the access she hadn't anticipated.

ON THE DRIVE to the apartment, Aidan let her theorize about what she'd found, unable to find any flaw with her concerns. While she changed clothes, he took another look at the pictures and skimmed every article he could find, taking one last minute to email a friend of his at Interpol.

What Frankie wanted to see as proof positive, Aidan saw as coincidence, until they had independent confirmation the picture looked like proverbial smoke. He had yet to pin down anything that resembled a fire. Paul and Sophia could very well be trying to help a friend overcome and take positive strides forward. But his opinion was met with a stony silence.

He pulled into Sophia's driveway and parked behind Paul's sedan. Frankie stared straight ahead, her frustration clear in the tight fists balanced on her thighs. He'd expected her to use the time in the car to launch another debate about her discovery. "You'll be okay during dinner?"

"What's not okay?" She gave him a patently false smile. "We're all nearly family, right?"

He didn't like the hard edge she put on *family*. "We don't have to stay long."

"Of course we do," Frankie countered. "This is a great chance to dig into Paul's background."

That made Aidan wary. "Are you bucking for a confrontation?"

"No way. It's too soon. I just want to know how *they* wound up building my dad's dream."

"Your parents dreamed up Leo Solutions together."

Frankie closed her eyes a moment and let loose a weary sigh. When she opened them again her gaze was sharp enough to cut glass. "Be warned, she's going to push for a wedding date. I told her we weren't in a rush, but apparently she is."

"I'll manage." He took her hand. "Do we need a safe word?"

"What?"

"If one of us gets in trouble or wants to bail, maybe we should have a code word or phrase so it's not obvious."

Her gaze drifted to the house, and her dark eyebrows plummeted into a scowl. "Not a bad idea."

"Baby," he said.

"Do *not* call me that," she snapped.

"Which makes it a perfect code word," he clarified, holding up his hands in surrender.

"Oh. Okay." With a resigned expression, she climbed out of the car and headed for the porch.

Right on her heels, he caught the subtle way she adjusted her stride at the steps, as if she anticipated pain with the short climb. "Are you feeling all right?"

She glared at him over her shoulder but didn't answer as her mother opened the door wide to welcome them in. Paul was at her shoulder and hugs and handshakes were exchanged.

Aidan seconded Frankie's reservations about Paul. He picked up a bad vibe from the older man, as if he didn't want to share Sophia or the company with Frankie or anyone else.

"We've got the salmon going out back," Sophia said. "I have drinks and appetizers to tide us over."

Aidan noticed Frankie didn't even turn her head

as they passed the formal dining room and the family portrait that had tripped her up during their first visit.

When the four of them were situated around a teak outdoor table sharing a plate of baked Brie and fruit, Aidan leaned back and draped his arm across the back of Frankie's chair. On the other side of the table, Paul mirrored the move with Sophia.

"What kind of flowers are those?" Aidan nodded at the flowering vines climbing the pergola.

"Moonflower," Frankie replied, sliding a glance at her mom. "Do you have a spot for sunflowers here?"

"Yes!" Sophia pointed to the other side of the yard. "That corner gets plenty of sun. I'm thinking of adding a swing or bench nearby."

"She means I'll have a new building project soon," Paul added.

As Sophia launched an unconvincing protest, Aidan asked Frankie about the sunflowers.

"We found a place to plant them whenever we moved."

"It was part of making each house a home, wasn't it?" Sophia smiled.

Frankie nodded, clearly uncomfortable.

"You'll have so much fun creating your own traditions with Aidan," her mom noted.

"They don't have any green space in the apartment," Paul observed.

"Aidan and I were just talking about starting a container garden on the balcony," Frankie said.

He nodded, supporting her improvisation. "Maybe you could share some plants, if that's how it works."

"What a great idea," Sophia said, twisting in her seat as if assessing the best choices.

"Wouldn't it be better all the way around to find your own place?" Paul queried, raising his drink to his lips.

Aidan watched him as Sophia insisted "the kids" were welcome to stay in the apartment as long as necessary. "Are you still driving the rental car?" she asked.

"We've been debating what to do about that," Aidan improvised.

Sophia nudged Paul, who said, "We can set you up with a company car."

"Mom, that's too much." Frankie patted Aidan's knee. "There's plenty of time to figure it out."

Aidan caught the flash of satisfaction on Paul's face, then did the mental calculations of buying a car for the sole purpose of the case. It wasn't impossible if he was smart. Driving back to Chicago when the job was done wasn't the worst scenario. Just as Frankie wanted to avoid living with her mother, Aidan didn't want to be saddled with a company car.

He and Frankie had enough stress with the assumption that the apartment was wired. A company car would have active GPS at the very least, if not a dash cam or mic that would pick up every word they exchanged. They needed more space to speak privately, not more places where they had to play the happily engaged, electrically attracted couple.

Sophia enlisted Paul's help getting the salmon to the table, and the delicious meal kept everyone distracted for a time. Frankie surprised Aidan by conversing amicably with Paul and her mother, getting both to open up—in the vaguest sense—about their friendship and the partnership.

Aidan hadn't expected her to have such a deft touch

with those questions. Sophia so obviously wanted Frankie and her fiancé to feel welcome. She wanted them to stay and was doing everything possible to nurture the olive branch Frankie had offered by showing up.

It would make Sophia miserable if she guessed her daughter's real purpose here. He had a feeling it would make Frankie miserable, too, if she found something to confirm her worst suspicions about her mother. She might believe she wanted to take her mom down, but Aidan wasn't convinced.

"So, have you decided on a wedding date?"

Frankie, caught off guard, lowered her loaded fork back to her plate. Under the table, he rubbed her knee with his for encouragement. "Not specifically," he answered. "Are there dates we should avoid?"

Sophia's dark hair swung gently as she shook her head. "I don't think so. Paul?"

He shrugged and dropped his gaze to his plate. "Whatever suits the happy couple."

"Do you have your heart set on a particular venue, Frankie?"

Beside him, Aidan felt Frankie tense up. "I really haven't thought about it. Being engaged is enough for us right now," she added, sticking with the excuse she fell back on whenever the topic came up.

He recalled her comments about expectations and realized what she meant. No one in either family had been quite this pushy after he proposed before. There hadn't been time. Shortly after the engagement parties they were planning a funeral rather than a wedding.

"We need to get started," Sophia said. "The best places are likely booked for June."

Frankie coughed and reached for her water glass.

While she sputtered, Aidan jumped into the fray. "June feels terribly quick. I'd marry her anywhere, anytime," he added, when Sophia's happy expression faltered. "To do it right, maybe we should look to the fall?"

"That would give your family more time to make travel arrangements," Sophia said. She glanced at Paul. "Maybe we can help with some of that. The company has an account with a charter airline service."

"Really?" Frankie asked. "I didn't realize we had clients that required so much travel."

Paul blotted his mouth with his napkin and set it beside his plate. "Primarily the charter service empowers accounts where personal security arrangements are necessary. Your mother and I worked out a strategy to give the company a global reach and relevance right away."

Sophia nodded, immediately returning to her preferred topic. "If your family comes all this way, I hope they'll take some extra time for enjoying the city in addition to the wedding."

"I'll certainly suggest it," Aidan said, once more grasping Frankie's hand. Despite his plan to take a step back, he couldn't quite keep his hands to himself. Of course, in public it was considered part of the job, he thought, justifying the pleasure he felt in the contact.

"Are there dates that are important to your family, Aidan?" Paul asked.

Aidan recognized the veiled interrogation. "My parents were married in late September."

"A lovely time of year." Sophia's smile bloomed on

her face, and her eyes crinkled with happiness. "Would you like a September wedding, Frankie?"

"That could work." She squeezed Aidan's hand. "Just don't get your hopes up for anything big like the officers' club," she said. "We'd prefer something simple."

Aidan watched the barb land perfectly. Sophia's enthusiasm dipped momentarily. "We can manage a simple, tasteful day that suits you both."

"We could just go to the courthouse," Frankie suggested, looking up at him. "What do you think?"

He wasn't about to let her off the hook or give her mom heart failure. "We could manage that next week," he pointed out, calling her bluff.

Frankie blanched. "Or in September, after we settle in here."

"Absolutely not," Sophia protested. "I only have one daughter, and while it's your day, I want it to be a celebration you'll remember."

Aidan decided this was another woman, family and case he'd never forget.

Sophia wagged a finger at her daughter. "Pull up a calendar and choose a date. It will give us a target even if we have to adjust it." The woman sounded as though she'd been the general in the family.

Obediently Frankie did as requested, and she and Aidan chose the last Saturday in September to appease the mother of the bride.

Aidan expected to feel snared. Instead, he heard himself laughing as he leaned over and kissed Frankie's temple. "Always a good idea to have a target for any successful operation. Does it feel too real, my love?"

"Maybe a little." She elbowed him in the side and

had all four of them grinning. "Just wait. You won't be laughing when we're confronted with dozens of choices over the smallest details."

"You know I trust your judgment." As he said the words he realized how true they were. Not just as her pretend fiancé. Watching how she'd handled this evening, he knew she'd play this investigation the smart way: patiently, until they had the necessary evidence to take action against the right person.

While Frankie would surely disagree, he was increasingly confident Sophia wasn't that person.

"I NEED A RUN," Frankie said as they entered the apartment. She wanted some space to sort out the crazy day and crazier dinner. In the navy, she'd never been required to maintain this sort of cover. The assignments had been handed out, planned and executed. There were gaps and improvisations, of course, but she'd never had to second-guess every breath the way she did now.

"You're going to the gym downstairs, right?"

"No." She stalked past Aidan, grabbed her running gear and ducked into the bathroom to change. He was sitting on the bed, glaring at her when she emerged. "What now?"

"You can go to the gym," he declared.

She laughed. "I'm a big girl, Aidan. I'm going running outside."

"Not alone at night."

"You're overprotective all of a sudden," she said, for the benefit of any prying surveillance. Reaching into her drawer, she showed him her knife, then tucked it into the sheath clipped at her waist. She tugged her T-shirt down to hide it. "I won't be long."

"We'll go together." He stood and she backpedaled out of the room before he could catch her or kiss her into submission.

"No." She gathered her hair into a ponytail. Frankie could hardly confess she needed to escape him. It seemed his intriguing scent filled her every breath. Here, in the car, at dinner. She had to stretch her legs, let her mind wander and just be herself for a bit. "I'll be back within the hour."

"Frankie—"

"I'm going alone. You won't change my mind."

"Fine." He scowled at her. "At least take your cell phone."

With a sigh, she grabbed it and dashed out the door. Considering it a good warm-up, she took the stairs down for a few flights, pausing to stretch on the landings.

Outside, the cool night air washed over her and she drew in a deep breath as she set out down the block toward a nearby green space that flowed along the waterfront. Using the app on her phone, she programmed a route that circled back to the building. That way she wouldn't be tempted to stay out later just to annoy Aidan.

Probably not smart to alienate her only ally in town. If she could call him that. He kept insinuating she wasn't capable of objectivity. It stung, knowing he was right. But couldn't he put himself in her shoes for just a few minutes?

The man had been a top investigator in Europe and he was a whiz with undercover work. He should be able to see her point of view on this. How was she supposed to frame her life if everything she'd learned about love and strength, and all she'd known about the two people who'd mattered most, was false? In her place, up against these terrible questions, she couldn't imagine Aidan doing anything different.

She ran, letting the questions float through her mind, releasing the pent-up stress with every exhale. Her father had been relocated to Washington during her senior year of high school. She and her mother had stayed behind so she could finish school with her friends. Had that decision also been motivated by trouble in their marriage Frankie hadn't seen?

She concentrated on her footfalls, rather than get sucked into that quagmire. She was out here to escape the situation, not wallow in it. Her legs were warm, her stride strong and powerful, though she was mindful of the smallest twinge in her back.

She knew the difference between healthy and a signal to ease up and evaluate. Every step was a victory over the initial, bleak prognosis. Good thing she didn't believe in quitting. Her mother must have been told the odds were slim that Frankie would even walk again. Odds were no match for grit and determination, though the navy wouldn't believe her. Their loss, she thought as she pressed on, feeling the welcome strain in her lungs now.

She checked the route on her phone, thinking about Aidan's comments that Sophia had chosen to be with her in those early days. It was a point in her mom's favor that she'd never once told Frankie a full recovery was impossible.

Giving a nod to passing runners, she was tempted to snap a picture for Aidan. There was nothing to fear out here, especially not for an armed woman trained by the military's best experts. She didn't take the picture, nearly turned off her phone, except he'd likely call out a search party if she did that. The mental image made her smile. No one had cared so much about her survival since she left the navy. Aidan would probably tell her Sophia cared, but Frankie didn't want to think about her mother any more tonight.

At the two-mile mark, she hit the sweet spot where it felt as though she could run forever, and she let herself relax into her stride. Following the programmed route, she turned at the next path and looped around, dutifully heading back toward the apartment.

She sensed trouble just before it lunged out of the deep shadows between the trees. A man in a blue sweatshirt and gray athletic shorts, wearing a dark cap and bright white shoes, blocked her path.

"Gimme your money!" His demand was slurred around the edges, but she didn't smell any alcohol on him.

"Why?" She hoped the question would buy her precious seconds as she stutter-stepped closer to the next streetlamp. He kept his head low and moved to tackle her. She spun, letting him flow by her, drawing her knife. "Better luck next time," she said, racing down the path toward safety.

He chased after her rather than giving up. She kicked into high gear, but he matched her pace, finally bumping her off the paved trail and down a grassy slope.

Her phone fell, but her grip on the knife was sure as she rolled, coming to her feet braced for battle. He charged, gravity and momentum aiding his attack.

She drove an elbow into his ribs when he went high,

but before she could follow through with a kick, some-one else dragged her to the ground from behind. Her battle-starved heart swelled at the challenge of two opponents.

"Stay put," Aidan ordered, leaping between her and her assailant.

Not an opponent, a teammate. She jumped up, re-fusing to cower while he handled it. Confronted with losing odds, the mugger grabbed her phone and ran off.

Frankie started after him, but Aidan caught her around the waist. "Are you nuts? Let him go."

"He's got my phone!"

"It's replaceable. You aren't." Aidan's hands swept over her, checking her for injuries.

"Give it a rest. I'm fine." She was in no mood for an "in character" exchange. "There's evidence on my phone," she added in a furious whisper.

"I don't care."

She tucked the knife back into the sheath and started up the slope to the path. He fell into step beside her. "What were you thinking? I could've stabbed you."

He snorted. "You're welcome. I told you it wasn't safe out here."

She let her breath out in a slow hiss. It didn't calm her down. "If you'd been paying attention, you would've noticed I had it under control."

"Oh, right."

"I can't believe you followed me." She pulled the tie out of her hair and shook it loose as they walked along the path. Her scalp was sweaty and the confrontation pissed her off. Aidan's interference only exacerbated the anger beating through her veins.

"Good thing I did. He had fifty pounds on you."

"I had it under control," she repeated, flexing her hands. "Why couldn't you let me have this one hour to myself?"

"Because your safety is my priority."

"Bull. Victoria sent you along so I don't create more scandal than my father did."

"That's not true," he snapped.

"You promised me honesty." She broke into a jog, needing to get away from him. She couldn't look at him right now, didn't want to hear his voice. If she had any choice at all, she'd pack up and run to her mother's, claiming a lovers' spat.

She was deep into that stupid scenario when Aidan caught up with her again. He earned points for not speaking until they were a block from the apartment. "The bugs are live," he murmured. "And we've earned an upgraded team." His gaze slid past a dark van at the end of the block.

"I noticed the van when I set out."

"Did you use an app for your run?"

"Yes." Her temper dissolved as she realized what he was saying. "Good grief." She stopped short and he moved in as if they were swept away by a romantic moment. His lips on her cheek, brushing over her ear, almost derailed her train of thought. "You think someone purposely set that mugger on me to get my phone?"

Leaning back, Aidan smiled down at her, and her foolish heart tripped and fell over the concern and affection shining in his blue eyes.

"I do," he said. His palm was warm at the small of her back as he turned her toward the entry. "I like the sound of those two words together," he added as they crossed the lobby to the elevators. "Are you sure we can't just go to the courthouse this weekend?"

So he'd decided the building staff couldn't be trusted, either. At the moment, she shared his paranoia. "You heard Mom at dinner. She'd be heartbroken if we did that."

"Well, I don't want to be responsible for that."

"You've been such a good sport about all this," Frankie said, leaning into his touch as the elevator arrived. She might've gripped him a little tighter than necessary, but he didn't seem to mind. As they boarded the elevator, she murmured, "I'm still mad at you."

"Get over it quickly," he suggested. "Once we cross that threshold, we're 'on' again."

Knowing he was right didn't make it any easier.

"You should call the police," he said as they walked in, rolling his hand so she'd follow his lead.

"And say what? The guy didn't hurt me and we left the scene. I'll just buy a new phone."

"You could give them a description."

Frankie stared at Aidan, shaking her head and holding up her hands. What did he want her to say? "I guess you're right. I'll call after I get a shower."

She walked toward the bathroom and started the water. "This is silly," she murmured, when he followed her in so they could talk for a minute.

"If you've got a better idea, I'm listening," he said.

"Fine. We'll come up with a new option tomorrow." She leaned back against the counter and crossed her arms. "Still think that 'recipe' I found is useless?"

"I never thought it was useless." He leaned forward, his arms caging her between his broad, lean chest and the countertop. "Tell me you backed it up somewhere besides your phone."

If he was trying to intimidate her, it wasn't working. It was turning her on. She reached under her shirt, nearly laughing when he jerked back.

"What are you doing?"

"I'm not jumping you," she said with more than a little regret. She pulled a small flash drive out of her bra. "Giving you something to work with."

Turning one of his hands palm-up, she placed the drive in his palm and curled his fingers around it. "Now get out of here." She set her knife on the counter and plucked at her T-shirt. She refused to undress in front of him. Kisses were one thing, but she didn't want to see his face shift to disgust when he saw the scars and divots where chunks of muscles had been blown away. "I really want a shower." It was no business of his if it was cold.

"Right." His gaze trailed from her head to her toes and back up again. "Right."

"Aidan." She waved a hand in front of his face. "Go away."

He shook his head briskly. "I need one more thing."

"Wh—"

He interrupted her with a kiss, drawing her flush against his body as he laid claim to her mouth. She clutched his shoulders as much for balance as for the sheer pleasure. No one could hear them. No one was watching. This kiss was just for him. Or her. *Them.* She stopped trying to analyze the purpose and just enjoyed the sensual beauty of the moment. The night air lingered in his hair and she tasted the rich flavor of the beer he'd had at dinner. His lips, warm and tender, moved over hers, coaxed a delicious, instinctive response from her.

"When he jumped at you..." His voice trailed off and he dropped his forehead to hers. "I'm glad you had it under control."

"Kissing me doesn't make me less mad at you."

"I know." He grinned and her heart fluttered in her chest. "That's part of the attraction."

She gulped in a deep breath when he walked out. Held it. Released it slowly. She peeled away her sweaty clothes and stepped into the shower. The cold water poured over her, bringing her back to her senses. So much for keeping him at arm's length. If Aidan's career as an investigator stalled out, he had a promising career in acting.

Pressing her fingertips to her lips, she wondered which one of them he was trying to convince or distract, with expert kisses like that one.

Chapter Nine

Tuesday, April 12, 8:30 a.m.

Aidan focused on the new job as soon as he hit the office Tuesday morning, catching up on the progress of trainees. He was searching the calendar for ways to implement his own ideas when Sophia's elegant shadow crossed his doorway.

"Good morning, Aidan."

He smiled at the woman who thought he'd be a son-in-law soon. "Good morning."

"I heard there was some trouble at the apartment last night. Is everything okay?"

He shouldn't be surprised she'd heard about the police report. Frankie and Victoria had warned him of Sophia's extensive connections, and he knew from experience that old habits were the last to die. "No trouble. Frankie performed a bit of community service during a run in the park."

"Pardon me?"

Aidan hesitated. "What exactly did Frankie tell you?"

"I haven't asked her. A friend of mine in the police department saw her name on an incident report.

According to it, she fought off a mugger and lost her phone. I assumed, incorrectly apparently, that you'd give me the full story."

Aidan leaned back in his chair. She was being candid, so he'd follow suit. "I'm not comfortable getting between you and Frankie. On anything."

"Was she really out for a run?"

"Yes."

Sophia beamed. "I thought maybe she'd exaggerated when she said that the other day. The girl *never* gives up. They called it a miracle she lived through that first night." She fanned her face, tears brimming on her lashes. "Forgive me. I'm so glad to have my daughter back, so glad she's found happiness with you. You have no idea what it means to me," she said before she hurried away.

Aidan disagreed. He had a clear sense how much the daughter mattered to the mother. And he was increasingly convinced, Frankie's opinion of the evidence aside, that Sophia was the one in the dark. If she knew the apartment was bugged, if she knew they were being tailed, she was a pro at hiding it.

He heard Frankie's voice in his head, reminding him of Sophia's career as a military analyst, of her contribution to the alphabet soup district in Washington, DC. So far, she'd proved herself a loving mother above all else.

He didn't care about Sophia's past; he felt like an ass for deceiving the woman this way. Making it worse was the knowledge that his fake affection for Frankie was growing into a serious fascination compounded by intense desire. Every tiny detail she revealed left him wanting to discover more.

When the mugger had jumped her last night, Aidan had felt murderous. He'd woken with a start in the middle of the night and left the couch to check on her. As he watched her sleep, it had hit him that this was more complicated than keeping her safe to avoid a repeat of his past.

He was doing the one thing he'd sworn never to do again: he was falling in love.

UPSTAIRS, FRANKIE KEPT her attention strictly on the job today. Aidan had asked her to give him time to verify some details and make some calls. She was basically cooperating, even as she explored the documentation about the formation of the company. She had valid reasons if anyone questioned her, although her reasoning got a little weak when it came to how the documentation landed in her personal cloud storage.

Her email chimed with an instant message from her mother, asking for a private meeting in fifteen minutes.

Nervous that she'd been caught, Frankie forced herself to sit back and take a deep breath, then one more for good measure. She'd been granted full access. She hadn't done anything wrong. Her new job was to look at the past and present to help with a proposal for a future client. Satisfied with her logic, she checked her appearance and reached for her phone—which wasn't there, because she hadn't replaced it yet.

When Frankie walked to the end of the corridor, Sophia's assistant wasn't at her desk and the office door was open, so Frankie peeked in. But her mother wasn't there. Being perpetually early was a curse of being raised by a top general. Her stiff back was a by-product of her ambitious career and a restless night after

the mugging, so Frankie decided to walk a lap around
the floor rather than sit and let her muscles lock up.

She heard voices as she approached the stairs near
the break room at the corner opposite Sophia's office.

"People get mugged in Seattle all the time."

Frankie recognized Paul's voice and froze, just out
of sight.

"She's my daughter, not a random stranger."

"That doesn't warrant a protective detail. How many
times have you told me she can take care of herself?"

"And she did," Sophia admitted. "I'm not pulling
them."

"Sophia. Call them off," Paul insisted. "The rumors…"

"Don't exist," Sophia snapped. "Anyone working
for *me* knows better than to talk about it."

Talk about what? Did that mean people working
for Paul were chatty? The facts lined up in a shocking revelation. Her mom was responsible for the team
tailing them? Frankie's stomach twisted and questions
tumbled through her mind. It was all she could do to
stand there when her body vibrated with the urge to
confront them both.

"We can't afford to show any weakness," Paul said.
"If this gets out, it could wreck everything."

"Please. Our clients have more sense than that."

"Sophia, think about it."

"I don't need to. I'm not pulling them until I'm sure."

Frankie gave herself a mental kick. If she'd had her
phone, she could be recording this. Aidan would have
to reconsider Sophia's innocence when he heard about
this exchange. Hearing them part ways, Frankie pushed
open the stairwell door as though she'd just walked
through it, turning for her mom's office.

Her palms were damp and her legs trembled, making her gait awkward. *Breathe, think, breathe.* She had to get herself under control before her mother spotted her.

"Oh, there you are." Sophia glided up, offering a half hug so Frankie had plenty of room to evade the contact. "How are you feeling today?"

She gave in and accepted the gesture. "Better than ever," she replied, pretending her mom wasn't privy to last night's problems.

"Aidan told me what happened," Sophia said, when they were alone in her office.

Frankie couldn't hide her surprise. "You spoke with him about me?" Why bother, when she'd hired a team to follow them?

"It wasn't like that," Sophia said quickly. "A friend of mine on the police force mentioned the report you filed. I know how you typically understate matters, so I asked Aidan about it."

Frankie folded her arms over her chest. "And you're asking me now in order to confirm his story?"

"No. He refused to tell me anything beyond the facts in the report. I can see you're okay."

Frankie immediately relaxed. She'd thank Aidan at the earliest opportunity.

"You've chosen a smart man," Sophia continued, muggers apparently forgotten as she crossed her office. A mobile wardrobe had been parked next to the couch by the window. She turned, fanning her face. "The way he *looks* at you, sweetheart. Well, it's reminiscent of my early days with your father. You're a lucky woman."

"Mom." Frankie's heart did a happy dance and she quickly reminded herself Aidan was an excellent actor.

While it would've been a compliment years ago, now the comparison felt all wrong. Dirty. Could she use the opening and ask about what had changed between her parents to have her mother assist with the general's conviction? Frankie wanted the relationship answers nearly as much as the professional ones.

And Aidan had asked for time. She pushed her questions to the back of her mind. "What did you want to discuss?" she asked, pasting a smile on her face.

Sophia grinned. "Feel free to tell me if I've overstepped, but I called in a favor or two."

To keep an eye on me, Frankie thought. Eventually all this would come out. "Do I want to know?"

Sophia pulled back the curtain on the wardrobe. "I couldn't resist."

Wedding dresses. Frankie was stunned. There had to be twenty gowns, individually bagged and crammed tightly together on the rack. It was so unexpected she just stood there gawking.

"I know you think we have months," Sophia said, "but September will be here before you know it."

"We— I— Mom." She rubbed a fist along the ache at the front of her hip. "Mom, this is your office."

"I know it's silly, but I thought we could at least narrow down the styles you prefer." She held up a stack of magazines. "I bought out the bridal section on my way into work. And a few planning guides." She tapped a pile of thick books on the corner of her desk.

"You have wedding fever."

Sophia's enthusiasm drained away. "You're unhappy."

On too many levels to count, Frankie thought, feeling terrible. *Play the part.* It wasn't just her life or reputation on the line. If she faltered, Aidan would be screwed, too. That fear helped her sell it. "It's just so much." She gave the dresses her full attention. "Too much. We could've made an appointment."

"Please. I know you. You inherited a double dose of drive and commitment from your father and me. The client proposal will be fine." She waved off the contract of the year as though it were an annoying fly. "Let's take half an hour for this."

"I can just imagine the staff's opinion of our meeting."

"I'd do this for any one of them," Sophia replied.

Frankie raised an eyebrow.

"Well," she amended, "maybe not this, precisely, but I take the time to know what's going on with my people. Now, tell me what you had in mind."

Frankie wondered how many surveillance teams Sophia had at her disposal. "I haven't had dresses in mind at all," she said. There wasn't room for much beyond her determination to clear her father. "No ruffles," she added, when her mother gave her an anxious look. "Simple is better."

"Clean lines. Got it." Sophia nodded and turned to the rack. "What about lace?"

Frankie struggled to come up with any fashion terms applicable to wedding gowns. "Wasn't your dress lace?"

"Yes," she said quietly. "It was fashionable at the time." She unzipped one of the garment bags. "Let's start with this one." She handed the gown to Frankie. The curtains that blocked the window to the rest of the floor were already closed. She locked the door and motioned for Frankie to undress.

"Here?"

"Our next appointment can be at the boutique with

champagne and the works." Sophia waved her hands. "Come on, sweetie."

Frankie thought about the burn scars on her thighs and the surgical scars on her back and sides. She hadn't let anyone see them since the rehab hospital declared the wounds healed. "Can we just look at the dresses today? I'm not comfortable doing this in here. At the office," she added, hoping to appeal to her mother's work ethic.

Sophia studied her with one of those X-ray gazes only mothers possessed. "What is it? Talk to me, sweetie."

How could Sophia have her followed—possibly mugged—one minute and turn the office into a bridal boutique the next?

"It's not how I imagined it, that's all. I haven't imagined it," she said, hoping the right words would tumble out of her mouth if she kept talking. "You know I was never the little girl who dreamed of walking down the aisle."

"Is it the scarring?"

Frankie shivered at Sophia's astute guess. "No," she lied. That was only vanity, anyway, though she'd forever think twice about wearing shorts and short skirts. "When my friend Jack got married, his wife had one of those big princess gowns with the, um, little tucks in the skirt." Jack had died in the attack that left Frankie wounded and paralyzed, but his wedding was the only one she'd attended. Hopefully his widow would forgive her for surviving.

"Here." Sophia put a bridal magazine in her hands and nudged her toward a chair. "Flip through that and dog-ear the pages that appeal to you. Don't analyze, just gut reactions."

Frankie obeyed, ignoring the slide of zippers and whooshes of fabrics behind her. Where was Aidan when she was in real trouble? Muggers were no problem compared to a determined mother of the bride.

"All right, turn around."

Again Frankie cooperated, helpless to remain aloof as Sophia beamed in front of a wall of white. "Do any of these resemble what you marked?"

There were gowns of every style, from a bell-skirted ball gown to a sleek and modern sheath with a band of sparkles at the waist. "Is it even possible to walk in a mermaid gown?" Frankie asked.

"I'll teach you, if it's the one," she promised. "All the more reason to choose early."

Unconvinced, Frankie walked over, standing by her mother to assess the dresses in the lineup. "I guess I like the sweetheart neckline," she said, flipping to a page in the magazine showing a similar style.

"Very romantic," Sophia said approvingly as she reached up and moved that dress to the far left. "Anything else?"

"I do want to try on an extravagant ball gown," Frankie admitted. "Just for fun. Aidan would laugh if I wore it," she lied. He wouldn't laugh, because they weren't getting married.

"Not a chance," Sophia declared. "I've never seen a man so adoring."

Frankie let that go, choosing two more gowns and handing her mother the magazine. Then she noticed the last dress. "Mom," she whispered. "That's *your* wedding dress."

Sophia smiled. "Your father swayed on his feet when he saw me. He never admitted it, but I was sure there were tears of joy in his eyes when I walked down that aisle. There's no pressure at all, but it might be a nice way to include him on your special day. We were married in May," she said, her voice full of memories. "It might not be right for a September wedding."

Overcome, Frankie barely kept it together as she promised to try on the column of lace with a chapel train. She endured the calendar search for the right date for the boutique and then escaped to the safety of her office.

She leaned back against the closed door, her heart lodged in her throat and her hands quaking. Ages ago, when they were stationed in Europe, she'd gone ice-skating on a frozen river, her mitten-covered hand safe in her father's big palm. She remembered that day so clearly, the bite of the wind, the squeal of laughter when he spun her around. She remembered standing hand in hand with him weeks later, watching from the bank as the thinning ice cracked and split, to float away with the current.

She felt that way now. Cold. Fractured. Drifting on a course she couldn't control. She wanted to know which woman was the real Sophia Leone. Was it the savvy businesswoman who hired covert teams and kept state secrets, or the warm mother devoted to her family? Were Sophia's two sides mutually exclusive? Frankie caught her reflection in the window glass, hating the haunting similarities between mother and daughter.

She'd told Victoria the truth mattered above all. Ideally, she wanted to clear her father's name. Barring that, she wanted her mother's full explanation for the part she'd played in his downfall. Suddenly, Frankie wasn't sure what truth she wanted or even how far she was willing to go to hear it.

She should just march down the hall and confront her mom, demanding an answer for each of her suspicions. But giving in would be selfish and blow any chance of justice. A confession without evidence was useless. Worse, if she was wrong, she'd destroy her relationship with her mother—something she'd been so sure she could live without. Now the possibility of that finality frightened her.

Frankie turned away from the window and dropped to the floor behind her desk, where no one could see her. On her back, she pulled her knees to her chest and just rested there, searching for a solution.

When had doing the right thing become so twisted and complex? If her mother went to prison for her crimes, Frankie would be alone. If she told her mom everything and was wrong, she'd face the same solitary fate, with an extra helping of guilt for doubting her mother's motives and actions.

The statement from the safe-deposit box was clear. That picture from Iraq didn't lie. The conversation Frankie had overheard an hour ago confirmed something wasn't right.

She heard Aidan's voice in her head, urging caution. The only time she'd mastered patience was during her navy career. Aidan had been involved in all this for a few days, while Frankie had been dealing with the storm cloud looming over her life for far too long. So why was she thinking about walking away? Could she spend the rest of her life pretending she'd come to terms with how her father died?

Which took precedence, family or country? She'd been raised by two people who preached the philosophy of God, country and family, in that order. Had her upbringing been a lie, and if so, what did that make her?

She closed her eyes, but her mother's face filled her mind. All her life Frankie had heard people say she had her mom's beauty and her dad's grit. She'd chosen the navy in an effort to make her own way, outside the reach of her father's influence and her mother's shadow.

What did it mean that so much of her identity and perception of self was tied up with two people who as of a year ago felt more like strangers?

Her office door opened with a soft squeak of hinges and Frankie opened her eyes. She might be new, but no one should feel free to walk in here without knocking. That someone had come snooping might turn into the break she needed.

She sat up and startled Aidan. "What are you doing?" Her question overlapped into his inquiry about whether she was all right or not. "Stop asking. I will let you know when I'm not feeling well."

"You're on the floor," he pointed out.

She clambered to her feet, hating the way her hip seized in the process. "I was thinking." He raised his eyebrows, but she refused to elaborate. "What brings you by?"

"Your mom suggested I take you to lunch."

"Why?"

"Beats me." He shrugged. "I'm just following orders."

"She's deliberately keeping me away from work today." Frankie made a fist and rubbed at the sore spot in her back. Rolling down the slope with the mugger had tweaked something. Not enough to matter, just enough to annoy.

Aidan looked to the ceiling. "She's watching out for you. She saw the police report."

"I heard."

"I'm glad she told you."

Frankie nodded. "Thanks for sticking up for me."

"Any fiancé worth his salt would do the same."

She was suddenly exhausted. "Is it bad form to go home early my second day on the job?"

"You're the boss's daughter." He tucked his hands into his pockets. "Let's have lunch and then you can ask me again."

During lunch, she told him about the conversation she'd overheard between Sophia and Paul. She kept the impromptu wedding dress exhibit to herself.

"I'll see what I can find on the team tailing us," he said. "Knowing Sophia planted them startles me."

Frankie let him have his objective delusions.

"Apartment or office?" he asked, when they finished eating.

"Office. I'll be damned if she keeps me out of there all day long."

"Frankie."

"I promise to behave, but I will get what I came for." It helped knowing he'd be researching, as well.

Back in her office, she sat down behind her desk and debated her options. There had to be something definitive. Something she and Aidan could agree on about her mother's involvement with her father's ruin.

What Frankie had considered black-and-white, starting with that damaging statement from the safe-deposit box, was becoming a foggy bank of gray. She was tired of words that weren't answers, weary of incomplete theories rolling around in her head. Frankie's focus narrowed to finding one inarguable piece of intel she could use to force her mother to talk.

She pulled up the research on crime trends and client services Leo Solutions had provided since opening its doors. Then she pulled up the current proposal. Present or past? Which research would pay off sooner?

Mentally, she flipped a coin, and wound up combing through her mother's email, for lack of any other option. Her mom was too smart to leave anything that might implicate her on the company server, but Frankie just wanted to see what was there.

The email address from a doctor caught her attention and Frankie dug a little deeper. The message, forwarded from Sophia's personal account, confirmed an appointment this afternoon. Frankie worked her way back through the correspondence, easily tracking the old trail of emails. Researching the doctor, she discovered he was a psychologist and her mother the patient.

Frankie wanted to give a victory shout. Something like this, in the wrong hands, could push Sophia out of the company and into an early retirement. As Paul had said earlier, investors and clients didn't like any sign of weakness at the top.

"Prepare for a shock, Mom," Frankie whispered. It would be a matter of a few keystrokes and Leo Solutions would be in serious trouble. "The truth will come out."

Better if she could figure out the connection and compel her mother to be honest—for once since her dad had died. Noting appointment dates, she was surprised they went back so many years. This wasn't a short-term grief counselor her mother had consulted to overcome anxiety during the recent family struggles. This was a long-term doctor-patient relationship that went back to when they'd moved to Seattle.

Troubled, Frankie switched gears, learning as much as she could from the doctor's website, skimming through articles ranging from marital counseling to drug abuse recovery and just about everything in between. She noted the shrink's address and clicked for directions. Visiting the office wasn't likely to get results, but it would give her a bit more leverage when she talked to her mom.

Frankie sat back, assessing the discovery. Sophia had been seeing a psychologist for years. One more skeleton lurking in her mother's closet. Did it have any bearing on the statement she'd written to ensure that General Leone was convicted of treason? Every step forward led to two sideways and one back.

Why would her mother see a psychologist?

The little girl inside Frankie wanted to deny her parents had dealt with marital trouble. They'd rarely fought and as far back as she could remember they'd always been close. Marital problems didn't explain why Sophia was still keeping the appointments.

Frankie's agenda app on her computer chimed with an alert for the afternoon meeting. Grabbing her company tablet, she headed for the conference room. The meeting was a simple status update on current antivirus and malware solutions. When asked, Frankie shared an update on recent cyber crimes and the latest scam alerts she'd gathered.

She listened, watching as Sophia took notes by

hand, asked questions, then moved along to the next topic. It was a rare glimpse of her in full business mode.

"Thanks, everyone," her mom finally said, flipping her notebook closed. "Keep up the great work."

Frankie caught her eye as the others filed out of the room. "One more thing, if you have just a minute?"

"Sure." Sophia gave her bright, happy smile. "You seem to have a handle on the job."

"It's great," Frankie said. "I was curious about our association with medical and mental health providers. Do we have products or programs to assist them?"

"We do," Sophia replied, unfazed. "Is there a particular area of concern?"

Frankie wanted to believe the doctor was a client now, but she'd seen the emails. "No." She swallowed. Why did she feel so terrible lying to her mom, when Sophia never told the truth? "I was just curious about the potential within the market," she said. "I have a few contacts that could benefit from our encryption products."

"Go on and talk it over with Sales if you have some ideas," Sophia said.

"Now? On my own?" Frankie wondered how her mom would slip out of this.

Sophia gave her an odd look. "I'd go with you, but I have another appointment. You can manage." She started for the door, only to turn back. "Did you and Aidan decide on a venue for the reception while you were at lunch?"

Frankie felt as though she was caught in a never-ending game of hide-and-seek. "No." She almost admitted he hadn't brought it up.

"Oh. That's fine. It will depend on the timing of the ceremony, too. We'll talk later tonight, okay?"

"Sure." Dread slithered between her shoulder blades as Sophia walked out.

Frankie didn't want to think of reception venues or anything else, and not just because this engagement was a farce. When she found the right guy and decided to marry, they were going to do it right and elope. It wasn't as if her dad was around to give her away, and she wouldn't want her wedding day shadowed by the secrets and lies her mother carried around.

Weddings were supposed to be celebrations of love, not burdened with bitterness and emotional baggage.

AIDAN WORRIED ABOUT Frankie the rest of the day. It was clear her patience was gone, and he used every spare minute of his afternoon to do the research that would give her the answers she needed. The pain and confusion in her eyes bothered him as much as the sharp glint of determination. The woman was drawn as tight as a bowstring and last night's attack put him right there with her. He didn't believe the mugging was random. They'd managed to threaten someone, but who and how?

Trusting his gut instincts, he used his phone and booked a hotel room under a different name. After work they could buy her a new phone and get checked in. They wouldn't spend the night—that would be too much temptation—but they could talk without fear of being overheard. He'd make sure they each had a key in case either of them needed an escape hatch.

With only a half hour left in the workday, he sat

down at his desk to address reports and office email, and to continue his research on his real case.

He proceeded carefully, knowing he garnered more attention from both partners because he was the fiancé rather than a typical new hire. He and Victoria had been exchanging emails since he left Chicago. She was searching for the mysterious man who'd pointed Frankie to the safe-deposit box, and Aidan was digging into Leo Solutions and their clients. Someone close to the Leone family had motive enough to embarrass and destroy them. The more he studied General Leone's service record, the more the treason charge baffled him. It felt like a smoke screen for something else. The more time he spent around Sophia, the more convinced he was she and Frankie had been used, as well.

Frankie had seen her father at Bagram, when Sophia was sure he'd been in Kabul. Sophia had claimed responsibility at the graveside, but the statement without more support was meaningless, though Aidan had passed all that on in his daily reports to Victoria.

Hearing the soft click of heels in the hallway, he wasn't surprised when Sophia stopped at his open door. "Can I bother you a minute?"

Hitting the screen saver on his computer monitor, he pushed to his feet. "Two visits in one day. I'm honored." He waited until she sat down before he did the same.

Her lips didn't quite smile. The expression reminded him of Frankie when she was trying too hard to pretend everything was fine. "I really don't want to cross a line here." She worried the edges of the folder in her hands.

"Is something wrong?"

"No." Her eyes went wide as she shook her head. "Nothing like that. It's actually not about work."

The wedding. Either she wasn't pestering Frankie about the details, or Frankie wasn't sharing with him. Aidan's money was on the latter.

"September will sneak up on us if we let it. We need to make some decisions quickly."

Aidan tried to sympathize with Sophia's urgency. She didn't know he'd be walking out of her life soon. "I didn't realize I'd have quite this much say in the process. My buddies teased me that it would be all bride all the time."

"With a normal bride it is," she assured him. "Frankie is…different."

Aidan smiled. "I know." He made a mental note to talk to Frankie about picking up the slack on the happy bride stuff.

Sophia's shoulders relaxed. "She doesn't say much about your side of the family."

"What don't you know from the background checks?" He kept it light, but the query was serious.

"Not that. We have all the time in the world to get to know them. I'm referring to the guest list." She handed him the folder. "This is a short list of venues in the area. I can't move forward until I have an idea of how many guests we're expecting."

Venues? Guests? Stuck, his skin prickled at the back of his neck. The best course on any undercover job was to keep it as true as possible. "I'm not sure any of my family will make the trip."

Sophia pursed her lips, concern in her brown eyes. "I worry about you."

He laughed that off. "Frankie and you are all the family I'll need on my wedding day." It sounded true enough when he said it out loud. He grabbed his pen, just to give himself a distraction.

"You say that now." She took a deep breath and crossed her ankles. "Yes, the wedding is about you and Frankie, but your family should be there to celebrate with you."

"I appreciate your concern," he said. "I'd planned to pay for the video and photographer."

"This isn't about who pays which bill," Sophia said with a flash of impatience. That was going around today. "We have the tech to stream it live, but it's not the same."

"My family isn't as close as yours," he began as a cloud fell over Sophia's face. Now he was concerned about two Leone women. Sophia didn't typically show this kind of agitation.

"I'm not pushing this because I want you to fit some perfect mold or expectation," she said. "I don't want you to have regrets."

Too late. He wasn't sure mother and daughter would overcome the pressure this engagement stunt would put on their fragile relationship when the truth came out. From his vantage point, it seemed Frankie and Sophia wanted the same things from each other: love, trust and respect.

The love was there, under the anger and pain. Although Frankie would vehemently deny it, the respect was there, too. All they needed was the trust. That would take time and practice, assuming this didn't shatter them.

"Honestly, I've never given much thought to who would be at my wedding," he said.

"You're a man," Sophia said with a wistful smile.

"Frank and I basically eloped. My parents were furious with me for a time and I always regretted upsetting them. Years later, I wondered if a longer engagement might've been smart."

"Frankie told me you had to hurry things along because of his orders."

Sophia's smile brightened, transforming her face to that of a young woman in love. "That was the least of it. We were impatient to get real life started."

"We could've eloped," he pointed out. "But Frankie wanted to tell you first. She wanted to reconnect with you."

Sophia studied him, her mouth tipped up in a wry smirk. "I imagine you exerted influence over that choice."

He shrugged. "Maybe just a little."

"It only underscores my concern about having your family here. Is there something I could do or say to help?"

"No, thank you." At this rate he'd be forced to explain the situation to his parents, without blowing the case. "I'll reach out," he said, recognizing an unwinnable argument. Creative problem solving was supposedly one of his strengths, though it didn't feel like it right now.

"Thank you. I know I'm pushing, but…"

"No worries," he assured her. "I know you want what's best for Frankie."

"And you," Sophia said suddenly. "I'm sure I sound like a romantic fool, but I see how you look at each other. It's love. Your family should be able to see that love, too, especially on your wedding day."

Leaving that hanging in the air, she walked out,

and he stared at the empty doorway for far too long. How exactly did Frankie look at him? He'd thought this was one-sided. Was she being convinced by the charade, too?

He thought about the way she responded to his kisses, the way her hand gripped his whenever they were together. The woman, tougher than anyone he knew, had a vulnerable side he instinctively wanted to shelter. Her search for the truth had become his cause. For her, he wanted go above and beyond the resolution of a challenging case.

There had to be a way to survive this tightrope he was walking. Any misstep could be his last and Aidan feared he wouldn't survive the fall.

He plucked the reception venue file off his desk and shoved it into his duffel bag. Refreshing his monitor, he returned to the task of gathering intel for Victoria. His new boss was the best in the private investigations business for a reason. After reviewing his last update, she'd pointed him in a new direction: the applicants who'd been *rejected* by Leo Solutions. Neither Aidan nor Victoria trusted the man who'd contacted Frankie in Savannah. They both suspected he was connected to the person behind this mess.

Due to the nature of the work at Leo Solutions, every application was screened and kept on file for reference. In a fortunate break, he discovered the rejected résumés weren't locked up behind firewalls like the personnel files of those who landed jobs. Aidan made swift work of it, wanting to get in and out without leaving a trace or raising suspicions. He had an excuse ready, but better all around if he didn't have to use it.

At last he found the man who'd approached Frankie,

and gave a mental fist pump. Reading the résumé, he wondered why John Lennox hadn't made the cut. He was a little older, but his military background, three tours in the Middle East and his fitness should've made him an automatic hire. Aidan frowned, downloading the data and notes from the man's interviews with both Paul and Sophia to his flash drive.

If the dates on the dossier were accurate, Lennox's overseas service had coincided with General Leone's on all three deployments. Immediately, Aidan's thoughts turned to Frankie and her likely interpretation of this news. She'd find a way to twist the interview and no-hire into her mother's prejudice against applicants who'd known her father.

Aidan's instincts were once more prickling as he read through Paul's vague post-interview notes on Lennox. Aidan cross-referenced the email address and searched through the corporate accounts, coming up empty. It was too coincidental to ignore.

He leaned back until his chair creaked. As an investigator, he would pass the intel on to his boss and keep Frankie out of it. Victoria would use her assets to follow up and track down this guy who seemed to know everything about Frankie's parents' histories. Still, the idea of hiding this from her made Aidan's gut twist.

"It doesn't add up," he muttered, after reading through the file again. The items Frankie had found were too personal, too specific. General Leone might've opened the account and rented the box, but it had to be Paul or Sophia who used it to get Frankie back to Seattle.

Which of them had stocked that safe-deposit box and given Lennox the key to pass on to her?

Aidan could make a case for Sophia; the woman knew only a serious catalyst would break Frankie's stubborn streak. But why paint herself so negatively in the process?

Considering Paul as a suspect had Aidan asking the same questions about making Sophia look bad. On top of that, he couldn't see what Paul gained by undermining the face of Leo Solutions on a professional or personal level.

Aidan copied the new intel to the cloud where Victoria could access it, then ejected the drive and tucked it into his pocket. If he shared it with Frankie, Victoria had cause to fire him. If he didn't, Frankie would never trust him. The obvious answer was career above client.

Could he live with that?

No. The answer tolled like a church bell in his head. It didn't matter that he and Frankie were playing at romance for the sole purpose of the case. Handling this incorrectly could destroy his career. It hit him like a roundhouse kick. As his dad often said, there was always work for a man willing to get his hands dirty.

Frankie mattered more. Damn it, he'd fallen for her. Handling *her* incorrectly could destroy him, along with his heart, his sense of self and his decency. If he kept her out of it, he had no hope of exploring a real relationship with her when they resolved this case.

He couldn't live with that. Couldn't accept a result that killed any chance he had with the one woman who challenged and captivated him so thoroughly. Frankie was in the fight of her life and he wanted to be sure she never had cause to consider him an enemy.

Decision made, he set up a secondary cloud account. He created a username and password for Frankie and uploaded the Lennox file, just in case something happened to him or the drive. Once they were done here for the day, she could take a look and they could discuss the possible ramifications over dinner out.

If he was lucky, this would be enough to make her listen to an alternate theory, though he knew it would be an uphill battle.

Everything worthwhile took effort and risk. In Frankie's case, Aidan knew the reward, gaining her trust and a chance to be with her for the long run, would be priceless.

Chapter Ten

7:55 p.m.

For the first time, Frankie believed they would figure this out. She had a new cell phone and a key card for an "in case of emergency" hotel room near the airport, and Aidan had identified her father's friend as John Lennox. Now they just had to connect a few more dots and she could confront her mother.

She could feel the weight easing off her.

After work, Aidan had managed to lose the team tailing them, giving them space and time to relax in the hotel room. Wisely, they'd worked on the case and managed to keep their hands and lips off each other. Over Chinese takeout they'd debated the significance of the psychologist, if her father had indeed asked Lennox to take action in the event of his death, or if Lennox was being controlled by someone else.

Having returned to the performance required of them at the corporate apartment, she decided progress was a beautiful thing. Even the small steps, she thought as she sent him a text message that she was back from her bakery run and headed upstairs. It bothered her that they couldn't just pull the trigger now.

What they'd found, revealed in the right way, could spell the end of Leo Solutions and leave her mother with no choice but to cooperate. If Frankie couldn't get justice for her father, maybe she'd finally get answers for her peace of mind.

She punched the call button for the elevator and tapped her phone on her palm while she waited. One second she felt absolutely certain about taking definitive action. About ruining her mother and the company. But before the next second could tick by, her resolve wavered. It seemed Aidan's warnings about family, lies and love were sinking in.

She stepped into the elevator and pressed the button for the apartment floor.

She'd been out for vengeance, if not exactly blood, ever since her father's disgrace and death. Would taking action, even righteous action, against her mother make her a hero or lump her into the category of another problem? Aidan had told her point-blank she'd be devastated if she tore her mother's professional life apart. Then again, his mom hadn't turned on his dad.

The elevator screeched and jerked to a stop, tossing Frankie down hard into a corner. She swore as the bakery bag fell and the emergency lights came on.

From her knees, she hit the red button to call for help. The emergency alarm sounded, but the elevator car jerked and dropped again. Moving slowly, she reached for her phone and checked the signal. Hopefully her text to Aidan would get out. Slinging her purse strap across her body, she pushed herself to her feet and tried to pry open the doors.

Her fingers pinched and cramped, her back ached from the effort and her shoulders burned, but the doors didn't part. "Damn it." She shook the tension out of her arms and tried again. Another screech of metal on metal sounded in the elevator shaft above her and the car tipped to the side like a sinking boat.

"Hey, lady! Can you hear me?"

Frankie followed the sound of the voice to the speaker in the instrument panel and then glanced up toward the security camera in the corner. She gave the camera lens a thumbs-up.

"Fire department is on the way. Just sit tight."

She didn't like it, but she didn't have much choice. She nodded and tried to breathe. Tight spaces weren't a big problem for her. Feeling helpless was her big hang-up and it had only become more pronounced following her injury. She fisted and stretched her fingers while she waited for the sound of sirens. It had to be her imagination, but even that small motion of her hands seemed to set the car swaying.

Determined to help herself, she looked for the service panel in the ceiling. There had to be some way out of here.

She heard a soft thud on the roof of the elevator. "Who's there?" No one answered. Whatever had landed wasn't heavy enough to cause the car to move, so she assumed it wasn't a rescue team.

But the pop and hiss, followed by a sizzle and puff of white smoke, startled her. "What the hell?" She didn't think the person monitoring the security camera could see the problem yet.

She waved her arms in front of the camera. "Hey! Help me! There's smoke or something—"

A chunk of the ceiling dropped into the elevator with her, and the smoke filled the small space with a stinging vapor and noxious odor. Her eyes watered and she covered her mouth and nose with the collar of her T-shirt.

She scrambled for the door, pulling and prying with all her might, ignoring how the car swayed with her efforts. She pounded the sleek paneling with her fists.

The voice on the other end of the intercom faded to static and she felt the gas taking effect. Thick gray smoke made her feet invisible and billowed up toward her knees. If she was meant to die here, she refused to go without a fight.

Using the railing on the back panel of the car as a toehold, she smeared the lens of the security camera with lip gloss. Then she popped open the emergency access in the ceiling. She wasn't sure what she'd do once she was in the elevator shaft, but as the smoke continued to build up, she knew she couldn't stay here.

The cleaner air in the elevator shaft cleared her head some as she pulled and wriggled her way to the roof. Looking around, she noted her slim-to-none options as the car swayed under her feet. She recognized the smell of a military-grade explosive and saw the frayed cable straining against the weight of the car. Someone had rigged this elevator and waited for the right moment to send it plummeting to the ground.

She used the flashlight on her phone to get her bearings in the dim, cavernous space, looking for the best path out. The cable creaked again and if she didn't move quickly, the saboteur would win and she'd wind up a smudge amid the debris.

Calculating the distance between her perch and the service ladder bolted to the wall between the runs, she thought she could get there. If she didn't fall, she'd climb up to the next floor and pry open those doors. The other option would be climbing down to the bottom of the shaft. With no alternative, she put away her phone and moved as cautiously as possible toward the safety of the ladder, using the cables and wiring for balance.

Light suddenly flooded the shaft and she peered up. "Frankie?"

Aidan! "I'm here." Her voice was raspy from the smoke. "The elevator cable blew. Gas grenade, too."

He swore as he flashed a beam of light around the elevator shaft. "Get to the ladder."

"That's the plan," she replied.

"Faster," he said, his voice low and urgent. "There's another charge on a timer."

How had she missed it? It didn't matter. She stretched for the ladder. The cable creaked; the car shifted away. She waited until it steadied, then, using a cluster of wiring, pulled herself close enough to make the jump for the ladder. The cable creaked again as the car swung away.

"Hurry, Frankie." Aidan was lying in the open doorway, his arm stretching down to her.

She kept her eyes on his face, on the light behind him as she climbed. One rung at a time, she focused on him, rather than the dark narrow elevator shaft lit with emergency glow strips.

Finally her hand met his, wrapping around his wrist, and his strength made the last few steps easier.

Beneath her, another pop sounded, then the rasp and whip of the cable, followed by the scream of metal as the car plummeted down the shaft.

Aidan jerked her up into the brightly lit hallway as

the crash swelled from fourteen stories below. Frankie trembled under his sheltering body as the explosion roared up the elevator shaft.

"Good Lord," she whispered into his chest. "I knew we were on the right track." A shiver rattled her body. "She tried to kill me." *Her mother wanted her dead.* The raw awareness was more of a shock than the attack.

"We're getting out of here," Aidan said. "No cops." He rolled to his feet, bringing her with him. "No statements." He gave her a hard look. "And no arguing."

She nodded. They were in and out of the apartment with essential gear in less than five minutes. Her back and hip protested, but she'd deal with that later. She let Aidan lead, following him up the stairs to the next floor, down the hall and into another stairwell. He pulled out a device that looked like a key fob and pressed the button.

"Signal jammer?"

He nodded. "Should mix up the building surveillance, too, if we're lucky."

Having scoped out the egress options after they'd accepted the corporate apartment, they needed only a few minutes' head start to disappear into the city. Aidan had his gun drawn and cleared each landing until they were all the way down and outside.

At street level they deftly avoided the police and fire departments. Several blocks away, he hailed a cab.

"Airport," he said, his voice gruff.

Frankie slid onto the seat beside him. "We can't leave," she said. They were too close to the goal. If they gave up now, she might never have another chance. And after that near miss, she refused to let anyone off the hook. "You realize—"

He shot her a quelling glance, his eyes harder than his voice had been.

Apparently the "no argument" rule hadn't been lifted yet. Fine. The silence gave her plenty of time to calm down so she could state her case in a way that left him no room to argue with *her*.

AIDAN WANTED TO hold her and never let go. He wanted to know she was safe, that her back was fine, but those questions would wait. If he touched her now, he'd lose his mind. He forced himself to assess their surroundings as the cab inched by the chaos in front of the building they'd just escaped. There was a killer on the loose, likely watching the result of his handiwork.

Unbidden, the image of Frankie on top of the lift filled Aidan's vision and his heart slammed against his rib cage. He'd nearly lost her. Mere seconds had separated her from certain death. Even if she hadn't fallen, she would've been wiped out by the explosion.

He pinched the bridge of his nose as the cabbie hit the freeway. In ten minutes they'd be safe in a hotel. In under an hour they could be out of the state or even the country. Not that Aidan would ever convince her to leave. She didn't have her answers yet.

For the first time since he'd taken the case, he considered cornering Sophia and forcing the issue. Not smart. Not professional.

He felt the soft touch of Frankie's hand and watched her lace her fingers through his. She gave a gentle squeeze. He could barely swallow through the lump in his throat. He rubbed the band of her engagement ring with his thumb, a welcome reminder that she'd survived. They were out of danger. For how long?

The question iced his skin. They weren't dealing with speculation or theory anymore. Something they'd discovered was making someone very nervous. The next strike was inevitable and he needed to be prepared.

"I have to report this," he said, so only she would hear him.

"Yes."

Her agreement startled him. He told the cabbie to drive through the departure area for the next group of airlines, then on to the circuit of hotels nearby.

Satisfied they hadn't been tailed, he directed the driver to stop at the next major chain. He wasn't going to expose their escape hatch just yet. He paid the fare and, with his arm at Frankie's waist, moved directly to the check-in desk. He used a false ID and credit card, requesting a room on the first floor. He felt her watching him, but there was no way in hell he could deal with an elevator right now.

He didn't care that it was irrational, only cared about keeping her alive.

They reached the room, and the moment he'd locked the door, his patience evaporated. He dropped the bags and wrapped his arms around her. Holding her close, his hands splayed across her back, he measured every breath. She was alive. In his arms.

He released her long enough to move their gear to the bed and pull the curtains closed. When he turned back to her, she hadn't moved. He hugged her again, tucking her head to his shoulder. "I was terrified," he confessed.

"Aidan."

"Don't ask me to let go." He couldn't do it, not yet.

His palm moved up and down her spine, lingering too long at her lower back.

"I'm fine," she said. Her hands slid under his jacket and fisted in his shirt. "I promise. Thank you for saving me."

"You had it under control." He moved just enough to tip up her chin and lay a soft kiss on her lips. Managing to push back the panic and terror, he knew the dam wouldn't hold for long. She was alive and well. He might remember that for all of five minutes without a touch or word, but he didn't want to chance it. He smoothed a loose tendril of her hair behind her ear. "I was just moral support."

"More than that," she whispered, gazing up at him, her eyes shining with a rush of need that matched his. She pushed her fingers into his hair and brought his mouth back to hers. Her lips parted with a sigh and his tongue swept inside, tangled with hers.

The abrasive odors of oil and machinery, explosives and the smoke grenade, clung to her hair. Her taste, sweet as honey and warm as a summer day, overwhelmed his other senses. He needed her. All of her. He needed to take her into himself and keep her safe. Always. He didn't want to think how impossible that was.

There was nothing of comfort or reassurance in this blatant mating of mouths, no simple curiosity of attraction. This kiss was full of need hemmed on all sides by sheer desperation. He'd nearly lost her before he had a chance to tell her how much she meant to him.

His hands spanned her trim waist, moved higher so her breasts filled his palms. He tweaked the hard tips through her shirt and she arched into his touch. Gripping her backside, he brought her hips close, pressing her against his erection. He bent his head and explored the softness of her skin, down the column of her throat and back up to her ear. "I need you."

When she trembled, whispered his name, he kissed her until they were both shaking and breathless.

He shrugged out of his jacket and reached for the hem of her shirt, pulling it up and over her head in one swift move.

Her skin glowed golden around the simple white fabric of her bra. "Francesca," he whispered across the sensitive skin of her breasts. She wasn't Frankie the client or pretend fiancée now. The case was irrelevant. The games were over. She was the woman he wanted more than his next breath. The woman he needed to give that breath meaning. His hands on her hips, he drew the stiff peak of her nipple into his mouth, teasing her through the fabric. She held him close, running her fingers through his hair, over his ears.

His hands learned her curves, the dips and hollows, in long, slow strokes from her waist across the flare of her hips.

She shoved at him and he stopped immediately. He had no time to ask what he'd done wrong, as she yanked his shirt from his waistband, gasping, "I need to touch you."

"I'm all yours." He'd never spoken words that meant as much.

FRANKIE PRESSED HER PALMS to Aidan's wide, lean chest and backed him toward the bed. She could feel the heat of him through the fabric, but she wanted skin. She pushed his shirt up and away and just stared. He was perfect. Smooth skin, hard muscle and ridges she couldn't wait to trace and taste.

Her heart was racing, and though the warning signs of stress were firing in her back, she was done with foreplay. She wouldn't be denied this moment. The twinges only served as a reminder of how fleeting life was. She'd survived an IED, paralysis, and now a sabotaged elevator. She deserved a little happiness and positive adrenaline. Just to change it up.

She flicked open the button of his jeans, eased the zipper down until she could wrap her hand around his thick erection. Her breath caught in her chest, her pulse throbbing in her ears at the feel of him. So close and yet not nearly close enough.

Moving in a passionate frenzy around and between searing kisses, they shed his interfering clothing until at last he stretched out on the bed, drawing her down beside him. She wanted him fast and hard. The slow and tender could wait. She needed him to hurry and blot out the terror crowding her, to affirm her survival.

She hesitated. In the midst of crawling over his amazing body, she froze.

The sudden bout of nerves surprised her. She hadn't been with anyone since her recovery, and she wasn't sure what might happen. Everything in her back felt normal most of the time and she didn't make a habit of expecting the worst. Sex wasn't any more rigorous than running, from a functional standpoint. She'd regained her mobility and fitness, but there was nothing she could do about the scars Aidan hadn't seen.

"Is there a problem?" He sat up, drawing her between his widespread knees. Spearing a hand into her hair, he pulled her lips to his and leveled her with another devastating kiss. "Second thoughts? Please say no."

She closed her eyes and blurted out an excuse. "No second thoughts. It's been a while, that's all."

He slid her bra straps down over her shoulders, his face so close his breath raised goose bumps on her sensitive skin. "I can't decide if that's more or less pressure on me."

She wanted to laugh, but it sputtered and died on a gasp when he unhooked her bra and took her bared breast into his mouth. "Francesca. You're beautiful."

Feeling his words more than she heard them, she decided. She'd shatter his illusions of beauty later. She leaned over to turn out the light.

"Don't." He stilled her hand. "Let me see you tonight. All of you."

"Aidan." She turned shy, an unprecedented sensation. "You don't know what you're asking." She spoke to his perfect, sculpted chest, unable to meet his eyes. "The repairs are…difficult." It was the least offensive word she could think of.

"You are perfect." He was soothing her, hypnotizing her with soft strokes over her shoulders, down her arms. "The strongest woman I know." His mouth followed, covering her, tasting her, chasing away the chill hiding in her bones. "Let me show you what I see."

She was no match for him when he looked into her eyes as he stripped away the rest of her clothes. He brought her hands to his shoulders, easing back so she practically melted on top of him, giving her the control and the choice.

"Francesca," he murmured over and over in that

mesmerizing voice. His hands flowed and coaxed, erasing her scars, until she felt her body as he did.

It was like floating through a beautiful, dynamic dream as she lowered her body, taking him in carefully when she wanted to rush. He filled her so well she didn't want to move. She wanted to savor. Gently at first, she lifted her hips, testing and teasing the limits of his desire and her patience. His hands gripped her hips and he changed the rhythm to suit him. Them.

The pleasure coursed through her with every stroke, building. The climax crashed over her and she cried out as her body shuddered around him. He flexed his hips, driving deep, deeper until she couldn't discern where he ended and she began. Her body instinctively clung, gripping him tight, reluctant to let go.

When he stretched out beside her with a satisfied sigh, she curled into him, her hand resting over his heart, the light glinting off the diamond on her finger. She stared at the stone and the setting, knowing she'd given him far more than her body.

His hand traced circles over her shoulder and he pressed a kiss to the top of her hair. She'd dropped her heart into his care. Worse, she realized as exhaustion claimed her, she trusted him not to break it.

FRANKIE WOKE IN the middle of the night, knowing she wouldn't get any more sleep. There wasn't a better sign of feeling safe than the fact that they'd slept soundly. She slipped out from under Aidan's arm, turned out the light and grabbed a T-shirt and yoga pants from her suitcase on her way to the shower. At some point she was going to have to assess what they'd just done in that bed. She'd have to address how she'd left herself open to him, body and soul. Right now she locked on to the easy fib that the sex had been about reaffirming life. They'd experienced a standard biological reaction to the adrenaline spike of survival. Simple.

Under the hot pulse of the shower spray, it didn't feel simple, but she ignored the new awareness pressing in on her. The priority had to be the work. Her search for answers had gotten her mugged and nearly killed. It was past time to take a stand against her mother's schemes. Frankie toweled off, dressed and twisted her wet hair into a loose braid.

There had to be hard evidence. Without it, Aidan would continue to do his job and offer conflicting theories. She couldn't bear the idea of him siding with Sophia on any topic. Worse, she couldn't bear the small voice in her head that suggested he could be right, that her mother wasn't guilty of awful things. That was the voice of the heartbroken child inside her, not the woman smart enough to know better.

She opened her laptop, turning it away from Aidan so she wouldn't wake him while she tried to put the pieces together. Rubbing her temples, she went back to the beginning, to the treason charge, looking at every piece in light of what she and Aidan had found along the way.

It helped, Aidan's identification of Lennox, and she pushed her research skills to the limit to make the connections between Lennox and her father, her father and the supposed act of treason. He'd been at Bagram, not Kabul. A general didn't travel around unnoticed. How had her mother, an expert analyst, made such a costly mistake?

Too quickly Frankie wanted to cycle back, pointing

to the blatant lies in her mother's statement, but she fought to stay objective. For Aidan.

She stood, stretching side to side and forward, loosening tight muscles as she let her mind work. Her team had been attacked. Units under her father's command had been ambushed, the objective compromised presumably because he'd tipped off the other side for money. Her husband found guilty, Sophia had chosen to retire and start her company. Who gained from taking down the Leone family?

"Come back to bed, love."

Aidan's voice, gravelly from sleep, tempted her. She didn't want to resist. "Can't sleep." She didn't dare look at him. "I'm almost there."

Behind her she heard the mattress give as he got up. He turned on the light and denim rustled as he pulled on his jeans.

His chest was warm on her back when he wrapped his arms around her, linking his hands at her waist. "I think you're trying too hard. Let it rest."

"I'll rest when I have answers. We're running out of time."

"Your mother may not have the answers, Frankie."

The nickname rang hollow in her ears, after he'd called her Francesca when his hands and mouth were heating her body. She shivered. If he was right, what would she do? She moved back to the table, easing into the chair.

"Why do you do that?" he asked. "Sit so carefully."

"Habit. Early in the rehab my hip would catch and lock up. I would jerk or wince and everyone stared or asked about it. I learned to move so my weaknesses didn't show."

His short laughter startled her and she stared at him as he knelt beside her chair. "What weaknesses?"

She loved him for that. Kissed him for that. She wrapped his bigger hand in both of hers, needing that contact as she asked a question of her own. "Why are you so convinced Sophia is innocent in all this?"

"I've been looking at both of you, past and present, with objective eyes."

"She's fooled you," Frankie protested. "That statement—"

"If the statement is real, she gave it in good faith. The intel might've been flawed. If the document you found is fake, who put it there?" His blue eyes were steady on hers. "I'm not fooled. Not by her or you." Aidan stood and pulled Frankie up with him, his arms banding tight around her. "You're hurting. You've been robbed of everything you valued and you want a hard target to attack."

She leaned back, just enough to meet his gaze, since she didn't want him to let go. "I was a target just a few hours ago."

His face blanched. "I'm well aware." His lips brushed over her forehead, her nose, then claimed her mouth. "Despite any flaws, Sophia is a mother delighted with her daughter. Awed and inspired by you. Whatever happened, she loves you."

That only made it worse. Frankie flinched. "Take that back."

"I won't."

"That was before." Frankie felt the facts dragging her down into a well of despair. She had to *know* or walk away. Walking away was weakness. "If you're so sure it wasn't Sophia, *show* me why."

She expected him to sit at the computer, call up something he and Victoria had found. Instead, he stalked over to the duffel bag he'd brought along and unzipped the end pocket. Tossing a folder full of brochures and information onto the table, he glared at her. "Go on. Take a look."

She poked at the pile, startled by the glossy images of handsome men in tuxedos, couples lounging on a cruise ship, dancing in a classroom. "What is this?"

"Your mother keeps dropping this stuff at my desk. I can pull up the emails, too, if you'd like to read them. Questions about my preferences on tux colors, buffet or plated meals, suggestions for honeymoon destinations. Seems she's traveled extensively."

"Well, of course. The army toted us all around the world."

"Uh-huh." He planted his hands on his hips. "She's been telling me which climates you enjoyed most, which excursions and discoveries made you light up."

"What?" The behavior he was describing baffled Frankie. Everything she found pointed to a woman all too eager to ditch her past for a better venture.

Aidan pressed his hands to his eyes and she imagined he was counting to ten. Or maybe one hundred.

"Your mother *loves* you. She wouldn't be working this hard on the wedding, wouldn't be sharing the highlights of your childhood with me, if she wanted you dead."

"She's hiding something," Frankie insisted, but the argument felt flat. "Playing us."

"No." He shook his head. "We're playing her."

"That was the plan." She wagged her finger between

them. "None of this pretense would be necessary if she'd been honest with me from the start."

"Think, Frankie! She can't give you answers she doesn't have. Take another perspective and consider the possibility that she's protecting *you*."

He spoke with such conviction she wanted to believe him. "We were close once. My family was a team. Someone twisted that into lies."

He gripped her elbows, gave her a gentle shake. "You deserve answers. I know you're hurting. But your mother is too direct, too efficient to waste this much time on wedding stuff if her goal is to kill you."

Aidan drew in a big breath. "You know her better, I'll grant you that. But your history and grief are clouding your view."

He had to be wrong. Frankie couldn't see how anyone else gained from this fiasco. Who else would care if she lived or died?

"All right." Frankie sat down at her computer, ignoring the wedding paraphernalia. She motioned for him to pull up a chair. "Walk me through it. If my mom's just a patsy, let's find the culprit."

Chapter Eleven

Wednesday, April 13, 7:50 a.m.

Frankie and Aidan arrived at work hand in hand, parting ways with a quick kiss in the lobby. They'd made this their routine from the start, but today it felt different. More real, far more significant.

It didn't take any investigation to know making love with Aidan changed her, she thought, taking the stairs up to her floor. Love? No. Her mind backpedaled in denial. It was excellent sex that left her feeling soft and mushy all over. Something in the way Aidan had touched her reached her heart, yes. The experience had definitely surpassed her expectations. Still, it was too soon to burden either of them with *love*.

She tugged open the stairwell door, refusing to dwell on the conversation she'd overheard, instead greeting the others on her floor as she hurried to her office.

At least she and Aidan had solid indications her mother had been involved, if not willingly, with her dad's downfall. As Aidan had reviewed the facts, Frankie had grudgingly admitted he was right. Everything she pointed to was circumstantial, some of it possibly fabricated. If they could just prove it, they could move on. She wished she knew what that next phase of her life would look like.

Frankie dropped her purse into her desk drawer and locked it. Booting up her computer, she thought about what Aidan had asked her to look for today while she pretended to analyze company data looking for criminal trends, security options and new clients to approach.

It still surprised her how much she enjoyed the work that was supposed to be short-term cover. If they didn't find something by the end of the week, she'd have to resign her post at the police station and stick this out, or else leave her mom in the lurch. Somehow the idea wasn't as appealing as it had been forty-eight hours ago.

Frankie closed her eyes and leaned back in her chair. She sure as hell never expected to carry away any guilt over what had to be done in her effort to clear her father's name.

At the sound of a soft rap on her office door, she sat up, her eyes popping open.

"Good morning," her mother said, peeking around the door. "Late night?"

Either her mother was diabolical, a theory Aidan dismissed, or her surveillance team had no idea someone had tried to kill her daughter last night. Frankie heard Aidan's voice urging her to play nice. "Hi, Mom. I just didn't sleep well."

"Wedding plans do that to a bride."

Frankie struggled to maintain the eye contact. "I suppose."

"Was it the elevator? I heard there was an emergency call with an elevator in your building. Do we need to move you and Aidan?"

"Some kind of mechanical failure," Frankie said slowly. Her mother had friends tailing them who'd surely seen the emergency personnel. If she was responsible for the bugs in the apartment, too, did she know the two of them had been gone all night? Frankie needed another cup of tea before tackling these mental gymnastics. "Don't worry about us."

"Okay. You know—" Sophia took a small step inside the office "—before your father and I rushed our wedding, the most fun we had was cake testing."

Frankie swallowed. It wasn't just the idea of cake at eight o'clock in the morning. It was the image of her parents' loving, romantic relationship spiraling into something so terrible. Did love ever last? Great, now she had one more impossible question in need of an answer. "I remember you made chocolate cake every time he returned from a deployment or business trip."

"His aunt Josie baked the cake for the reception my parents hosted and she gave me the recipe," Sophia said. "Does Aidan like chocolate cake?"

Frankie nodded, hoping it was true.

"I'll email you the recipe."

"Thanks." Frankie deliberately turned her attention to her computer monitor.

Sophia ignored the hint to leave. "I don't want to step on any toes," she said, her hands clasped tight around the travel mug of coffee in her hands. "But I, um, made a few calls and if you'd like we can preview some bakers this afternoon."

"What?"

"Just to streamline the process," she said with a tentative smile. "Naturally you and Aidan will want to make the final choice together."

"Mom." Frankie was appalled at the soft sound of her own voice. The love shining in her mother's gaze was worse. Aidan was right, this wasn't the face of a woman who wanted to destroy her daughter.

Frankie cleared her throat and reminded herself she had nothing to lose by playing along with wedding plans that wouldn't happen. It didn't help. She was in too deep with her mom and the fake fiancé who'd become her real lover. "That's thoughtful. Thanks."

"I sifted through the recommendations and reviews and chose bakers who still had openings in September."

It was such a caring-mother move. Frankie managed to get air in and out of her lungs without choking. The misery over what had begun as a white lie mounted. Worse, this morning it was surprisingly easy to imagine exchanging vows with Aidan. She gave herself a mental kick. They were here for a purpose and she was letting herself get carried away by the game.

Sophia caught her lip between her teeth. "Are you angry?"

"No." Not the way she had been. "It just sort of hit me that we do need to make plans. I'd thought I'd have time to enjoy being engaged."

"And you should." Her mother sank gracefully into a chair. "We can always shift the date."

"Maybe." Frankie mustered a smile. "I'll probably want to move it up after we meet with the bakers."

The tension fled from Sophia's face. "Oh, good. Afterward maybe you and I can have dinner down in Pike Place Market."

"That would be great, Mom." If a mother-daughter dinner worked, she wouldn't squander the opportunity.

Sophia's phone chimed from her pocket. "Meeting

alarm," she said. "It's so hard to think business when my daughter is getting married!"

Frankie admired her mother's ability to hurry without a single outward sign of stress. Years of maintaining her composure as the general's wife had been good training. It should serve as a warning that Sophia Leone was capable of saying one thing while doing another.

Thanks to Aidan planting doubts in her mind, Frankie no longer believed her mother could book wedding cake tasting after ordering a hit on her only child.

Frankie dug into the work. It was the only way to get her mind off the not-going-to-happen wedding plans. She even gave the cyber-crime trends her full attention for over an hour before turning her focus back to her quest for the truth, coming up empty again. She swore under her breath. Either her mother had disposed of all evidence or, as Aidan and Victoria would happily point out, Sophia was innocent. Frankie needed to find something soon. Victoria wouldn't let her monopolize a Colby investigator indefinitely.

"Think!" She drummed her fingertips on her desktop as she considered her next move. There had to be some confirmation of Sophia's source, or a trace of her obligations at the time of the operation that ended Frank Leone's military career.

Frankie worked her way through the company directory, focusing on the legal and organizational angles as the company came together. How long had Sophia and Paul kicked around this idea before taking action?

And suddenly, there it was, the validation Frankie had been looking for. According to the official statement, Sophia had been consulting in Washington, DC, when Frankie was injured. So why did these travel documents show her mother and Paul traveling on a military flight from Germany to New York? Paul had then returned to Seattle, while Sophia met Frankie at Walter Reed Hospital in Maryland.

Her stomach sank. It was the proof she'd wanted to find, what she'd put all her energy into for months. Forty-eight hours ago she would've marched into her mother's office for a confrontation. Today, she saved the information for Aidan to review first. It was still a file in a database and, as he'd pointed out repeatedly, possibly manufactured.

If her mother wasn't guilty of taking down her dad, who would want to make it look that way? Frustrated, Frankie used every computer skill she possessed to catalog the information and store it securely until she and Aidan could plan the next move.

AIDAN SPENT EVERY free minute of his day working on Frankie's case. Now that he had her on his side, he didn't want to relinquish the advantage. Paul found him as he and the trainees wrapped up a session on hand-to-hand strategies. "Looks good," the older man said.

"They're coming along," Aidan agreed.

Despite the words, Aidan couldn't shake the sensation that Paul wasn't happy with anything at Leo Solutions right now. Aidan didn't have anything solid to pin that on and it made him think he was becoming as paranoid about the man as Frankie was about her mother. Still, his investigative instincts were in high gear.

Paul gestured with the phone in his hand. "Sophia tells me she set up a preview of bakeries for tonight.

Says she and Frankie need some time to narrow down the style and choices before they invite you to a tasting. It's code for 'girls' night out,'" he said, looking less than happy.

"All right." It required a little too much effort today to remember this was a cover story. After last night—before, if Aidan was honest with himself—he couldn't quite see his future without Frankie in it. "As long as she doesn't leave me out of everything."

"Ha!" Paul's sharp bark of laughter gave way to a rare, genuine smile. "Trust me, you'll want to leave the details to the women. The days after the ceremony are when the heavy lifting begins."

Aidan just nodded. That wasn't how he envisioned marriage, but he'd never gotten that far, so what did he know? "Thanks for the heads-up. I should get back to it." With his evening free he could spend the time digging into the company's records for the source behind the ruination of Frankie's family.

Paul cleared his throat and managed to keep a smile in place. "How about you and I head to my club for dinner? There's a weekly card game if you're interested."

"Sounds great." Anything that gave him a better glimpse of Paul could be helpful.

"I have a six o'clock meeting. Then I can swing by the apartment and pick you up by seven-thirty."

"We can leave from here," Aidan offered, seizing the excuse to stay late. "I'll have time to clean up and change clothes between classes and the paperwork."

"All right," Paul agreed. "I'll send a text when my meeting ends."

Busy man, and he liked to keep it that way, Aidan

thought as Paul walked off. More accurately, he liked to make others believe he was indispensable.

Aidan wasn't convinced, no matter how Sophia explained the professional partnership. Granted, he hadn't been on-site long, but the vibe he picked up was interesting. Employees seemed utterly devoted to Sophia and wary of Paul. There had to be a reason, beyond the man's reticent nature.

Unfortunately, Aidan hadn't been on the job long enough for anyone to confide in him about specifics. And with the elevator attack, he didn't want to drag this out. He sent a text message to Frankie about his plans with Paul and then headed to the mat for the next lesson. When the classes ended, Aidan cleaned up for dinner and retreated to his desk while he waited for Paul.

It hadn't been easy worming his way past the corporate security protocols, but Aidan had experience and tenacity on his side. He'd given up the direct approach— leaving that to Frankie—and started his investigation through lower-level personnel. As a trainer he used his access to review how each personal security officer was connected to Paul, Sophia or both. It made sense that the men and women who'd been with the company since the outset had worked with one or both of them on other endeavors.

He found his way back to the Lennox file and continued searching for the man who'd approached Frankie in Savannah. The guy couldn't just show up and disappear. Aidan had just found a plane ticket matching Lennox's ID when the text message from Paul came through.

At least he had something to chew on as soon as dinner was over. Quickly, Aidan copied the information to the cloud storage sites for Victoria. He'd tell Frankie in person, hopefully over wedding cake samples.

Paul was uncharacteristically chatty in the car and Aidan struggled to keep up with the conversation while his mind worked through the case.

"Scotch?" Paul offered, pulling down a panel of the backseat to reveal two highball glasses and a decanter of pale amber liquid.

"I'll pass," Aidan replied. "Thanks."

"Suit yourself." He poured a generous serving into one glass. "Has to be the best perk of having a driver in this city," he said.

"You're not from Seattle?"

"Hell, no." He sipped the Scotch. "I tried to convince Sophia there were areas more conducive to our business, but she was determined to pin the headquarters here." He gazed about, eyeing the traffic through the windows.

They had plenty of time to enjoy the view of Seattle sparkling at twilight at the edge of Puget Sound, since the freeway was clogged with commuters. As traffic jams went, this wasn't bad. This part of the world was so different from his other experiences, Aidan soaked it up.

Paul raised his glass, draining the contents. "So, how are things going?"

"Well, thanks," Aidan replied honestly. "It's good work—"

A car rear-ended the sedan, cutting him off.

"What was that?" Paul demanded, twisting around in his seat.

His pulse jumping into high gear, Aidan looked in

turn. A bullet screamed through the rear window, exiting through the windshield. Aidan hunkered down, resisting the urge to go for the weapon in his ankle holster.

"Get us out of here," Paul roared to the driver.

The man jerked the wheel and slammed his hand on the horn as he aimed for the left shoulder, searching for any opening on the crowded roadway. The acrid odor of burning rubber tinged the air when he gunned the engine through tight spaces. The car that hit them gave pursuit. Aidan and Paul were tossed back into the seat and then side to side as the driver evaded within his limited options.

"Where's a cop when you need one?" Paul grumbled. Keeping his head low, he managed to get the glassware back into the console and tuck the liquor station away.

Aidan muttered something agreeable as he mentally weighed his limited options. He hoped Frankie and Sophia weren't experiencing a similar attack.

Paul's driver cut across traffic from the left shoulder, aiming for the next exit. Aidan couldn't understand the decision. The surface streets would give the maniac behind them better access as they jerked in a stop-and-go pattern between lanes.

Bullets started to fly again. One after another struck the window closest to Aidan, creating spiderweb patterns in the glass. He ducked down, taking Paul with him. "Are you hit?"

"No," the older man said. "What about you?"

"I'm good." Aidan pulled a pen from his sport coat and wrote down the plate number of the car that had hit them. "Got the license," he muttered.

Paul gave him a small smile. "Good job."

"We're clear, boss," the driver said.

Aidan followed Paul's lead, resuming his place in the backseat as they merged with traffic exiting the freeway. "What now?" he asked.

The remnants of the rear window exploded and Paul's answer was swallowed by a spray of sparkling glass and a violent oath. Aidan felt a burning in his back and across his arm as a wet warmth seeped slowly down his side. The coppery tang of blood filled his nostrils. "I'm hit." Had he managed to get the words out or had he only thought them?

It was his first gunshot wound and he hadn't expected it to make him woozy. He didn't understand how the shot was even possible until he looked back over his shoulder and caught the movement of a sniper on the overpass above and behind them.

He'd been set up, he thought, afraid this time he had said it aloud. "Hospital," he rasped, reaching for his phone.

Paul shouted orders to the driver while applying pressure to Aidan's back.

Aidan reached into his pocket, relieved his phone was in one piece. He pulled up Frankie's contact page.

"What are you doing?" Paul demanded.

The call went to voice mail. The sound of the greeting Frankie had recorded on her new phone made him feel better immediately.

"Fr-Frankie," Aidan stammered. "Baby," he said, using the code word for trouble. "Got shot." It was only a small fib, not an outright lie. "Here's Paul."

He handed over the phone. "Tell her what hospital."

He listened as Paul explained where they were headed, and then he reclaimed his phone.

"I'll call Sophia as soon as we get to the ER," Paul assured him. "Just in case they don't get the voice mail."

"Good." Aidan let his head drop back onto the seat, hoping that didn't make him a better target. The wind rushed through the destroyed rear window, the sound and chill keeping him awake as the driver sped to the nearest hospital.

It felt like a small eternity before the car stopped. Aidan was soon surrounded by people in scrubs helping him from the vehicle. He heard Paul explain they'd been attacked on the freeway and then, finally, he heard nothing more than the orders of medical staff around him.

"It's not that bad," he murmured as they cut away his clothing. "I need my phone."

A nurse argued with him, but he had to tell Victoria. "Aidan Abbot, Interpol," he said, hoping they wouldn't ask for official ID. "I need five seconds to send a text, and then you can have at it."

Over the gurney a doctor exchanged a look and a shrug with the nurse. The woman handed him his phone and he managed to send the text. Victoria would know what to do next. "Thank you," he said. His head was swimming again, just from that small effort. "What the hell happened to my head?"

His questions went unanswered as the medical team worked to assess and address his injuries. At least he was out of Paul's reach for the moment. Assuming that bastard was behind the whole mess.

More important, if he didn't survive this, the Colby Agency would protect Frankie and could flush out the mole inside Leo Solutions.

Chapter Twelve

Frankie was completely overwhelmed and more than a little worried when her mother drove out to a small, private airfield on the west side. "We're flying to interview bakers?"

Sophia chuckled and reached across the console to pat Frankie's knee. "No. I just needed neutral territory to bring them all together. A friend of mine let me use the conference room here. And I didn't want any distractions from the office."

Frankie was distracted enough with all the details and emotions she could barely fit into the box in the corner of her mind. This woman didn't reconcile with the distant widow Frankie remembered after her dad's suicide. She was much closer to the vibrant, reliable mother from Frankie's childhood. "You didn't have to do this," she said, her guilt riding heavy on her shoulders.

"I want to. You're going to marry a wonderful man and your wedding should be perfect from start to finish."

Only in her dreams, Frankie thought. "You barely know him."

"I know you," Sophia countered. "You're smart and

an excellent judge of character. If he wasn't worthy, you never would've said yes when he proposed."

Frankie knew that no matter how delicious the presentation, she would taste only bitterness today. Sophia put the car in Park and wiggled her fingers. "A man who puts a ring like that on your hand is serious about forever."

Oh, God. This wedding business was way out of control.

Sophia patted her arm. "Sweetheart, you're starting a life together and I want to celebrate that moment with you to the fullest." She reached for her door handle. "Let's go eat cake!"

Frankie managed to make a sound that resembled laughter. If she was such an excellent judge of character, why did she feel that her family was one lie on top of another? She had believed her parents were in love, devoted and committed to each other and to her. She'd believed her mother had supported her dad through the accusations. Then she'd believed her mother had set him up. And now she believed, as Aidan did, that something bigger and darker had manipulated them all.

What did she know about anyone's true character? She barely recognized herself anymore, running around pretending one thing while thinking and feeling ten others.

Further self-assessment took a backseat as she walked into the conference room. Her mother had pulled out all the stops. Tables were draped in white, and seven different bakeries had created elaborate displays. "Holy cow," Frankie whispered. "Mom."

"This is fabulous," Sophia gushed, striding forward

to greet the bakers. "Thank you all so much for doing this at the last minute."

Frankie marveled at the effort she had made, as well as the bakers. This had taken more than a few phone calls. Would the real Sophia Leone please stand up?

She and her mother set out to evaluate each display. They tasted two samples from each baker and flipped through presentation books of designs. Overwhelmed didn't begin to cover it. Sophia conducted a group interview of sorts and Frankie chimed in with an occasional opinion. No pricing was discussed, just options and preferences. It was clear to everyone in the room Sophia wasn't putting a limit on the wedding budget.

If Frankie could've crawled into a hole, she would have.

"If we have a family recipe for a specific cake, is that something any of you would consider? Not for the formal cake," Sophia clarified, "but for a groom's cake or a honeymoon suite surprise. I don't want my daughter or me worried about baking on the day of, you understand."

That generated more favorable responses and Frankie found herself as enamored as the bakers by Sophia's bright, happy smile.

Her phone vibrated in her pocket and she checked the display, irrationally hoping it was Aidan. Seeing that she'd missed a call from his number, she excused herself to listen to the voice mail.

He stammered her name, sounding drunk.

Her heart lunged into her throat.

"Baby." Hearing the code word for trouble, Frankie rapped on the glass window to get Sophia's attention. "Got shot," Aidan's message went on.

Frankie swayed at the news. "Oh, my God!" Suddenly Paul's voice was telling her the car had been attacked on the freeway and they were headed to the hospital.

Frankie fought down a tidal wave of panic as her mother joined her. "We have to go," she told Sophia, her hands shaking. "Aidan's been shot."

Her mom's eyes went wide. "How? Where?" She dashed back into the conference room for her purse. "He and Paul were together," she said as they ran for the car.

"Paul sounded fine," Frankie assured her through clenched teeth. She used her phone to search the news networks for any reports of a freeway sniper. No results. Either the story was too new or the attack had been focused solely on Paul and Aidan.

Sophia reached over and clutched Frankie's hand as she drove. "Paul won't let anything happen to Aidan. Just hang in there."

Frankie hoped she was right. It felt like hours rather than minutes before they reached the ER, and her heart threatened to beat out of her chest. Sophia dropped Frankie at the door and then drove off to find a parking space.

Frankie raced up to the emergency room information desk. "Aidan Abbot." She paused, the words jammed behind the panicked beating of her heart. "My fiancé. Gunshot wound."

The nurse behind the desk nodded in recognition. "He's stable. If you'll have a seat, we'll tell you more when we know something."

"I need to see him right now." A rush of tears blurred her vision. "Now," she repeated. She hadn't been this frantic since waking in that hospital bed with no feeling below her waist.

"Frankie." His hand at her elbow, Paul drew her aside.

She looked up, wiping the tears from her cheeks as he put his arm around her. Where had he come from? Why wasn't there a mark on him? Was that Aidan's blood on his jacket? Fear tore through her. She shrugged off Paul's touch and stepped out of his reach. "You did this. Somehow." She thought of the travel documents and the Lennox interview. If not Sophia, it had to be Paul pulling the strings. "You set this up."

"You're upset." The man's voice was gentle, but his eyes were cold. "Understandable. Just take a breath." His gaze slid past her and she heard high heels clicking rapidly on the tile flooring.

Frankie attacked, drilling a finger into his chest. "It's you. Last night you tried to kill me, and now him. No way I'll let you get away with this."

"Frankie," her mother said. "What's going on? How is Aidan?"

"He's stable," Paul answered before Frankie could.

"Thank God for that." Sophia pressed a hand to her chest. "What happened?"

"Road rage, I guess," he explained, without explaining anything at all. "Aidan claims he caught some of the license plate of the car. We were rear-ended and then shot at."

Sophia sucked in a breath. "Are you sure you're not hurt?" She gestured to the bloodstains on his clothes.

"I'm fine."

Frankie had calmed down enough to speak again. Though she doubted anyone would like what she had to say. "Of course he's fine. The attack was aimed at Aidan. Paul here wants us off his trail."

"You're out of your mind," Paul accused.

"I'm right." Frankie fisted her hand, eager to reach for the knife in her purse. "We've been tailed and mugged, attacked and shot at. You even bugged the apartment."

Staring at her in bewilderment, Sophia echoed, "Bugged?" She looked to Paul. "What is she talking about?"

"This is hardly the place to discuss these things," he chided, his voice low. "Your mother is the public face of a prominent security company."

"I want to see Aidan," Frankie demanded. Her mother's arms went around her, drawing her close. Frankie's first instinct was to pull away, but she simply didn't possess the wherewithal.

"He's going to be fine," Paul insisted. "The police are on their way."

"As if I'd believe anything you say." Frankie jerked out of her mother's embrace. "Either of you. I came here, we came here because—" She caught herself in the nick of time and dragged in a deep breath. "Because I thought we could be a family," she said to her mom. "It was Aidan's idea." She tried to remember more of the cover story and couldn't. She pushed her hands through her hair. "I just need to see him."

Her mother's full lips compressed to a straight line and she stalked back to the registration desk.

"How's that family idea working?" Paul stuffed his hands into his pockets. "Since you showed up with that chip on your shoulder, she's bent over backward for you and you—"

"Frankie." Sophia snapped her fingers and pointed to a nurse wearing a harried expression. "Hurry."

Frankie didn't have time to figure out what Paul meant or listen to a lecture from the sullen man. With a parting glare for him, she joined the nurse and tried to pull herself together before seeing Aidan.

She supposed it couldn't be too bad if he wasn't in surgery. Still, she'd be the one to decide if he was fine. Not Paul, standing out there without a scratch on him, lecturing her about family. Bastard.

Another nurse stepped out of the emergency treatment bay. "You're the fiancée?"

Frankie nodded. The fake fiancée dumb enough to have fallen in love with her undercover groom.

"He's been asking for you."

"Thanks." She walked through the split in the curtain and, seeing him alert and smiling, her anger and worry faded. He motioned her closer to the bed and laced his fingers with hers. *Relief* wasn't a strong enough word. He was pale, but the monitor showed steady vitals. "You're okay?"

She examined every inch she could see as the words *I love you* and *don't scare me* danced on the tip of her tongue. She wouldn't say them, not here. She couldn't put that pressure on him. It wasn't his fault she'd fallen so hard and fast.

"Stop looking for trouble," he said. "I'm fine, I promise." He raised her hand to his lips.

"Hardly fine. You're in an ER," she pointed out. "You've been shot."

He laughed a little and then winced at the resulting pain.

"Tell me what happened." She kept her voice low

and bent to give him a kiss on the cheek. "Did you find something?"

He shook his head, but the gleam in his eyes told her the answer was yes. He didn't want to discuss it here.

"None of the news agencies are reporting a freeway sniper."

He grunted. "I gave the plate number to the cops who came by a few minutes ago."

"How bad is it, really?"

"I'm fine," he insisted. "It's all superficial. I got clocked behind the ear with debris and have a mild concussion. That gave me more trouble than the gunshot."

When the doctor came around an hour later to discharge him, Frankie verified that he'd left nothing out regarding his injuries and that she understood the instructions and danger signs to watch for overnight.

IT WAS NICE, in a strange way, to have Frankie fuss over him. To watch her dark, expressive eyes fill with relief when he finally convinced her the bullet had done little more than graze him. He had a few stitches, and thanks to the concussion he was bordering on exhausted by the time they convinced her mother he was fine and escaped to the hotel where they'd spent last night.

"What do you need?" she asked, pushing the U-lock and dead bolt into place.

"I'm good." He eased himself onto the bed and smiled at her. "Just relax."

"How? You were attacked—"

He wanted to tell her the attack was sloppy, to point out—again—that he'd survived. She needed to hear something else. He understood. "Now you know how I felt last night."

Her mouth closed and her eyes went wide, her dark eyebrows arching, and then she scowled. "Yeah, okay."

She dropped into the chair across the room and he stifled a smirk. "How was the cake tasting?"

"Cake is the least of our concerns," she replied.

He eyed the ring on her finger, liking the look of it there. "They didn't send any samples with you?" That earned him a sharp glare. A smarter man wouldn't bait this particular woman, but he happened to be fond of the way her eyes sparked when she was annoyed.

Fond. Yeah, that was an understatement. Despite the close call, it didn't feel like the right time to tell her how "fond" he was.

"We left in a rush." She stood up and pushed her hands through her hair. "Are you sore? Do you need something for pain?"

"No," he answered. "I only need one thing."

"Tell me," she said, eager to help.

"Come here and kiss me." He hoped it would distract them both from the inevitable talk about the case. When she learned that he'd sent his latest findings and theories to Victoria without consulting her, Frankie would be angry. At the very least.

Before he faced that, he wanted some tangible reassurance they were both still breathing, and committed to this case. To each other. He shoved the errant thought aside. Yes, he needed her touch more than he wanted to admit, but he'd just been shot. Sappy, random things were supposed to wander through his concussed brain.

She walked over, pulled a chair close to the bed and took his hand between hers. "You scared me."

Her quiet admission surprised him. "Given a choice, I'd never do that." He tugged on her hand until she was in range of his lips. For a long moment, he savored the sweet, soft kiss.

Her mouth curved in a gentle smile when she broke away. Then she caught her plump lower lip between her teeth. Stepping out of his reach, she hooked her thumbs into the back pockets of her khaki slacks. "I did something stupid while you were back there," she said. "Before they let me see you."

"How stupid?"

"I lost it." She fixed her gaze on the ceiling and blinked a few times. Her eyes were clear when she focused on him again. "I was scared and mad and confused. I started tossing around accusations about..." She waved a hand in the general direction of his injuries.

"Sophia didn't do this," he blurted.

Frankie dropped her head into her hands, embarrassed. "I blamed Paul, actually."

"What?"

"That's not the worst of it."

Aidan waited, impatience and worry clawing at him.

"I nearly blew our cover. I was just so mad. It's one thing to take a shot at me, but you're just along for the ride." Her hands raked through her hair again and she scooped it up on top of her head before letting it fall. "Whether it's Paul, Sophia or both of them behind this, I think I've wrecked the case."

"Frankie—"

She barreled on, "I'm going to confront Mom in the morning." Standing, Frankie paced back and forth along the foot of the bed. "I'll show her what I've found and be satisfied with whatever she does or doesn't say. Then I'll send everything to Victoria for a final decision about notifying any authorities."

"What did you find?" Aidan willed her to stop pacing and look at him. It was hard enough to concentrate right now without the distraction of her tantalizing body and cascading hair. "Frankie."

She stopped short. "I found travel documents buried in the corporate organization files. They show Mom and Paul returning from Europe the day my unit was attacked. The statement filed in my father's treason case listed her in DC on those days."

"Where were the documents?"

"Archived on the main server."

"You know that can be faked."

She nodded. "Her trips to see me in Bethesda and Atlanta were there, too. I couldn't see any difference. I copied everything for you to review."

"Thanks," he said, watching her place the drive on the table as if it might explode at any second. "I found something today, too."

"Tell me. I have to know, Aidan."

Hearing the pain in her voice, he cleared his throat, wishing he'd had a better choice. "I found Lennox's trail and a charter flight record signed with Sophia's signature stamp. I'd planned to work on it more tonight."

"That's it. I'm going over there right now."

He shook his head, dreading what he needed to say. "No." How did he tell her it was too late? "You can't confront Sophia tonight or tomorrow. I sent everything we've gathered to Victoria. She'll take it to the right people for confirmation."

"You did *what*?"

He watched shock and hurt twist Frankie's beautiful features. He knew she felt betrayed, and with good reason. When he'd walked her through his investigation early this morning, he promised to share everything with her first. "I'm sorry. I was still in the car and I didn't want to take a chance that Paul would finish me off before I reached the hospital."

"Paul?"

Aidan nodded. "I'm sure that's really why he invited me to dinner tonight. My investigation was getting too close. He had to act."

She was on her feet again. "Were they working together? Why did they need to get my dad out of the way?"

"I don't have those answers yet. Victoria—"

Frankie spun around, her long hair fanning out and then settling over her shoulders as the anger returned in a rush. "This was *my* fight, Aidan. Sophia won't ever be honest with me now."

Aidan felt as if he'd taken a punch to the gut. He'd blown it. Not with the case; he'd done the right thing as an investigator. When she calmed down, maybe by the turn of the next century, Frankie would see that, too.

But he'd done it the wrong way for her. Frankie's quest might have looked like vengeance days ago, but he knew better now. He knew *her* better. Frankie was a woman trying to reconcile inconceivable events for the brokenhearted little girl she kept locked away inside. Her father had been her hero. The charges, verdict and suicide were irrelevant. Her mother had been her anchor, the one constant in her life.

Hell, logic and justice were irrelevant at this point. She just wanted to hear the whole story, to understand, if that was possible. She'd never be satisfied, never move forward until she had the truth. And now she'd never trust him enough to give him a chance to share that life.

"I—I'm going out," she said, starting for the door.

Aidan pushed himself to his feet and the room did a slow spin. "Frankie, wait." He couldn't let her leave. Not upset, not alone.

She shook her head. "I can't stay here with you," she said over her shoulder. "I can't trust you."

The words slid through him like one of her lethal knives. The bullet hadn't caused him this much pain. "It's too dangerous. You're a target." They just couldn't be sure about the method of the next attack.

Her shoulders rolled back, her spine ramrod straight. "I can take care of myself, Mr. Abbot. You should ask Victoria to check in on you per the concussion protocol."

He swore as Frankie left the room, the door closing with a heavy clack. He wanted to follow her, but with him in this condition she'd easily outpace him. Damned concussion. He wouldn't leave her safety to chance, not after all that had happened. There had to be something he could do, someone he could call to keep an eye on her. Who could he trust?

He stared helplessly at his cell phone. He trusted Frankie. She was the only person in the city he felt he could count on. No one else was worth the risk. Aidan swore again and called her number, praying she'd pick up.

Naturally she didn't. The woman had a temper and this time he couldn't blame her. He'd promised to bring everything to her first and he'd meant to. But he'd mentally applied a caveat that he would bypass her if it kept her out of harm's way.

"How's that working out for you, Abbot?" The answering silence felt like judge and jury.

Aidan used the app on his cell phone to verify that the GPS on her cell was active and working. When the location came back that she hadn't left the hotel, he breathed a sigh of relief. Assuming she hadn't tossed the device into the trash on her way out the door.

He'd screwed this up beyond all recognition. He could make it right. Ignoring the headache and vertigo, he booted up his laptop and grabbed her flash drive.

She wanted answers? He'd find them, to hell with caution. He did a quick calculation of the time difference as he sorted through the files. One by one, he sent her findings on Sophia and his research of Paul on to an old friend at Interpol. With any luck, an objective opinion would shed some light on what he and Frankie were too close to see.

Whether she could forgive him or not for breaking her trust was another question entirely. Aidan sighed. That answer would have to come later and most likely after much groveling.

He smiled. If it worked, if he won her trust, it would all be worth it.

Chapter Thirteen

Frankie knew Aidan had done the right thing. Though she hated giving in to his safety warning, she went only as far as the hotel bar. She nursed her beer, trying to sort out this ridiculous mess. In his place, targeted by a sniper and sitting next to a potential enemy, she would've done the same thing. Understanding his choice wasn't the same as approving it. Who was she kidding? Holding a grudge against her only ally wouldn't help her unveil the truth.

Ally. What a crock. He'd become far more important than that. Shutting Aidan down only made her stubborn. She ordered a second beer while she figured out her next step with the man and the situation.

She signed the bar tab at the last possible moment and trudged back upstairs. It wasn't safe to leave him alone, no matter how mild the concussion. He was asleep when she walked in, but she could tell he'd tried to work, because his computer was still on and open. She walked over and shook his shoulder, asking him a few standard questions about the day, his name and hers. Satisfied with the answers, she let him drift off to sleep once more.

What a difference twenty-four hours could make.

After she was attacked they'd wound up in that bed. Hot. Naked. Together. Her pulse leaped into overdrive at the recollection.

It had been more than wonderful how he'd held her, scars and all. She would savor the memory once they finished here and went their separate ways. Taking a pillow and the extra blanket from the closet, she curled into the lumpy chair to get some rest.

Thursday, April 14, 6:00 a.m.

SHE WOKE TO the sound of her cell phone buzzing near her pillow. It was too early for an alarm, but she was wide-awake when she saw the text message. Her mother wanted her to come to the house, alone, to clear the air. This wasn't a talk for the office. Sophia had definitely figured out the happily engaged, prodigal daughter routine was an act.

Answers at last. Rolling to her back, Frankie sent a quick affirmative reply.

Last night Aidan's decision about the case had felt like a kick in the teeth. Now it might just be her ace in the hole. It was small comfort that if she and Aidan did wind up dead, the Colby Agency could pursue their killer.

Quietly, she showered and dressed, simultaneously pleased and worried that Aidan slept through it. She roused him just enough for the concussion protocol before leaving him a note about the message from her mother. If Sophia was ready to talk about Frank Leone's downfall, Frankie certainly wasn't going to ignore the summons.

She took the rental car and drove out to Queen

Anne, enjoying the lack of traffic at this early hour. She parked at the curb and gave herself a moment to breathe. Which Sophia would be waiting for her, the mother who was eager to salvage a relationship or the professional analyst with layer upon layer of secrets? That was the crux; Frankie didn't know which mom to trust, only which mom she *wanted* to believe.

The front door opened and her mother hovered in the doorway, the smile on her face loaded with tension. Like mother, like daughter, Frankie thought, climbing out of the car. She ignored the catch in her back as she mounted the steps, taking her time so she wouldn't reveal any weakness.

As Frankie reached the porch, Sophia moved as if to hug her, then jerked back. Apparently she didn't know which woman to be in the moment any more than Frankie did. "I made tea," Sophia said, inviting her inside.

The door closed with a bang and Frankie spun around in time to see Paul throwing the lock. "What are *you* doing here?"

"Think of me as a mediator," he said.

Something in his smooth voice made Frankie's skin crawl. "This conversation doesn't concern you." She shot a look at her mother, but Sophia only gave a small shake of her head and a look that told her not to argue. But the days of her blindly obeying her mom were long gone. "What the hell is going on?"

"It does concern me," Paul said, giving her a shove into the kitchen. "You wanted answers, Frankie. I have them." He pulled a gun from his back and a silencer from his pocket, slowly mating the two pieces. "Not that you'll get much time to enjoy the truth."

"You said you loved me." Sophia stared him down, her voice hard as steel. "Prove it. Let her go."

"I loved you once." Paul shoved Frankie into a kitchen chair. "You told me you were giving Frankie space and the next thing I know she winds up in the heart of the company," he countered, his voice rising before he regained control. "With full access. You pushed me into this corner. Now I'm cashing out."

"I don't care about the company," Frankie said, trying to distract him, to get him away from her mom.

"No one does," he announced. "Not like I do."

"Paul, think about what you're doing," Sophia pleaded.

His gaze shifted from Sophia to Frankie and back. "I've thought it all through. I've exhausted the options. We'll have a tidy double homicide, capped with a suicide."

A cold shiver raced down Frankie's back. The hardware in her spine made it worse, driving that chill into her bones. "Leave Aidan out of it." She couldn't bear to know her case had killed him.

"You are clever," Paul said with obvious approval. "But you're weak." He tapped Sophia's shoulder with the silencer. "When I realized you wouldn't see things my way, I knew it was time to make my move."

"See what your way?" Sophia's voice was quiet, urgent. "We're partners! What are you doing?"

"You've blocked me at every turn, darling. It's time for the overseas expansion—"

"The company isn't ready for that," Sophia interrupted.

Paul gestured with the gun and rolled his eyes. "See what I'm up against? The point is, Frankie, I had to do something after she met with Legal and changed the ownership so you had a say in whatever moves we made as a company."

"You did that?" Frankie couldn't believe it. "When were you going to tell me?"

"When I was sure you wouldn't consider it an emotional bribe," Sophia admitted.

A few more pieces clicked into place. She glanced at Paul. "You couldn't kill her until she changed the legalities back in your favor."

"Or unless you die, too."

"You used her," Sophia said through gritted teeth. "You bastard."

Frankie gasped, horrified that his plan had nearly worked.

Paul shrugged. "A man's entitled to hope for an easy road once in a while."

Frankie's stomach twisted. As Aidan and Victoria had feared, she'd been played, from the moment Lennox showed up in Savannah. "You tampered with her statement. Made sure I saw it. The false passports, the safe-deposit box. Everything was a setup to prod a move out of me."

Paul stepped close to her, his eyes sharp and mean. "You wanted to believe the worst of your mother, a woman who's done nothing but agonize over your distance. It was easy enough to get you out here, wasn't it?" He paced away, turning back before Frankie could make a move. "You idolized your father. It was so easy. You latched on to the 'evidence' against her like a dog with a bone."

An ugly image, but she couldn't argue with the truth of it. "You sent me on a wild-goose chase."

"So predictable," he said with a sneer. "I had to do something when I caught her watching your career in Savannah."

"Of course I watched her career," Sophia snapped, tears spilling down her cheeks. "She's my *daughter*."

Paul shook his head. "Women are soft. Shortsighted. Family and sentiment have no place in business. Trust me, Sophia, I will take good care of Leo Solutions."

Sophia swore at him. "It was never *your* dream."

Frankie looked at her mother and didn't see anything that resembled soft right now. Her face was set with a grim determination, and Frankie knew she was looking for a way to get them out of this.

"You set up my dad," she guessed, trying to keep Paul talking while she racked her brain for the right maneuver. "You insinuated yourself into a place that should've been his."

"He got himself into that mess. I just made sure the pieces fell where I could pick them up." Paul gave a sharp bark of bitter laughter. "You should've been mine all along." He sneered at Sophia. "Frank stole you from me. I waited a very long time to take him out of the picture and reclaim what belonged to me."

Sophia's eyes went wide. "You blew that operation and pinned it on Frank?" She leaped forward and slapped Paul across the cheek, leaving a red handprint behind. "Innocent people died that day."

Frankie felt equally blindsided. She'd misinterpreted everything. Her mother hadn't been any more informed about her father's treason than anyone else. Her sworn statement had been little more than a report. Paul had been the one who'd painted the gray area and ruined the Leones and the lives of countless others in the process.

He gripped Sophia's arm and shoved her hard into the counter. Frankie jumped up, but Paul leveled the gun at her mother's forehead. "You ready to say goodbye?"

"No!" Frankie held up her hands and sat down again, ruthlessly ignoring the catch in her hip. "You don't have to do this, Paul. Dad's gone. Walk away now."

"You won't let me go that easy."

"Let us live and I'll forget you ever existed," Frankie promised.

"I know better. I've watched you." Paul glowered at her. "You should've died, but you're as stubborn as your father. I'm not leaving anything more to chance. Consider this a hostile takeover."

Sophia stood there, silent, unmoving, Paul's hand ruthlessly gripping her arm. Frankie recognized her intention. Her husband had been framed and murdered, her family destroyed, and Sophia was calculating how to save her daughter. Frankie sent a silent plea with her eyes for her mom to be patient. She refused to lose her to this madman the way she'd lost her dad.

"Don't do it," Frankie screamed, though her mother hadn't moved a muscle.

Startled, Paul whipped around, leading with his gun. Frankie lunged, going for his knees. The weapon fired with a muffled pop and she could only pray the bullet had missed her mom.

The gun clattered across the tile and Frankie grappled with Paul, trying to keep him down. Her navy training kept her in the fight, but he was bigger, with a longer reach. He punched her and rolled away. She pulled her knife from the sheath at her waist and put herself between him and the gun, between him and her mother.

He lunged, she ducked under his defenses, her blade slicing through his shirt, and a thin line of blood followed. She heard her mother calling the police. All she had to do was keep him here, keep him busy, and it would all be over.

Sophia threw herself at him. Somewhere across the room Frankie could hear the 9-1-1 operator asking the nature of the emergency. Paul punched Sophia in the face. When she hit the floor, he grabbed her by the hair and pounded her head against the hardwood.

"Mom!" Frankie rushed toward him.

AIDAN HEARD THE noisy fight as he broke through the back door and into the kitchen, gun drawn. Sophia was on the floor. Not moving. Frankie was fighting Paul. Aidan lined up a shot, but they flipped and he couldn't take it without risking hitting her. Sweat poured down his face. His body shook with the effort of staying vertical.

He shouted a warning, but Paul didn't heed it. He plowed a fist into Frankie's stomach, followed by a shoulder, driving her back into the wall. Aidan rushed forward and the room spun. Damn it! His vision cleared just in time for him to see Frankie trying to get up and Paul smirking down at her.

"Move away from her," Aidan shouted. "Or I will blow your damn head off."

"Whatever you say." Paul raised his hands as if in surrender, but then twisted and kicked Frankie in the back.

Aidan fired twice, putting the first bullet in Paul's knee, the second in his shoulder. The coward howled in pain. "Stay down or the next one will be between your eyes."

Aidan rushed to Frankie and fell to his knees beside her. Almost too terrified to touch her, he took stock. She was breathing, blood smearing her nose and lip. Paul had given her hell in the brief fight, but she'd held her own.

"Frankie," he said. She didn't respond. The vicious bastard had executed that last kick where he knew it would do the most damage. Aidan had no idea if it was safe to touch her or to move her. He wouldn't take any chances. "Talk to me. Come on. Please, Francesca."

He smoothed her hair back from her face. He'd called for help en route. Where the hell were the authorities? If he'd only moved faster…

"Frankie?" Sophia was up on her hands and knees, crawling toward them. "Oh, my God." A keening sound issued from her throat.

Aidan handed her his weapon. "Make sure he stays put until the authorities arrive."

Sophia, her face swollen and battered, accepted the weapon and turned it on her lover. "Devil," she spat.

"Come on, Frankie." Aidan clutched her limp hand between his, raising it to his lips. She had to wake up. She had to survive so he could beg her forgiveness and tell her he loved her. He couldn't accept any other outcome.

"She's strong," Sophia said quietly. "Strong and stubborn."

"He kicked her in the back," Aidan said, his voice cracking with fear. This couldn't be happening again.

"You'll see," Sophia promised. "She'll be fine." A sob choked out of her. "She has to be."

Aidan wasn't convinced. There was a bruise blooming on her cheek, a thin line of blood just showing in her hairline. "I'll kill him," he whispered. He aimed a look at the worthless coward now curled in the fetal position. "For every scratch, I'll—"

"Aidan?"

Frankie's thin voice yanked him away from his dark thoughts. "I'm right here." He squeezed her hand.

"How?" She tried to look around, grimaced for her trouble. "When…did you get here?"

"Not soon enough," he said. Sirens sounded in the distance. "Help is almost here."

The police arrived, bringing a new onslaught of chaos. Paul was arrested and taken away, while paramedics rushed in to tend to the injured.

"I'm okay," Frankie insisted. She tried to push herself upright, but Aidan stopped her.

"Let the paramedics do their job," he ordered.

Relieved of holding the gun on Paul, Sophia moved closer to her daughter. "Where does it hurt, honey?"

"Everywhere," Frankie admitted.

"Thank God," Aidan breathed. He'd been worried Paul's malicious attack might have paralyzed her again. Frankie was strong, but he'd do anything to spare her another debilitating injury and arduous recovery. "You're still going to the hospital."

She tried to shake her head. "I don't need to go."

"Just a precaution," Sophia added as paramedics treated her. "Don't argue with your mother."

"But I do it so well," Frankie said, her lips twitching into a lopsided grin.

Her hand still in his, Aidan kissed her. "Play nice," he reminded her, much as he'd done their first day here.

"Yes, dear," she replied in kind.

He stayed by her side, releasing her hand only when ordered to do so by the paramedic team. He rode with her in the ambulance and walked beside her until they wheeled her away for testing at the hospital.

Over two hours later, Sophia found him in the waiting area and he accepted the coffee she'd brought along. "Any word?"

"Not yet."

"She's a fighter."

"I'm aware," he said.

"She's lucky to have a fiancé like you."

"I'm the lucky one." He studied his coffee, certain that if he looked Sophia in the eye, she'd see his guilt over lying to her about their engagement. Would it take the sting out of the deception if he told her he loved Frankie and planned to convince her to marry him?

"She loves you, too, you know," Sophia said.

Aidan kept his mouth shut. Any reply would only make things worse.

"I think it's best if we reschedule the wedding for the spring. It will give your family more time to adjust to the news."

Now Aidan looked up. "My family?" The Colby Agency should've intercepted any inquiries about his real family to maintain the cover.

"I may be a romantic," Sophia admitted with a shy smile, "but I'm not a complete idiot. Not about my daughter, anyway."

Aidan leaned back in the waiting room chair, laughing. "You knew from the beginning."

"I knew she wanted me to believe it," Sophia said. "And I might confess to making extravagant plans in an effort to break her. You're not going to let her off the hook, are you?"

"I love her," Aidan said. "And I like the look of that diamond ring on her finger."

"You have excellent taste. In women and jewelry." Sophia stood, urging him up as well so she could give him a real hug. "Welcome to the family."

"That might be premature. It could take some time to sell your daughter on that whole love, marriage and commitment idea."

"Do you like chocolate cake?"

"It's my favorite."

Sophia nodded as if that answered everything. "Have faith. My daughter's a smart girl. She'll come around."

He hoped she was right. "The Leone women are a tough breed."

"Don't you ever forget it, young man."

Aidan thought his future mother-in-law, though a little daunting, would be an asset. He checked the clock on the wall, hoping it wouldn't be much longer before he could see the woman who'd captured his heart. While they waited, he and Sophia tossed around real wedding plans, just in case Frankie agreed to stick with him.

Medical staff came and went, and Aidan's patience was gone by the time the doors parted and Frankie appeared.

She walked toward him carefully, her face pale and her smile wide. It took him a minute to process that it was her, upright and steady. Leaping to his feet, he hurried forward, wrapping his arms around her and breathing her in. "You're okay? You're really okay?"

Her cheek rubbed against his chest as she nodded. "Told you I wouldn't break." She hugged him gingerly, mindful of his stitches. "Thanks for saving the day."

"Anytime. Every time. You can trust me." He dropped to one knee, holding her left hand in his.

"What are you doing?" Her big brown eyes were round with surprise.

He felt people staring at them and didn't give a damn. "I won't waste one more second. I love you, Francesca Leone. Marry me."

"Oh, Aidan." She covered her lips with her free hand. "I—"

"Say yes." He cut her off, terrified she wouldn't say what he needed to hear. Gently, his thumb stroked her finger just above the ring. "Please, say yes, make me the happiest man on the planet. Say yes, for real this time. Forever."

He heard a sniffle and knew Sophia's heart was on her sleeve. But Frankie continued staring at him with an unreadable expression. What was going on behind those stunning eyes?

"Aidan." She pulled him to his feet and kissed him as tears slid down her cheeks. "Yes," she whispered against his lips. "You're more than I deserve." She stopped his protest with another soft kiss. "I love you, too. For real. Forever."

Chapter Fourteen

Chicago,
Friday, April 15, 6:30 a.m.

Victoria sipped her coffee and hummed in satisfaction. "Lucas, this coffee is amazing. Is it something new?"

Her handsome husband winked at her. "I selected various beans and ground it myself."

Victoria smiled. "Well, it's wonderful."

"Thank you, my dear."

She thought of her friend Sophia and all she had suffered with the devastation leading up to her husband's death last year. Not to mention all those months of being estranged from her daughter. The mystery shrouding that terrible time remained unsolved. Aidan and Frankie had uncovered the evil that had kept mother and daughter apart, but the rest…there were still few answers.

"You're worried about Sophia," Lucas guessed.

He could always read her so well. "She's flying to Chicago on Monday. We're having dinner. I told her you'd be joining us."

"Of course. Is this about what happened to the general?"

"She says she has a business appointment, but I'm hoping she'll allow the Colby Agency to help her find the truth."

Lucas nodded. "If anyone can find it, the agency can."

"I'm certain we'll hear all about Aidan and Frankie's wedding plans."

Lucas reached across the table and squeezed his wife's hand. "There's nothing like a wedding celebration to remind us all how special true love is."

Victoria was lucky to have found true love twice in her life. She hoped Sophia Leone would be as fortunate.

Only time would tell.

* * * * *

The soft denim molded to a fantastic specimen of a man that she missed as soon as he was around the corner.

Time to get on with her day and just move forward. Last night, her thoughts had taken her into dreams that had been mixed with murder and lovemaking and decaying bodies and excellent bodies. She was exhausted from sleeping. That was a fact.

How was this supposed to work? Did she really think she could just calmly take care of business? As if being chased by a serial killer/assassin wasn't enough, she had to be partnered with a man totally oblivious to her attraction.

"I'm in so much trouble."

SHOTGUN JUSTICE

BY
ANGI MORGAN

First Published in Great Britain 2016
By Mills & Boon, an imprint of HarperCollins*Publishers*
1 London Bridge Street, London, SE1 9GF

© 2016 Angela Platt

ISBN: 978-0-263-91898-4

46-0316

Our policy is to use papers that are natural, renewable and recyclable products and made from wood grown in sustainable forests. The logging and manufacturing processes conform to the legal environmental regulations of the country of origin.

Printed and bound in Spain
by CPI, Barcelona

Angi Morgan writes Mills & Boon Intrigue novels "where honor and danger collide with love." She combines actual Texas settings with characters who are in realistic and dangerous situations. Angi and her husband live in north Texas, with only the four-legged "kids" left in the house to interrupt her writing. They recently began volunteering for a local Labrador retriever foster program. Visit her website, www.angimorgan.com, or hang out with her on Facebook.

There is never a book without my pals Jan and Robin. Thanks for the crazy cabin inspiration, Nicki, JoAnna and Lizbeth. Ruth. . .thanks for the idea for my "pal" Snake Eyes. And a special shout-out to Julie for helping me at the beginning and end of this book.

Prologue

"My twin brother is the one wanted for murder. You have no right to lock me up, Dan." Avery Travis was experiencing insane fury. She'd been disappointed, been angry, had even been fighting mad, but this was worse. Her head just might explode.

Jesse Ryder had absolutely no right to suggest she be thrown in jail for her own safety. When she got out she might…she might just… Well, she knew how to hurt him.

"Dan, you know Garrison needs help to get him out of this mess and clear his name." She could help him. Just as soon as she sweet-talked her way out of this holding cell.

"What I know is that you're upset and have a reason to be." The older sheriff of Dallam County locked the cell and gestured for her to back up to the bars—just like he did to every common prisoner.

"Okay, you win, Dan. I'll give you my word as a deputy that I won't take off to Austin." She crossed her fingers. "You know you can't spare me right now. Who's going to answer to keep the reckless juveniles in line?"

"I'm not arguing about you being the best deputy I

have. I'm only doing what that Texas Ranger friend of yours suggested."

She walked to the cell doors for him to remove the handcuffs, her fingers definitely uncrossed. "You didn't have to cuff me."

"Now, darlin', you know that's not true." Dan drew another circle in the air and Avery turned around. "If I hadn't surprised you, then you wouldn't be here."

He removed the cuffs and she rubbed her wrists, glad to be free. Well, almost free. She looked at the three walls of the small county jail. "You can't be serious about keeping me here. How long?"

"Until the Rangers have everything under control. It shouldn't take long. They're very capable men who know what they're doing."

Right. *Men.*

"He didn't do it, you know." She stated the fact without having spoken to her brother. He hadn't called her or their mom during all the confusion, but she knew it was true. She knew that he'd been framed. And she knew that she could find out the person responsible—if she was allowed to help. But the Texas Rangers were on top of it and didn't need her.

"I haven't met him, but I've never thought he murdered those two women. He's your brother." Dan turned to leave. "But that makes no never mind. If he were here, I'd have to take him in. Since I don't believe it and a criminal family is involved, I tend to agree with your friend—I mean Lieutenant Ryder. You need to stay safe and won't be if you go traipsing off to Austin trying to help your brother from this predicament."

"I promise to stay out of trouble," she said with crossed fingers.

"I tend not to believe you, Avery. Don't get me wrong. You're a blasted good deputy and can take over this office in a New York minute. But staying out of trouble when your brother's being hunted for murder?" Dan shook his head and pursed his lips, rubbing the graying whiskers on his chin. "No, missy, I just don't believe you'll stay in Dalhart voluntarily. So this is the best solution."

"I can't believe you are seriously going to keep me locked up." She threw her hands in the air and walked over to the very visible toilet. "Are you really going to make me stay here while my fellow deputies watch me tinkle on a video screen?"

"Avery, we'll make it work and find a way to keep your privacy. But I guarantee you one thing… I like you being alive more than I'm worried about any of that." Dan waved his hand in the air toward the toilet area. "I'll have someone bring your standing order from the Dairy Barn for dinner. You can have the bag you packed as soon as Julie goes through it for weapons."

"What weapons?"

"Anything sharp or heavy you can use to hurt Bo and Derek." He laughed over his shoulder as he walked away. Probably because he used her movie-reference nicknames for his two perfect-ten deputies.

She'd packed too fast to think about a heavy object that could be used to hit anyone over the head. She'd had no idea that she'd need anything sturdier than extra undies, socks and a toothbrush. Carrying her service weapon would have been enough for what she'd intended.

Well, then again, it wouldn't take much to get the jump on the two young men. She'd put both of them on the training mat right after she arrived. At least she could do that six months ago. After the first training workout, they wouldn't come with her again. They were afraid to hurt her. Big laugh. She predicted their moves as soon as they faced her because they thought of her as a woman. She'd practiced with Jesse her entire life.

Jesse. The man behind all her problems.

None of that mattered at the moment unless it would help her get free of this place. This was all Jesse's fault. She plopped down on the thin mattress and right back up. They'd forgotten to take her cell out of her back pocket. She tapped a number still on speed dial and waited.

"Hey, Avery. Been a long time. Like your new job?"

Oh, that voice. She'd missed it. Even being embarrassed beyond anything she could have imagined, she'd still missed him. "Jesse Ryder, if anything happens to my brother because you won't let me help…"

"Whoa, whoa, whoa, Avery. You know me better than that. I'm doing everything I can. We all are."

She recognized his sincerity. He believed the best of the best were on the case. And she hadn't been good enough to be a part of *the best.* "I need you to make a call to my boss and get me out of here."

"Where's 'here,' babe?"

Oh man, there had been a time when she yearned for him to use that endearment. Now was not it. "Exactly where you suggested Dan hold me until my brother's problem is over."

Laughter. Lots of laughter. And then a little more laughter. "Are you serious? I made a tiny suggestion and he put you behind bars? How did anybody get the drop on you?"

"Your sweet-talking won't work this time. I'm going to stay angry forever. Especially now. I am not one of those girls who hangs on your every word. So you make that call and get me out of here."

She'd been exactly one of those girls. From the time she could run, she'd followed her brother and his best friend everywhere. She'd pined for Jesse and gone unnoticed when they were teens. And for just a short period of three months last year, she'd been the happiest girl on the planet.

"There's nothing to be done, Avery. I'll be a pal and call in a couple of days to update you. Even that's against the rules and you know it."

"I wouldn't call you a pal at this particular moment."

He cleared his throat. She could tell he was about to mention that horrible night when they'd almost made love. That sounded pathetic and she wasn't even saying it out loud. If he apologized for walking out on her...

"I haven't had a chance to explain—"

"I don't want to hear it. It's done. Over. I've moved on. Moved to the far northwest of Texas, in fact."

Living in Austin after the guys had been promoted had become impossible. Everywhere she'd gone there had been a memory of one of them. She might have been able to handle missing her brother—eventually.

But Jesse? She'd been head over heels in love with him her entire life. One day out of the blue last year, she'd caught him looking at her differently. Then it was three months of clandestine, sexy kisses. Three months of sensual foreplay. And one night they'd almost made love. Whatever she'd done wrong, it had scared Jesse into walking out.

"I grew up next door to you, too. Remember? It

doesn't sound like you've moved on. So when are you going to let me explain?"

She pressed the disconnect button. She was angry and needed to stay that way. Focusing on her job was the only thing keeping her sane in this little town. There wasn't anything to really worry about. Right? Seriously, this was her brother. Of course she was worried. It was the first time they hadn't been together for a crisis.

Dan might have turned the key in the lock, but Jesse was responsible. She could focus her anger on that man. He deserved it for putting the idea into Dan's head.

"Oh yeah. The next time I see Jesse Ryder...I'm definitely going to kill him."

Chapter One

Late April, the South Texas Desert

"Please, please. I beg you. I…I have money. Lots of money. I can pay you more than Tenoreno."

Rosco had awakened from the drug and would soon become annoying. The drive was almost over. The first part of his assignment almost complete.

"Sorry, man. It's nothing personal. Just a job," he answered, trying to prevent the inevitable. He still had to make a decision on how to kill this man.

Gun. Knife. Swizzle stick. He chuckled at the idea. Of course, he could do the job with anything. He was that good. The swizzle stick he chewed on, however, would retain his DNA and he'd never be that stupid.

The perfect set of gloves sat on the seat next to him along with the rest of his tools. Some killers went so far as to shave their bodies so as not to drop a single hair. For him, the diving suit worked just as well. He'd changed a few minutes ago before continuing down Texas 349 to find just the right abandoned spot.

There were no witnesses on this stretch of deserted road. No cameras. No recording devices of any type. Rarely a car or driver that would think twice about seeing his ordinary vehicle. He'd deliberately left the burner phone at the Kerrville hotel. An automatic text message would be sent to indicate he was hundreds of miles away on Interstate 10. Not that anyone would call, but it was there in any case. No one in the nearby town would notice a plain blue rental car that looked black on this moonless night.

No one ever noticed. As he'd said many times—at least to himself—he was very good at his job.

He didn't tire at becoming better, striving for more. He was a professional, after all. Thomas Rosco kicked his seat.

"Stop that. What do you hope to accomplish by annoying me?"

"I want you to see reason. Let me go."

"Mr. Rosco, don't you know who I am?"

"I haven't seen your face. You could leave me here and I'd never be able to identify you."

Pulling onto a dirt road leading under an old faded gate, the single windmill made him feel lonesome. That was ridiculous. He was completely at ease in this desolate country and never tired of his work. The fun was just about to begin.

"I'm hurt that you thought Tenoreno would hire anyone other than myself."

"You...you...you're Snake Eyes?"

"It seems an appropriate name." He turned around to stare directly at his prey. "Don't you think?"

He knew what the crime boss saw. Almost glowing eyes, slanted and the color of a reptile's. The contacts added a dimension to his persona that made his victims quake. He laughed, the sound deliberately sinister. It normally put fear in his victims' eyes.

Rosco wasn't any different than the other men. A sad example of a tough guy. Tough men bled just like the rest. Their bodies rotted under the sun just like that of a man with a good soul.

The gloves slid over his hands, and then he helped Rosco stand from the car. No rough stuff was necessary.

The man was about to die. The fear rushed through Rosco's veins. The poor fellow might get a burst of adrenaline. Might make a run for it. Whatever. It didn't matter.

"You should make peace with your God, if you have one. Maybe ask forgiveness for all the men and women you're responsible for killing."

"Do you tell that to all the people you're about to murder?"

"Let's get moving."

The answer was yes. It was his thing. He believed in a higher power and that he'd be punished accordingly. But he had a calling to be the best at his work as he could.

They walked into the field. The knee-high tobosa grass crackled under their feet as they shuffled through. Near the dried-out gully was the perfect place to leave a body. He doubted anyone would find Rosco for months. Not until the hunters returned for wild turkey or deer in the fall.

"No wailing? No more pleading?" he asked, curious.

"I know you get the job done. That's why we employed your services so often. I... There is nothing I can say?" Rosco sank to his knees near some mesquite scrub. "Nothing you'll accept in payment over what Tenoreno is paying you?"

"No. This is a waste. I wish I had time to play, but sometimes work comes first."

With one stroke he pulled his knife and sliced left to right across the windpipe before him. Rosco's eyes widened as he realized he couldn't take a breath. The gurgling sound of him choking wasn't unpleasant. It was satisfying to Snake Eyes that he'd completed the job. Rosco fell forward, hands secured behind him, twitching as his lifeblood soaked the parched earth.

Slicing easily through the plastic handcuffs, he gathered the remnants and shoved them inside the diver's bag at his side.

Now the fun really began.

He flipped Rosco to his back, not bothering to wait for the body to grow cold. He methodically removed the lifeless eyes in Rosco's face. He wouldn't keep them. He wasn't sentimental and didn't need a souvenir, just a way to identify himself as the killer.

He'd studied serial killers, read up on them. If it had been possible, he could have shared his checklists of how to get away without a trace. But then...if everyone knew his methods, he wouldn't be in such high demand.

Laughing, he withdrew the artificial snakelike eyes, using a cleaning solution and a polishing cloth to make them shine. Then he meticulously placed the stones in Rosco's face, leaving him staring at the heavens.

The eyes would be anonymously shipped to his employer. Proof of the completion of his task. He popped them into the jewelry case he carried in his bag.

Many of his victims had never been found. Some never would. But those who were...the eyes were an eerie sight when his handiwork was discovered. As a calling card, they were unique and rarely reported to the press.

But they knew. He was precise and unique. He methodically went through his mental list. Then he opened the notebook and verified he'd performed everything on the list again. He would not get sloppy and make a mistake.

Or bored.

Admitting that he was bored was why he took on the next challenge. Keeping a captive alive long enough to extract information. A definite challenge that needed a new notebook of lists. He flipped the pocket spiral closed, satisfied that he'd covered everything.

Now it was time to discover the details of his next victim. How she lived her mundane life. What drove her to make a mistake. He had a short time to get to know Avery Travis. His new commission would be a test case. Careful planning would be the key to a successful kill.

Chapter Two

"Thomas Rosco is dead. His throat was slit by the Snake Eyes Killer."

Texas Ranger Lieutenant Jesse Ryder had to replay the words in his mind to verify that he'd heard the major correctly. There really wasn't another interpretation of *Thomas Rosco is dead.* Everyone in the room quieted, probably replaying the same words.

Rosco was a crime boss, rumored to have been partnered with Paul Tenoreno—brought to justice earlier that year. The Rangers received the credit, but the man mainly responsible had been his best friend, Garrison Travis, and his witness, Kenderly Tyler, a beautician. They'd witnessed a double homicide orchestrated by Tenoreno. Her courage, along with detailed files left by the murder victims, provided the prosecution with an excellent case.

Then they'd turned Rosco to testify against his partner, but he'd been missing for the past week. Tenoreno had one play left…eliminating the witnesses. Rosco was just the first. He'd be after Garrison and Kenderly next.

Major Josh Parker stood at his office door to make the

announcement. If he expected a response, there wasn't one. It looked as though the other rangers in the room were just as dumbfounded.

Tenoreno had hired an assassin who left no trace of evidence. He was a virtual ghost. Law-enforcement agencies across the country hadn't collected more than a page of notes on the man. Or woman, whatever the case may be, since they had no DNA to prove either.

So far, Snake Eyes was known for killing bad guys. The bodies found had all been those of people wanted for other crimes. If there had been more evidence, maybe someone would look harder.

"Property owners came across the body off of Texas 349 south of Sheffield," the major finally continued. "The medical examiner estimates he's been dead six days. Pure luck on our part that the owners were dropping off a hunting blind."

"His death blows a huge chunk of the case against Tenoreno." Bryce Johnson hadn't realized what he'd said until the sputters grew in number around the room. "Okay, okay. Huge chunks. Got it. Ha-ha. We all know that it has to be Tenoreno pulling the strings from his jail cell to order something like this."

Bryce was the resident expert on Texas organized crime. He knew better than any of them how much the state's prosecutor was depending on the rival crime family's testimony.

"Tenoreno's been in solitary. No visitors. No communication other than his lawyer." The major might have been waiting on answers or ideas, but none came forth. "No apparent connection to Rosco's murder. No one believes that to be true."

"How was he killed?" someone behind him asked.

"What does that do for Garrison's detail?" It was no secret that Jesse was more concerned about his best friend's safety than putting Tenoreno away. One couldn't happen without the other, but Jesse knew what his priority would be.

"Who's taking the lead on the investigation?" Bryce asked.

The major gestured for the two of them to come to his office. Jesse followed Bryce, ready to work with him, ready to get some real action instead of tracking criminal activity through the internet.

"The murder of Thomas Rosco will be handled by the local PD with the aid of Company A. Headquarters is ready to roll if they think there's a problem. They've got it covered and don't need our help. Before you begin objecting, the two of you are needed other places."

Jesse was ready to object anyway, but his commanding officer turned his back as he walked around his desk. He sat and propped his feet on the corner, taking his thinking position.

"Prosecutors have asked for your help, Bryce," he continued. "They have a lead that needs your knowledge and expertise. Vivian has the information. Hand over anything you're working on to her and we'll get it taken care of."

Bryce didn't hesitate. He was out the door and gathering his things after a hurried "Yes, sir." Jesse's nerves began twitching. Whatever was about to come, he didn't get the feeling that Major Parker felt comfortable, either.

"What's happened? Did they discover the location of Garrison's detail?"

"No, nothing like that. But while Tenoreno was at the pretrial, he plainly stated that no one close to Garrison would be safe. It's a threat most criminals make. That's nothing new. But we have intel that someone accepted a contract on Garrison's sister."

"Avery's a deputy in the Panhandle. Has she been made aware of the situation? Have you alerted Sheriff Myers?"

"Headquarters believes this could be another nail in Tenoreno's coffin if we can capture the assassin and get him to turn state's evidence."

"That would mean they're using Avery as bait. Did anyone tell her?"

"It's been handled. Her participation, on the other hand… Well, Jesse, the attorneys think it would be better coming from you when you arrive in Dalhart."

"Then they should think about that again, sir. I'm the last person Avery wants to see. The title's mine with Garrison a close second."

He actually missed Avery. They'd grown up together, gone to the same schools, same concentration of studies. He'd made the Rangers and she hadn't. She quit everything, packed up, left and hadn't spoken to him since. Of course, the real reason for not talking to him was a little more involved.

"Our information is credible, Jesse. The hit is happening soon, so you don't have much time." Major Parker wasn't pondering any longer. He had both feet on the floor and leaned forward on his desk. "It's already been decided, Lieutenant. Already in motion. This isn't a debate."

"I had her thrown in jail to protect her the last time this happened, sir. She's not going to listen to me. And I doubt I can get her near the county lockup again."

"Make her listen. The last thing we need is for Garrison Travis to be lured from the safe house and be killed. Take care of his sister or you'll be searching for her murderer instead."

The two choices hit him between the eyes like the baseball Avery had thrown when they were nine. His head was whirring just as badly as back then. Murdered?

No one else would try as hard as him. That was a certainty. And if something happened to her, he'd never forgive himself. Neither would Garrison.

"We call. Now. She needs to be warned." *And Garrison needs to be kept in the dark.*

"The state's attorney informed the sheriff as soon as we knew about the threat."

"Who else is on the protection detail?"

"Did I mention a detail? One riot, one ranger. That's our motto. Right?" Parker stood, looking ready to dismiss Jesse. "You'll be coordinating with the county sheriff. Keep the element of surprise on your side. You know the hit man is coming. He doesn't know about you. Handle it."

"Of course, sir. I'll catch the next available flight."

"Vivian arranged a private flight to Amarillo that leaves as soon as you arrive. Then a rental car. We've got Tenoreno on lockdown, but somehow he's getting directives to his men." Josh Parker picked up a stack of papers and tapped them into a neat pile. "Did I ever tell you why you have Garrison as a partner here?"

"We both knew it was improbable." The suspicions he'd had for eight months were going to be confirmed. The major waited. "You mean why it's me and Garrison. Not me and Avery."

"Exactly. You've had a relationship with her. A close

one, from what I gathered. You didn't lie to cover it up. If you had…"

"If I had, sir, none of us would be rangers."

"That's true." He nodded his agreement.

It was a fact. *He* was the reason Avery hadn't become a Texas Ranger. Somewhere while they were being secret, kissing in corners, or sneaking glances at each other… Someone had seen them.

When asked about it at the end of their training, he'd come clean. Avery had discovered she wasn't selected, then said the Texas Rangers was an old-boy organization and would never consider her good enough. Well, he'd known she'd never forgive him for what he'd said in the interview.

Of course, she didn't know and she'd left anyway.

"This isn't the time to rebuild bridges. There's no evidence that will help you pick out the Snake Eyes Killer. He's good at what he does. Killing. You're there to protect Deputy Avery Travis. It's not going to be easy. If it were, a ranger wouldn't be needed. Go on. Vivian's waving information for you on the other side of the door." Parker opened the first file, ready to get to work. "And, Jesse, remember, we want to interrogate the man hired to kill her. Try not to kill him."

"Always up for the challenge, sir."

If he survived the assault of the green-eyed deputy he was being sent to protect, he might be able to capture Snake Eyes.

Definite challenge.

Dalhart, Texas

AVERY TRAVIS IGNORED the readout on her radar gun. Five miles over the speed limit was forgivable in her opinion.

She'd told herself for months that sitting here wasn't a speed trap. Drivers had enough time to slow down before they reached her spot at the tractor store.

Or they slowed down as soon as they spotted her. It was the ones who ignored both that she'd stop for a ticket.

Midweek shifts were easy to hate. Especially in the middle of the night on a Texas Panhandle road. But it was her turn. Life was totally different here as a Dalhart deputy after four wasted years trying to become a Texas Ranger.

Her brother was the one fighting real criminals. He'd uncovered evidence against one of the biggest crime bosses in the state. Garrison rescued witnesses, saved the day and who knew what else. The anger was building up again. It was definitely easier to tap it back into place, buried under the surface of everything job related.

Safe zone. Find a safe place to park all this emotion.

Knowing what to do and accomplishing it were definitely different, but she'd manage. Her self-improvement tapes would be easier to understand the second time through. But if she began listening to one tonight, she'd fall asleep.

This. Is. Boring. With a capital *B*, boring after being posted in Austin. No, after working anywhere.

An occasional flat tire. Watch a lot of shooting stars. Watch a lot of dust. Watch a lot of snow. Watch a lot of grass grow. Did she mention giving a ride to an occasional driver with a flat? Yep. Boring in every sense of the word.

"Car two-twenty-two. You around, Avery?" Julie Dunks's perky voice broke the silence. "Are you still out on Highway 385 at the Supply Company?"

"Where else would I be, Julie? I always tell you when I go on break or move locations."

"Oh good. But you know Bo sometimes doesn't bother to tell me. Sheriff Dan always takes a break when his coffee kicks in—if you know what I mean. So it'd be understandable if you did the same while you're out and about. I know you drink coffee."

"You switched me to tea." She yawned, wishing for some coffee.

"Did I tell you what Miss Wags did this morning? That terrorizing little diva wouldn't let me leave the house today without feeding her a bacon treat. Isn't that just too cute?"

"Julie, was there a reason you needed me?"

"Why, yes, there is."

"And…"

"Oh. Right. You had a visitor here looking for you. He said he was a family friend. Pretty nice lookin,' if you ask me. Of course, you didn't ask, but I didn't think that would matter."

A good-looking family friend could mean only one person. Jesse Ryder. Avery was forced to listen. She couldn't interrupt Julie on a two-way radio. Besides, what else did she have to do?

As Julie kept being her natural chatty self, Avery tuned her out and wondered what had gone wrong. What or who would force Lieutenant Jesse Ryder to come barging into her life? Barging all the way up here to the Texas Panhandle?

It wasn't fair. She'd left Austin and Waco behind because she'd been upset for being passed over. But it was also because everywhere she looked there was a memory of her with the man. Memories she no longer wanted to think about. If he was coming to see her…there would be images of him at the café to haunt her mind every time she ate there.

Then at the Main Street Motel—where he would definitely spend the night, because he wasn't staying with her. Each time she passed it, she would imagine seeing his car return for another visit.

"No way he's staying with me." She released the talk button and sank in her seat, knowing that Julie had heard her.

"What was that, Avery? Actually, he said he was on his way to find you. Isn't that excitin'? He couldn't wait until the morning when your shift ends."

"Thanks for letting me know, Julie. Over and out."

Jesse was on his way? To her? Right here at her favorite spot? Well, she wouldn't be here. Her future would not be parking here night after night and picturing him sitting on the hood of her patrol car.

Nope. No way. No how.

She'd arrest him. Throw him in jail. He'd had her boss do it to her three months ago when Garrison got in trouble. Now, that was a good place she could picture Jesse…behind bars.

The second favorite place to park and wait for speeders was a little over two miles down the road. If she hurried, she could be waiting on Jesse as he sped past. This was going to be a blast.

A few minutes later she parked and took out the radar gun, pointing it toward town. It wouldn't take him long if he'd left right before Julie checked in with her. But she waited and kept waiting. Maybe he'd changed his mind.

No headlights. It was more likely that he'd stopped

at the motel first. And less likely that Jesse would get caught in her speed trap.

Disappointment. Plain and simple disappointment. Maybe she could give him a ticket for jaywalking tomorrow. Or maybe vagrancy. Something obscure where he'd never agree to pay the fine. Then off to jail he'd go.

Before Avery cut the engine, she lowered the window, letting the fresh summer air into the car. She leaned her head back after readying the radar gun on the dash. The stars were sparkling on a blanket of black. Her plan about limiting where Jesse created memories was completely shot now.

She'd remember him here because she thought about him here. In the jail, in the back of her patrol car and the same places she always thought of him. Just about everywhere.

"What I need more than anything else is to learn how to live with Jesse around. As long as he's Garrison's best friend, he's going to be in my life." She closed her eyes and let out a long soulful sigh, continuing her lonely conversation. "This is my life. I've worked hard to become independent, but I refuse to live in isolation any longer, because I'm petulant. I can be an adult about this."

On a clear night like this, she could see a vehicle miles away. Out of nowhere, headlights were on the highway from the opposite direction. A local heading to town for an emergency?

She pointed the radar, placed her foot on the brake and shifted the car into Drive—ready to perform her duty. Ninety-two flashed in red. High school kids on a dare or a rancher in serious need of an escort to Keen Hospital in town. Either way required her deputy services.

The car lurched forward, the radar gun dropped to the

seat and she flipped the lights on in one smooth motion as she raced after the speeder. She followed less than a minute when the car pulled onto the shoulder. The tags were obscured by mud.

It might not be Jesse, but it was a little bit of work. Anything was better than being bored.

Chapter Three

The car pulled over well onto the grass at the side of the road. Plenty of blacktop was to their left as her vehicle lit up the area in red, white and blue. Avery ran the tag number, found it was a rental and got out of her truck.

What were the odds of two visitors in separate cars showing up in Dalhart within the same hour? Extremely high. If something had happened to Garrison, Jesse would come to take her home. But two cars?

The tiny hairs on the back of her neck were prickling. Avery unsnapped the thumb break on her sidearm holster. The door opened and a man swung one leg and then the other from the vehicle.

How pathetic of her…she recognized his boots. Relaxing a little during the seconds it took Jesse Ryder to unfold his tall body from the sports car, she snapped the thumb break back into place. Why hadn't he phoned? It still irritated her that she didn't know why he'd come in person.

Irritated or scared. The feelings caused similar nerves to gurgle in her stomach. Or maybe anticipation because…

Lord have mercy, he looks good. Bo and Derek are attractive young men. But they had nothing on Jesse.

Six foot two, dark walnut hair that was neat and close
to his head. She'd looked into those mischievous brown
eyes before. Looking again wasn't going to resolve any
problem. He was lean, with shoulders wide enough to
make her feel small. And she wasn't.

At six feet minus an inch—as her mother referred
to her—she was not small by any means. Not as tall as
her brother, but she'd learned to be as strong as possible. Jesse got partial credit for that. They'd always gone
toe-to-toe in wrestling or racing or even at the shooting range.

"Do you know how fast you were going?"

He wrinkled his brow, looking concerned. His eyes
were searching the landscape. Didn't he know there was
nothing around? Maybe a couple of cows or deer, but
no threats.

"I think it was close to eighty or eighty-five. What are
you doing out here without backup, Avery?"

The ice around her heart melted a little at the sound
of her name. It was so good to see him. And so embarrassing. "That's well over the speed limit." She took a
defensive stance, stabilizing her shaking knees. "What
are *you* doing here?"

Her heart shook a little at the possibilities. He didn't
look as though he was bearing bad news. But if he
wasn't, then why had he come?

"Can't a guy visit a friend?"

He was lying. She'd known him too long not to hear
the warble in his voice. The one she'd recognized as he
said being with her was great.

"We're not friends anymore. I haven't returned any of
your calls. A Texas Ranger like yourself would be able
to pick up on that clue. So why are you here?"

"Vacation?"

"Are you asking me if you're on vacation? Like I'd ever believe that. You've never taken a vacation. And your first wouldn't be to Dallam County."

"Okay, you got me." The smile left his face and his demeanor changed. "Enough kidding around. You seriously don't have backup? We need to get you secured."

"Secured? What's happened?"

"I'd rather talk about it at the sheriff's office. Let's go." He extended his hand her direction and she flinched. He looked shocked. She didn't have a memory of that expression on his face before.

Had she really never surprised him by following her own mind? *Wow, I really was desperate if I never disagreed with him about anything.*

"I asked you a question, Mr. Ryder. What business do you have in Dalhart?"

His handsomely chiseled face searched the road both directions. "I'd rather talk to you in private back at county."

"In case you didn't notice…" She expanded her arms into the darkness lit by only her patrol lights. "This is pretty private. If you refuse to cooperate, I'm going to have to take you in."

Okay, she knew it was a stretch and she really didn't have any reason to haul his backside to jail. But he deserved it. She remembered the three days of no privacy behind bars. Three days of trying to occupy the time by pretending to read a book. But most of all, the three days of being worried sick about her twin.

The moonlight made her rarely used handcuffs sparkle when she pulled them from their pouch. "Turn around and put your hands on the car."

"You're not arresting me." He laughed, throwing back

his head. Then he focused on her and squinted when she took a step forward. "Wait a minute... You *are* arresting me?" He took a step back, something on his belt clinking when it hit the rental. "What did I do? I'm here in an official capacity, Avery. You know I am."

Avery hadn't heard Jesse's voice this high-pitched since it changed in the seventh grade. She covered the laugh, trying to escape by clearing her throat as she pulled his left hand down and snapped the handcuffs around his wrist. "You're refusing to cooperate. I don't see that you've given me any choice."

"I've done nothing *but* cooperate. I didn't have to stop, you know. I only did because I thought it might be you." He slipped around to face her. "No one's going to believe that I didn't cooperate."

"This—" she pointed to him facing her instead of remaining where he was against the car "—this is not cooperating, Ranger Ryder."

"I can understand if you're still angry about the last time we saw each other. We've never really gotten a chance to talk about what happened. Unfortunately, we don't have time now except for an apology. You would have had one sooner if you'd returned my calls." Jesse placed his hands on either side of her waist and began to lean closer.

"That's it." She knocked his hand away, stepped to the side, whipped his arm behind him and forced him to kneel. "Nobody goes for my weapon and doesn't go straight to a cell."

"I wasn't going for your weapon and you know it."

"Well, we'll just see what the judge has to say. Your word against mine. And I live here."

"Avery, I'm a Texas Ranger, for gosh sakes. This ludicrous charge will never stick. It's not going to keep me from doing my job while I'm here. As soon as Sheriff Myers finds out I've arrived—"

"Oh, don't give me that, Jesse. Julie told me you were asking about me at the office."

His body stiffened. Something changed in his posture. He seemed worried or anxious. "Let go, Avery. This has gone far enough. I don't want to hurt you, but I will if I have to." The playfulness was gone from his voice. "Didn't you get the message about Rosco and the threat?"

She reached for his other hand, but he jerked it away, twisting out of her grasp. "No one's given me a message and you're not talking…your way…out of this." She stuck a knee in the small of his back, taking his chest to the ground.

He was halfway struggling with her now. Only halfway, since she was familiar with what he could do if he put his strength into a shove or his elbow into her gut.

"I'm serious, Avery. Tenoreno put—" Jesse twisted to his back under her. "He hired someone to take you— Ow. Dammit, that hurts."

"Stop struggling and the cuffs won't pinch you." She still had hold of his arm that he'd pulled above his head. She was pulling it back to her when he got very still. It hit her just where she sat—straddled across his lap. She scrambled off. "Get up."

"Are you still going to arrest me?"

"I owe you a night in jail. Two, actually, if I'm getting technical."

"I'm serious. Call it in, Avery. I haven't been to Dalhart yet."

"Julie said a family friend asked where I was. You're the only person that could be."

"Don't you see? It's the hit man. We can get a description—"

"Oh, good grief. This is too much, Jesse. You don't have to lie."

"They said they called, spoke to the sheriff and explained everything." He remained on the ground. "I'm going to kill a state official."

She watched him, aware of his every move. He was tense, waiting for her to make a mistake. Maybe move the wrong way.

"Tenoreno doesn't care about me. I'm not a witness." All the anger that she'd been suppressing seemed to bubble up to the surface. "I can't believe you'd come up here and…and what? What could you possibly want to do? Sabotage my new career?"

"Okay now." He raised his hands above his chest. "I think you need to calm down."

Acting like a cop with a perp at her feet, she used her boot to flip him downhill to his chest, swiped his arm behind him and flicked the second handcuff onto his wrist before he could work his way free. "Do. Not. Tell me to calm down."

AVERY GROUND HER knee into his kidney as she forced her words between her locked jaws. She was furious, and if he reacted, she'd get hurt.

Deliberate or by mistake, it didn't matter. He resisted the temptation to buck her onto the road behind them. Her pride had been hurt enough. It probably would be again. But not by him.

"I knew this was a bad idea." He'd never live this story down if it got out.

"You think?"

"Look, Elf Face—"

"Come on, Jesse. You can't call me that. Your face is the one in the dirt. I'm in my uniform, for crying out loud. Using my nickname stopped working on me ages ago."

He didn't believe that for a minute. She'd already removed her knee and her voice had spunk again instead of anger. So, yeah, using the name worked.

With her knee gone, he rolled uncomfortably to his back. Her voice might have calmed, but the look on her face hadn't. Intense. Jaded. The anger made her eyes narrow. Of course, they'd been narrowed and upset like that each time she looked at him since they'd slept—well, didn't sleep—together.

If he explained everything, she wouldn't listen. He should have called her before he got on the plane. He dialed when he was waiting on the rental car. Somehow telling her over the phone just didn't seem like a good idea. He'd gone through the pros and cons of telling her.

The cons won out. He simply didn't trust her not to take matters into her own hands. He'd driven like a race-car driver to get to her side before something happened. Or before she led Snake Eyes into a trap of her own.

"You're seriously going to put me in jail?"

Her lips turned up in a smile. It was easier to give in. At least she'd be indoors and protected, not running around searching for the man who'd asked about her at the desk. Once he spoke with the sheriff, they could work together to set the ground rules for Avery.

"Let's get this over with." He rolled onto the grass

again. Loose gravel from the side of the road stuck in his knees as he tried to get up without his hands. "You'll have to help."

"It's pretty funny watching you."

"Come on, Avery. If our man was at the sheriff's office, we should get out of here. He might be stalking you right now." He cursed under his breath for bringing attention to the man bold enough to walk into the county jail. It didn't matter. Avery ignored the warning and stood strong.

Acting as if it was against her better judgment to touch him, she helped him stand. Hands on the cuffs, she guided him to the patrol car, shoving him inside and locking the doors.

She opened her own and dropped her hat on the passenger seat.

"Will you at least get my stuff? There's a bag in the trunk. Maybe lock the car, grab the keys. It's a rental."

She stood and tapped the roof. Slow taps. One fingernail. He recognized the signal of the internal debate she was having. He remembered when that action became a habit right after her dad had been killed.

Tap. Tap. Tap.

That was when she stopped arguing as much. The more her brother's feeling had been disguised with charm, the more hers had been pushed down deep. He hadn't realized it until years later. Way past the point of return. He'd always been in the middle between her and her brother. Their parents called him the peacekeeper.

Some peacekeeper.

Tap. Tap. Tap.

Avery and Garrison had been inseparable twins before their father was killed in the line of duty. Afterward, they became fierce competitors. She'd even tried out for the football team with them.

It wasn't pleasant around the neighborhood when she was forced by her mother to play volleyball. Even if she had been their star player for four years. She was so damn tall it was a given. Didn't hurt that she could actually spike the ball and scare the other girls from the net.

The fingernail against the metal roof stopped. He heard her feet crunching gravel, then the click of the radio as she walked away. The duffel he'd packed was lifted from the trunk and dropped to the ground.

"Check inside," he told her. If she did, she'd see his weapons. She'd know he was telling the truth.

She ignored his command to look, locked the car and engaged the alarm. There wasn't anything else he could do at this point. He had to wait to have his story verified by Sheriff Myers.

And he had to keep his mouth shut. He couldn't afford to tick her off any more—as evidenced by her fast and false arrest. She needed him whether she liked it or not.

"Julie, I'm coming in with a… ETA is six minutes. Out."

"That's great. I'll let everybody know."

"Could you ask her to have the sheriff meet us there? I'm sure he'll be able to straighten out this whole mess."

"No."

"Dammit, Avery. Enough is enough. I've got a job to do."

"It's not up to me. Dan's in Dallas. His daughter just had a baby. He won't be back for another four days."

"When did he leave?"

"Three days ago."

No one from the State's Attorney's Office had ex-

plained the situation to the Dallam County Sheriff's Department. Hell. He was on his own.

"Elf Face?"

"Stop calling me that." She shifted back and forth
uncomfortably in her seat as she buckled up.

"You're not really going to put me in jail. Are you?"

"You bet your last dollar I'm going to. Of course, the
cell isn't as comfy as Dan made mine, but it's not bad.
Hardly any privacy, but that shouldn't bother you. Right?"
She pulled onto the deserted highway and pushed the gas
to the floor. "I mean, you don't care for anyone's privacy.
Or their private life. Or things like suggesting their boss
incarcerate them for their own good. Things like that
are second nature to you. They don't bother you at all."

Jesse closed his eyes and let her rip into him, knowing he was the only person around who could save her
life. She was going to force him to take that night in jail.
He'd be lucky if he didn't receive life in prison for wanting to hug a deputy.

Chapter Four

There she was… Avery Travis had returned early to process a prisoner. A Texas Ranger prisoner. How fun was that?

The foot traffic in and out of the county jail was higher than Snake Eyes had anticipated. A point in his favor that his employer hadn't put a rush on the job. He'd have to get creative with this one…a deputy and the additional bonus of a real Texas Ranger.

He couldn't take one without the other. If he did, there would be too many complications. Both were quite competent. He was aware of their history, of them growing up as neighbors. He had expected that Jesse Ryder would come when Avery went missing.

This was better. Much better.

Now he could widen his plan to include them both and not be bothered with searches. How convenient.

Finding out the prisoner was Jesse Ryder took no skill. Walking in the shadows across the street from the jail, he'd overheard Jesse as they'd gone inside. Not all the conversation, just what had bounced between the buildings.

It was time to go. There was no longer a need to discover vulnerable extraction points. Unfortunately, Jesse's arrival would delay the extraction while he fortified his plan. If the Rangers were involved, then it meant they knew about his contract. Maybe not the details, or his name—

Well, no one knew his name, as he was very careful not to be identified. He'd taken precautions. Lots of precautions. Even the criminals who employed him didn't know. Frustrated officers referred to him as the Snake Eyes Killer.

Assassin was the more accurate description. After he'd successfully completed his third murder, he let himself be hired. Then proof of a completed assignment had been needed.

The first pair of replacement eyes had been simple marbles. The next had been fashioned after the venomous creature his victims called him. He rather liked it. Kept it. Made it easy for the police to identify him.

If they found the body.

He pulled away, leaving the jail and sheriff's office behind. He had work today. Lists to make. A new plan would require a new spiral.

Did their argument indicate they were more than close friends?

The arguing would work to his advantage. He snapped a couple of pictures of back doors and guards on cigarette breaks, noting the time. But he already knew how he'd take Avery Travis. He knew exactly what he was going to do with her and where it would happen.

Smaller towns created a challenge to blend in and not be noticed. He'd handled them before. The extra element of this job required him to obtain information. A nice challenge. A new string of contingencies. He must be detailed. Thorough.

His camper was in Clayton, New Mexico. He'd develop his plan during the ninety-minute return drive.

The ranger needed further study. Killing Jesse was too common. Too predictable. Patience equaled reward. Yes, life would be interesting for the next several days.

The Snake Eyes Killer deserved some fun.

Chapter Five

"This has gone far enough, Avery. You've had your fun, now unlock the door. You can't leave me here even overnight. We need to call the state's attorney."

Did she really want Jesse to spend the night in jail? It wasn't as if he'd really broken the law or anything. She was exacting her revenge the best way she could. The only way she could, really. So, yes, he would.

She smiled, doing an about-face straight into Martha Coburn. She'd followed them through the booking area asking why they'd bypassed it. "Jesse Ryder is definitely staying the night with us."

He cursed. Martha jerked at the profanity.

"Sorry, ma'am. When I get out of here, Avery, I'm going to paddle your behind like I used to in junior high," he shouted.

She shut the hall door on the loud clang of his boot kicking the bars. She recognized the sound well, having made the same gesture once or twice herself during her stay. "I think he needs to calm down a bit before we do any paperwork."

"You know that's not protocol, Avery. Is there something wrong with him?" Martha asked, tapping her temple. "I mean, he's claiming to be a Texas Ranger."

"How do we go about getting a psych evaluation?" She tried to be serious. If Martha's reaction was an indicator, Avery had been successful. "Oh, I'm just kidding. We knew each other a long time ago and he…" She raised her hand to whisper behind it even though no one else was there. "He got a little fresh, if you know what I mean. I'm just teaching him a lesson."

"I see." Martha crossed her arms, looking completely like an old-fashioned schoolmarm. "Dan's done that a time or two in his day. I'm not one for telling stories that aren't mine to tell, but he has a couple of doozies."

"I can't wait to hear those. I better get back out there. Never can tell who's breaking the law before dawn on the weeknight." She did look forward to those stories about Dan setting someone straight. Maybe it would lessen the rampage she already expected when he found out what she'd done.

Or maybe it would lessen the concern her boss had about her safety when he discovered she'd taken care of herself. It didn't really matter. The satisfaction of keeping Jesse in jail was worth the chiding she'd receive from Dan.

Now that her heart wasn't racing ninety to nothing, it bothered her that Jesse would come up with a wild tale about an assassin…or was it? After Garrison had volunteered to spend his time until trial in a safe house, she'd done her own investigation into the Tenoreno family. She'd taken extra precautions.

Just because she was on her own didn't mean she was an idiot. She'd installed extra locks on the windows and doors of her rental house. Installed security lights to the point her neighbors had raised their concerns with Dan. She'd even spent a day trimming back the hedge and trees so she had line of sight to the road and sidewalks. Her landlord nearly had a cow, but admitted it was safer for a single woman—even if that woman carried a gun.

Maybe she was an idiot after all. Jesse wouldn't lie about his concerns for her safety. He was the one guy she'd known who just didn't lie. And he wouldn't take off work and come all this way for…for what?

Just because Paul Tenoreno was in jail didn't mean that the crime family's money and influence would be stopped. She sat in her truck and waited, watching the jail instead of heading back to the highway. Some of that Texas Mafia money could have prevented the warning Jesse claimed the State's Attorney's Office should have made. But what if…?

She jumped from the truck, locking it on her run across the street to the office. "Julie?" She raised her voice to get their dispatcher's attention in the back.

"Oh, hi, Avery." She poked her head around the corner. Her cute wireless headset still sat on top of her head. "I thought you said you were—"

"Did Dan have any messages you were keeping until he got back?"

"Avery, you told me to keep all his messages. Remember? You said the big guy deserved time with his family." She thumbed through a pad of sticky notes. "This is everything that's come in since he's been gone. Well, his calls, that is. All three of us are keeping them in the same place."

"May I take a look?"

"Sure." Julie passed the notes.

Each page of the lined pad that had been used was folded back, easy to thumb through. One had a scribble about teenagers shooting beer bottles and a note that it had been passed on to Derek to check out. Another from an unfamiliar number. The last on the list that afternoon was from a 512 area code and marked urgent.

"What about this one? Did they leave a message?"

Julie looked closely. "I bet Mrs. Lena took that. She said they asked for Dan and wouldn't talk with anyone else. Was it important? Should I call him now and pass on the number?"

"No. It's okay. I'll take care of it." An Austin area code, asking for Dan and no one else meant… "Shoot. Jesse's telling the truth. You mentioned a man came in to see me. What did he look like? How was he dressed?"

"Oh, I don't know, Avery. Nice looking enough, about late thirties or early forties. Sort of stylish in a Western kind of way. Hair hung below his collar. It was the only thing that just didn't seem to match the rest of him."

"That's not Jesse. Man alive, I've messed up." She pushed the pads of her hands into the corners of her eyes, blocking all the light, wishing she could block the image of Jesse's face when she'd mentioned this stranger. "Does Dan ever need a forensic artist?"

"I can ask Mrs. Lena when she gets here in the morning. Why?"

"I have a feeling that the man avoided the camera and we'll need a drawing from your description. I'll check the video, but I'd like a name to call if I'm correct."

"You mean a criminal came in here tonight? I was talking to a genuine criminal?" Julie's face lit up in a smile.

There was no way Avery was going to tell Julie the truth. But she'd need someone to stay with her until this man was caught. If she could identify him, then she was in danger.

"I'd just like to know who was claiming to be a close family friend."

Hopefully that would quiet Julie's curiosity. And unfortunately, she'd have to let Jesse out. Or maybe not. Perhaps the safest way to talk to him was with steel bars between them. It might become very public, though. And once she was mad enough, she might just ask about their fated night.

The night she thought things were changing between them. She'd changed clothes and he'd changed locations. *Think of something calming.*

So maybe a nonconfrontational approach to his release was a better idea. She'd send word to release Jesse with the shift change, leave instructions to take him to his rental car and give him directions to her house. She'd apologize first thing.

Privately apologize for not listening more carefully about the possible assassin. But for sticking him in jail… never. He deserved that. When the yelling began, they'd be in the privacy of her home. Then they could work out a plan to catch whoever the Tenorenos had hired.

Yes, she believed him. Now that she was calm and could reason without his Texas-size smile in her face. But she wouldn't leave her job. Nope. She had responsibilities. Dan was counting on her to keep things under control while he was gone. She couldn't pick up and run every time someone threatened her brother.

Or threatened her pride.

Logically, that meant releasing Jesse and getting started immediately on whatever he'd come to do. They shouldn't wait for morning. She should face him and get everything done.

"Julie, can you get Tosh and Tolbert Jennings out

here to go pick up a car on 287?" She dug in her pocket and placed the rental keys on the counter. "Have them leave the car here and leave you the invoice and keys. I'll pay for it."

"Sure thing." Julie raised a finger, paused in thought. "The county usually tows, but you know that, so this must be different."

"Yeah. There's one person who gets under my skin and, well...he did. Let Martha know when it's back, please."

"I can do that."

Avery walked back to her truck, changed her mind and went inside the county jail. "No loud banging. That's a good sign."

Martha tossed her head back, looking up from her paperwork. "At the moment. That is one angry gent in there. Keeps ranting that you're in danger. You back to process him?"

"Yeah, about that." Her choice was a private conversation. It didn't mean she was a coward. Facing Jesse and exposing their complicated past just wasn't an option. "The Jennings boys are going to bring his car here. Julie will call when it's back. Do you mind letting him out?"

Martha closed her eyes and shook her head. "Well, it won't be the first and I doubt it's the last. Should I direct him to the nearest motel or tell him they're all full?"

"I'm sure he has my address. You could tell him I should be there. If he asks." Tapping the counter, she was hesitant to place Jesse's wrath on Martha's shoulders. Private or not, it was definitely the cowardly way out. "Thanks. I owe you."

"Two margaritas at Consuelo's. There's no doubt in my mind that this man is a handful. He's really a Texas Ranger?"

Avery nodded. "My brother's partner and best friend. He's also the guy who grew up next door to me and felt that it was his job to persecute me until the day I left for college. Oh, wait…it didn't stop, because we all went to Baylor. My social life was horrible with not one, but two, men claiming to be my brother."

"Whew. I don't know what went wrong out there tonight, but I'm glad I'm not hanging around you when he gets out." Martha laughed. "Really, really glad."

"Yeah. I better get going. Lots to do before the big confrontation."

"I have faith in you, Avery. And, hon?"

Confidence wasn't one of the feelings overwhelming her at the moment. "Yes, ma'am?"

"I trust that you'll let the rest of us help you with whatever is going on as soon as you can. And you might consider calling Dan—even if he is on vacation. He won't like it that you're in danger and kept him out of the loop."

"Sure thing. As soon as I know what's what." She stepped onto the covered porch just outside the door, noticing the Jennings truck across the street.

Trying not to be obvious, she looked without moving her head. Nothing was moving accept Tosh's dog. He barked a couple of times at her until she closed the door to her truck and sat inside. Tosh waved at her as he came out of the county building.

A couple of cars were heading north on the business route through town. Other than that, nothing was moving besides a southwest breeze.

It wouldn't take long for them to bring back Jesse's rental. She needed to check the videotape. Whether the man had hidden his face or not would determine how she moved forward.

She had about an hour before Jesse would be waiting on her porch, waiting for answers. And an apology.

JESSE KNEW AVERY almost as well as he knew himself... maybe better. Predictable, a woman with efficient routines that worked, and a woman who did not like him at the moment.

Moment? It would be days. Months that might add up to the rest of his life. The reaction to him on the highway proved she wouldn't work with him. Now or in the future. Walking out on her that night without an explanation was a relationship destroyer. There was no coming back from something like that. He'd known it before he'd seen her cry the next day.

He'd messed up. Hell...she'd left him in jail.

An hour alone, behind bars, was plenty of time to think himself into every possible corner. Or not think his way out of any. Major Parker needed information from him to find whoever said the county sheriff had been notified of this threat. They should know who had screwed up or been bought off by the Tenoreno family.

He had to convince Avery's coworkers that she was in danger and to let him go. So far they'd left him alone. He wanted to see a confident, satisfied Avery waltz through and tease him. He'd imagined her barely speaking to him. Maybe making him beg to be released. Or putting her hands on her hips while stating dramatically to get out of town.

Okay, that was a little on the Clint Eastwood side. She'd try to tell him she could take care of herself. He knew that much and had his argument ready.

The door at the end of the hall opened, and a young deputy with a couple of bottles of water in one hand and cell keys in the other approached him. He began reformulating his arguments.

Jesse had studied a lot of people. When you were best friends with a man as outgoing as Garrison, you weren't required to say much to fit in.

Garrison thought of what to say faster and usually better. Jesse required time to think things through. Then react. Which, admittedly, he could have and should have done better when Avery pulled him over.

The deputy's body movements indicated he didn't know if he could trust Jesse. He dangled freedom from one finger as if he wanted to be convinced, then dropped the keys in his pocket.

"Mind telling me who you are?" the deputy asked, extending a water bottle through the bars. "No one logged you into the system."

"Lieutenant Jesse Ryder, Texas Rangers. My ID's in that duffel you're holding, unless Avery took it with her." He gulped the water, letting it cool not only his parched throat but his temper. "And you?"

"Deputy Bo Jackson. Why are you here?"

"Where's Avery?"

"Good question." He shifted his weight to his other foot, attempting to look casual. He didn't succeed. "We're hoping you could tell us if she's not coming back here because of you. Or if you're here because something's up with that thing her brother's involved in."

Jesse's heart rate sped out of control. He lost his grip on the plastic, then watched the bottle bounce and roll, spilling cold water across the old tile. *He has her.* His gut and mind were in sync. *Snake Eyes has her already.* "Get me out of here. Now."

The deputy jumped back a little. Maybe from the spilling water but more likely because of the animalism Jesse barely recognized in his own voice.

"Just hold on a minute and don't get worked up again. Nothing's happened to her, but I think you answered my first question. This is about her brother, but you're here because of you. She's been tight-lipped for the past hour and I wanted some answers."

"Deputy Jackson, you're smarter than I gave you credit."

"Thanks. I think. Easy mistake. I'm a lot older than I look." The deputy retrieved the key and swung the door open. "Avery had your car brought to the office. Keys are across the street."

"You aren't going to keep me here till I spill what's going on?" Jesse slid through the water on the floor and darted through the door before the deputy could change his mind.

"Smarter. You should remember that later." He smiled, making himself look younger than before. Then he handed over the blue duffel. "Go inside the office across the street and collect your keys. Avery wanted to know if you needed directions to her house."

"I got it, thanks."

Keys. Paperwork. A short drive down unfamiliar streets. Jesse's mind was blank following the directions on the map he'd printed out. He hadn't thought of what he was going to say this time. As he pulled into a driveway, a motion detector flooded the yard with light. His eyes adjusted and he saw her sitting casually on the front porch.

Relief coursed through him like dousing a sunbaked

body in a cool stream. She was safe. Exposed. Beer in one hand. Shotgun lying next to her bare thigh.

Very short shorts. But who was he to complain? She was safe. Avery had long, terrific legs that he'd admired for most of his life. Sand volleyball at Baylor had been eye-opening when he was eighteen.

"Sorry for losing my head on the highway." She took a short sip from the bottle, never taking her eyes from him. Her short pixie cut—and he knew that only because of his mother telling him years ago—was under a black hat.

"Sorry that I didn't give you a heads-up before arriving." He took a couple of steps closer, wondering if that shotgun was for him or Tenoreno's hired man. "Got another one of those?"

"Didn't you bring your own weapons?" She sipped, then set her bottle on top of the water ring already on the old porch. "Oh, you meant a beer. Sure."

The amber bottle had been sitting behind her for a while. Evidenced by the moisture dripping from its surface. He didn't care if the beer inside was hotter than hell; he'd guzzle the peace offering he recognized being offered to him.

"Nice hat." They tapped the bottle bottoms together and each drew a long drink.

"I bought it when I moved here. Symbolic. Rangers wear white, et cetera."

Crickets chirped, the floodlight went off. It was a calm he could be thankful for. No words were necessary. In spite of their differences, they could work together. Old friends, falling into sync with...

"Your assassin waltzed into the sheriff's office this evening." Avery tipped the bottle for another swallow. "Want to see his picture?"

Chapter Six

Warm beer shot from Jesse's mouth and up through his nose. Avery remained on the step, calmly finishing her last swallow. Her eyes sparkled from the porch light but mainly with laughter. Or maybe it was satisfaction.

No one had caught a picture of the Snake Eyes Killer. If they had, they didn't know it. Completely at home with her, he untucked his shirttail and used it to dry his face. "You're lucky I wasn't facing you when you shared that news."

"It's all about the timing. Have a seat." She patted the space on the far side of her daddy's shotgun.

He recognized the initials carved into the wood. *A.T.* Hers. He'd helped her do it when they were ten. They'd both been grounded two weeks for ruining it, according to their dads. He took his seat and tried to be patient.

She pulled a folded piece of paper from her back pocket and flipped it on top of the gun. "I'm not convinced. Too easy for someone who's never left a trace."

"You know?"

"I'm not helpless, Jesse. I already admitted that I lost it on the highway. But honestly, when have you ever known me to lose the good sense God gave me during a case? I called Major Parker. I got all the details you didn't tell me." She spun sideways, leaning against the porch rail. "You sort of buried the most important part of your story when you got out of the car."

"I apologized."

"Yes, you did. So, moving on." She leaned forward and tapped the paper with a short nail. "Professional hit men don't curiously face a video camera like this guy did. He smiled at it, for crying out loud."

"I agree. Probably not our man, but—"

"It's someone who's met him," she finished with him.

Jesse unfolded the picture of a guy who looked normal enough. Looking directly at the camera with a big grin. "Did you send it to Major Parker?"

"Yes. He has someone working on facial recognition. I issued an all-points bulletin." She shook her head. "We both know that's just busywork. Why do you think this Snake Eyes character would show his hand, letting us know that he's here?"

"To draw you out? Think he was waiting for you at the jail?"

"If he was…then he knows you're here." Her palms covered her eyes. An old habit she'd had since a kid. "There goes that bit of surprise."

"I may be wrong."

"I doubt it. Makes too much sense."

"So I guess you're on board with flushing this guy out. No way to talk you out of it?"

"I said yes to Parker. He explained why it's important and asked that I remind you to take Snake Eyes alive. I don't understand why he thinks you'd shoot him. I mean, you haven't killed anyone in the line of duty."

Jesse knew. Watching her, he'd kept an eye on her legs, her waist, the curve of her lips. There wasn't a night that went by that he didn't wish his hands were stroking her silky skin. He remembered how she'd felt against his flesh, how she'd eagerly responded to his kisses.

He'd defend her with his life. He'd rather shoot the other guy first. Yeah, he knew why his commander needed to remind him.

"You know he's not going to approach me if you're around."

"Probably won't be tonight, then." He chugged the rest of his beer, listening to her small pretend gasp. "I'm not heading anywhere."

"I put sheets and a pillow on the couch. I don't have a guest room."

The security light popped on. They both went for the shotgun. Both realized it was just a tree branch blowing in front of the sensor. No one stood in the driveway ready to kill them. She slid the gun across her lap anyway.

"You're not going to like the couch," she added with a grin.

"It's okay. I didn't plan on getting much sleep."

Avery stood on the step, shotgun resting on her arm as she looked up and down the street. He understood that she was silently waiting on him to gather his things and come inside. He did, watching as intently as her.

Once inside, he dropped his bag and laptop, then began checking window locks.

"They haven't been open since I was locked up."

Focus. They'd apologized. No need to go back and dredge up another hurt. If they were going to do that, he'd talk about their last night together. Explain how things had seemed different.

Later. Now was the time to talk strategy.

"When's your shift start tomorrow? How much do

you plan to tell your staff?" He checked the back door and paused for her answers back in the living area.

"Are you even curious why I didn't get the message that Rosco was dead?"

"You said Sheriff Myers is out of town and you released me before daylight." He returned from the small bedroom that was just big enough for her queen mattress sitting without a frame in the corner. "We both have deductive skills that we utilize fairly well. All the windows are secured. You spoke to Parker. If there's a problem, he'll find it."

"Glad nothing's changed in the last ten minutes. I checked them when I got home."

"Just making sure."

"Well, you could have asked."

"Come on, Avery. We both need to be on our toes. We can't get emotional about this situation." He dug through his bag, removed weapons and ammo. Unzipped carrying cases, setting a rifle and three handguns on the coffee table.

She placed the shotgun between the door and porch window. Easy access. Then she huffed to the kitchen. "I suppose some things will never change."

"I'm the same man I was before. I'm not changing who that is for this assignment. It's the reason they sent me." It sounded as if a metal pot hit the floor. "I never wanted to let you down, Avery."

"Ha."

They were there. Emotional. A night of mistakes between them. "There's no way to avoid this conversation. Is there?"

"You seem to have done a good job avoiding it for at

least eight months," she said, not quite shouting from behind a wall.

"I'm sorry."

Half her body appeared at the kitchen entrance. She pointed a wooden spoon at him. He would have ducked if it had been in her throwing hand.

"For what part? Not speaking to me? Not making love to me? Leaving me embarrassed in my apartment without a word of explanation? Why are you apologizing?"

"All of the above?"

"That's what Garrison would say." She left him alone.

If she was using the spoon, she used it silently. He barely heard a sound for several minutes. The microwave beeped and a pretty good aroma wafted into the living area.

"I want to ask if any of that is for me. Then again, I believe it is. We might be arguing, but we're family and you wouldn't leave me hungry." He was joking, trying to lighten the mood. It always worked for Garrison.

"Come get your plate. I'm not waiting on you."

He joined her in the kitchen, where she was filling two plates—one more than the other. She shoved his plate complete with a fork into his chest.

"Jesse Thomas Ryder, we are not family. You're my brother's best friend and a Texas Ranger who I'm being forced to work with. But we are not family." That answer was loud and through gritted teeth. "My brother hasn't seen me naked since we were four years old." She had her head down, looking a little embarrassed at what she'd implied.

And I have seen her beautifully naked. "You're right, of course. Avery, about that night—"

Shotgun Justice

She nodded to the refrigerator. "There's soda." She left him standing there.

He followed, shoveling a forkful of some sort of cheesy casserole into his mouth. It wasn't bad. "Did you start cooking? I don't think it's restaurant quality and doesn't taste store bought. Did you start watching food shows?" He looked around the house. "You know, this is pretty cozy, with the exception of the mattress on the floor."

"Fully furnished," she said while setting her plate down. "I needed a bigger bed and haven't found a frame yet."

The confident woman sitting in front of him was gorgeous. Even more so than when he'd taken her to his bed. The smoldering in her eyes and the slight arch of her eyebrow would have implied sexy reasons why she'd needed a bigger bed. He'd believe that look from anyone other than Avery.

If she'd been seeing someone, not only would Garrison have spilled his guts, but their mom would probably have asked for a background check. Things had changed, though. So was she…?

"You're teasing me?"

She jumped up and tapped his shoulder as she passed with her plate. "Good grief, Jesse. You aren't the only guy around. And it's none of your business."

"Yeah, I know. I just thought—"

"You thought that because you wouldn't have sex with me, no one would? Or did you think I was still upset about it?" She hugged him from behind. Her arms wrapped around his chest.

He could feel her warm breath through his shirt as she pressed her cheek to his back. His hands were occupied with a half-eaten plate of the mystery casserole or he would have hugged her in return.

"Get serious. I'm not upset because you were drunk and obviously had some…um…problems. I'm totally angry because you suggested that I spend three days in jail and my boss listened to you over me. Is that misunderstanding all cleared up?"

Forgiven as if their embarrassing encounter meant nothing? Or it hadn't caused her to quit the Highway Patrol and move hundreds of miles away? He couldn't tell if she was lying. Not without looking straight into her eyes. If she was, they always opened wider. Or she'd accidentally wink, forcing them not to open. She knew that he would know.

"Yeah, we're good. Let's get started." He pushed the last three bites into his mouth and took his plate to the kitchen.

She grabbed a laptop from the bedroom and sat cross-legged on the couch. He took an uncomfortable chair across from her. If Avery was lying about how she felt, she'd learned how to fake it. She didn't seem fazed in the least that he was there. He couldn't say the same from his view and those legs.

"Major Parker said he'd email you the research they'd gathered on Snake Eyes and possible homicides he's linked to. Do you have them?" She never looked up from the keyboard.

Whatever she was doing…she kept at it with that same sexy upturn to her lips. He opened his laptop and she told him how to access her network. A loaded question that he ignored.

"Got it. We should probably print these. Looks like there's a dozen possible matches."

"The printer is wireless. Same password." She let him know but kept typing.

"Why Snake Eyes?" She tipped the lid toward her and looked at him as the printer zinged to life. "I mean, the rocks are polished like flattened marbles, hand-painted with reptile-like features. Why snakes? Why not human eyes?"

"Something in his past maybe?"

"Or present."

"These bodies all have one thing in common—they were found in wilderness. Doesn't matter what state, they're miles from the closest town. Nothing else around them except nature."

"Is there a profile?"

"No. He hasn't been considered a serial killer. More like an assassin for Mafia or gangs. These deaths weren't all connected until today." He thumbed through the photos. They almost all showed the same scene.

"So we know he likes snakes. He's comfortable in the outdoors. He has money." Avery typed her list.

"By the looks of these pictures, he doesn't care if the bodies are found. He probably *wants* them found. The decomposition and the fact that he's in the middle of nowhere would cover any DNA mistakes he might make." Jesse pointed to different remains that used to be humans.

"Do you think he's proud of his work?"

"He took the real eyes and left fakes for a reason. He wouldn't have if he didn't want to connect all the murders." What kind of man were they facing?

"True." Her eyes dropped to the keyboard. The familiar *click click click* began. "A lot of serial killers are eventually caught because of their egos. Oh, I know you said Snake Eyes hasn't been classified as that. He might be getting paid, but he has all the markings of a serial."

"Agreed. The person who did this…" He paused, flipped a photo of a corpse toward her so she could take a good look. "He would still be killing if he wasn't getting paid."

"Elements, animals or him?" She reached for the paper.

They'd analyzed cases before. Shoulder to shoulder, for years studying to become better than the best. He could do his job and protect her.

"Jesse?"

"What?"

"I asked if there was anything in those files that indicated how the victims disappeared."

"Sorry. I must have drifted. It's been a long day." He wasn't lying, just not admitting how worried this guy made him.

"Oh man, don't I know it? Covering for Dan is exhausting." If that wasn't the complete truth, she hid it well. "So we'll leave it for the morning and have something to discuss for polite breakfast conversation."

She picked up the shotgun as she went to the bedroom. "If you need to use the facilities, better do it now. I'm taking a shower in about three minutes."

He nodded his confirmation before she shut the door.

Polite conversation discussing the motives of a deranged serial killer. Why did the prospect of more than one such breakfast discussion turn him on and give him hope for the future?

Chapter Seven

The smell of strong coffee woke Avery. She wasn't startled or frightened. Jesse had slept in the front room, insisting the door to the hall remain open. She was cool with that.

Stretching her arms wide, she patted where her daddy's favorite weapon rested next to her. "Better protection than any man."

She giggled, something that just didn't happen anymore. It was her joke. Not that Jesse—whether she was upset with him or not—was close by. And he'd already made coffee.

"What's so funny? Want a cup?"

Jesse extended a mug. The steam encouraged her to sit first before accepting his morning gift. She had to blink a couple of times to make her eyes work as she blew across the coffee's surface to cool it a bit.

The fact that Jesse had his shirt off shouldn't have disturbed her. She'd seen that rock-hard chest before. Her view from the floor gave her a more in-depth view of the contours of his muscles. Nothing had changed except that she knew what was below the snug fit of his jeans.

She sipped, forgetting to cool the coffee first. "Shoot."

She reached across and set the cup on the old wood floor. "I should get up. Do you need something?"

She should have been grateful. More polite. Her mother had raised her better. His bare chest was just so...so...

"I came for the copies you slept on—literally. I couldn't get them out from under you. Thought I'd give them a once-over before I showered. We eating in or going to a drive-through?"

He'd already been in her room? She glanced down at her chest, verifying she'd slept in full pajamas and was still covered up. "I usually just have a protein bar."

"Mind if I take a couple of eggs, then?"

"Go right ahead."

"Come on, Elf Face. Time's a wastin'." He hooked a thumb over his shoulder.

"I'd forgotten you were a morning person," she called out, watching his backside leave her bedroom. The faded tight jeans were different than the dark black he'd worn the day before.

The soft denim molded to a fantastic specimen of a man that she missed as soon as he was around the corner.

Time to get on with her day and just flat move forward. Her thoughts had taken her to dreams mixed with murder and lovemaking and decaying bodies and excellent bodies. She was exhausted from sleeping. That was a fact.

How was this supposed to work? Did she really think she could take care of county business while Dan was out of town? As if being chased by a serial killer/assassin wasn't enough, she had to be partnered with a man totally oblivious of her attraction.

"Oh Lord, I'm in so much trouble." She tossed back

the covers, changing her mind about being alone with Jesse. "Hey! On second thought, let's go to the diner."

"Sure. Give me your word you won't leave the house and make me follow you. I need a shower, but I'm not wet behind the ears." He wandered in front of the door, two eggs balanced in one hand, a frying pan in the other.

Very conscious of rolling her lip between her teeth, she stopped herself by biting it. Then stopped again at the first brush of her tongue to wet them. She'd be professional. Especially with him. Even if he was shirtless, abs abounding naked in front of her.

"I'm not going anywhere alone until we have a plan," she finally admitted, knowing he'd get his way. And knowing it was the smart thing to do. If she was being watched, it only made sense to stick close to Jesse.

"I sort of need to hear the words, Avery."

"All right. I promise." She did the childish symbol of crossing her heart. "Do I need to pinkie swear or something?"

Half of his mouth turned up in a grin. "Next time."

She heard noise in the kitchen and had to mumble to herself, "I wonder if he knows how sexy that makes him look?"

Yes, she said it out loud for her ears only. It was just a true statement that she needed to remember. Jesse was sexy. That particular thought had floated around in her head since sex education.

She'd never understood why girls flocked to Garrison and left Jesse alone. It seemed that he was always out with girls, but never anyone steady. Garrison seemed to have a girlfriend every other week. It had been worse in college. They'd go to Austin and her best friend would insist to her twin that she'd be okay. They'd sit in the background and watch Garrison do his thing. Without a doubt, her brother was charming.

So yes, there always seemed to be girls around. Thinking back, they were leftovers. So what was it about Jesse she wasn't seeing?

The shower started and she got dressed quickly. Gathering papers and straightening the linens on the couch, she left them there. It was no use to ask him to stay at a hotel. He wouldn't. At least not until Snake Eyes was apprehended.

Just as he'd had to hear the words, sometimes talking through ideas made them more real for her. The past eight months here, she'd done a lot of talking to herself. It stopped her from picking up the phone to ask Jesse why he'd left. And it stopped her from calling her mom to see how Jesse was doing.

"Yes, Jesse is sexy. But... He's off-limits. He's out of your league. He's your brother's best friend. He stood you up—that's a nice way of putting that traumatic night. He's a professional colleague, a partner, even." She wagged her finger into the mirror at herself. "No fraternizing with partners."

Oh man, I spend way too much time alone.

Sweeping her short—massively tangled after a sleepless night—hair away from her face, she dabbed on some eye makeup and stuck her tongue out at the image. The same eyes that gave her brother such a carefree, bright-eyed friendly look... Well, they made her look weird in her opinion. Jade. A bright green that people accused her of wearing contacts to create.

No color change required. They were even greener today wearing her Kiss Me I'm Irish T-shirt. Soft, stretched out and comfy. Along with her favorite pair of jeans with worn spots in the knees that showed white threads. Fashionable in the real way—not that store-bought look with frayed edges. It was her day off.

His bag was gone. He'd taken it into the bath with him so he'd come out fully dressed. She wanted to be completely ready to walk out the door. Her small satchel held her laptop and the paperwork. Her service weapon was in its holster on her belt. And her pink toenails peeked out under the very worn edges of her jeans.

"Shoot. Shoes."

She'd grown up wearing Western boots and had half a dozen pairs on the floor of her closet. Along with a backup Glock in the pair reserved for dancing. *Like that has happened recently.* She sat on the couch and tapped her feet into her everyday boots.

The bathroom door opened, steam billowing to the ceiling.

"Whoa. You're…um…ready." He sounded genuinely surprised.

Thank God he wasn't wrapped in only a towel. The realization that she just couldn't have handled that came with the desire to pull his dark T-shirt over his head.

It's the danger of the unknown. It has my adrenaline pumping and doing crazy things with my hormones.

"I've collected the paperwork. We can use Dan's office to spread out and make some real notes about the homicides."

"Sounds good. Can we run the sirens to wherever we're eating? I'm starved." He laughed, but he meant it.

The diner wasn't far. It was a converted old storefront in the historic district. She ate there all the time, since it was between her house and the sheriff's office.

"This place fast? I am seriously hungry." Jesse pulled the door open for her.

"Is there a time you're not famished?"

"As a matter of fact—"

"Oh, don't bother saying that in a public place."

His grin and wink told her that his mind had gone to the same scenario hers had raced to. *Sex*.

"One day, Elf Face."

"You blew that chance." She left him behind her and found the rear booth, placing her back to the wall. He shook his head at leaving himself in a vulnerable position and slid into the booth next to her, pushing her over with his hip.

"Have you lost your mind? You can't sit next to me."

"I'm sure as hell not sitting with a window and the door behind me," he whispered firmly.

Curious looks were expected. Avery was still considered new. This morning there were double takes from the customers and waitress. She was the new kid in town and had been working her butt off to prove she was capable. There had been no time to make friends or form any real relationships other than at work.

But even the cook sneaked a quick look by strolling past to collect a syrup bottle in the next booth.

"Now look at what you've done. Everybody's going to think you're something special."

"I'm not?"

She ignored him.

The restaurant had limited seating, since it was open for only breakfast and lunch. Half the chairs were bar stools that kids loved to spin around on until they were dizzy. Jesse placed a huge order as a tall, lanky man entered. Avery hadn't seen him around before. He sat on the first stool and looked around anxiously.

Funny because he was looking at the ceiling and stopped his gaze on the security camera pointing at the register. Older... Longish hair over his collar...

"Is that the guy who claims to be my old family friend? Come on." She shoved at Jesse's rib cage to get him out of the booth. "He ordered coffee to go."

Jesse began moving, but slower than she wanted. "Couldn't we get Bo to follow him while we eat?" He joked because he already had his weapon drawn and resting at the back of his thigh, pointing at the floor. He waved at her to stay put as he quickened his pace.

Avery shooed the customers back. Jesse stood next to the man they'd barely begun searching for. The front glass shattered. A split second later, the man slumped and fell to Jesse's feet.

"Everybody down." Jesse lunged toward her, tackling her backward to the floor and covering her with his body. "Call 911."

The window was pierced again. Then a coffee carafe burst.

"Crawl behind the counter! Get to the kitchen!" Jesse shouted into the room, then gave her a shove under him. "You, too."

"What do you have planned?" she asked him as the customers belly crawled around the end.

"To keep you alive."

"But we can get this guy. He's right across the street."

Jesse shook his head. "He'll be gone before we decide which building."

"We're wasting time. There's an exit by the restrooms." They were far enough away from the window front that

Snake Eyes couldn't see them. Not from the roof. So she stood and ran.

"Avery. Stop!"

THE GIRL HE'D grown up next door to had always been fearless. The officer she'd grown up to be wasn't afraid, but she wasn't foolish, either. He was out the door two seconds after, following in her footsteps, crouching behind her, waiting for the next shot to hit.

"You know he could have help, a partner." He tried to catch her before she darted along the back of the buildings. At least it wasn't the most direct route to Snake Eyes. Jesse didn't have any doubts about who was firing.

"Not this guy. He just killed the man working for him."

He heard a car speeding up. Avery jumped out, waving her arms before he reached her. A deputy stopped the vehicle and began asking what was going on. Avery explained as she holstered her weapon and took a pump-action shotgun from the trunk. "I don't miss with this."

The deputy followed Avery's lead, staying to her right. Jesse followed on the left. "I've heard four rifle shots since we left the diner, but not in the past two minutes. He's probably on the move."

"You take the south side." She pointed. "I'll take Spencer around the north."

There was no time to argue or make a different decision. He had to trust her direction and the man who worked with Avery to have her back. He ran under the sidewalk awning. People should have stayed indoors at the sound of a sniper. But he yelled at them to get inside and lock their doors.

Stealthily arriving wasn't going to happen. So he got

louder, shouting, waving his gun. People cleared faster and perhaps he drew attention away from Avery's approach.

Jesse rounded the corner. No vehicles sped away from the block of buildings. He continued and spotted the deputy he hadn't met. "Where's Avery?"

The older man pointed up. "I gave her a boost."

"Dammit! I thought she was staying with you."

"Have you tried telling that *chica* anything?" He pointed his weapon where he scanned behind him.

"It's all clear," Avery stated from the roof, shotgun on her hip. "He got away and I have no clue how. I'm coming down."

The deputy caught Avery's shotgun and she propelled her legs over the faded red brick. She had a couple of handholds before she dropped to a covered Dumpster, then slid off the top to the ground.

"I could see the streets from there and no one was running or driving away. I'm not certain how he escaped so easily."

"He planned it. Like everything else he's done."

A few people joined them from the main street through town. One with a rifle in hand. Jesse pulled his badge and hooked it on his belt. "Texas Ranger, folks."

"Call the funeral home for me, Spencer."

"Who?"

"Not sure yet. I don't think he's from around here, but there are a lot of seasonal guys who fill up the hotels this time of year who I'm unfamiliar with."

"I'll take care of the scene." Spencer shuffled off. A handful of people followed along with Avery.

"Hey." Jesse stopped the deputy with a hand on her

upper arm, but immediately released her with the narrowed gaze he received. "Don't—"

"Let me save you the trouble, Lieutenant Ryder. You're in my town by my invitation. I get to say what I do and don't do. I was safe."

"Not hardly."

"You said it yourself. Neither of us expected Snake Eyes to be there."

"Do you have a forensics team to see...?"

"You're looking at her. It's one of the reasons I was hired, because of my training. But there's nothing up there. No casings. No cigarettes. Nothing except evidence of a bit of drinking over spring break. We need to get to the diner."

He admired her quick decision making, but it might just get her killed if she moved around in the open. His job was to protect her, and he meant to do it. "Look, before we assess the scene, I've got to remind both of us that this killer isn't what we're used to dealing with. We need to be as smart as him, which is going to be hard."

"I know, Jesse. We'll be careful." She patted his cheek and left.

Snake Eyes scared him. He admitted it.

Simply put, the man was complicated and dangerous. He had everything to lose—whatever everything was. This killer wasn't going to make mistakes like the average drug dealer.

Snake Eyes needed Avery alive or she'd already be dead. He'd been waiting on John Doe to walk into the diner. Probably sent him there in order to eliminate a witness.

Jesse took a long look, gauging the trajectory of the

bullets. He could have shot either one of them when they'd parked. This stunt was to prove he was in charge.

Snake Eyes knew it. He wanted Jesse and Avery to know it.

Chapter Eight

Dan's office walls were covered in copies of crime-scene photos, sticky notes and autopsy reports. It had started on his bulletin board and just kept spreading both directions. The back of the door and window were covered in one piece of tape at a time.

"Looking at the photos and sheer volume of information, I can't believe some of these victims weren't linked together sooner." Or as Jesse had pointed out the night before, law enforcement wasn't as concerned because the dead bodies were criminals.

Her partner nodded as he finished off the last bite of a hamburger Spencer had picked up for him. He tossed the wrapper in the trash can and ceremoniously gave himself two points. Avery didn't know how the man could put away as much food as he did. She'd never noticed just how much before she was constantly ordering it for him.

"Leonard Nelson was working with one of the harvesting crews. Did we find out what motel? And did he have a vehicle?" he asked, looking up from his constant internet searches.

"Yes to the first, no to the second." Her stomach growled. "In fact, the motel is over a mile to the diner. And there's a twenty-four-hour restaurant across the street. So it wasn't a coincidence that he came to the place I frequent."

Each time Jesse had eaten, she'd been a little put off by the thought of food. An empty stomach was catching up with her. She had to admit that one particular photo was making her a bit queasy.

"Snake Eyes told him to be there."

"Yes. But how did he know *we* would be there? *I* didn't even know." She stared at the tire tracks at one scene. *Duh.* "He had Nelson with him and followed us. He killed him to make a point."

Jesse acknowledged her with a "right." Meaning he'd come to that conclusion much earlier but let her get to it on her own with the evidence. It made an impact. Probably more than if he'd told her they were being followed. It also made sense now that they'd returned to her house, retrieved his weapons and car, then come straight back to the office.

"I've been through all the evidence collected. The only strange thing is a wet-suit fragment found close to the third victim. Strange because the body was discovered in the desert and the wet suit was over thirty years old. No DNA." He leaned back in the chair, rocking a bit, deep in thought with the pen tapping his lip.

She wrote the info on another sticky note and stuck it to the picture.

Was it horrible that her brain was a mishmash of emotions and thoughts? Every other one involved the case. The window made her think that she was freaked out about a serial killer stalking her. Each crime-scene photo made her think about each missing victim and their families, sending her right back to her dad's death.

Then she'd glance at Jesse and feel the support he'd

been all through her life with the exception of one lone night. And he was here now. Working next to her even after she'd thrown him in jail. Or he'd let her throw him in jail because he could have overpowered her and stopped it.

But he hadn't.

So even now, amid a room full of horror, he was her source of comfort and confidence. She could manage, but it was so much nicer working the case with her best friend.

"There really is nothing connecting these murders except the fake eyes." He hit the laptop keys a little harder. Frustration showed in his compressed lips and furrowed brow. "He has to be making them himself. The police from several of these cities canvassed hobbyists with rock polishers. But nothing."

"Polished river rocks. Hand-painted to look like eyes of reptiles."

Jesse tossed the ballpoint onto the desk. They both watched it bounce to the floor and roll to the wall. "There's got to be a connection."

"Are these just snakes? They look different."

He stood and went to the far side of the room. "These are gray. Brown. More detailed gray. In fact, these get progressively more detailed. Solid black."

She followed him back to his laptop, where he started searching for pictures of snake eyes.

"Each of these pictures matches a variety of snake." Jesse put in another search, then slapped the desk. "He's going through a damn alphabetical list. Each of the replacement eyes seems to be increasing in detail. He's obsessed with getting better each time."

"Or he's proud about his work. There are a dozen victims here. How long do you think he's been killing?"

"No way to tell from his calling card. I thought he might be connected with snakes somehow. You know, like a zookeeper or have them for pets or something. The different types just means he's looking at a book or online."

"In other words, it's another dead end with no way to connect him to a place." She pressed her palms into her eyes, completely and totally discouraged.

"Why don't we take a break from this and look at something—"

"Everything we've accomplished can be filed right next to a likely place where he lives. Nowhere." She couldn't bottle up the frustration any longer. "He's all over the country. Arizona. Texas three times. New York. Pennsylvania. And half a dozen more. Even Florida— that's such a lovely picture, by the way. Makes me want to throw up."

Jesse was out of the chair, pulling her into his arms. She let him. She might be trying to keep her distance, but the fruitlessness of the situation hit her hard. She felt like…like a girl.

The tears surprised her. She sniffed, raised her hand to wipe one away, and Jesse beat her to it. The back of his knuckle was gentle under her eye. Instead of drying up the rest, his caring opened a flood.

"Hey, it's going to be okay." Jesse held her tighter.

"There's… No… We can't…" She couldn't suppress the hopelessness of the situation. She also couldn't finish a sentence, so she stopped trying.

Jesse held her. They swayed and she heard the lock on the door being pushed. It really didn't help that he was such a nice, thoughtful man. She cried until his T-shirt was wet.

"We can catch this sick bastard, Avery." He gently tugged her face from his shoulder, looking in her eyes. He filled her with confidence. "It may not seem like this is giving us much to go on. But even a lack of anything is something. You're smarter than me. You can do this."

As she was about to step out of the intimate circle, Jesse pulled her back to him and leaned forward. Cheek to cheek. It seemed natural for them. Just a kiss between friends. Turned out as anything but…

Their lips gravitated to each other, locked together and struggled to come apart. It wasn't just her. She opened her eyes to see what Jesse was doing. His eyes were open, checking out her reaction.

They held each other's shoulders, keeping each other in place with little pressure from their hands. Just a whisper of their bodies touched. It was the weirdest moment.

Jesse's eyes closed. The pressure of his hands holding her in place eased, but his arms swooped around her, pulling her to conform to the mold of him. Her arms stretched around him, helping the process.

His tongue pierced between her lips, seeking what she wanted to give. Or filling a void she had known was there but wanted to ignore. It seemed inappropriate. Bad timing. Impossible.

Yet perfect, replenishing, just what she needed.

They drifted apart.

The grin was back on his face. "You going to knock me into the next room or pull out those handcuffs again? Your shirt does say to kiss you, even if I know you're not Irish."

She could only shake her head. She'd participated.

He wasn't alone in avoiding the problem of Snake Eyes. "I'm guilty this time."

"Guess we should…" They broke apart and went back to their respective corners. Jesse unlocked the door as he passed.

Avery wiped any makeup residue from under her eyes and took a peek using the reflective surface on her cell.

"I didn't mean to fall to pieces," she said softly. "Sorry about that."

He shuffled, raising a hand mimicking a schoolkid with something to say. He thought too hard on his word choice. "Not a problem. It's frustrating. What if we set this aside and see what we can come up with as far as trapping this guy instead of the other way around?"

"What do you have in mind?"

"He's told us that he's here. He thinks there's nothing we can do. All of this—" he pointed to the papers hanging on the walls "—tells us that he's meticulous. He's a planner. The longer he waits, the better his plan will seem."

"That's partly what I'm afraid of."

"You can call this off, Avery. We can get you a protective detail or you can stay in a safe house."

"That might be exactly what he's looking for us to do. Retreat like Garrison. It might give him a clue where my brother is located." She picked up the pen Jesse had tossed earlier and gave it back to him. "Could we trap him that way? Make him think I was being escorted to a secure location?"

"It might work. I need to call Major Parker."

"What's going on out there?" She could hear noises. Telephones. Chairs scraping the linoleum. Frantic tones. A couple of shouts. She had her hand wrapped around the doorknob to see for herself and take charge if necessary.

"Don't!" Jesse shouted. "Let me confirm what's going on."

A frantic knock decided things. She opened the door and found Julie. It must be late if she was already on duty.

"There's been an explosion north of town, Avery. We've dispatched the guys, but now there's been a second and third explosion east and west. All grain silos. People are freaking out."

"You can't go," Jesse said behind her.

"I have to. There's not enough of us. You'll just have to follow me." She swiped the address from Julie's hand before she left to answer another call, but turned to him. "You understand, right?"

"Be careful. You'll be completely exposed."

AVERY STOPPED LONG enough to put on a windbreaker marked Sheriff across the back. They needed everyone possible.

"Are you calling all off-duty personnel?"

"Yes. I've sent the men on duty to all three sites. A fourth was just called in, so I'll be changing where Bo's headed. The off-duty officers are headed at the first three to help out local PD. This is crazy."

"It's a trap. Call in surrounding volunteer firefighters. You're going to need all the help you can get."

"That's not—"

"Trust me on this, Julie. Call Amarillo for anyone they can spare."

"But they haven't evaluated the fires yet," the receptionist said, her worried expression indicating that she wasn't comfortable.

"They're going to be big and keep everyone pinned down and spread out. He's after Avery and just might get her. Here's my cell number. Keep me informed."

"Okay, but I think I need to check with Avery about all this."

"You need to hurry." He pushed open the door, stopping to ask, "Where the hell is Avery going?"

Julie looked overwhelmed, but handed him an address. He tapped it into his phone, calling up a map before he left a coverage zone. Avery had a head start. Every minute she was alone, she'd be more vulnerable.

Map on his phone, he sped behind her in the rental. Out past the city limits, he could see a fire on the horizon. He didn't need a map to see where he wanted to go.

Taking a turn onto a dirt road, he fishtailed a bit, straightened up, and the car sputtered. Then it lost momentum, cruising to a stop. The engine light was on. He had no idea what might have happened. Except...

He hit the steering wheel. "That son of a bitch!"

Chapter Nine

Avery was sliding her truck around corners, taking them as fast as possible without rolling it. If she caught the drop-off on the edge of the road, she was sure to lose control. Yet there was a set of headlights in her mirror, gaining speed. Her first thought was that it was Jesse catching up.

As the vehicle got closer, she wondered if it could be Snake Eyes. His logical move was at the fire. Catch her in a vulnerable spot and drag her into the darkness. He was methodical. The fire was the best bet that he'd approach to abduct her. She'd keep herself safe. She wouldn't stand alone, especially on the perimeter of the scene. Jesse would be there, focused on locating Snake Eyes.

The car kept gaining and the blinker indicated whoever it was wanted to pass.

"Are you crazy? Slow down."

Maybe it was a volunteer firefighter? Another officer? She slowed and drove on the side of the road as far over as it was safe. The car never slowed, just gained more speed until it disappeared around the next curve.

No other car headlights were visible. "Where is Jesse?"

She tried calling him. There was no answer on his cell that went straight to voice mail.

The open country let her see a flash of lights ahead of her. Then she rounded the corner and saw the disabled car that had just passed. "I had a feeling that was going to happen."

"Dispatch. Julie?" she called before she pulled to a stop.

"Something wrong, Avery?"

"There's been a single-vehicle accident on 3212 just past 807 toward the fire. They were going pretty fast. I'm checking for injuries. Redirect someone to the fire."

"Bo's the only one still in his car. You want me to send him as backup?" Julie was very professional for once.

"I got this. The car's blocking the road, so tell Bo to take another route and you send a tow truck out here."

"Copy that, Avery."

Blaze in the distance. Lights flashing around her. Smoke poured from the front of the vehicle. She approached the car with caution, running quickly through different scenarios in her head. Each time, she came back to a volunteer rushing to the fire. A hired murderer wouldn't want her approaching his stolen vehicle with her weapon drawn.

"Hello? Are you all right?" She looked at the mirror, which was pointing oddly toward the ground. She drew her gun, stood in line with the back door, leaning forward to tap on the window. It descended.

"I think I'm…having a heart attack. Officer?" A man's voice. Pleasant. Adult. "I know I was going a little fast. I think I blacked out for a minute. Can you help me? Am I going to die?"

Once again she ran through scenarios. Would the Snake Eyes Killer actually have an accident? Would he know which fire she'd be headed to?

"I'm a volunteer firefighter at home…thought I could help."

"Is anyone else in the car with you?"

He did nothing to make her on edge. She needed to holster her weapon to check out his injuries, but her experience working as a state trooper kept her ready for anything.

No, it was the situation with Jesse that had her on edge. The fact that an unidentified man was threatening to kill her. She kept her weapon drawn, ready to do business. "Stay calm. Are you injured?"

"I…can't breathe… It hurts," he cried out.

Oh God, what if he dies while I play frightened schoolgirl?

She holstered her gun and reached out to take his pulse. As quick as the flicking tongue of a lizard, he pierced the back of her hand with a needle. The hypodermic swayed back and forth, almost hypnotizing her with the surprise.

She knew she collapsed to the ground, but barely felt the impact. Her thoughts got fuzzy as the door opened and a black snakelike man stepped from it. *Shoot the poisonous snake.* She tried. He kicked her gun away.

A man. A snake man all in black except his glowing green snake eyes.

Fade to black took on a whole new meaning. She tried to hang on to consciousness. She could feel the gravel pressed into her cheek. It couldn't end this way. She'd promised her mom she'd be careful. She heard a man speaking to her, but the words didn't make sense.

Then the darkness grew more real. More frightening. She was about to die on the side of the road…just like her dad.

Comprehension shifted from logic to dreamland as her body floated and curled into a shadowy, bumpy place. She couldn't wake up.

Chased. Stung. Falling. The green-slit eyes of a snake monster kept coming for her, pushing her deeper into nightmare land.

Chapter Ten

"I was supposed to meet Deputy Travis here. I was delayed with car trouble, but I hitched a ride. I can't get her on her cell. Have you seen her?" Jesse asked a firefighter coming away from the fire.

"Only county guy I saw was over by the car. Other side of the fire."

The deputy by the car was Bo. *Keep it real. She would be busy.*

"Where's Avery?" he asked once within shouting distance.

Bo met him halfway, raising his radio to his mouth. "Julie? Has Avery cleared that vehicle yet?"

"She's not there? I got a garbled message that everything was okay."

Recognition hit the deputy's eyes. "How long since the first message?"

"Half an hour, Bo. After she sent you to the fire, I got the other message about six minutes later. I've been pretty busy. Everything okay?"

"Is that normal for her?" Jesse knew instantly it wasn't. "Where was the accident?"

Avery's father had been killed in a routine traffic stop and found by a stranger on the side of the highway. Her mother had worked for months to find out what happened when the papers accused him of not following procedure. Avery had always been a fanatic about following protocol. She wouldn't change that habit no matter how laid-back her county coworkers were.

Jesse could feel the blood rushing in his ears. He was a couple of minutes from panic mode. "She's in danger, man. You gotta listen to me. Tell me where she is."

"Bo?" Julie's voice called through the deputy's radio. "There's a call for Jesse Ryder. They say it's important. Should I put it through?"

Jesse took the hand radio from the stunned young man. "It could be him. Don't let him hang up," he shouted after pushing the talk button.

Julie was unaware of who it might be. Bo dialed his cell. He'd make certain she knew that the situation was serious. There were a couple of clicks. "You should be able to talk now."

"What have you done with her?"

"You sound out of breath, Jesse."

Jesse locked eyes with Bo and mouthed, "It's him."

Bo removed the radio from his shoulder, pulled his cell from his pocket and walked away. Jesse could hardly catch his breath. Snake Eyes was right about that. "What have you done with her?"

"I know all about you, Ranger. If you want Garrison's sister alive, you give me his location and let him take his chances. He comes out of hiding, sissy gets a pass."

"Where is she?" Jesse asked too late. The call ended before he finished. He looked to Bo. "Anything?"

"We barely got on the call. Did you recognize the voice? Man? Woman?"

"Disguised." The young men and women in Avery's

department would be unprepared to face a killer like Snake Eyes. "I need a phone with reception. You need to call Dan Myers and get him up here pronto."

"What's going on? Is Avery in trouble?" Julie asked through the radio.

The staff would be spooked, but there was only one way to deal with this...truthfully. "Yes. This is what I need from—"

Everybody spoke over the other. Donny Ray broke in on the radio, panicked. Jesse let them have their minute. Everything was still in his bag that he'd tossed in the backseat of Bo's vehicle when he'd found him. He was about to leave the deputy stranded at the fire. But he was needed here and Jesse needed to check out the scene where Avery disappeared.

His commanding officer answered on the first ring. "Parker."

"It's Ryder, sir. We were outsmarted. He's got her and wants the location of Travis." He pulled away from the fire. No one took off after him.

"Hang tight. I'll get you backup from Company C."

"He wants this to go public, sir. If it does, it's a sure way to let Garrison know his sister's in trouble. You know him. He won't trust us to take care of this without his help."

"Witnesses don't have access to the news or social media. But I'll verify no one slips up with Travis. Don't do anything foolish, Ryder."

"No, sir."

Jesse took a deep breath to keep his voice calm in spite of the apprehension rising in his chest. The odds of finding Avery alive were... He was ready to find Avery, but something caught his eye.

Movement at the corner of an outbuilding. Someone was creeping in the shadows.

Stopping the car, he fought with himself. He took a couple of paces onto the gravel, hesitating. Backup in the form of a nervous Bo, who might shoot the person watching? Or approach the shadowy figure on his own. It didn't matter what was in the dark. It wouldn't help Avery if anybody got shot.

He did an about-face, heading back to the car.

There wasn't time to react to the two-by-four that hit his head. He fell onto the trunk, then to the ground. He was pulled by his feet into the dark, and his blurred vision prevented him from seeing much, but not from kicking weakly at his attacker.

His boot connected with something solid that let go. Released, he flipped over, ignoring the pain, struggling to get to his feet.

"You're bleeding," a man's voice said behind his ear.

He felt the sting of a needle. Felt the thick liquid enter his body and travel to his limbs. He was helpless to respond.

The glow got closer to his face. Green horizontal slits in a sea of black. He was pretty much paralyzed.

This was it. The end. He didn't want his final thought to be of failure. Instead, he chose to remember Avery's face just at the moment he kissed her that afternoon.

Then there was the first kiss that seemed so long ago. Second in their lifetime, but the first as adults. Her sweet eyes lit up like a fragile dogwood blossom. Easy to remember because that was how she'd smelled. All sweet and sumptuous.

It was a good last thought.

Chapter Eleven

"Wake up, silly." A sweet singsong voice penetrated Jesse's dreams.

"Avery?" Jesse pushed his face from the dirt. He wasn't dead. Neither was the girl he'd been dreaming about. He was in her arms, skin to skin. No secrets in their way. "It's still dark. Let me sleep."

"To misquote one of your favorite movies, this is a hell of a rescue." When his eyes focused, he could see that her hands were secured around a fence post.

"Drugs?"

"Yeah. Fast-acting, too. Son of a B must have been following me and faked an accident. He got me while reaching to take his pulse."

"Edge of the fire…then took a board to my head." He rubbed the wound that felt like the size of a golf ball. Wait. His hands were free.

"That's right. Snake Eyes didn't secure your hands. Can you untie me? Soon?" she asked.

"Sure."

Strange that he was free to move and not Avery. He took in their surroundings. Nothing close. Not a fence to go with the post in the ground. Which after his eyes focused a little he could tell was the end of a picnic table.

"I imagine you've got a whopper of a hangover. I do. And you know I never get hangovers from drinking. If this is what it feels like, I'll pass. I am sort of light-headed."

"You didn't eat anything all day." He struggled to pull himself upright.

Blurred vision and a sicker-than-he-could-remember gut had him moving slower than a slug. He hauled himself across the dirt to get close enough to work on the knots around her wrists, slowly getting her free.

For a second, Jesse thought Avery was stretching to get life back in her arms. Then those arms dropped around his shoulders to hug him. He remained barely upright, she was on her knees and all he wanted was to stay there awhile to be thankful neither of them was dead.

"What the heck's around your neck?" They both got to their bare feet and she began tugging.

"Whatever it is, it won't come off."

He ran his hands around the entire metal collar and couldn't find a release button or catch, just a lock. "Does it hurt?"

"It's snug, heavy and feels huge. It makes me want to swallow."

He'd never seen anything like what was clamped tightly around her throat. Whatever it was, it couldn't be good. "Any idea where we are? Or how long we've been here?"

"I think it's still Saturday night. I can see smoke on the horizon from the fires. Based on that, I think it's been four or five hours. That's just a guess, since he took my watch. But I know where we are. This is Thompson Grove Recreation Area. It's about an hour or so north of Dalhart. Not far by car. Might take us a while to walk to the nearest house with no shoes."

"I agree on the timeline." He shook his head, trying to free himself from the emotion of the moment. Drugs. Relief. He didn't know which, but it was doing a number on his head. And his gut was objecting to any fast change in any direction, especially up and down. "You don't know how relieved I am that you're still alive. Think I'll sit for a minute until we decide what we're doing."

"I'll join you."

The moon was rising high in the sky, reflecting off the picnic tables and structures across a small white gravel parking lot. As his vision cleared, he could see well, considering the circumstances. Moonlight seemed to bounce off everything.

"I have no idea why he'd dump us here." He laced his fingers with hers. "It doesn't fit his MO at all."

"I'm sort of relieved that something's happened. But totally confused over what he plans. Do you think someone scared him off or that he's hiding close by?"

"Honestly, Avery, anything's possible with this killer. We're not certain that the victims were killed where the bodies were found. This might be how he does things." Jesse scratched the scalp under his short cropped hair.

"So keeping victims out in the open like this might be his thing," she agreed with a long sigh and another tug on her metal collar.

"You don't think he's going to hunt us or something? There are a lot of farms and houses close by. Plenty of possibilities for an escape."

"It might not be that easy." He had a feeling they were being watched. The moon might be keeping their surroundings from being pitch-black, but it didn't permeate every corner of Thompson Grove.

"Ready to get moving? We have a long way back to

town and can talk about this dude's crazy motives all
you want." She jumped up and he caught her upper arm,
gently pulling her to a stop.

"We have to work together on this, Avery."

"All we're doing is walking. Unless you know something I don't." Her eyes narrowed and she visibly clenched
her jaw. She twisted her arm free and fisted her fingers.
"I suppose you're wishing you'd thrown me in jail this
time, too."

"You know, I didn't think he'd lock you up, Avery."

"It was humiliating."

"I hope it wasn't too insulting. And your people don't
think anything about it. They respect and care about
you." He wanted to regret the suggestion of putting her
behind bars. He didn't, though. She'd been kept safely
out of the picture while the state searched for her brother.

He'd keep that opinion to himself. He could see the
similarities to her twin brother when she was in deep
concentration. But nothing could make him picture Garrison.

Not right now. This situation had everything to do
with Avery. He was haunted with the last drugged memory he'd kept in his head. The sexy dreams had left him
wanting to pull her into his arms as soon as he'd seen
her face. Holding her hand reassured him she was really
alive and unharmed.

"You shouldn't butt into my business. I know it's difficult for you to understand. I'm all grown up." She patted his hand politely and started toward the parking lot.
"I won't hide just because Garrison's in trouble."

"We're probably in more trouble than he ever was."

It wasn't his fault she was so damn stubborn. Or that
she hadn't listened to him when she pulled him over for

speeding. But he kept his mouth shut. They needed to work together like partners even if they weren't.

The only words coming to his mind would make their situation worse. He had to ignore the urge to respond. If they were ever going to move past arguing and work together, that was what he had to do.

He shook his head, determined to bite his tongue in half before he argued with her. "I thought Dalhart was south of here?"

"If we walk due east we'll hit 385 if no one comes along before that." She was about twenty feet from him, still tugging on the silver collar around her neck.

"Wait—" He heard an electronic beep. A red light glowed from the back of the collar by the lock. "Do you hear that? Avery? Stop."

"We really need…" Her body convulsed and she fell to the ground.

Jesse ran to her. Whatever had just happened, she was still breathing. "Do me a favor and wake up, Avery. You've got to be okay."

Jesse smoothed back her hair, wiped away a few beads of sweat and worried about her clammy cheeks. There was nothing outwardly wrong with her. He'd seen the light, heard a beep—not a gunshot.

"And I thought…I had a headache before," she whispered as she came around. "What happened?"

"This thing around your neck is a…a shock collar. I don't know how—"

Avery's eyes fluttered closed again as she fainted. Jesse picked her up and placed her on the picnic table. Why put a collar and shock Avery? How would that get what Snake Eyes wanted?

Because Jesse knew the location of Garrison's safe

house. The Snake Eyes Killer had found where he was vulnerable. He couldn't watch Avery suffer like this and didn't know how many times she could be shocked without it disrupting her heart.

He wanted to be strong.

Wanted to keep his oath as a Texas Ranger.

But Avery was more than a colleague or family. He wouldn't let her die.

AVERY SLOWLY OPENED her eyes. Every muscle ached like it never had before. She turned her head cautiously, uncertain what the heavy weight was at her waist. Pretty sure a man had hold of her hand.

She recognized the back of his head. "Jesse?"

He popped upright, quickly taking in their surroundings, which were completely strange. Her back was stiff from whatever she was lying on. Trees swayed overhead. The beginning streaks of a sunrise peeked through the trees in front of her. The grasslands to her right. A cow mooed somewhere close by.

"How do you feel?" he whispered.

"I don't understand. What's going on?" She should probably remove her hand from his, since they weren't on really good terms at the moment. But her body felt chilled and his fingers were warm. He didn't seem in a hurry to let go, either.

"What do you remember?"

The outline of his features were worried expressions or frowns—but not because of something she'd done. No, this was different and frightened her. Her stomach tightened.

She couldn't let him see her scared, so she reacted the only way allowed in this new phase of their relationship.

"Throwing you in jail. How did you get out and where the heck have you brought me?"

"Thompson Grove Recreation Area. You said it's not far from Dalhart."

"What? Why?"

Glowing reptile eyes.

The image was so vivid it jump-started the memories that flooded back in one fast whack. "Shoot. Wow. For a minute there I lost a full day. Snake Eyes drugged you, too?"

"Yeah. You…um…you don't remember waking up before?"

"Why are you acting this way?" She shooed his hand from her side and swung her legs over the edge of the picnic table, sitting up, feet next to him on the bench. Sort of woozy, but determined not to let Jesse see. "You look worried about…me. And I know that's not what you should be thinking about. We need to get out of here before Snake Eyes returns."

"I guess we need to go over the details again." He shoved away from her and the table, cursing the hodge-podge of dirt, twigs and stones that he walked across without his shoes.

"Again?" She wiggled her toes…also free of shoes.

He cursed and pulled up his foot, brushing aside something that caused him pain. Facing the sun, she stared as he bent in half and grabbed the back of his head. When he straightened, he faced her with so much worry and concern in his eyes it scared her. "Dammit, Avery. It doesn't matter. Nothing does. I thought you were dead."

Dead?

Confused, she took a deep breath, noticing for the first time that her chest hurt. Swallowing hard, she felt the tightness inside her throat and out. Her fingers touched cool metal like a tight choker. "What is this thing? And what do you mean by 'dead'?"

"A shock collar."

"Like for a dog?" She tugged at it, barely able to get her fingers between it and her skin. "Get it off."

"I can't. He'll zap you again if I touch it. You've been unconscious most of the night. I can't believe you're standing up."

"He who?"

"Snake Eyes wants me to divulge information about your brother. Info I don't have, by the way. If I don't..."

"He plans to shock me to death? Is that even possible?"

"You damn well came close already." Jesse shoved his hands into his pockets, spun to face the sun, cursed at something under his foot and bent at the waist, rapidly drawing air into his lungs. "And you don't seem to remember any of it."

She had nothing. Couldn't think of a word to say. No response and couldn't even say that. Her former best friend was clearly upset...with good reason. She was speechless because he'd said "dead." Meaning, she might have been close to it.

Jesse was a smart man. He'd know if she was breathing or if her heart was beating. She'd never seen him like this. Ever. Through all the scrapes and bruises growing up. Or the awkwardness in junior high. Or even going to the spring dance with her to shut up Garrison's bragging about taking the homecoming queen. This quiet man had never broken down.

If she didn't know him so well, she'd swear he was halfway crying with relief. He pressed the corner of his palms into his eyes—her habit—before standing straight and throwing back his wide shoulders.

Absolutely not. That was impossible. Jesse didn't cry. Nothing affected him that deeply.

"You're obviously tired," she concluded. "But are you ready to get back to Dalhart?"

"No!" He marched to her side and pressed on her shoulders to hold her in place. "We aren't going anywhere. He said to stay put."

"He's talking to you? How? Is he watching? Is that how he knows when you mess with the collar?"

"He knows when *you* mess with it or when *you* try to leave. He's either triggering it or there's a sensor embedded. It starts beeping before you're shocked."

"I can handle a couple of shocks until we can get to a hospital."

"Avery, honey." He rubbed his palms up and down her arms. "You've already tried that. This time you can't remember trying it. We aren't doing it again. We're waiting."

"You can't really expect me to just sit here. Until what? He kills both of us?" She could rest a little longer while she figured this out. She headed back to the picnic table. "What about Garrison? Who's going to warn him?"

"It's already been taken care of."

"Right. And that's the reason you personally came to rescue his little sister." She crossed her arms, not meaning to huff, but sort of huffing all the same. She didn't mean it and regretted the words as soon as they were out, causing a continued tension between them.

Jesse was talking about things they'd experienced a couple of hours ago that she couldn't remember. She wasn't angry at him or his help. She was frightened and didn't know how to admit it.

"Would you put being angry at me on hold? I know I'm the bad guy in your life. I'm willing to accept that responsibility most days. I just think we have a bigger problem at the moment."

Put her anger on hold? That was a ridiculous suggestion and made her want to laugh out loud. But it was also very logical. It was very...Jesse.

"Agreed."

Shoot. Shoot. Shoot. Her heart took a little tumble as she watched his surprised expression and the backward step that he took. His hands drifted from her shoulders to her knees and the outline of her body in between.

Time for her to put distance between them and keep it there. She sat confused on the picnic table. Suddenly cold and warm and severely attracted to him. Even here. She wanted his warmth, his comfort, his concern.

"So how do you know what Snake Eyes wants?" she asked, pulling her knees to her body and weakly wrapping her arms around them. She couldn't dwell on how her body felt. She could stay as strong as Jesse. She could remain strong and logical.

But to think logically, like a law-enforcement officer, she needed the facts, which were all fuzzy. Some danced around in her brain but not as complete sentences. Everything was fragmented like a puzzle.

"Snake Eyes called the sheriff's office when I arrived at the fire—where you were supposed to be. He admitted he had you, asked where Garrison is hiding. Said he'd kill you if I didn't spill the beans."

"Well, you can't tell what you don't know."

Just a flash but she knew he had that answer. The quick

narrowing of his eyes and a slight arch of his eyebrow...
That was his tell. She'd learned it years ago when he tried
to cover for her twin brother.

So he knew where Garrison was staying, but he wasn't
letting anyone else know that he knew. Probably a wise
decision. If Snake Eyes was watching them, it made sense
that he had a listening device somewhere close, too.

"He hasn't made contact since we've been here. I'm
drawing the conclusion that he wants us to stay, since
he shocks you each time you try to leave."

Jesse leaned on the end of the picnic bench, stretching his arms over his head. Avery wanted to reach across
and rub his shoulders. Lord knew, she'd done it often
throughout college. But not now.

Touching him that night... It was what had started the
greatest embarrassment of her life. She laced her fingers
together, holding tighter, pulling her legs closer. She was
still a little chilled and very unwilling to let her compan-
ion know it. She could manage.

"I'm at a loss here, Avery." He shook his head. The
early sunlight reflected off the natural highlights in his
hair. "I honestly don't know what to do except sit tight.
I've combed through this parking lot for a sliver of metal
to pick the lock on that collar. I've got a pair of bloody
kneecaps but nothing else."

"I could try now that it's daylight."

"Too risky if he's watching."

"We just wait? For what?" Fear was pushing its way
to the forefront of her emotions. It was hard to control
it. "I'm attempting to walk this through from the killer's
point of view. We know his purpose is to secure information. How does he plan on doing that? Telepathy?"

Right on cue a phone rang. Faint. Covered by something. They both jumped to follow the sound, searching the brush and tall grass. Not too hard to find when you knew where to look. They found the plastic bag pushed deep in the hollowed part of a tree.

Jesse held it, paused. She had the same thought… What if there were prints inside? What if there was trace evidence? She shrugged, gestured for him to answer. He flipped the phone open and pushed the speaker button.

"Yeah?"

"I'll skip the pleasantries," a voice disguised by a mechanical device said swiftly. "It's been a long night and I'm ready to move on. Are you ready to give me the location?"

"I swear that I—" The collar beeped. "Wait. I can't provide you an address I don't have."

"You have half an hour before the next phase of our game begins."

The screen went blank.

"Is it locked? Make sure you can't dial out. Don't shush me. I know he's probably listening. Just try it." She pointed, wanting to take it into her hands, realizing at that moment just how tingly her hands felt. As if they'd been asleep for a while.

Jesse punched in numbers on the old basic phone. Nothing happened. He flipped it over and tried to remove the back to gain access to the battery. They could see the glue around the edges. Glue around the on and off button.

The screen was locked, just as she'd feared. He stuffed the cheap phone back into the bag, not trying further. He spread his arms wide, ready for her to be comforted, then wrapped her in his hug.

"What the he—"

His hand clamped over her mouth even as his eyes

scanned the horizon like a machine. He held her tight, chest to chest, his lips brushing her ear as his hot breath lifted the tendrils of hair falling free from her ponytail, tickling the sensitive skin.

"Just listen for a second," he barely whispered. "Keep your eyes peeled for movement. I haven't seen a glint of a scope, haven't heard anything to even stop the bugs from chirping. We're casually going to find the way he's hearing us. Don't do anything that will get you shocked. You start beeping, you move back to the table."

"Why can't you leave without me and bring help?" she asked just as softly against his ear.

"Been there. Done that. The second shock knocked you off your feet before I made it to the road."

She pulled back to look into his eyes. Searching for that small squint that happened when he lied. "How many times?"

"Three." His voice cracked. He was telling the truth. "You really don't remember? You don't feel weird or anything? You're good. Not faking it?"

Reading him was so easy for her. Weird because she seemed to have a handle on so few others. "I'm a little sore and my chest hurts, but not half as much as my neck from the weight of this thing."

"I'm surprised you're walking around."

Genuine concern poured from the look he gave her. So much that she opened her mouth to ask him why he'd left her that night. Ironically, even with all the questions floating around in her supercharged brain, that night was clearer than most.

The long kisses, the yearning looks, the feel of his hand hesitantly touching her breast for the first time... It was as if she could feel all of it at that exact moment. Her mind was playing tricks on her. Jesse was only skimming the skin above the monster necklace. She cleared her throat and his hand dropped to his lap. They scooted a little farther apart. Of course, they had more relevant problems—as in how to survive the next few hours.

"Are you sure there's nothing around here to pry this off? This collar weighs a ton."

Searching the back edge of the picnic area with her eyes, there was something lighter in the brush. The sun highlighted a patch that looked a lot like skin.

"Is that a...a body?"

Chapter Twelve

"Can you estimate how long they've been dead?" Avery asked behind him.

When Jesse had searched the picnic area before, he'd missed the two bodies on the edge of the back fence. He carried them closer to the parking lot. Avery was still shaky, but not admitting it to him. Her normally tanned features were pale. He'd heard people talking about turning as white as a sheet. He'd never seen it until today.

"I assume they arrived with us. No animals have been at them. Stripped to their underwear. No ID. No shoes."

His feet were missing shoes, too. Probably a deterrent to running away. He was going to miss those boots.

Scooting off the bench, she stood to take a look at their faces. "I recognize one of them. He's come through Dalhart driving New Mexico plates. But I don't recall his name. The other one, I haven't ever seen."

"They must have set the fires. Snake Eyes doesn't leave witnesses."

"Shoot, Jesse. Snake Eyes doesn't even work with anyone for very long. I can't imagine how many people have been a casualty of his crimes." She sighed.

The shock collar was having more effect on her than she'd admit. "He's left us alive but we're in a public area? It's daylight. People will be driving by. We can ask for help."

"He wants Garrison and Kenderly Tyler, his witness. Without them the state has no case. The remaining evidence would be thrown out."

"We can still ask for help."

"How can we possibly get out of this?"

"Together. I don't suppose there's extra ranger training for this sort of thing?" She tugged at the collar.

"The subject of how to remove a shock collar hasn't come up." Just in case Snake Eyes could listen via the phone, Jesse left it with the dead men, then sat next to her.

The sun was full in the sky, almost topping the trees on the east side of the grove. They could see more clearly and had about ten minutes left before Snake Eyes was supposed to call them.

"What would he do if you gave him a false address?" she whispered.

"Kill anyone there or some other innocent man he asks to check it out. I don't know where they are." He wished he didn't know. Then there'd be no chance in hell he'd share the information.

As it was, he didn't know if Avery would survive a fourth shock. He had no idea how much electricity was flowing through her body. The third time had lasted quite a while and her heart had stopped. She'd come back, but would she the next time?

"Any good ideas? If not, I'm going to the restroom over there. Shock or no shock." She stood and spoke while turning in a circle. "You hear me, Snake Eyes?

I'm going to cross the parking lot and have a private moment."

His mind was a blank. Maybe it was a side effect of the drug he'd been given, but he couldn't think of a single thing to do. Not a damn way to protect her.

"Ah!" she cried out as she opened the door. "It's all right. I'm okay. There are more moths in here than I've ever seen in one spot."

He'd jumped up, ready to do battle as he was, dressed in jeans, a T-shirt and bare feet.

"Ah! More moths. They're creepy."

More creepy than two dead strangers about thirty feet away?

"Oh man, Jesse, can you help me? I'm going to be sick."

He ran across the gravel parking lot, not caring that every step was painful.

"What?" He pushed through the door. Avery had a finger over her lips, instructing him to be quiet.

"I'm all right. I checked every crevice in here. No listening devices or cameras, so I'm testing something," she whispered. "I think you might be able to get the toilet-paper holder off the wall."

"I could have kicked this off easy if I had my boots." He bent to one knee, taking a closer look. "I need something thin enough to work as a screwdriver or a heavy rock. He took everything from my pockets. I've already tried to break my zipper pull. No luck."

"I'm going to pretend to remain sick. Maybe that will give you time to find how he's watching us. Or find something to knock this loose. There has got to be something around here that you can pick a lock with."

They might be in a tight spot—some might call it

hopeless—but Avery wasn't about to go out without swinging. It hadn't crossed her mind to give up. Her color was coming back, so she might be feeling better but wasn't about to let Snake Eyes realize it.

She reached around him to open the door and he saw the solution. "Our answer has been staring me in the face. Literally."

"What are you talking about?"

"Do you still wear an underwire bra?"

She nodded.

"Take it off. I can use that to jam open the lock on that collar."

"Are you sure?"

"It's worth a try. Let me help." He reached under her T-shirt and unhooked the hooks. The collar began beeping.

Without removing her shirt, she slipped the bra off and pushed her arms through the holes.

"I'll get sick again in a few and we'll come back in here to try it." She stumbled out the door, and the red light stopped blinking. Twirling in the parking lot, she spoke to the trees. "There is a lot I want to say to you, Snake Eyes. A lot of words I'd like to call you. I'll wait until we're face-to-face."

Standing half in and half out of the restroom, Jesse held the bra behind his back, working until one of the wire ends ripped through the material. He pulled it out and stowed it under his shirt.

Their situation wasn't good, but he'd never been prouder to watch Avery shake her fist at anyone. They'd both get out of this alive because they'd work together to get the job done.

Avery didn't receive a shock, but the phone rang. She carefully picked up the bag and flipped it open.

"Here are the rules," the altered voice said. "I need an address. You and your ranger stay. I'll let you go once my friend has verified he's there. If someone happens by… It's your choice. I'm glad to kill anyone you invite to the party."

"We know you're going to kill us. Why should we give you my brother, too?"

"There is so much more fun we can have."

Avery dropped the phone, shaking back and forth. If Jesse touched her, he'd be useless.

"How much can you take, Ranger Ryder?"

The shaking stopped and Jesse caught her before she hit the ground.

"Son of a B, that hurts."

"At least this time you're not passing out. Must have been a lighter current."

"Restroom, please." She squeaked out the words as she clung to him.

"I hope you're faking this. At least a little," he whispered and picked her up in his arms. He left the phone on the ground. His only concern was Avery. "You can't take much more of this."

She sat on the closed toilet seat. "Then get me out of this thing."

"I'm with you there, sweetheart." He stuck the underwire into the lock. "This thing looks like a cylinder lock that can sometimes be opened with just a credit card. Worst type of lock there is. So maybe…"

The collar began beeping. A bead of sweat rolled into Jesse's eye.

"Oh God, please hurry, Jesse. I can't—"

"Almost…" He jammed and twisted. "Got it."

The collar fell to the concrete floor, stinging his fingertips as he released it. Avery pressed herself into his body so fast they both fell backward.

"I've never been so thankful something worked before in my life." She kissed his mouth.

Quick with gratitude. It was better than handcuffs for sure.

"You going to be able to run? He's got to have eyes on us. He's going to know you aren't wearing that thing and he has no control any longer."

"There's an empty house on the corner. It's been on the market for months. I don't know what's inside, but it's not in the open like this."

"You said it would be faster to stay on the dirt road and not cut across the field. Yeah, that's where we were heading before the second shock. We've got to blast out of here and not stop. Something happens to me, just keep going. Don't look back."

"There'll be none of your Texas Ranger heroics. This is my county. Remember? We stay together. Don't worry. I can keep up." She held out her hand. "Just as soon as you get me off this filthy floor, because I don't think I can move."

"Elf Face?"

She winked. "Just kidding. I can run a marathon to get out of here. Come on."

JESSE LED THE way from the restroom as the collar beeped and buzzed behind them. The parking-lot gravel hurt. Avery ignored the pain, pushing through the sharp bruising.

"Okay?" Jesse reached back and took her hand.

"Just winded and braless."

They hadn't made it to the road yet. How was she supposed to run a half mile? Blessed relief hit her feet as she stepped onto the soft dirt road. She stayed in the tire tracks, where it was packed down and a little easier to run through.

Jesse ran in sand, imitating an ocean sand dune. If he'd let go, he could take the other tire rut. But he held on tight to Avery.

The wind whooshed by, much different than the stillness of the grove. She barely saw the dirt kick up in front of them. There were definite pops and puffs of sand in the air.

"Snake Eyes is shooting," she panted.

"We can't turn back. Keep going." They both slowed and turned toward the sound of shots. "Down."

He pulled her to the dirt, covering her with his body. Bullets peppered the road. He rolled them closer to the ditch, which was more like an extension of the field.

"What now?"

"I can't tell where the bastard's shooting from." He raised his head even with the wildflowers and some kind of flowy grass. Nothing happened. "Can you run?"

They shifted to where they were looking not only at each other but at the perimeter behind the other.

"I'm slower than normal. But I'm not going back, so it has to be forward."

The dang house looked farther away than before. She could see the roof and more trees. But around them was nothing. No tree or wood fence post or telephone pole... no anything except grass and flowers.

"Make a dash for the house."

She saw the desperation in his eyes. He was about to do something stupid.

"What happens when he shoots you? I can't—" Even now it was hard to admit it out loud. "I can't do this alone, Jesse. Please don't make me."

Weaving her fingers in his, she began to stand. Shots brought them back to their bellies.

"Can you crawl?"

"Watch me." Their arms would be raw from the plants that had dried like tumbleweed.

"This is going to hurt," Jesse said, moving a couple of feet.

"Not as much as being dead."

He sort of snickered as they moved forward. Ten arm pulls along the ground and he tapped her shoulder. "You ready to make another try?"

"Absolutely."

They stayed low to the ground, began running, kicking up dirt behind them. Jesse had a tight grip on her upper arm. She heard the shot. A rifle behind her and on the side of the grove.

"Keep going!" Jesse shouted, instead of falling to the ground again.

The house was closer. Another hundred feet and they'd be on pavement. It was tempting to stop and crawl through the barbed wire, but it might give him time enough to make a shot.

If Snake Eyes was back around the grove, he wouldn't have a shot as they rounded the corner. They kept running past the fence to the driveway. A broken swing set had been left in the yard. They kept running.

The door was locked. Jesse didn't hesitate. He broke the window with something left on the porch. They were inside, leaning against the walls at the base of a stairway, breathing so hard she didn't think she would ever catch her breath. She really needed water and prayed it had been left turned on.

"Now what?"

Chapter Thirteen

The inside of the house was dark with the exception of a morning shaft of light from the broken window next to the door. There was a staircase opposite the front door, a closet under it and two rooms on either side. Jesse couldn't shake the bad feeling.

"I'm going to see if the water's running." Avery dusted off debris from her feet and cautiously moved around corners.

"He has to be following us. Let's stay together."

"Jesse, we've been drugged. I've been shocked to unconsciousness. We just ran a half mile. We're both dehydrated. Water is a necessity for us to be able to think." Avery slid her hand down his arm and laced her fingers through his. "Come into the kitchen."

"We need a plan."

"Dehydration keeps us from thinking clearly. My brain's muddled enough." She turned the handle and cupped her hands to drink. "Your turn. I'll watch. I can see the front door and out back from here."

He'd been staring out one window without a memory of what he'd just seen. She was right. They both needed water, food, sleep…a weapon. Essentials. He splashed his face, scrubbed it to wake up. He began looking through cabinets and drawers.

Avery stood watch at the door. "We can't look for a weapon and keep watch on both sides of the house. He's going to come after us."

"He's probably already here. Maybe already gone through here for a weapon. It's unlikely there's anything to hold him off."

"Okay. We've been quiet. We would have heard him if he came through another window." She had lowered her voice, emphasizing the quiet that surrounded them. "I'll follow your lead on this, Jesse. My mind... Seriously, I'm having problems thinking straight."

"He hasn't gotten what he wanted. His goal is Garrison, not us. We're just a necessary step—even if he enjoys killing." Jesse forced his mind to work.

"You're a smart man. If the positions were reversed, what would you do?"

"Wound us? Drug us so he could start over? He could have shot us on the road, but he didn't. He needs his information. He likes the hunt, wants us to run."

"So we make a stand." She nodded. "With what?"

"A banister rail? Maybe there's something that got left behind." He turned, opened a door. Nothing. "What about the barn? And I noticed a shed."

Avery leaned close to the window, taking in as much of the perimeter as possible. "I haven't seen him come down the road."

"That's it! We've got to find his vehicle. That's how we'll both get out of here alive."

"Together. You promised. Don't go sacrificing yourself for me. You know Garrison would kill me." She smiled.

The thing was…he would sacrifice himself for her. And it had nothing to do with his friendship with her brother.

The strong emotions that rushed through him would have set him on his ear under normal circumstances. Yeah, they already had. Here he had to push them aside until they were safe. Eight months ago he'd pushed them aside and run. He'd be running again, but not away from Avery.

"Let's get out of here before he has us pinned down again."

"We can do this, Jesse."

"We zigzag across the open yard. I don't see a lock on the shed, so we're good. You hear shots, run faster. We're out the door on three." He turned the lock and removed the chain. "One—"

"Wait. Wait."

"Did you see something? What's wrong?"

"I…I can't remember." There was pure panic in her eyes. "Don't laugh, but I can't remember what comes after one."

"Must be the shocks your body has had. Don't worry. It'll come back." He surveyed outside again.

No sun reflected off anything. No one in sight, but Snake Eyes was out there. He was certain of that. Maybe he should leave Avery hidden in the house and take the bastard on by himself. If she couldn't remember how to count, what else would her mind blank on?

It was a fleeting thought. Gone almost as fast as it came. He couldn't leave her alone… She'd never allow it.

"I asked you not to laugh."

"I'm not. I'll wave you forward. Okay?"

She nodded, her eyes big with tears, her heart full of courage. *She must be frightened out of her mind*.

Once again, they held hands and moved as silently as possible across the yard, staying low, darting between the few trees. They made it to the old wooden shed and heard breaking glass inside the house.

"Take cover."

They ducked behind a rusty wheelbarrow with a hole in the bottom. Rapid shots hit the wood, penetrating it and ricocheting off the rusted wheelbarrow.

"I don't think he's trying to take us alive anymore," Avery said, pointing to a rake.

It was equal in rust to the other smaller tools in the shed and not a surprise that it was left behind in the move. The handle looked as if it might break by picking it up. It was the closest thing to a weapon that they had.

"See anything to pry these back planks apart. If we're lucky, Snake Eyes might not see us leave." Another round of fire had them ducking again. Another broadside to the shed, but just a short burst.

Jesse leaned against the bottom support of the wheelbarrow and it moved. Staying low, he worked the screws back and forth until the support popped off. They wedged it and shoved, prying the old planks to where the nails lifted free. A second plank and they were free.

Again.

They squeezed through, dragging the rake and wheelbarrow support along with them. They were behind the barn when another blast of bullets hit the shed.

"How many more times do you think we can escape this guy?" Avery asked.

"None," a voice said.

POINTING A GUN at them, a man dressed entirely in a black rubber skin waved them to the wall. The black material was almost like a wet suit. It wasn't quite like anything Avery had seen. Old-fashioned. He was hooded, wearing thick old rubber gloves duct-taped at his wrists.

Yet with modern reptile contacts. She'd seen them before on kids around Halloween. Yellow with horizontal pupils. A memory of them flashed for a moment. "You were dressed like this when you drugged me."

"Looks like we're repeating the same act," he said, confident he had them. "No one I've ever hunted has gotten away, Deputy. If you won't tell me what I need to know, I'll get the information somewhere else. There's always a backup plan."

"Duck!"

Avery flattened herself on the ground. Snake Eyes realized the rake was coming at him a fraction too late. Jesse made contact with their attacker's side. The man screamed, pulling the trigger, but the handgun was pointed at the sky.

Jesse pulled for another swing, but the handle broke in half, leaving the rusty prongs in their assailant. Snake Eyes screamed again as he tugged himself free. Jesse tried to help Avery up, but she'd seen where the gun had flown.

Snake Eyes stepped on her leg as she scrambled forward. Pain blasted through her calf. She stopped the scream inside her chest. She didn't want to stop her partner.

"Scott, you idiot, get over here," Snake Eyes called out.

Jesse caught the man's arm, spun around and elbowed him in his face. He staggered backward, grabbing his nose.

Snake Eyes had another man with him. Avery crawled toward the only real hope they had...the gun.

Punches flew behind her. She heard fists connecting with flesh. The solid thumps against ribs and jaws. She couldn't take the time to look. Finding the gun was their way out. She got to her knees, searching the overgrown johnsongrass. She'd heard the gun clank against something metal but didn't know exactly where.

Unable to stop herself, she caught glimpses of Jesse's right cross and Snake Eyes responding with two solid body punches. "Where is it?" She smoothed the grass, going through it all, found an old garden tool, then...

"Got it!" Her fingers wrapped around the butt of the gun and she rolled to her back in time to see the second guy round the corner of the barn. "Hold it! Stop!"

The men staggered apart. The young man with the rifle planted his feet and aimed at her. Snake Eyes narrowed his contact slits and backed toward his accomplice.

"Looks like we have a standoff." He got next to the rifle, tapped the guy on the shoulder, and they ran around the corner. "You'll be hearing from me soon."

Avery tried to stand and follow. Her calf was cramping from earlier, her arms could barely point the gun and she was still barefoot. "Are you all right, Jesse?"

"I don't think I can follow, either." They both ran as far as the barn, where they watched the men jump into an old Jeep and drive away.

The younger guy fired his rifle wildly, pinning them at the corner of the barn. He whooped and hollered as Snake Eyes drove south.

"He's getting away," she croaked.

"We're alive," Jesse replied. He took the handgun from her. "Maybe we'll get lucky with this thing. Prints or registration."

"When do we begin walking back?" Avery did not look forward to moving at all. She needed to massage the cramp in her leg and might even need to throw up. "Not before we get some more water."

After a couple of steps, limping back toward the house, Jesse slipped his shoulder under her arm to help.

"I think we can wait five or ten minutes." He panted and pulled her to a stop.

"Good idea. It won't take too long if we double back and cut across a field. If we're lucky, someone heard the gunfire and reported it."

"Yeah. I feel real lucky."

Chapter Fourteen

Scott what's-his-name was increasingly annoying. Snake Eyes should be on his way to find Garrison Travis and the hairdresser witness. Instead, he watched a young man who had shown his face to the enemy. He'd also nearly shot them in that shed.

"You do not take instruction well, Scott."

"Man, I was getting the job done. It's not my fault that collar had a cheap lock." He danced around the hotel room, trying to imitate an American Indian war dance. He wasn't close.

"Stop that at once."

"Hand over my money, and me and my Jeep are out of here, man. You can find your own way back to wherever you crawled from."

The sharp knife sliced deeper through Scott's throat than Snake Eyes had intended. He watched the younger man grab at the wound. Both of them knew there was nothing to do but die.

"This is the reason I don't work with amateurs. Pathetic. What did you expect after you moved the other two bodies to the grove? You actually thought you were better? Perhaps good enough to work with me?"

Scott's blood gurgled to the floor when he dropped.

The life left his eyes. There was no reason to take the kid's eyes. It would just delay his next move having to make another pair. Leaving the body in a hotel room without his signature was against his principles. He gathered his tools.

Still in his suit, he removed the keys from the front pocket of the twitching body. It amazed him how instinct clung to life. He could dispose of Scott's eyes later. Somewhere down the road where animals would use them for nourishment.

From his bag, he removed the eye rocks he'd especially painted for Ranger Ryder. He'd need to find another. Yes, the yellow-faced whip snake's amber around the eye would match well enough. It would be easy and quick to paint in its simplicity.

The black river rocks were a snug fit in the small eye cavity, but looked good. "Oh, to be a fly on the wall when you're found, Scott."

The nosebleed he'd received during the fight would give Avery and Jesse a mental boost. An injury to your opponent would always give hope. As would the blood they were sure to collect from the rake. He wasn't in any of their systems. They'd never discover his identity through DNA, but that wouldn't stop them from searching.

"Finish or die," his father would laugh and joke. He wasn't talking in a literal sense, of course. His father had actually taught him survival skills. He'd been a terrific father.

No regular education or training would have provided the opportunity to become who he was. Or could have taught him to be so independent. Depending upon only himself.

Finish or die.

He would do just that. Finish this job or... There was no *or*. He started. He must finish.

The towels he used on his side were still there as he left the room. No hotel cameras caught him. He'd made certain they didn't work beforehand. He got in the Jeep to drive back to his camper.

A week ago, he'd wanted a greater challenge. Well, now he had one. His prey were wounded. They'd be on guard, wary. They might be protected by others. Yes, this was a challenge.

He'd have to drive into Tucumcari, New Mexico, for additional supplies. Ha. The shortest route was straight through Dalhart. The risk would be... Not any real risk. No one knew him or what he looked like. He'd taken care of the witnesses.

The next phase would be stealth instead of torture. He'd made a huge mistake counting on anyone other than himself to watch the picnic grove. Lesson learned. He sniffed at the blood dripping yet again.

First the information. Then he'd terminate the two people responsible for bloodying his nose. That was a guarantee. He tossed his bag on the seat next to him and put the Jeep in gear.

"Thanks for the ride, Scott."

Chapter Fifteen

Avery should feel safe. Two Texas Rangers were sitting on her porch and another was in her living room. So why couldn't she sleep or even stop her heart from racing with every sound?

A green-slanted-eyed monster haunted every minute she closed her eyes. She was starving, but the thought of eating got her stomach in knots. She kept drinking water, then had to get up every half hour. Both she and Jesse had been seriously dehydrated by the time they got to the hospital.

The Amarillo doctors had wanted them to stay overnight, but Jesse had insisted they'd be safer in Dalhart. She agreed and they were escorted to her house. That was—she looked at the clock—two hours and forty-seven minutes ago.

Almost three hours that she'd been lying on her mattress with the door cracked open—as Jesse insisted. Whatever conversation the rangers had in the other room had been whispered so they wouldn't disturb her sleep.

Avery tossed back the covers and tried to get up. She wanted to act as if everything was normal, but her body caused her to moan. She thought she'd been sore this morning. Every muscle had forgotten how they worked, screaming in agony. The moan couldn't be helped.

And Jesse heard it. His bare feet slapped the hardwood floors as he came through the hall. Head poking through the opening, he was quiet and obviously trying not to wake her. Truth time.

"I can't sleep. I haven't been asleep. I doubt I will be asleep anytime soon."

"Me neither." He extended a hand to help her up but withdrew it. "What do you need? I'll get it for you."

"An ice pack for the back of this leg." The one Snake Eyes had stepped on. "And company. If you help me up, I can sit on the couch."

"I can get the ice pack, but you're staying put. Wyatt and Kayden are chatty and I can hear them through the window." He tapped the door frame and was gone.

"But, Jesse—"

"Let me get the ice."

Avery piled all the pillows in the corner and scooted so she could lean against them. Then alternated pointing her toe away and pulling it back, trying to stretch the pain into submission. Maybe if she asked real nice, Jesse wouldn't mind rubbing the cramping muscle. Maybe.

"Hey, I was thinking." He came through the door empty-handed. "Do you have a heating pad or something? A sore muscle needs to relax, not tighten up from the cold."

"No heating pad."

"I could call one of the deputies—"

"Please don't. Once this is all over, I'd be running errands for them forever. It's bad enough that Dan had to come back from Dallas when we went missing."

"You didn't expect him not to. Did you?" He sat on

the mattress, pulled off his belt and made himself comfortable. "Give me your leg."

Just as if no time or an ill-fated night had transpired between them, he massaged her aching muscle. The rest of her body tingled at the thought it might also get attention. It wasn't fair. She couldn't return the favor.

"Can you count to ten for me?"

"You're joking." She looked at his eyebrow quirked high onto his forehead. "I guess you're not. One, three, five, seven, nine, ten."

"Was that for real? Dammit, Avery. I shouldn't have listened to those guys about moving you. Get dressed. I'm taking you back. You should be kept under observation—"

"Wait. Sorry. I was joking. Whatever it was this morning has passed. Sort of like a concussion. My counting ability returned at the hospital."

"Don't mess with me that way." He'd shoved her legs to the side when he was ready to rush her to the hospital. Now he wrapped his firm grip around them and continued an absentminded rub.

"Yes, sir. Promise. I didn't mean it."

During their captivity he hadn't looked as panicked as right then. He began working the muscles again, but this time a stern look invaded his features. She could see him pretty clearly with the light that came between the window and sill. He clenched his square jaw. His eyebrows were drawn straight and close together.

Since they had been driven back to Dalhart after their fight with Snake Eyes, he hadn't let her out of his sight. That was how she knew that his eyes had lost their usual sparkle.

"Hey. Earth to Jesse. You can stop playing Twister with my leg now."

"Huh? Was I hurting you? I must have drifted."

"I could tell." She didn't pull her legs from on top of his. She was comfortable and the contact felt reassuring. "You know that I've been in some tough scrapes before. We both have. But this… This was…"

"Intense."

"And very personal. Why do I feel…invaded?"

"Snake Eyes did his homework. He messed with us personally. That hasn't happened before."

"Dan said your car had bleach in the radiator. Did he tell you that?" Topics of conversation were limited—at least in her head—to Jesse or the case. She chose to ignore the Jesse topic. "Do you think we'll find that Scott guy dead somewhere soon?"

"Yes. Unfortunately. I couldn't get the plate number to help find him sooner."

"If the Jeep had any at all." She shook his shoulder. "There was nothing you could have done. That teenage hellion almost killed us in that shed."

"Snake Eyes knew more than he should have. Like how I wouldn't leave you. Knew that threatening your life would eventually get the information he wanted."

"I might have told him if I'd known." She rubbed her throat where the collar had been.

Some tech somewhere was analyzing it to see exactly how it worked and all the grim details. The doctors said she'd be feeling the aftereffects of the multiple shocks until she didn't. In other words, they didn't have answers. Especially answers about her returning to work. Or about anything, really.

Those same techs had been here to sweep the house

for electronic devices, had taken their phones, their laptops and had even checked her cable for suspicious whatever. But they'd found nothing. The powers above her pay grade believed Snake Eyes hired someone to gain information to them.

She didn't. The experience was too...

"I advised Major Parker that they should move your brother. When they do, he's going to know something's wrong."

"Are they going to move him? Snake Eyes might find out his location if he's moved." Mixed emotions rushed through her. Was it the thought that her brother might face the insane man who wanted to torture her and kill him? Or a little envy that someone else—maybe him— might catch the bastard before she could?

"That's a risk they're going to take."

"We have to find him. Snake Eyes." It wasn't sibling envy for once. She was scared for her brother. "There's got to be something we've missed." She tried to move past him to get off the bed, but he stopped her. "Come on, Jesse. Neither of us is going to sleep tonight. You know that."

"We're not looking at another crime-scene photo tonight." He cupped her cheeks and gently brought her face even with his. "We're just...not."

Avery wanted to lean in and kiss him. Unusual and stressed circumstances might have brought them back together. Okay, there was the tense part where she threw him in jail. But after that, they'd worked together well. So...

Jesse dropped his hands, leaned back against the wall and crossed his arms over his chest, burying his hands in his armpits. If that didn't speak volumes, she didn't know what did.

Leaning back against her pile of pillows, she wasn't just frustrated. She was on the verge of being angry. More like one step away from already angry. *I'm tired. Exhausted. This isn't the right time. There won't ever be a right time.*

"I want to know why you left me that night. I know I didn't have much experience, but was it that bad?" She bit her lip, anticipating his answer. Preparing for the worst. If he didn't answer at all, that would tell her everything she needed to hear.

She impatiently waited. He didn't move and didn't look lost in thought. He looked worried, sort of ashamed—just like when he confessed he was about to tell Snake Eyes what he wanted to know.

"I'm your brother's best friend."

"Sometimes you seem to forget that I was a third of that trio. I have no doubt that you were closer to Garrison, being guys and all." She popped his biceps with her fist. "We were close, too, you know."

"But I never made a promise to you not to sleep with Garrison."

"Oh, good grief. You slept with Garrison?" She knew what he meant, but couldn't help teasing him. He was so serious all the time. "Are you gay? Bisexual?"

"No! HELL NO! I meant that I..." Jesse squirmed. "You know what I mean. I swore to Garrison that I'd never sleep with *you*."

"Is that all?"

He could tell from her smile that she was ribbing her friend. She knew the answer and had definitely got blood pumping through him again. Life went on. No matter how dire their circumstances, he still enjoyed being with her and wondered if she felt the same.

Then she began laughing. Hard, holding-her-belly kind of laughing. "Oh, Jesse. You're such a goofball. He forced every guy that spoke to me to make that promise. Why do you think I had so little experience?"

Her laughter was infectious and had him going a bit until he asked, "Garrison chased off all your boyfriends?"

"Um...yeah." She laughed some more. "High school was horrible. You were there. What did you think he was saying to them while they waited at the door?"

"I never gave it a thought. You were always hanging around with us. I didn't date that much, so it didn't seem like a big deal."

"Maybe not to you." Avery's elfin-like face lit up. She feathered her bangs to the side. "You had a beautiful date for your prom."

He got the reference, remembering the sexy backless dress that she'd worn. He'd been very aware of how beautiful she'd been. And he could repeat the threats from Garrison about laying a hand on her. "Are you saying I wasn't handsome enough?"

"You wore boots."

"There was nothing wrong with wearing boots with a tux. Men do it all the time."

"Maybe you should have cleaned the hunting mire off them first."

"Hey, I was just a kid. Guarantee it wouldn't happen again. I'm more sensitive to those kinds of things now."

She pulled back, looking at him with a serious question in her eyes. Did she want to slap him because of high school? Wait. He hadn't been sensitive when walking out while she was naked in bed waiting on him to get over his panic attack.

He put his hand over his heart, wanting like a fool to get out of this conversation. "The rest of those guys may not have meant it. But I swore an oath. I don't go back on those."

"So what part of sneaking into corners and kissing on me for three months was keeping your promise?"

"I didn't promise not to kiss you."

"Aha. Manipulating the meaning of words. So you can't sleep with me. I guess you didn't swear not to touch me." Her eyes followed the direction of his hands, both casually dropped across her knees.

He shook his head and caressed the sensitive skin along the inside of her thigh just above her knee and back.

"I don't feel guilty."

Lying through his teeth. He was guilty, just not about touching her. He couldn't tell her the other half of the truth. The real reason he hadn't followed through on making love to her was that he didn't want her to be disgusted after she found out what he'd done.

The truth always had a way of coming to the surface. If he knew anything, he knew that as a fact. Coming clean would make him feel better for the few seconds it took her to utter the words that she never wanted to see him again. If she knew…that was what she'd say.

"Come here." They shifted and he pulled her close, encouraging her to rest her head on his chest and enveloping her in his hug.

It would break her heart to know the truth. He loved her too much to do that. Better to let her think he was a fool. Or a stand-up guy who couldn't lie to his best friend. Not one refusing to lie so she could have fulfilled her lifelong dream of becoming a Texas Ranger.

It was either her or her brother. That was what the choice had been. She'd see it that he chose her brother. And no one could blame her for interpreting the facts that way.

"Let me get you out of here, Avery. Right now before something else happens."

"What about catching this guy in the act? Isn't that why we're here?"

"How do you think that's going?" Jesse's heart might just beat out of his chest. All the feelings and thoughts while she'd been unconscious kept hammering at him. He should have done something sooner to save her.

"Probably about as good as you think it's going. But you have orders to try to catch this murderer alive. The attorneys need him to put away Tenoreno."

"Shoot, Avery. I can't follow orders at the cost of your life."

"And what about yours? Snake Eyes wants you dead as much as he wants me out of the picture. Besides, we're not even certain he'll come back."

Her chest expanded deeply and her warm breath escaped across his arm. It felt comfortable to have her where she was. If circumstances were different… They weren't. Two armed guards were on the other side of the old wooden walls, patrolling the house because they'd both been caught off guard.

Avery was right. Snake Eyes might not come back. What scared Jesse—yeah, he was scared—was that it was the first time anyone had seen the murderer and walked away. That in itself was bothersome. What if the killer didn't return? How long would they be forced to look over their shoulders?

"I'm glad you came in here to check on me. Thanks." She sleepily patted his chest. "Have I mentioned how tired I am? This is exactly what I needed. A friend to help me get rid of the nightmares."

"Or just plain worry." He rubbed her arm. The house seemed secure enough. Then again, they'd had a plan before Snake Eyes drugged them. "Will you consider getting someplace safer?"

"I'm safe right here." She yawned into his chest. "I hope you're okay sitting up the rest of the night, because I'm so…so comfy."

Her last words were barely audible mixed with a long yawn. She relaxed against him completely. She wasn't kidding about getting comfortable.

"I wish you'd let me take you out of here. You could join your mom and aunt." He spoke over her head. His arms held her tight. "Or you could sleep on my chest while I hold you all night…keeping you safe."

She was asleep. That last little bit of resistance was gone as she sank both lower and closer. He helped her roll over onto the pillows without waking. She curled one hand under her face, the other under her chin.

The second he backed away, Avery whimpered. He shifted the unused pillows to under his head, turned on his side and draped his arm across her body. She wiggled a little, getting closer, and continued sleeping.

Did she have any idea what she was doing to him?

Concentrating on his breathing, and not waking Avery as he did, distracted him from the arousal of lying next to her. Every memory of her naked in his arms sneaked between the rapid heartbeats, exciting him all over again.

The sure way to temper the desire was simple. When—not if—Avery found out what him sniffing around her last year had cost…he'd never be allowed back in her life.

It seemed like the way to go. Fast, easy, truthful… But not if he wanted her out of here. Safe. Away from the possibility of Snake Eyes returning to kill them…

"The problem is…" he whispered, spreading his hand across her abdomen when she jerked, already dreaming. "I'm not ready to let you go. So there's gotta be another solution."

Chapter Sixteen

"Did you hear me, Ranger? I said to knock until you wake them up. No, I don't want you to break down the door. Use your common sense."

Sore beyond thought and even more tired, Avery heard Dan's voice on her porch. The tap on the window would have been enough to scare her out of bed. But the heavy arm and light popping noise of the man sleeping soundly against her back had her checking to make certain she was still dressed.

"Thank goodness."

"Is someone knocking on the window?" Jesse asked with a voice full of sleep. He didn't budge.

Avery moved his arm off her midsection. "Dan's outside. He might have news."

Jesse rolled over, falling off the mattress to the floor.

"Avery, darlin'." Dan interrupted her laughter. "Sorry to disturb you, but I need to talk to you a minute. Then you can get back to whatever."

"We're not doing—" She pulled the curtain open, but her boss's back was to the glass. She started to raise her voice. "Oh, forget it. I'll be right there."

It was Jesse's turn to laugh. He pushed himself up from the floor, extending a hand once on his feet. Let him laugh. She'd straighten Dan out on the circumstances. Of course, it wasn't anybody's business, so she didn't have to bother.

She moved slowly to the couch. Much slower than Jesse, who had opened the door, let Dan inside and already headed to make coffee.

"I'm sorry to wake you up or…" Dan winked.

"Nothing was going on, even if it is my personal life." She felt her lips flatten, then tried to relax her face to look normal. "Is there news?"

"Want some coffee, Sheriff?" Jesse asked from the kitchen.

"Had my limit hours ago."

"Holy smokes, is it really four?" No wonder she was stiff. They'd been asleep for thirteen hours and had barely moved. That hadn't happened…well, ever.

"We figured you were both just sleeping, but I told everybody involved that I'd come by personally and check when you didn't answer the door."

Jesse joined her on the small couch after moving the folded linens. Dan raised an eyebrow and she shook her head. Jesse just grinned like an idiot and then frowned. "They must have found the kid who was shooting at us. Right?"

"Ten this morning. A motel over in Clayton, New Mexico. The maid found the body. No Jeep in the parking lot. And all the towels were missing."

"Knife?" she asked.

"Sliced him all the way to his spine." Dan shook his head. "People in Clayton didn't recognize him. They think he might have been part of the harvest crew. Same as the other two at Thompson Grove."

"I imagine they're canvassing the other motels," Jesse said.

Dan nodded.

"I'd like to see the crime scene. Who's got jurisdiction? Who's collecting evidence? Do I have time for a shower?"

"Hold on, Deputy. They're practically done. I've been there and back."

Jesse shrugged when she looked at him for backup.

"Mainly here to see how you're both doing. And to tell you that Bo will go get anything you need. Including a cot." Dan gave a fatherly glance in Jesse's direction.

"I'm good."

Dan awkwardly cleared his throat. "I bet you are. Think I'll have him bring by a cot anyway."

Avery was sufficiently embarrassed admitting to herself that the possibility of sharing a bed hadn't left her mind. "House arrest, then, huh?"

"Protective custody," Jesse corrected her. "I'm getting coffee."

"Before you step out…" Dan paused. "Here are some new phones, courtesy of the state of Texas. There's a couple of people expecting some calls from you both. Your personal phones and laptops will come back after they're checked out for tracers or hackers or traces of a hack. You know more about that stuff than I do."

"Working on the case will be harder without a laptop."

"Guess you'll have to do your detecting the old-fashioned way with pen and paper and tape."

"Maybe a whiteboard," Jesse said before she could.

"No one comes in or knocks on the door. That's the way this works. Just making certain you understand that those two rangers, Bo and me…that's it. If anyone else comes or calls—"

"Something's wrong," she finished for him.

"Is it better if we leave, Sheriff? I suggested it last night, but we didn't really have a chance to talk about it yet."

"The powers that be agreed for you to come back here. Here's good." Dan was matter-of-fact most days, but this wasn't one of them. "This is important, Avery."

"I know, sir. I wouldn't put anyone else at risk. Everyone at the office knows what's going on? They'll be careful? Work in twos?"

"We got it covered. We brought in extra help from Amarillo. I better be on my way so you can get on with your…um…breakfast." He looked toward Jesse. "Make a list. Bo will pick it up."

"Sounds good. And you'll copy the Clayton crime scene?" she asked.

"Got my word and the word of your Major Parker." He nodded at Jesse. "Nice fella."

"Yes, sir." Jesse politely excused himself with a motion for coffee.

"Just say the word and I'll put him up at the jail." Dan winked.

"Who told? Julie, I bet."

"Well now, you can't blame her for being forthcoming with information. This has all been on the exciting side of our lives." Dan leaned forward and took her hands in his. "You're very fortunate to be alive. You know that?"

"Yes, sir." She wouldn't let herself cry because Dan or the others in the office cared. It was natural, and she needed to do her job.

"You need these days to recover."

"You could say the same thing for Snake Eyes. They should check all the hospitals and clinics—don't forget veterinarian offices, but I don't know if they carry tetanus, which he'd probably want a dose of. That rake was pretty rusty and he might be worried."

"Make a list, Avery. You aren't shut out from the case. Speak with Major Parker. He's waiting on you to feel up to a debriefing." Dan stood. "I better be going for real this time." He got to the door and nodded at the shotgun. "That thing loaded?"

"Always."

"I'll add that to *my* list. You'll need a couple of weapons. Glock okay?"

"Sure. Please stay safe out there, Dan."

He left, and once the door was locked, he said, "Boys, you take care of my girl in there."

"Throw me in jail again?" Jesse handed her the coffee with a wicked grin. "If I go, so do you."

"No privacy, remember?" She sipped. "Are you ready to get started?"

"Not really. We've missed breakfast and lunch. I want to begin with those. Where's the food?" He'd leaned toward the door and spoke louder. "Isn't the state supposed to provide food?"

"Under house arrest two minutes and already complaining," one of the rangers said. "Whoever you send, choose something for us, please?"

Jesse affirmed.

"Thin walls," he mouthed at her.

"I'll have to remember to keep my voice down."

Jesse grinned like a man with a secret. "Coffee good?" he asked instead of stating the off-color remark she was certain had passed through his male brain.

"I'm going to shower. Alone," she said, loud enough for the ranger at the door. "But I'm starving. There's frozen hash browns and eggs."

"Guess that's my cue."

In spite of the headache, she managed to move quickly through a shower. She imagined all sorts of scenes in a sordid little motel in Clayton. With the spray adjusted to beat on her shoulders, she thought of hundreds of ways to collect evidence and crossed her fingers that it would be done correctly.

Normally, she wasn't good with anyone doing her work for her. If they were shut out of the case, she would probably go cabin crazy in a matter of hours. Her list of potential items grew. She'd have to give Bo her debit card to pay for everything.

She was reminded that she was really recuperating when she stepped from the shower and landed on the side of the tub. No thuds or screams or even an "oops." Jesse didn't rush to the door, so she didn't have to be embarrassed. But her hands were shaking until she weaved her fingers together and took a couple of trembling breaths.

No warning. Her legs just seemed to stop holding her for a moment. It seemed the shocks her body had tolerated had left her with a physical problem after all. She got dressed carefully and could only manage finger-combing her hair.

The smell of eggs and pepper hit her nose, and a migraine headache seemed to arrive without any warning. Her legs started shaking again, so she curled up on the couch and pulled Jesse's blanket over her.

"Still hungry?" Jesse asked, smoothing back her damp hair.

"Not really. Can I have that notebook and pen?"

He'd used it a couple of times, so she didn't have to use more words to be specific about where or what.

"You could rest instead of making a list." He handed her the writing tools anyway.

"I'm okay. I want to get a list written while it's fresh in my mind."

"I'll hold off scrambling your eggs, then."

She propped up the notebook and held the pen, but couldn't make it move on the page. The letters were there. She could see them. One at a time they danced around just like the numbers from the day before. She shoved the notebook to the floor and tossed the pen.

Of course Jesse looked at her from the small dining table in the corner. If their roles had been reversed, she'd be searching him critically, too. She'd have sympathy for him and the challenges he'd be facing.

"You're right. I'm too tired and think I need some aspirin." She pushed at the covers, but he jumped up and lifted a hand, indicating to wait. Water, aspirin, no pity and no "I told you so."

Jesse Ryder was a good man.

WYATT MCDONALD AND Kayden Cross were rotating shifts. One catnapped in the truck in the driveway, since they hadn't got a room yet. Jesse was very aware how often they changed out positions. He'd walked onto the porch only to be confronted and politely—yet firmly—asked to return inside.

Avery had been asleep about four hours. His first call had been to the doctor to see if that was normal. This was a woman who rarely slept six hours a night, so yeah, he was concerned. The doc had said he'd be more concerned if she wasn't.

The second phone call was to Major Parker. He'd gone to the back corner of the kitchen to place it. As far away from Avery as he could get. You could hear everything in this house. Small and compact. He hadn't meant to listen to Avery and the sheriff, but it had been impossible not to.

Dan didn't have anything to worry about. Jesse wasn't going to sleep with Avery when she was in this shape. But he also wouldn't sleep with her having a lie between them.

"Sir, I think you should reconsider adding me to the guard detail outside." He tried one more time to do something useful.

"If there's something wrong with your detail…"

"No, sir, nothing like that. It would just be easier with four-hour shifts split three ways."

"I'll reconsider it next week. Right now your rest is as critical as Miss Travis's. I have the doctor reports. Severe dehydration. Possible concussion. If you were here you'd be on leave at least a week. I doubt you'll have that long. Did you get the laptop?"

"They delivered it a half hour ago."

"I'll be back in touch in the morning with decisions on how we'll proceed."

"Yes, sir."

"Rest up. This isn't over yet."

Jesse wanted to throw the phone across the room. He didn't normally throw a tantrum. He wasn't the person in the room raising a ruckus or who questioned authority. Garrison had always been around to ask the questions and Avery had been close by to voice objections.

He missed their three-ring circus.

"Finally off the phone?" Avery asked from the table.

"I think I could eat those eggs now if you don't mind. Or we could ask Bo to pick something up from the diner if you need to sit awhile."

"I think I can handle scrambling eggs. I ate all the hash browns, though. Want this teakettle thing going?"

She leaned against the counter. "Eggs, tea and toast would be great."

"When did you start drinking hot tea?" He set to work. He could scramble eggs in his sleep and it was a good thing. Most of his attention was on observing Avery. She didn't look as pale as she had before she'd fallen asleep. She was resting her head in her left hand and not using her right nearly as much.

"Julie introduced me to it. Got me hooked, actually. She was concerned with the amount of coffee I consumed."

"I remember your mom voicing that a couple of times. I gave a list to Bo. He said he doesn't mind making another trip in the morning if I forgot something. I, um... had him pick up a puzzle and a card table."

"Since when do you work puzzles? You hate puzzles. We both do."

"I noticed..." Did he have to say it? She looked away. "The doc said a puzzle might help."

"Don't you think we have a big Snake Eyes puzzle to solve?"

He removed the eggs and scooped them onto a plate, handing them to her. She leaned back and let him set it on the table. "I'm just trying to help."

"Each time you call the doctor, he's probably telling Dan I need more time to sit here."

"If he doesn't I will. You can't go back on the job like this."

"What do you know? I'm fine, just tired." She took a bite and glared at him.

"Then use your right hand."

"I'm good."

He couldn't strong-arm her. She'd keep pushing until they were angry. He didn't want that. "Avery, please use your right hand."

She shook her head. "It feels like it's asleep and sort of disconnected. I…I just want it to be over."

"You need some time. Eat and try not to think about the case while I clean up." He pushed bread into the toaster. "I forgot your tea."

The knock in front saved him from making a complete fool of himself. It was on the tip of his tongue to tell her not to worry about anything. She could come home; he'd take care of her. *Those words would have been grounds to throw me out on my ear.*

"That must be Bo." He tossed the hand towel to the counter.

"I can see that."

"Right," he mumbled, opening the door. "Looks like he has everything on the list and then some."

"Hey. I got you two whiteboards. The bed frame was harder to locate. That's what took me a bit longer. It's about time she bought one." Bo, laden with paper and plastic sacks, pushed past him. His demeanor brightened when he faced Avery. "How you feeling?"

"Pretty good, Bo. We appreciate you doing all this."

"Beats waiting for speeders out on Highway 57. I better get the rest of the sacks."

"Let me help," Jesse offered, glaring at Avery when she got up and headed to the door.

"I got this. You aren't supposed to be out of the house. More than one person told me to keep you both indoors."

Jesse held the door and noticed Avery eating left-handed but stopping when Bo entered the house. Kayden stood on the corner of the porch obviously watching for movement—other than Bo coming in and out.

Bo brought in the bed frame and whipped out a multi-tool to put it together. Avery just rolled her eyes. She couldn't like rolling out of bed every morning instead of sitting on the side.

"I'm paying for it," he blurted.

"Oh, I know. And you can take it with you when you leave because you aren't using it while you're here."

"The thought didn't enter my mind."

"I bet it didn't." She took her plate to the kitchen. "Did you see the puzzle Bo got?"

"Popcorn. Colored popcorn. Sort of made me hungry. Maybe I'll add that to my list."

"All done," Bo said, wiping his hands. "I'll stop by around lunch tomorrow if you want me to pick you up anything from the Dairy Barn."

"Thanks," they answered together. He might have been a little oversensitive, but he got the impression Bo was only asking if Avery wanted her standing order for lunch.

It was totally dark by the time he finished putting everything away. The card table was stuck against the wall by the television after they'd moved the couch closer to the door. Cards, dice and a puzzle sat on top. But the main, clear focus for Avery was the crime-scene photos getting taped to the hall wall. First up were the photos from Clayton, then the picnic grove.

"You ready to look at all this?"

"I need to catch this sicko, Jesse. Are you?"

Chapter Seventeen

Five days, four nights sounded absolutely perfect for a vacation. All winter Avery had dreamed about five days on a sunny beach, baking to a crisp golden brown. The cold Panhandle wind had cut through her until she learned to buy pants a size bigger and wear long underwear.

Five days going on five nights stuck in the same sixteen hundred square feet was absolute torture.

Not that Jesse wasn't a perfect gentleman. He was. A perfect gentleman all the way. Considerate to the point of ridiculous. He let her use all the hot water for her shower. Always put the toilet seat down. He cleaned up after himself. And he slept on the cot.

After the first night when he'd held her close to him and she'd slept so soundly...nothing. Not so much as an accidental touch. Which was hard to do in a one-bedroom, no-dining-area, overcrowded cracker box.

Oh yeah, she was good and ready to be sent to the funny farm.

The window unit in the front room was working overtime. She'd kicked off most of the covers and the bedroom door was open wide. Spring had taken a turn toward summer today. She needed to install ceiling fans or buy a box fan. She'd lived here during only the winter, so she had no idea how hot the place got when it heated up outside.

"Avery?" her forced roommate called.

"Yes?"

"You're not asleep?" He was just outside the door and could have checked for himself.

"Too hot."

"Want to trade?"

"Quit being so damned nice!" she shouted. She was ready for a rousing discussion, excitement, a break in the case, some sighting of Snake Eyes or even a good old-fashioned fight with Jesse.

No workouts. She couldn't handle it if Jesse discovered just how dizzy she was all the time. She never knew when her hand or her leg might give way and she'd fall flat on her face... Everything had taken its toll on her. She needed a change.

"What was that for?" He stood in her doorway as pretty as you please with only his boxers. He had been standing in the hall.

"Do you remember that discussion about me *not* being your sister?"

"Yes." He crossed his arms, covering his muscles.

"Then why don't you have clothes on?"

"You got me, Avery. Why do people tend to not sleep in their clothes. Sorry. I'm tired of sleeping on that cramped cot. However I'm dressed doesn't matter." He did an about-face and left. "I didn't exactly bring pajamas with me."

"Sorry."

"Can't hear you," he bleated.

"All right, you can have the bed tonight and I'll take the AC." She gathered her pillows and turned right smack into his chest. She still wasn't 100 percent stable on her feet. His arms caught her before she wobbled.

Their eyes met. She hoped hers weren't shouting as loudly as Jesse's. His told her just how much he wanted her, like nothing else mattered but her. All in one close-up.

He swallowed hard.

She swallowed hard. "I'm good."

"I'm not."

This wasn't how she pictured their first real kiss after everything—that horrible night or Thompson Grove. She dropped the pillows as soon as his lips touched hers. Her arms circled his back, getting their fill of his bare skin. Tough-guy skin stretched tight across his muscles, yet smooth.

Jesse didn't wait to get reacquainted slowly. His tongue darted into her mouth, teasing her, making her want more of him. His hands circled under her backside and drew her closer to his...boxers. She wanted him, but he couldn't hide how much he wanted her.

His lips moved to her shoulder. He tugged the over-size T-shirt down and nipped at her skin. She tried to take a step back to the bed, but he trapped her closer. He kissed her faster, completely in control. Taking and not asking permission.

Man, did she love it. Her mind kept repeating "it's about time, it's about time." Her heart felt...everything. The firmness of his lips smashed the softness of hers and she didn't care. His hands kept a firm grip at her hips, but she longed for him to explore, to pull off her shirt and tease her breasts.

She backed up again, trying to let him know she was

ready for the next step. They could finally discover what they were like together. If he'd only…

She broke off his kisses. She hated to bring it up, but she also didn't want a repeat of their night in Austin. "I thought we were past the whole promise thing to Garrison."

"We are."

"Then if I want to be with you and you want to be with me… What's wrong with the bed?" She smiled as best she could, but something was wrong. "This feels like your party night all over again. But this time you're completely sober and unable to run away. Darn my overprotective brother. I could wring Garrison's neck, in a loving sisterly fashion, of course."

"It was never about Garrison."

"But you said…"

"Yeah. I thought I could do this. I wanted to have at least one night. Make love to you one time. You know, then I'd have memories."

"Are you dying? Even living as far apart as we do, we could still—" She inhaled so fast she choked on air but still managed to yelp out, "You're… You…you…you found someone?"

"No. Of course not. I would never do that to you. Do you really think I'd fool around if I had a girlfriend?"

"You aren't fooling around, Jesse."

She pulled the sheet off the bed and wrapped it around her. She felt vulnerable standing there braless, in PJ shorts, about to cry. Tears were in her very near future. He'd never seen that. Or at least not since ninth grade when her mother had forced her to stop trying out for football.

"Get out." Her voice was surprisingly somber, considering she wanted to scream.

"I need to tell you why I can't do this."

"I don't want to hear it." She kept her back to him as the first tear slid down her cheek. She tried to wipe it inconspicuously with a knuckle.

"I don't want to tell you, but that doesn't matter." He cupped her shoulders in his hands.

Hot skin to hot skin just made her burn for him more. She dipped a shoulder, attempting to free herself. He wouldn't let her go.

"It's nothing to do with your body or mind or anything like that. I want you till I ache, Avery," he whispered near her ear. "So bad it hurts. Every night on that cot has been hell, knowing you were here craving the same thing. I didn't want to do this to you. Or hurt you."

"What could be worse than humiliating me like this a second time?"

"I swore to myself I wouldn't put you into this position. If I just kept my distance, I'd never hurt you."

"I got news for you, Jesse. *This* hurts."

JESSE SWALLOWED HARD, needing water to wet his suddenly dry mouth. "It was me. Okay? I'm the reason you aren't a Texas Ranger. It had nothing to do with the fact that you're a woman. I mean, it did. That's the whole reason for me, but not *their* reason. It was my reason."

Avery turned to face him. He could see the wet paths her tears had made. She tucked the sheet under her arm and put her palms into her eyes. She slapped her thighs and sat on the mattress.

"I'm not quite following. You're trying to take the blame for me not being selected as a ranger. My being passed over wasn't because I was a woman, but it was wholly because I was a woman." She clapped her hands together and shrugged. "I can't possibly be mad at you, Jesse. At least not yet. I can't understand anything you've said."

"It made more sense inside my head when I planned it out. I think you're going to get mad. I just hope you can forgive me one day."

"Then I'll reserve the right for both."

"Let's sit in the living room, where it's cooler." Jesse took her hand and led her from the room. She slipped her feet under the swishing sheet wrapped around her. Then leaned on the arm of the couch, waiting for his explanation.

"Oh gosh, it's better in here. Now, what's this all about? Why am I going to be angry?"

"You see, the higher-ups at the highway patrol thought you and I were having an affair. Someone must have reported seeing us together, kissing. You know they have a strict no-fraternization rule."

"No one mentioned an affair to me."

"They didn't mention it to me, at least not first thing. But it's what instigated the situation they presented to me."

"Please stop trying to word everything perfectly, Jesse. Just tell me."

Explaining to her was difficult. Or maybe explaining by trying to make himself *not* look as guilty as he felt. Which wasn't the truth. She needed the truth before they could move forward in a relationship.

"All right. They pulled me into the office one day, reminded me of the rule, then said there were three candidates for two ranger positions. I had one. The next on the list was you. If I could swear there was nothing between us and wouldn't be in the future, then they'd send us to Waco."

"And your conscience wouldn't allow you to do that. I see."

"It was an impossible position to be put into. Garrison wasn't just my best friend. He was my partner."

"So you chose him."

"But I didn't choose. I didn't know Garrison was one of the three. Don't you see?"

"I see perfectly."

Could she? He couldn't swear that they weren't involved because he wanted to become completely involved with her. Did she understand? Why couldn't he just say what was in his head?

"I see that you couldn't lie to your boss, but you could lie to me." She stood, straightening the sheet, tucking it under her arm tightly like a wall of protection. "We were sneaking behind Garrison's back and hiding from everyone. As I recall, you kissed me. You started the whole thing. But what you really did was set me up. I should be wearing that badge. Not you. You never even wanted to be a ranger. Garrison pulled you kicking and screaming to the Texas DPS and...you went along for the ride."

"That's not—"

"Please don't. I'll finish this assignment with you. I'd be stupid to turn away your experience. You might be telling the truth about it being an innocent mistake. But you're right. I don't see how there can be anything between us if you felt like you had to lie."

Whether she was calm or not, she put on a good front

as she walked to her bedroom. "You've had to choose between me and Garrison for the last time."

She cried herself to sleep and he heard every tear.

JESSE HAD TO hand it to Avery. She was a professional in every sense of the word. Until she closed the bedroom door. For two nights, under the hum of the air conditioner in his ear, he could still hear the echoes of her crying.

He'd predicted her reaction and it was killing him that he'd been right. It might be killing him a bit more because he wanted to hold and comfort her. He hated being the bad guy. Never liked it when he was the robber to Garrison's cop. And he didn't like breaking the rules.

Yeah, he'd cleared his conscience, but he'd lost his best friend. *Professional* was the word of the day. Polite. Shared the coffee. Fix your own dinner—or get Deputy Bo to bring it to you. Then sit and laugh over a burger.

I am not going to be jealous of that kid.

Aw, hell, he was very jealous of the man who had just left after a painstakingly boring conversation. It had taken nearly an hour to update Avery on everyone in their county. Long enough to set Jesse's teeth to grinding.

"Dammit." It wasn't the conversation. It was her laughter. She wasn't smiling or laughing around him any longer. He caused her to cry.

Avery joined him in the hall. "I guess lunch is over. Where were we?"

"The DNA familial tie led us back to this guy." He tapped the latest picture on her bedroom door. "Father, grandfather or brother—we were trying to decide before Mr. Smiley Face showed up."

His dig didn't receive even an arched eyebrow from

her. She took the rushed DNA report from his hand and was reading it for the third or fourth time. He'd been staring at the thing for the past hour and hadn't made any headway.

Most likely because he'd been listening to how Julie chased Miss Wags through the yard with bubbles all over the little dog. Avery had laughed. Bo had laughed. Jesse had read the same paragraph six times.

"Ted Hopkins, aka T-Bone Hop, was covert ops in the '80s. So, yes, he could be any of those connections. But we'll never know. He's off the grid and has been for over a decade." Avery closed the file and stared at the photo. "Since Snake Eyes wore the hood hiding his face, there's no way to even compare bone structure for a possible match."

"Do you think it's a dead end? Maybe we get someone from headquarters to keep searching?"

She tapped her finger against the wall, thinking. "I believe our resources and energy are better used to analyze what he'll do. Even if we know who he is…our personal experience with him tells us more."

"Still no reports of anyone with abdominal rake wounds at hospitals in two hundred miles. They widened the search—"

"I don't think he'd use a hospital. He was obviously trained by someone. Maybe T-Bone Hop?" Excitement—real excitement—had returned to her eyes. "He was military and disappeared. What if he taught Snake Eyes his survival secrets?"

"So we're looking for a ghost."

"A ghost who got sloppy and left us alive." She turned her attention to thumbing through the file they'd printed.

"What if it wasn't sloppy work?" Jesse wondered.

"This man has been excellent working alone. No trace. Hell, no one really put together how many murders he's committed. He could have taken us anywhere, Avery. Why leave me untied? I can't stop going back to the very public place he left us. Why there? What good did it do *him*?"

"You mean why out in the open with a house a quarter of a mile away? Why involve a kid who could and seemingly did mess up his plan?"

"It's almost been a week and he hasn't resurfaced. Not even an attempt to finish us off."

"This man is a hunter. Remember, he called us his prey. He's patient. He lies in wait until the perfect opportunity." Avery dropped the file to the floor and put her palms over her eyes, concentrating.

"I don't think so. Yes, that he's a hunter, but he didn't wait for us to be alone before drugging us. He created a perfectly planned and executed trap."

She looked at him, excited. "So Thompson Grove was just a cog in the wheel he's turning to get to his real prey…my brother. But what did he expect to happen?"

"I need to talk with Major Parker." He pushed past her, taking a couple of the pictures down with him. "We recommended they move the witnesses."

Pure and simple panic ramped up his adrenaline. He grabbed his phone. Dialed. "Come on. Come on."

"If something had happened, we would have been notified. Right?"

Even during this moment of fear for Garrison and the men protecting him, he wanted to comfort Avery. His hand reached out to pat her shoulder. "Snake Eyes wouldn't do anything rash. He'd have a plan. He'd take his time to plan it. But he's had six days."

She pulled away from his touch. "You think he's going to act soon."

"Yeah. They should— Dammit, there's no answer. They should take extra precautions."

He wanted to smooth away the worry line on her brow. He wanted to swoosh back those crazy long bangs so he could see her eyes more clearly. But he'd lost the right to touch her. She wasn't his and wouldn't be.

"Jesse, he said he had a plan B. If he can't get the information from us, he thinks he can obtain it from somewhere else. But where? From who?"

"I know how to catch this bastard."

"What do you want to do?" She watched him dial the phone.

If the powers above him went for this crazy, half-baked plan, Snake Eyes wouldn't be a threat to anyone else. "We're leaving. Whether they know it or not, they're going to need us to finish this thing."

Chapter Eighteen

Snake Eyes to his enemies. Buster Hopkins to his family, but that was a long time ago. Of course, none of his family were left, so no one really knew him by that name any longer. Back when his dad was alive, they'd got several IDs from different states.

Although Snake Eyes fit him better than Buster, Carl, Sanchez or Nigel, he couldn't walk around in a thirty-year-old diving suit while in town. So for the moment Nigel Washington was checked into a five-star hotel in Austin. He couldn't imagine anyone visiting him in the camper owned by Carl.

After stitching his wounds and resting a day, he was living it up until his plans came to fruition. He knew how to play a role and that looks made all the difference. He'd exceeded his father's ability to blend in or hunt.

Today was the part of a potential campaign donor who was hard on crime. Yes, Nigel was a do-gooder, but he required a little proof in exchange for his monetary contributions. Dinner tonight would be interesting, eye-opening, in fact.

No, he laughed at his faux pas, this woman would keep her eyes. Information only. No one would realize who he really was or why he wanted to know details about Texas Mafia families. Nigel's looks were different than the killer Snake Eyes. They still wouldn't be traced back to him. The real him.

The computer system he'd breached prior to Rosco's death had been secured since his attack on Avery. Nigel's approach—money, love and blackmail—that normally found a vulnerable spot with anyone. The good Avery had made certain her mother and aunt were hidden away, so finding his prey required imagination now.

Dinner drinks would be quite amusing. There were so many ways to compel information from actual people. He stopped thinking about the steps needed for his venture this evening when Avery's pale face replaced the glass elevator zooming to his level. She seemed to push her way more and more into his thoughts.

Returning for the deputy and her ranger had consumed him the first two days after leaving them. He wanted completion. Needed their deaths. Desired another confrontation.

No one had attacked him like that before. It wasn't revenge, just more of a need. Finishing the job should come first. His reputation…that was all that should matter. When his last job was finalized, it could possibly be five-star hotels around the world.

What he should do and what his plan was…two very different things. Avery Travis fascinated him. She'd survived the collar and still fought back. She had a will to live that would be amazing to watch die. How much would it take to break her? His curious nature couldn't stop wondering what satisfaction would be gained from discovering that answer.

Yes, it would be a mistake to get sidetracked, but it was also a mistake to continue with the Tenoreno job that he wouldn't walk away from. He didn't need the money. He only needed to finish. Avery was only a part of the need to conclude his business.

Mistakes had delayed shutting the file on the Tenoreno family. His father would have been upset to find out how careless—or maybe arrogant—he'd been with his work. Which led to thinking about his father. That was probably because of the DNA they'd be processing.

Someone would discover who T-Bone Hop was and they might find out how he was related to Buster. But not to Snake Eyes. T-Bone had drilled it into Buster's childhood that he could be tracked through DNA. His father had left the navy a decorated hero, but his DNA was in the system. That was before he met the love of his life and before he killed her. Before he'd raised Buster to be a competent huntsman. Before Buster had surpassed his father's ability.

There would be no love of a lifetime for Snake Eyes or Buster. Love was for weaklings, for people who had nothing else to do other than conform to an everyday existence. He was above everyday anything.

He took a deep breath, jerked and remembered that he wasn't above making a bad decision. Scott. That cocky kid had been a mistake who caused Nigel's chest to hurt and brought Buster's father into the picture.

Finish the Tenoreno job and Snake Eyes would be gone forever. Perhaps Carl or Sanchez would take on a new lifestyle. He could try big-game hunting. He'd always wanted to hunt a tiger. That might be fun.

Leaving any of his identities behind would be strange. He'd been moving between them so easily for two decades. He liked living as them all. Snake Eyes was special. By being completely cloaked in black, he was able to tap into the hidden depths of his darkest curiosity.

The new prey arrived. They had a drink and conversation. But he changed his mind about dinner. He tossed down the three pictures he'd printed in his room. Three photos of a child playing at school.

"Where did you get pictures of my son?" the young woman asked.

"Anybody can park across the street from a school and click a few pictures. What's the world coming to?"

"What do you really want, Mr. Washington?"

"I need the location where a witness is being held. That's all."

"I might not have access," she said, her voice already filled with fright and cooperation.

"Sweet woman, I wouldn't be wasting my time with you if you didn't."

She shivered and began to cry.

Whatever he decided about Avery and her Texas Ranger, it wouldn't involve hiring another person for quite some time. He patted the stitches Jesse Ryder had caused. He needed to make certain that man was alive and suffering for days. He'd be his final kill. The one that he'd remember for his lifetime.

Chapter Nineteen

Avery had her bag packed sitting by the door with her daddy's shotgun on top. The files were stacked on the table. The cot Jesse had been sleeping on was upended on the wall by the puzzle table. Jesse had walked Dan through their conclusions. Then they'd both answered questions on a conference call with the State's Attorney's Office.

But they were still sitting here. Not being allowed to leave. Two Texas Rangers blocked the door and had taken their keys.

"I was right the first time. House arrest."

"Still protective custody," Jesse said pensively. "They haven't agreed that we're necessary for our plan. Even though we know this bastard."

"Can't a citizen refuse protective custody? Is there something I can sign?" She'd been reduced to walking her floor in as large a square as possible to make sure she moved.

"That means going against what they're all advising. If we leave, we won't know where Garrison's being kept. Won't know if Snake Eyes is following them."

She circled her arms and stretched them above her head. The button-down shirt wasn't ideal for optimum movement. She didn't care. She was dressed to leave as soon as someone came to their senses. "We'll know if he's following us."

"True. But if we're right and he's already in place, then we won't be allowed to help. Won't be a part of the solution. They could jail us to keep us out of their way."

"They they they they they." She pointed a different direction with each word to emphasize her frustration. "If you only knew how sick I was of hearing that pronoun. They this. They that."

Jesse ducked his head. She could tell he knew he was part of her frustration.

"Sixteen hundred square feet. Feels more like six hundred. Every day we're stuck in here feels like we lose footage." She stretched her arms over her head, wondering if there was anything else she could do. "I need to go for a run. Oh, wait, give me a punching bag. I need a serious workout."

She threw some air punches, feeling the tension in her shoulders. Not feeling any of the tingly leftover insecurity of being shocked. She was back. She turned to tell Jesse, then remembered that she was keeping it professional.

The only time she allowed herself to think about his confession was late at night…alone in her bedroom. It saddened her to be second best to her twin brother. Always. That was natural. Or at least she hoped it was natural and that she wasn't just being an insecure child.

The reason she cried? She missed her friend. Sure, she wanted more. But truth be told, if nothing else had developed between them, she'd never imagined her life without Jesse in it. Even during the past eight months while she'd been upset with him…he was there.

Idiot. He's still there. Sitting right there. What would you have done? *Lied?*

"During the conference call, didn't someone ask why you were still here in Dalhart?"

He shrugged. "Maybe."

"You're in a mood. I just wanted to say that you don't have to stay here and babysit me. I already have two rangers outside the door." She raised her voice and Wyatt didn't move from leaning on the porch post. "You could take all that work to Company F. Let them validate, analyze or whatever you guys do. The state's attorney might believe us then and do something about the threat."

"And you'd stay here doing what?"

"I have a popcorn puzzle. I'm good for three days." Okay, she'd offered an olive branch and he had to recognize it wasn't poison oak. He had a look.

Oh my goodness.

He had a look, all right. It simmered and made her bubble to a boil. She was standing in front of the air conditioner. She knew it was working but could swear she was heating up like a kettle. No hot jasmine-blossom tea for her. "Want some iced tea? I think I need a glass to cool down. Something chilly."

"Sure."

She escaped to the kitchen. Standing at the sink, she stared mindlessly out the window until the tea steeped. The pitcher was ready with a tray of ice and a cup of sugar. Two glasses poured. Her hands were around them and she couldn't move.

"I've been thinking."

She jumped so hard the tea seemed to hop from the top of the glasses.

"I didn't mean to scare you." His deep rich voice comforted.

She grabbed a dish towel, dabbed at the counter, then lifted the glasses. "I was just thinking. My fault."

"So was I. And you're right. I should go back to Waco. My job's been done here. I've been off my mandatory week. I should get back to work." He took his glass, steadying her fingers, keeping them wrapped gently within his.

The man's eyes were just incredible. He had a quiet strength. A mixture of confidence and concern that set her up for instant attraction. And when he smiled, he changed his chiseled features into a movie-star grin.

"There's not a reason to stay if you're mad or if I'm just going to continue to upset you." He wasn't smiling and still had a magnetism she didn't understand. No other man made her feel this way.

"I...um... I... Dammit, Jesse. I stopped being angry ten minutes ago. I don't want to lose your friendship."

Jesse pulled her to him, his fingers across her lips stopping her words. The tea she held spilled between their bodies. "I'm not just your friend, Avery. And I most definitely do not think of you as my sister."

The smoldering look he gave from her eyes to her lips devoured her before really kissing her. His fingertips were smooth across her lips while his thumb tipped her chin. He lowered his mouth and that was all she could see as she watched his lips take possession of her.

Soft, long luxuriating kisses. Then his thumb trailed down her throat. Shocks ran through her body, pleasant palpitations that had her pulse racing harder than any workout she remembered. His mouth followed the nails he scraped along her collarbone. He nipped, skimmed, then licked. She could only watch and...feel.

One arm encircled her back, bending her slightly so he could have more access. His free hand unbuttoned her shirt, one excruciatingly slow button at a time. Her knees weakened when his lips skimmed the top of her breast.

Sometime along the way, Jesse's skilled hands had untucked her shirt. Unbuttoned, he pushed it back to her elbows. His thumbs slipped higher under the edge of her bra, brushing skin, slowly advancing until the fastener released, giving him carte blanche.

Had time stood still or was Jesse memorizing every freckle she had? Her world went from slow motion to fast-forward. Jesse pushed her shirt off and tugged her arms free from the bra. When his lips and tongue circled her nipple, she stumbled backward with the sparks of delight.

Glass cracked under their boots, taking them both by surprise. "The tea glasses. I should clean— Oh…maybe… not…"

Jesse took advantage of the small space between them and sucked, alternating between her breasts until both were puckered and more alive than ever before. He worked his way back up her neck, then kissed her mouth, consuming any doubts she had.

"Might get dangerous if we stay in here." He lifted her in his arms, walking across wet glass and her favorite lacy bra. Her arms went around his neck and tugged his face back to hers.

She hoped that the curtains were still closed or the ranger on the porch was going to get an eyeful.

JESSE CAUGHT AVERY'S chest to his as they left the kitchen. He protected her from the window, locked lips, then realized he'd frozen that way while walking around the corner and into her bedroom.

They broke apart and laughed when he set her on the bed. He tilted his head to the porch. "You're going to have to keep the wildness down. Remember, there's someone listening for trouble."

Avery was wide-eyed innocent. He had no idea how much that "little experience" that she'd referred to actually meant.

"You know, I'm usually good with words, but around you it's like there's no connection to my brain." He unbuttoned his shirt as she tugged the sheet loose from under the pillows. He had no intention of letting her cover up the perfection he was gazing upon. But he was also so dang nervous he didn't know how to prevent it.

His mind was blank of ideas. He got to the last button and dropped his hands to his sides, totally in awe. That was what he should tell her.

"You are the most beautiful person I've ever known, Elf Face. Completely beautiful all the way through." He leaned on the bed and feathered her hair away from her jade eyes.

He stretched out next to her, kissing every inch of skin he could reach. Gently pulling the sheet to the side, he lightly drew circles and skimmed her breasts with his fingertips.

"Jesse?" She tugged his shirt off. "Why in the world do you call me Elf Face?"

There was no rush as their hands explored the other. "Remember when you got your hair cut?" he whispered. "Your mom was having fits, but my mom said it fit your elfin-shaped face. I thought it was cool...at least at the time. I might have been into a couple of movies that had elves. I know the nickname irritates you."

"No it doesn't. I could never let you know, but I sort of liked it."

His circles continued across her flat stomach to the top of her jeans. They were loose on her hips, enough that he could get the button through the hole one-handed.

"You sure about this?" He paused with his hand on the zipper pull.

"I swear, Jesse. If you stop…you won't walk out of this room alive."

Sexual frustration was something he was familiar with. He didn't question what they were doing any longer. This was right for them both. He unzipped her jeans and she unzipped his, hesitating only a second with what was hiding behind the cloth.

He brushed his hands up her thighs to her hips.

Skin to skin. Finally. He'd been dreaming about this since they'd crept into the dorm after a late-night party. There had been something about that night. Something different in the way she'd looked at him all bright-eyed and ready.

The same way she was looking at him…right now.

"Well?" she whispered.

"I can't stop looking."

"But you've seen it before." Her fingers searched for the edge of the sheet.

"No, ma'am." He shoved the cover away from her. "I want to remember this. Broad daylight. No alcohol involved. And no regrets for either of us."

"I can go with that." She skimmed a fingernail on the outside of his thigh, mimicking in her own way.

Jesse stretched out next to her, loving that she matched

him inch for inch. No one ever had. She was the only woman he'd ever looked at eye to eye when he was standing. The only woman he wanted.

Kissing her was something he should have been doing all his life. He shouldn't have avoided their attraction. He shouldn't have listened to Garrison all those years.

Part of the hesitation came because Avery was important to him. No second-guessing now. They had an instinct when they worked together. They meshed even when they were angry at each other.

The slow burn of kissing soon built into a wildfire of sampling every part of her. Touching her brought her to life. He loved seeing how skimming her skin sent shivers throughout her. Kissing her skin and tasting her made his blood run hot.

Intimacy with her was taking him to a new level of sensuality. He didn't want to rush, but waiting was infinitely painful.

"I swear, Jesse, I'm as flammable as I was days ago. Dammit, do something." Her nails dug into his arms.

He reached for the nightstand. The first night he was here, he'd seen the condoms. A small discreet unopened box shoved in the back.

"What are you grinning at?" she asked when he paused.

"The box is open."

"Would you do whatever you need to do and get this over with?"

"Believe me, Elf Face, this isn't going to be over for a long while. No matter how much *I* want it to be. I'm going to make certain of that."

Powerful and concentrated. That was how he would describe the way Avery watched him. But before he could move to join her, she took him in her hands.

He could die right there in her bed. Maybe he did a little. He shuddered with her gentle caress and almost made a fool of himself. He'd had no idea that her feeling the weight of him would be his undoing. If he was going to make good on…

He slid the condom into place with shaking hands. Caught himself breathing deeply in an effort to slow his blood. This was Avery. His Avery. She might think that she wanted quick until he showed her slow. Their lips met for a second or two and then he kissed her jawline, up to her ear and then down the column of her neck. She was trying to tug him on top of her, using those long legs to lock her ankles behind his back.

Jesse found Avery's wrists and, in one motion, pinned them to the bed above her head. "There's no rush, babe. We've got nowhere to go."

Avery bucked underneath him. "Please, Jesse, no more waiting."

His lips skated to the pulse beating at the base of her throat and continued down her rib cage. It was difficult to stay focused when Avery was hell-bent on fast and furious. Her hips thrust upward, trying to make contact with his.

He wanted to touch her breasts but couldn't trust her to keep her hands to herself. "Jess—ee." She said his name on a groan as his lips grazed her nipple.

He loved hearing the catch in her voice. Loved knowing that she wanted him as much as he wanted her. He licked one nipple before gliding his tongue across her chest to taste the other one. Her legs loosened from around his waist.

"I need to touch you," she said. "Not fair."

He nearly laughed, but knew it would break his concentration. If he thought too much about how he could have taken her, could have satisfied both their needs in less than two minutes, he'd already be inside her.

But this wasn't just sex. This was his chance to explore every inch of her body knowing she wanted him just as badly. Her chest arched against his lips and he released her hands. Wanted to feel her touch against his skin.

Wanted her. Now. "Avery." Her name felt like a prayer and he wasn't sure if he was saying it out loud or only in his head. He found her lips, kissed her as her hands gripped his arms.

He entered slowly and made her completely his. They quickened their pace with even strokes. None of their past would get in their way. Her hands gripped his arms as their bodies became one. Their bodies burned, climbed and met thrust for thrust. She wrapped her legs around his, opening to him, keeping him meshed with her.

With a few frenzied moments, they both cried out in fulfillment. Shuddering for real, he made a connection he'd never had. One that Avery might not understand.

The woman, the girl, the best friend, the partner-in-crime... She was his lifeblood. His for keeps. He loved her with his heart, body and soul.

Convincing her, on the other hand, was going to take careful planning. Or maybe for once he shouldn't censor himself, because it never seemed to work with her anyway.

Chapter Twenty

Avery flung her arms wide, one falling on Jesse's chest, patting him with the back of her hand. Totally, 100 percent exhaustingly satisfied…that was her.

"Oh. Wow." She had never experienced anything so complete. "That was better than amazing."

Who cared if she inflated his big ego? It didn't really matter. The truth was the truth. "I think I'm going to re-gret every minute we spent *not* doing this while we were stuck inside this house. Wow."

Avery finally caught her breath and propped herself up on one elbow. Jesse remained flat on his back, his chest still visibly rising and falling. She drew circles in a per-fect amount of chest hair and fell silent. She'd been the only one talking. He hadn't mentioned anything about it being the best sex he'd had.

Or how good she was.

Looking at him, at the sheer power she'd felt with each thrust of his hips, she wanted him all over again. Then the awkward "after" moment began. She rolled to her back, reaching for the sheet to cover her nakedness. And maybe his if she could manage it.

His arm crossed over her body, stopping her from moving.

"You taste like sweet tea," he finally said.

"That's because you spilled it all over us with the first kiss in the kitchen." *That* was all he could say?

Here she was, sharing from her heart about how wonderful he was as a lover, and he wanted to talk about the tea on her skin? He laced his fingers through hers, then pulled their hands to his chest.

"I love you."

"Is that normal pillow talk? It's really not necessary if you want to do this again." Did he think she needed to hear that to feel better about herself or them together? She didn't.

If the words had been true, he would have picked a better time to let her know. Or even looked at her when he told her.

"I thought—"

"Stop thinking." She moved her lips to his chest. "You taste a bit like tea, too."

She'd ignore this lie. It was probably just the heat of the moment. Something he thought she needed to hear. Jesse was just like every other guy. So what? They were still stuck here together and should enjoy the time.

"Avery, I—"

This time she raised a finger to stop his words. She was a grown woman and didn't need them. "Shh. There's only one thing I need to know. How soon can we do this again?"

THE FLOOR WAS clean from the tea and broken glass. So was her skin after a long shower. Jesse seemed sort of quiet, though…even for him. They'd made love again. She'd imagined feeling this way.

Life had a strange way of making things happen. She

and Jesse had been so close all these years. She'd been head over heels for him on so many occasions that she'd let other guys and opportunities pass her by.

Now this.

She was putting the mop away and heard banging on the door. Before she could run to the front, Jesse answered wrapped in a towel from his shower.

"What now?"

Kayden handed him a phone. "Major Parker's been trying to reach you."

The phone was up to his ear. He stood in the open door for all her neighbors to see his bare-chested glory. Not to mention the look on Kayden's face that said he was slightly embarrassed.

Thin walls.

"I got it. We'll leave immediately." Jesse returned the phone, acknowledged Kayden with a nod and shut the door. "Ready to get out of this town?"

"They're going with our plan?"

"Sounds like it. There's a plane waiting to take us to Fort Worth as soon as possible." He didn't look at her.

In fact, he frowned, covered his eyes with his free hand—the hand that wasn't wrapped in the edge of the towel, keeping it in place. Was he worried about her seeing something? Hadn't they—

"Avery, about what I said earlier."

"Don't think a thing about it. I didn't take you seriously, so we're good. Really. Don't waste any more time on it."

Jesse shook his head. "I need to get dressed."

Had she said something wrong? What was bothering him? She'd forgiven that he'd spoken honestly about their relationship before he became a ranger. She'd forgiven that he'd misspoken in the heat of passion.

She wanted to play it cool. She didn't expect anything from him.

"Are you upset because you broke your word to Garrison? I promise I'm not ever going to tell him." She raised her voice a little so she could be heard through the door.

His reply was several curse words at himself. Not her...definitely himself.

"I have no idea what to do." She wasn't certain he'd heard her or not. She walked away to sit on the arm of the couch. Her bag was packed. Things were put away.

The little house was perfect for her. Her life in Dalhart was good. Without Jesse living here with her, it would feel big here again. *And lonely.* But she'd manage.

Jesse was dressed this time and clean shaven. There was a nick on his chin where he'd cut himself. Probably the source of his four-letter-word vocabulary. He grabbed his bag and the files, pausing at the door.

"You really bringing your dad's shotgun?"

"You can transport it on the plane. Right? I'd really like it there." If the State's Attorney's Office had approved the plan to try to trap Snake Eyes, she was a much better shot with her daddy by her side.

"That's not a problem." Another simple nod to Wyatt and Kayden and they were on both sides escorting her to the car. Then they were the armed escorts on the drive to Amarillo.

After their afternoon, Avery was full of energy—exhausted, good energy. Why was it so different for Jesse? He put his hat over his eyes and pretended to sleep for the hour to Amarillo.

There was no way he'd stay asleep without relaxing

a little. She'd witnessed it over and over during the past week. Nap-time features were totally different than the closed-off, tightly wound man next to her.

The newly topped road was smooth and steady. She made notes of things that could go wrong. Possible scenarios. The one thing that would help would be to know the location of the safe house. Then variables would be limited and she could present a finalized plan.

They arrived at a private hangar. Jesse even yawned a couple of times for show. *Smile. Please.* She wanted him to confess what was wrong. If he withdrew like this every time after seeing her naked, she was going to end up with a complex.

Calling on the fact that they were lifelong friends, she decided to speak to him before they boarded. "Stick out your tongue."

"What?" He looked at her almost as strangely as after getting the call from Parker.

"Just do it."

He hesitatingly obeyed.

"Dab your finger and wipe the dried blood from your shaving nick."

He obeyed. "Why didn't you just say that to begin with?"

"You're welcome. Now are you going to tell me what's wrong?"

"Nothing's wrong." They leaned on the car, waiting for the crew to tell them to board. "Drop it, Avery. You want to talk about Dalhart, your job, the long drive to nowhere... I can accommodate those subjects. But right now everything else is off-limits. Do you understand?"

"Of course. I understand English. I also understand that we're not supposed to talk about particular plans in a public venue or even on this private plane. I get it. What I don't understand is how you went from a very cool friend with benefits to a complete a—"

"Good evening and thanks for flying with us."

The flight attendant had interrupted her at an appropriate time. They sat. They belted up. They took off and landed in silence.

JESSE'S THOUGHTS SHOULD be occupied with their plan. Details, how to act, potential pitfalls. But no. He was staring at the woman across the table from him. In a room with some of the best law enforcement in the state—he could hardly hear them.

One hand mindlessly spun a ballpoint pen on the oak table. The other propped up his head, sort of like being exhausted from a long stakeout. Neither was true.

Maybe the answer was a very exasperating woman.

"Have we had any luck tracking down a mailing address for the contacts?"

"We have our people looking, but it's a long shot. Some of the companies are overseas. The field is so wide. We can't even narrow it down to one state," Avery said.

They had been invited to participate in a planning session. A secret meeting in Fort Worth in some law offices he'd never heard of—a friend of one of the men barking out orders. Jesse half listened, slumped enough in his chair that he looked like an uncaring slouch.

He knew this was a time he should be impressive with knowledge and skill. If he hadn't known it when they walked into this conference room, the darting glares from Avery were stressing that he appeared like a kid who didn't want to be in church.

The chatter at the front of the room became more and

more about the traditional way to fend off an attack on witnesses. Escorts. Routes. Secrecy. Limited resources.

"The hell with this." The pen bounced across the wide table right into Avery's breakfast roll.

"Do you have something to say, Ryder?" the lead prosecuting attorney asked.

"It might get me kicked out of this room, but this isn't the plan I was told we'd be executing. You're asking Avery—Deputy Travis—to put her life at risk again for—"

"Hold on, Jesse. You don't speak for me." She spoke on top of him, even after his own glare at her to keep quiet.

"—for nothing. We've already been toe-to-toe with this bastard. Don't you think we know a thing or two? You had a profiler look at some pictures. I gave Snake Eyes a bloody nose and stabbed him with a rake." He pushed the rolling chair a little too hard when clearing the table to stand.

"We get the picture, Jesse," Parker said from behind him.

"I don't think they understand this killer at all, sir. He's nothing like what we've encountered—"

"Enough." The major said the word softly and laid a hand on Jesse's shoulder.

It took the steam from his actions and put his brain back in control. Avery sat straighter in her chair, fingers over her lips. When she caught his eyes, she silently shushed him.

He shook his head. "I won't be quiet. This guy is everything your profiler says but more. He's calm in a fight. Things went wrong and he didn't panic. He didn't yell. Didn't run. He's a planner, not a reactor. It was like he had a contingency for everything."

"This procedure has been proven to draw out threats," one of the men said. "Especially assassins."

"And that's exactly why it won't work with Snake Eyes," Avery spoke out. "I—we—respect how you're drawing your conclusions. But this man isn't just an assassin. He's more like a serial killer who's learned how to make money at what he loves."

"Good description, b—Deputy." He'd just come very close to ruining their credibility by calling her "babe." "He's got a plan."

"And we believe we figured it out," she added.

"What do you think, Major Parker?" the lead guy asked.

"I think they're right. We have a possible way to catch this guy. The information these two have given us over the past week has connected at least eleven murders from different states. And those are just the victims we discovered." Parker relaxed against the wall, totally at ease, arms crossed. "You should hear them out."

Jesse took note of the major's relaxed, authoritative posture while the men argued at the front of the room. Jesse was normally the laid-back guy, but these men hadn't stared into the eyes of a soulless reptile. It was more than that. The bastard had held a gun on the woman Jesse loved. He'd electrocuted her until her heart had stopped.

Looking at her now, no one would know that she'd died for a few seconds a week ago. She was a confident, strong Amazon. If she wasn't carrying a badge and gun, they might have taken her for a model. But there was a badge. More than one gun.

God, I love her. How can I make her see that?

"Major, we need to keep our witnesses alive. Understanding that the outcome rests completely on your shoulders, what plan do you want us to hear?"

"Go ahead, Ranger." Parker nodded.

"Right. We know Snake Eyes had a backup plan to discover the location of the witnesses being held in protective custody," he began.

"We also know that your state office computers were breached three weeks ago," Parker said, taking a seat at the table.

"No one told us about this," the attorney blustered.

"We didn't know until the attack on Travis and Ryder." Parker nodded to Bryce Johnson to distribute material. "Their abduction prompted a check of the system."

"That might have been his original plan B that he mentioned. Security was tightened and he's punting." Jesse caught the pen that skidded across the table from Avery. He also noted the tilt of the corner of her mouth.

"This is all just a theory." Came from the front of the room.

"Supported by the fact that Snake Eyes hasn't been seen or taken any action since our confrontation." Avery was a professional who knew her facts. She could handle the lead attorney. "So we asked ourselves, what did the man want? To kill? He'd just killed four people in two days. So no. It was pride."

"Ego. Serial killers can be caught through their egos," said one of the analysts who worked for the state.

The attorney's palms were flat on the table. Then he began tapping his fingers. Was he waiting for a pause in their explanation to respond or a flaw in their reasoning?

It didn't matter. If the state wanted to draw Snake Eyes out with their worthless plan, he'd throw Avery over his shoulder and resign. They'd contact Garrison and protect themselves the old-fashioned way. But they could catch this madman. He knew it. They just had to convince the six people sitting at this table.

He imitated his boss with relaxed self-confidence. "Snake Eyes threatened Avery to get the information he needed. When I showed up, I made it easier for him because of our long-standing friendship. When it didn't work, there was only one modification to the plan that he needed to make. Find another target."

He finished, flattening his palms on the table, too. A symbolic gesture that all his cards had been played. He didn't look at the attorney making the decisions. He looked at the woman who had stolen his heart and wondered how he was going to keep her alive while they trapped a serial assassin.

Chapter Twenty-One

Waiting was the hardest part. It was day two at the address leaked to nonessentials. The house was perfect for a trap. The plan was to lure Snake Eyes inside the house. Unless he attempted murder, they might not get more than trespassing. They needed a DNA sample and needed a crime to compel one.

Limited access in or out at the end of a cul-de-sac. There was an empty house across the circle where backup could stay and keep watch. It felt like a fishbowl, and yet she was so nervous she had trouble thinking straight.

Pacing the house wearing a blond wig and bulletproof vest, she passed in front of windows exposing herself to sniper fire. As long as he didn't take a head shot, she might only get the breath knocked out of her.

"I thought for certain they were going to kick you out of that meeting the other day." Avery had been full of excitement as they walked into the hotel. They'd won. They were setting a trap for Snake Eyes.

But could she face him? This wasn't the first time she'd had a moment of doubt creep inside her that she wouldn't be able to do it. Then again, if she didn't have that fear, she'd be more worried.

"You convinced them a little too well." Jesse had the

shotgun on his hip, leaning against the inside wall by the television.

"What do you mean?"

"There are other cops or rangers who could pose for Kenderly Tyler. It doesn't have to be you." He shook his head. "We could still bring someone on board to take your place."

"This is my case." She fingered a see-through curtain panel, pulling it slightly to the side to view the street. Nothing. Not even a street lamp in this new housing division.

"You've been through a lot."

"Haven't you?" She didn't blame him for doubting her. It did sort of hurt, though. She wouldn't want to work with anyone else. "Are you worried I'll fall apart or something?"

"Of course not."

"You're lying, Jesse Ryder."

"Of course I'm worried about you. But not that you can't do your job." Jesse cupped her shoulders.

Should she? Should she kiss him or even go to bed with him right now? Wow, that answer was a definite *of course not*. They were on the job and the idea shouldn't have even popped into her brain. But it had. And she would.

Her hands lifted to his cheeks and she drew his lips to hers. A gentle touch, firm, a little rough around the edges because he hadn't shaved that morning. His hands skimmed her shoulders, then her neck and into her hair.

She was next to him but wanted his body closer. She broke her mouth free. "We don't have time."

"We do if we hurry." He swooped in for another assault on her senses.

"Would you be thinking about making love to *me*? I have a lot of mixed images in my mind. I'm not really sure I can concentrate." The photos of murders popped into her head. She shivered and started pacing again.

"Who said timing was everything?" Jesse was dressed like her brother. He'd even ridden a motorcycle from Fort Worth and parked it in the garage. "I'm sure Garrison will appreciate what you're doing for Kenderly."

"I'm not doing this for Garrison. Or his girlfriend."

"Fiancée," Jesse corrected her. "He told us on the phone that he'd asked her. This isn't up for debate."

"He's marrying a woman we haven't even met after knowing her a couple of weeks. Don't you find that odd? I also find it very hard to believe that he'd settle down after so many." She stopped, and Jesse motioned her to keep moving. She did. "It's completely unrealistic that the witness would be moving in front of the window *all* the time." She went to the drapes and pulled them closer together. Anyone watching could see her silhouette because the light was on behind her.

"We agreed that we'd stop at eight thirty-five. So you have five more minutes."

She twisted her hands, flipped the long hair of the wig off her sweaty neck. "This thing is so hot. I don't miss long hair at all. It weighs a ton."

"Yep."

He agreed with her, just as he had the other twenty times she'd complained about it. She needed to stop but was afraid he'd want to really talk.

Laughing off that he'd said the *L* word... She still didn't know if that was good or bad. She hadn't determined if he wasn't talking to her because they'd simply been too busy getting this sting operation organized. Or because he didn't have anything left to say. Or it was a slim possibility—yet highly unlikely—that he'd actually meant it.

She wished it was the highly unlikely scenario. Loving him was second nature to her. But after their conversation about Garrison and the promise, she didn't want Jesse to feel obligated to say he loved her.

"Time."

Jesse turned the lights off. Turned the TV on. They both sat close on the couch as if they were Garrison and his girl, Kenderly—the second witness for the Tenoreno case.

"You have your second Glock on your ankle?"

"Do you?"

"Don't hesitate, Avery. You pull the trigger and don't think about taking this guy alive." He pointed his finger toward the kitchen doorway, then imitated pulling a trigger.

"We need him alive. You know we do. Everyone has emphasized—"

"I don't care. We both know what he's capable of. If he's gotten past the security outside, it means we don't have any backup close enough to help." Jesse squeezed her hand. "No matter what you want to think or hope, no one will get here in time if he gets near you."

"You are so full of optimistic enthusiasm. That was sarcasm, in case you didn't recognize it." She searched his expressive eyes. He meant what he'd said. "Jesse, I'm not sure about just pulling the trigger. I mean, we're law officers. Deadly force is a last resort. Promise me."

He watched the game and didn't answer. He'd said before that he kept his promises. By not giving his word about this…he was sort of promising he would shoot first.

It didn't matter. After everything they'd been through, she knew he'd do the right thing.

The TV could barely be heard. The house they'd chosen had basic cable and they were watching a previously broadcast Major League Baseball game. The organ played. The crowd yelled, "Charge."

And nothing happened.

"We can't do this much longer. Two days is sort of my limit to be stuck inside again. Are we sure that he obtained this address?"

"Relax, Avery," Jesse whispered. But when he dropped his hand on her thigh, she bolted off the couch.

"I need a shower."

"Not unless you want me in there with you." It was obvious that he meant it. "I don't think the vest is that waterproof."

She returned to her assigned seating, tugging on the protection she wore that he'd refused. "Don't read anything into that. I'm not afraid of you, just jumpy."

"Right."

"Do you think this will work?"

"Last chance."

Leaping out of her skin hadn't stimulated the conversation. To prove she wasn't afraid of his touch, she rested her head on his shoulder. Her eyes got heavy. She had dozed several times, hearing different high points of the game. Then it was two different teams playing.

This time when her eyes opened, more than her head was hot. Jesse had his hand over her mouth. She lifted his fingers away when she realized he wasn't looking at her. His focus was on the rear window.

A shadow.

This is it.

They had elected not to use outside electronic surveillance just in case Snake Eyes was watching the area. No panel van or utility vehicle was anywhere near the place. The team was just down the street, a phone call away from saving the day. With the hacking ability their target had shown or hired, she'd talked them out of video cameras in the corner of every room.

Jesse texted a message to Major Parker. The phone vibrated with a message that the shadow they'd seen was not one of the rangers stationed on the perimeter. Everyone outside was ready.

The stakeout team listened to them through their phones. Undercover units did this all the time. Let the screen go black and no one could tell it was on. Both their phones were activated, recording.

The clock was ticking.

"I'm tired. Are you ready for bed?" She opened her eyes wide as she delivered her preassigned dialogue.

His response would be... "I think I'll shower and work this kink out of my neck."

"Meet you in bed, then," she answered.

The television went off and everything was eerily silent. Jesse stood and stretched out his hand, pulling her into his arms. "Shoot him. As much as you'd like to take my head off...just make sure it's him you're aiming at," he whispered, then kissed her forehead.

Snake Eyes wouldn't take them by surprise. They could do this. They were prepared. Avery went to the bedroom and heard the shower turn on. She set the dummies under the covers and took her place in the dark corner. Phone in her pocket, she wanted to talk to the men who had her back. It was better if she let them concentrate on their jobs.

The plan was to have the men guarding the perimeter meet, and instead of immediately turning around, they would carry on a conversation for a few minutes. It would give Snake Eyes an opportunity to breach the house without killing the men.

Shoving off the hot wig, she let it fall to the floor and pulled her Glock, wishing it was a "make my day" .44 Magnum that she held instead. The recoil would have been murder, but if Snake Eyes got that near to her...

Could she kill him as Jesse had instructed?

Could the man she cared for more than any other really want her to? She heard the shower start up.

The Glock rested between her knees from her cut-off corner of the house. She'd set her phone on the nightstand. Over there she had less chance of accidentally disconnecting if she was in a fight.

She sort of wished for the comfort of it in her jeans pocket. *No, stay put and concentrate.* There was no one to protect except herself. At least for the moment. She rested her shoulders propped against the corner, but she wouldn't last long in this position.

Someone *oofed* as they ran into the coffee table in the television room. Their target must have hired another accomplice. She couldn't imagine the professional killer they had set a trap for bumping into a table.

The next sound was a curse word in a familiar voice. She slid up the wall, keeping her weapon in a ready position, but she was pretty sure the body coming through her bedroom door would be...

The lights flipped on.

Garrison.

"What the hell do you two think you're doing?" he shouted.

Her brother looked good. Fit. Rested. The normal

twinkle in his eye contradicted his words. So did his arms that were spread wide waiting for her to enter them. She stayed put.

"I could have shot you." Jesse's voice came from directly behind her twin.

"I should shoot you," Garrison retorted. "What are you thinking dragging my sister into this mess?"

"Me? Drag? You need to get your facts straight."

"Guys." She tried to interrupt.

"I know what I'm talking about. I've been fully briefed in spite of your efforts to prevent it." Garrison's fingers rested through his belt loops. He looked at ease, not worried about a thing—at least at first glance. All of his body language had changed as soon as he laid eyes on Jesse.

"Guys," she tried again. It reminded her of the summer she'd been invisible. No matter what she did, she couldn't get the attention of either of the boys. She'd even pretended to drown in the swimming pool. They'd both gone on with their horsing around while the lifeguard rescued her.

"If you knew your sister, you'd have figured out a long time ago that no one drags her anywhere. You've been practically on vacation for the last month."

"Vacation? I was on assignment, nearly getting my head blown—"

It might have been easier to go around them, but she shoved through, successfully separating them. She placed her weapon on top of the dresser. Jesse's was at least holstered.

She elbowed her way through again to get to the nightstand, where she'd left her phone, switching it off and cutting one of the connections. Those on the other end of the line must be laughing or seriously cursing. But they would stay where they were, hoping to salvage this mess.

Both men stared at her. "What?" she asked. "Hello, Garrison. What are you doing here? And, Jesse, you should probably have the team stand down."

She led the way out of the bedroom, pausing to turn the water off in the shower then sitting in one of the armchairs. She pressed her palms to her eyes, unable to envision anything but chaos for the next several minutes.

The attempt to block the men's arguing voices from her mind battled with the images of Snake Eyes laughing at their entire sting operation. If he was watching the house, he'd just seen her brother enter. And if he wasn't watching...well, then it had completely failed.

"Oh, would you both just hug it out or something? I need to think." She'd raised her voice. They were both looking at her strangely. "I can tell that you aren't used to me being in charge. Well, guys, I hate to break it to you, but if we're voting...mine's the only one that counts."

"Who asked for a vote?"

"What are we voting on?"

They both spoke at the same time and each poked the other in the chest as if they were teens. "Enough. Seriously. We are all adults and we have a rather difficult problem to solve."

"There's no discussion. You're heading to the house where they're guarding Kenderly." Garrison sat closest to her on the couch. "I'm here to take care of this problem."

"You aren't in charge, pal." Jesse propped the shotgun along the wall and took a seat. He reached for her hand.

What was that supposed to be? A statement of comfort between them or a statement that Garrison didn't have any say over her but Jesse did? *Unreal.*

"Both of you need to shut up and listen."

Surprisingly, they both relaxed against the cushions, waiting. It took a couple of seconds for her to decide where to start. It was with her twin and his tendency to sweep in and come to her rescue.

"I outgrew you bossing me around about ten years ago. You missed it. I let you because I enjoyed hanging around the two of you. I followed after you like a bad habit I refused to kick."

"You don't have to do this tonight, Avery." Jesse had a cautious look that she understood, but ignored.

"Garrison, you haven't explained why you stuck your nose in here during the middle of the night. You probably blew our sting." She popped out of the armchair, adrenaline pumping hard through her veins. "I'm sure you convinced yourself that leaving your protective detail was necessary in order to protect me, but you're wrong."

Exploding like this felt a little freeing. She was ready to bang some heads together, but kept her cool.

"You're overreacting, Avery."

Her brother didn't get it. Until that very minute she hadn't completely understood what living apart from the important people in her life had taught her. Somewhere between the boring, mundane speeding tickets and flat tires she had become an adult. She was capable of making decisions and living on her own.

"I don't need your help, Garrison. Do. Not. Need. Your. Help. Brand it across your forehead or simply repeat after me... 'Avery does *not* need my help.' Can you hear me this time? You've made a very big mistake coming here."

"You might be right about that," her brother mumbled.

"Oh, I know I am. Why would you put this operation at risk? Not to mention that one of your ranger friends could have mistakenly killed you."

"I thought you could use some help, but I needed to eliminate any threat against Kenderly, too." Garrison folded his hands together in his lap, tilting his eyes to the floor.

"Aw...the fiancée we've heard nothing about. If Snake Eyes is watching, he saw you. The whole thing's a bust. Your entire hero routine is for nothing."

Garrison popped his head up to stare at her. She shoved his shoulders back to the couch when he tried to stand. He could stay put; she was the one who needed to move around.

"You know there's more to why I'm here." Garrison's knuckles turned white gripping a throw pillow. "I got you into this mess. It's my responsibility. I'm not going to let you face it alone."

"I'm not. Jesse's here. An entire team of Texas Rangers is across the street. Someday you're going to have to have faith that I'm capable of doing my job."

"Faith has nothing to do with it. I know you're capable, but this wasn't—or shouldn't be—your fight. I didn't jeopardize the operation. Nobody saw me come in here. Nobody. Which in itself is a problem."

"It's part of the trap. Oh, I give up." She turned away, staring out the window.

"Man, you haven't faced this son of a bitch. He's a ghost with connections. We didn't make it a secret we were here waiting on him." Jesse acted relaxed, but his jaw muscles flexed continuously. "That was the plan."

"I guess I sort of messed things up," Garrison admitted.

"I bet that hurt to admit." Jesse snickered behind her. "You knew I was here taking care of things. You could have at least trusted me."

Had he forgotten his role in this debacle? Or that he'd lied to her all those months? She'd barely been angry with him, but suddenly the whole situation seemed to irritate her again.

"You aren't innocent in all this, Jesse Thomas Ryder. Your decisions changed my life last year. Just because we've slept together, that doesn't give you the right to make decisions for me. Or try to talk me out of doing my duty as a cop. This is who I am as much as you. Especially after the week we spent together." She blurted the words, then cringed, realizing that Garrison was still in the room. Well, it didn't matter. She turned to address both of the men in her life. "I am perfectly capable of making my own decisions. You two need to…to just… grow up."

Before her brother or Jesse could react, she bolted from the room. She couldn't referee their arguments or face what they might say about her love life. And she couldn't hang around any longer just waiting for something to happen.

Leave the investigation and manhunt to the competent Texas Rangers. She'd left her own department shorthanded long enough. It was time to go home. She returned to the bedroom, locked the door and dialed Major Parker.

Chapter Twenty-Two

Jesse watched Avery retreat to the bedroom. He wanted to go after her, but she was already upset with him sticking his opinion into her life. He didn't know he'd stood until Garrison's blow knocked him to the couch.

"You slept with my sister!"

Jesse rubbed his jaw. "I probably deserved that from her brother. And because I did, I'm not getting up to pound your face."

"You swore to me," the man who was like his brother whispered. "When? Last year? Is that what she meant about changing her life? Have you been lying to me for a year?"

"You have to calm down, Garrison. We have bigger catfish to fry."

"Dammit, Jesse. I came as soon as I heard what was going on. They should have told me sooner." He crashed back to the couch looking very defeated and speaking softly. "How could you do this to her? Now she'll never come home from the Panhandle."

"Don't let her hear you say that. You haven't spoken to her about her job or her life since she left. So don't blame me for what's going on between you guys." He'd accept the blame. He just wouldn't admit that to anyone but Avery. That was between him and her.

"You slept with her, man."

"It's not what you think."

Jesse's lifelong friend jumped up and paced the inside wall, obviously shaken by Avery's revelation. "I don't see how it could be much different unless you tell me it didn't happen."

"I can't do that. It happened, and if I have my way, it'll happen again." Jesse slumped in his chair, matching Garrison's dismayed attitude look for look. "I know I broke my promise to you. But like I said. It's not what you think. I'm trying to keep a promise to myself. And if she'll have me, one to Avery. I told her I loved her."

"You mean that? So you two are getting married." His best friend looked surprised.

Why? Was it so hard to believe that someone would fall in love with his sister? Or was it that Jesse Ryder had fallen for her?

"She accused me of kidding around." Resulting in the longest three days of his life.

"But you meant it? You weren't joking? You're really in love with Avery?" He glared down from above his chair. "So why didn't you just set her straight?"

"You seriously don't know your sister." Jesse shook his head, wondering how long he had to put up with the Garrison grilling. And when the roller coaster of up-and-down emotions would end. "She never gave me a chance to say it was for real. We haven't had much of a chance to talk since then. Well, we've been a little busy."

"I see."

Jesse looked at his friend, who shouldn't have a clue. The charmer who could talk his way out of every situation had nothing more to say? Maybe he did understand. They hadn't spoken more than a couple of sentences in the time that he claimed to have fallen in love.

Jesse looked around the dark room, wondering not only what to say but what would go wrong next. "Dammit, the phone. The team is still listening to this."

He leaped to where he'd left the cell a few feet away. The conversation was one way, but he knew they were there. The guys who would use his confession to razz him for the rest of his career. They'd never let him live this down.

As soon as he disconnected, it vibrated.

"I stuck my neck out for you," Parker said. "Can you explain why one Travis is there instead of at a safe house under protective custody? And the other Travis just notified me she's returning to Dalhart?"

"The first Travis can answer for himself. I'll find out what's up with Avery." He handed the phone over to Garrison and in two shakes was knocking on the bedroom door.

"Avery, we need to talk." He couldn't hear anything on the other side of the door. Had she already slipped by him to leave through the back? She was too smart to leave on her own and had already requested an escort from Parker. "Avery? Open the door."

Training kicked in. He didn't think, just trusted his instincts that something was wrong. Gun in hand, his boot was on the door handle busting through. He felt Garrison behind him, hand on his shoulder, tapping him forward.

They'd practiced the entry hundreds of times over the years. This time meant everything. And there was nothing there.

No Avery. No weapon. No bag on top of the dresser.

And no cell.

"Call Parker. Snake Eyes is out there."

"You don't know that, man." Garrison argued, but holstered his SIG and swiped numbers on the phone.

"She's gone and the bastard has her because Parker doesn't."

"The patrol may not have— No, you're right. He has to have her."

Jesse had to think fast. Snake Eyes would. He'd leave the talking and explanations to Garrison. Forensics would be too late and they wouldn't find anything. So he left through the yard.

The guards were out cold, drugged but alive. It was doubtful they'd seen anything. And if they had, it would be too late by the time they woke up.

"Why take her? Why not just kill her here? He doesn't need her. He should have known that Garrison was in the next room." Jesse weighed one side then the other. He and Avery had made more progress when they approached from the view of Snake Eyes, but he couldn't find a logical reason for the man's actions.

Their adversary had taken an unpredictable road. That was the rub. They thought Snake Eyes was obsessed with completing this job. So why was Garrison still alive?

It was no longer about the Tenoreno contract. Now it was about the woman he loved.

"Avery!" he shouted, his voice carrying into the dark. "Avery!"

Chapter Twenty-Three

Avery had walked straight into his arms, seeking a protective escort. Straight from the men she loved most in life to the animal who scared the life from her.

"Avery!" Jesse's voice called in the distance. "Avery!"

"Keep walking, Deputy Travis."

It was one of the oldest tricks in the book. "You took out one of the guards and dressed in his shirt. I practically tripped over you coming out of the house."

As the ranger posted on the west side of the house, he'd grunted, had a hand on her weapon and turned to stare at her with those reptile contacts. Then he'd dropped her phone. Never appearing in a hurry or as if he was worried about a thing. Especially a bunch of Texas Rangers following his trail.

Hooded, he pointed for her to lead the way between houses with no fences. Old neighborhoods that didn't fear the people who lived next door. Three streets behind her, she'd left the new edition of unfinished rooms where they'd set their trap.

But it was the middle of the night and everyone was asleep. She'd been warned first thing that if she cried out for help, whoever answered that plea would be shot with her gun.

"You're fascinating, Avery. And smart. Probably smart enough to know that you don't have long to live." Snake Eyes found an entrance gate from the utility-access path between the homes. "Your problem isn't that you aren't good enough to bring me down. It's that all the people surrounding you aren't as good. The best defense is usually the best offense. Don't you agree?"

"If we'd known where to take the fight, you're right— we would have taken it to you."

"I'm very glad to learn you've suffered no ill effects from the shocking experience in Thompson Grove."

"I turn on lightbulbs when I hold them now, but everybody thinks it's a good party trick."

"Aw, a sense of humor about your misadventure. As charming as your brother."

Avery felt sick to her stomach. The question of why he hadn't just burst into the house and killed them all as they were arguing still loomed as bright as that bulb she nervously joked about. Then he used the words *fascinating* and *glad* and *charming*. Yeah, she was getting sick at the thought he liked her.

For a man who'd never left behind a trace of himself, it bothered her that he was pushing through gates and lifting latches as if no one would be following them.

It bothered her a lot. Even after hearing Jesse shout her name into the night, Snake Eyes hadn't run or even walked faster. *He doesn't think anyone can catch him.*

The road they were on had no street lamps. The houses were farther apart. He shoved her into the side of a luxury car. *I can't get inside that car.*

The thought that it was all over if she did was all she could focus on. The thought repeated over and over in her mind. He had a gun and the knife he'd placed to her throat before. But she turned from the car, hands in a single fist, and hit him in the side where Jesse had stabbed the rake. He hissed in pain.

She prepared for his backhanded slap, rolling with the sting but losing a lot of the force behind it. She spun away from Snake Eyes, dropping to the ground, searching for a stick or rock. Hoping for a piece of glass. Nothing but dirt.

The reptile contacts glowed brighter with him surrounded by the dark.

Dirt. She dug her nails into the earth, coming up with a fistful when he lifted her to her feet.

"I would expect nothing less from you, Avery. If you didn't give me your best, I wouldn't be compelled to try my worst. But I've brought you an incentive to behave."

"There's nothing that's going to make me get in that car easily. I'm surprised you haven't used your knockout drug."

He opened the door to where a young woman sat. Her eyes were wide with fright, makeup smeared from crying a long time. She was gagged and both her hands and feet were bound.

"You see, Avery? Incentive."

"This doesn't involve her."

The woman tried to scream as he shut the door and clicked a lock. She was hysterical, thinking that Snake Eyes intended to kill her. Avery knew, too. It was a one-way ticket if she got in that car.

"Well, she has kept her part of the bargain. She did give me the address where you were staying. I could let her go if you promised to cooperate." Snake Eyes gestured for her to get into the car.

Avery shook her head. "Not...not until you let her

out. Leave her on the street just like she is…but she's left here. Then I'll go with you."

"Deal, Deputy." He pointed her weapon at her again. "Now give me your word."

"Why do you need me to promise?"

"I trust you, Avery." He cocked his head to the side, waiting for her answer.

Avery shoved her hand with the dirt into her pocket. If she gave him a face full of dirt now, the car was locked and she wouldn't get the keys before he reacted. She could wait until the door was open, but the woman was so hysterical she might think they were taking her into the trees to kill her.

Unfortunately, the best scenario was to get the woman out and wait for a chance to get away.

"I promise, on my father's grave…" …*that I will take you down tonight or die trying.*

"Good. Good." He opened the door again, grabbed the woman's ropes and yanked her from the car. He pulled her across the grass, gun pointed first at the woman, then at Avery.

To her credit, the woman didn't make it easy. She tried to be difficult, bucking with muffled screaming. Avery got halfway into the car, waiting to see if the gun fell away from her direction so she could run.

Snake Eyes didn't drop her from his aim. He moved the girl behind some bushes and left her there, then came back to Avery. He took plastic cuffs from his pocket and tightened them around her wrists. She sat and he placed another pair around her ankles after removing her boots.

Then he laughed, throwing back his head. As he did, she finagled a boot to slip to the ground. The door shut and she prayed that her father was keeping an eye on her tonight.

Jesse would find it. He'd find her. They'd get out of this mess. There had to be a way out.

IT HAD BEEN almost ten minutes when Jesse pulled onto the third street. The surveillance team agreed that Snake Eyes had to be on foot. Garrison had taken the north streets and Jesse headed south. Back and forth along the streets, one extra block either direction. The team was out beyond the first three blocks.

One more turn and he'd have to admit defeat. How had Snake Eyes got her cooperation? It didn't make—

A boot was next to the curb. He cut the engine of the motorcycle to pick it up, taking a close look at the darkened homes along the unlit sidewalk.

"Help!"

It was a muffled "help," but still a cry for help. He came off the bike so fast it toppled to its side. He hurdled a shrub, nearly landing on a woman. He knelt, removing the gag.

"Please help me. He's crazy. I think…I think he's going to kill her."

Jesse didn't have to ask who. Avery's boot on the side of the road told him she had got inside the car. He dialed Parker, giving him the address. Then Garrison.

"He's got her, buddy. Meet me three blocks my direction. Can't miss me."

"I'm Texas Ranger Jesse Ryder, ma'am. What's your name?"

"Um… Cindy Crouch. He had pictures of my little boy and said if I didn't find the address for him that he'd… He said horrible things. I brought it to him and then he drugged me."

"You're very lucky to be alive." Those were the wrong words. She'd been coherent before. Now she was just hysterically crying. "It'll be okay. Help's on its way."

"You. You might…catch them," she managed to say between gulps of air. "I'm okay. Go."

"Can you describe the vehicle?" He propped her up against a tree.

"Black Lexus, tinted windows, Texas tags KWX198."

"You're sure about that?"

"I took a good look when he moved me over here. I… She only got in that car to save me." Cindy began crying again.

"Give them the car's description first. You can save her." Jesse started the bike as cars rushed up behind him. He didn't stay for a plan to be developed.

His only hope was that Snake Eyes would be driving the speed limit so as not to draw attention to himself. There was one way out of the subdivision. Two directions from there.

"Garrison, I'm hitting the main road and taking it west. You've got east. Black Lexus, dark windows, KWX189. We have to find her."

"Taking it east and we will, man. We will."

He put the phone away and sped up. He had a fifty-fifty chance Snake Eyes was heading west. The open fields seemed to fit what they knew about him when he killed. He took the hill, searching for taillights.

Nothing.

Remember that this bastard is smart. He might have turned off the lights. If he did…he'd be going slower.

There wasn't a moon, no way to naturally light up the two-lane road.

Jesse would find him. There was no way Snake Eyes would be terrorizing anyone else.

THEY WERE OUT of the subdivision. Snake Eyes was humming under his hood. It wasn't a song that Avery recognized. Why did it matter? It didn't. Another distraction. Good for her because he was less likely to hear her popping the plastic cuffs against the seat next to her.

For the past eight months, nights off meant cable television or studying on the internet. She'd decided to test the plastic handcuffs normally used with riots. If you hit them hard enough, they'd break. Just like the instruction video had suggested.

The humming wouldn't cover the noise. She had to wait or he'd have the gun back in her face.

"Why me? I thought Tenoreno hired you to take care of the witnesses to his wife's murder." Avery wanted to see his face, wanted to rip the contacts out of his eyes and make him normal.

"I have special plans for you, Avery. I think you and Snake Eyes are going to have hours of fun together."

That was *not* normal. Her imagination didn't need a lot of help figuring out what this awful man meant. "Wait. Aren't *you* Snake Eyes?"

"There is a little bit of him in all of us, I suppose."

"All of you? If you aren't him, then who are you?" This was freakier than anything she'd had to deal with throughout her career. This was the same man she and Jesse had faced in Dalhart. He had the wounds proving it.

"I wouldn't be a good associate if I gave my name to you so easily."

"Then maybe you can explain why Snake Eyes wants me? Why is he fascinated with me?" She could see around the front headrest and noticed that the lights were off. There was no one around for miles.

"I see you inching toward the middle of the car. Please move toward the door."

Avery replayed the man's voice in her head. It had the slightest British accent. A different cadence in the phrasing. If she didn't know that the same man who put her in the car was still driving it, she might have thought a second had been waiting to drive them away.

There was just one man. Snake Eyes, the murderer.

"We never got to finish phase two of my project with you and Jesse. I'm afraid you took me by surprise by escaping the collar. And I'm afraid that Scott was just too useless. The other two young men, well… They were fine with setting the fires for the right amount of money. But when it came to abducting a deputy sheriff and a Texas Ranger… Let's just say I won the argument."

That sounded just like the man behind the hood.

"Phase two?"

"That's right. I never got to explain it." He slapped his thigh and hummed his tune. He wasn't going to give her any extra time to think her way out of his plan by giving her a warning.

Avery heard the motorcycle. Seconds later, Snake Eyes turned off the road. She wasn't certain he knew where he was, but she could tell it was unplanned by the way he looked around the field. It was easy enough to decipher that even if it wasn't Jesse, he didn't want the car he was driving spotted.

It was her last chance at getting help.

She twisted her body and grabbed the dirt in her pockets, then hit the cuffs against the seat. Then hit them again.

Snake Eyes swerved enough that the tires fell off the smoother ruts of the dirt road. She hit the seat and pulled, breaking the cuffs from her wrists. Her captor stepped on the gas, throwing her to the side. Her feet were behind him, so she kicked while he swerved.

When he turned to see what she was doing, she threw the dirt in his face.

He stomped on the brakes and threw the car in Park. The gun must have slid away from him, because he began searching around his legs. While his body was bent, she climbed on top of him and honked the horn.

Short. Short. Short. Long. Long. Long. Short. Short. Short.

Short. Short.

Snake Eyes stuck the gun against her jawbone. "Valiant effort, Avery. Too bad no one can hear you."

She raised her hands and sat on the smooth leather seat.

"Out of the car. Do it. Now." He popped the trunk.

Her first thought was that he was going to put her inside. She could break a taillight, get someone's attention. Then she saw the wire, the duct tape, the vials of drugs. And just as a chef unrolled his knives before he began cooking, Snake Eyes displayed his instruments of death.

Chapter Twenty-Four

The horn had been faint at seventy miles an hour on a motorcycle. Jesse almost ignored it. Then he came to a skidding stop and knew the SOS was Avery and did a U-turn.

Leaving the bike on the side of the road, he used Avery's shotgun to hold the barbwire fence away from his face as she went through. On the other side, he sent a text to Garrison and Parker, then switched his cell to silent mode before stuffing it in his jeans pocket. He watched the dirt road, listened without hearing anything—even bugs.

On the next rise he got low to the ground and shoved his way behind a pile of dry brush and dead branches. He could see the black car's silhouette, along with Avery.

Snake Eyes had her on her knees and was wrapping something around her neck. She wasn't attempting to get away or struggling. He bent and yanked her head backward, then connected whatever was around her neck to her hands. She cried out in surprised pain.

Whatever the madman had planned to do with Avery when he casually left the subdivision, it was clear that things had changed. Snake Eyes paced the length of the car, hitting his forehead, clearly shaken by whatever had given Avery the opportunity to sound the horn.

He walked to the trunk. The light reflected off a slew of knives neatly laid out in rows. Jesse had to get to Avery fast. Her captor had changed. He was no longer cool and collected, and his hands shook with such force Jesse could see them.

Snake Eyes fingered several knives before dropping the largest and walking away. Jesse began breathing a little easier, but then his target hurried to the trunk and placed the knives in order, talking to himself.

"He's nuts," Jesse mumbled.

No time to lose, Jesse backed out of the brush to approach from the front of the car. It was darker there and should give him an advantage. The closer he got, the more he heard Snake Eyes mumbling.

"Kill her now and forget your fun." He pivoted.

"But you left her new eyes at home," he answered in a different voice.

"Forget your signature—everyone will know it's you. Kill her!" He twisted his head as if listening for Jesse. Then kept up his argument.

Totally nuts.

Closer, Jesse crawled on his belly. If Snake Eyes came to this side of Avery, one blast from the shotgun and he'd be stunned for a few minutes. As luck would have it, he continued his debate with himself at the trunk. He'd lift a knife, walk in front of Avery, point it, shake his head, then return it to his stash.

Avery was in the light from the car door. Jesse could see that she was wrapped in wire. Loops around her feet stretching to her hands, multiple wraps around her hands connecting tightly to strands around her neck.

If she moved her hands or feet, she'd pull the wire into her neck. Hell, if she fell forward she might slice her neck open.

He couldn't get her free from that mess without wire cutters. He'd have to unwrap the wire by hand. And he had no time. There wouldn't be any distractions, then swooping in to pull her out.

His only choice was to remove the threat. And he had to get closer if he intended to use this shotgun to do it. At her Dalhart house, having buckshot wasn't a terrible decision. It gave Avery enough range and power inside.

Here was a different story. He might hit his target from twenty yards, but he was at least thirty or thirty-five from Avery. To his right, the car blocked everything. To his left, the only cover was well over seventy-five yards away.

Snake Eyes was sure to hear him moving through the grass and twigs before he got close enough. Opposite was the road. Pretty much flat and bare about ten yards on either side. This was his only route.

Getting to Avery would be tricky, and once there, he couldn't get her free, couldn't knock her over. She was close enough to Snake Eyes for him to slice her open or just shoot and kill her. Jesse didn't like his odds. He could save Avery by simply eliminating the target.

This was one time in his life that he wished he could just damn the consequences and head in guns blazing without thinking about it. No thinking. Avery needed him to save her. But he had to think. It was who he was.

Who he was... A planner who thought about everything too much.

Weapons... He'd take the shotgun and keep his handgun ready. Safer. Better coverage. But he'd still have to aim. If Snake Eyes kept up his monologue with the knives, Jesse would be aiming at a moving target for eight or nine more passes. He'd be hard to hit.

Position... He moved to his left for a better line of sight.

Rescue... Then what?

No choice... Take out the target so the hostage would no longer be threatened.

Execution... He inched his way through the field. He had a decent shot. He aimed. He tried to pull the trigger.

All he heard was Avery's voice telling him she wouldn't use deadly force as long as there was a chance. She would shoot to defend herself. This was why they practiced and trained...so they wouldn't think; they'd just do.

Delay... She was right. He loved her with everything and he still couldn't just shoot a man in cold blood. No matter what kind of man the target was.

With his hesitation, he'd lost opportunity.

Snake Eyes had something in his hand and quickly got behind Avery. *I can't be off six inches or I'll hit her.* "Raise your hand, you son of a—"

His body was braced. He was ready with a follow-through shot and began squeezing. But he immediately stopped when Snake Eyes snipped the wire connecting to Avery's feet.

What was the perp going to do now?

"You are quite a subject, Avery Travis," Snake Eyes said. "I haven't had many who could balance without their panic forcing me to intervene."

She continued to be perfectly still. Jesse didn't know how she was doing it. He kept his finger ready. He'd shoot before she could be hurt.

Snake Eyes forced her to her feet. She turned, refusing to get inside the car.

"You can do whatever you want. Do you understand me?" She'd raised her voice.

The words were for him. She knew—or hoped—he was there. She stepped away from her captor. One small step, then another long one before Snake Eyes realized why.

Jesse pulled the trigger, sending buckshot into the man's side.

Avery ran. Arms twisted high behind her, she ran.

Snake Eyes dropped to the ground, then half crawled, half dragged himself into the backseat.

"Jesse!"

"Over here!" They met a little off the road. "This is the fastest way to the bike."

"He's got the car. Can you…?" She stretched her neck and turned for him to help untie her. "Two guns that I know of."

Headlights bathed them in light as Snake Eyes bore down on them. If she fell, the thin wire could slice her windpipe, but they ran anyway. Jesse couldn't stop to untwist the wire yet. Up and over the slight rise. The car followed, bouncing through the uneven field, heading to cut them off.

"This way. Do you see them? He can't follow through the stacked hay bales," Avery said, sliding to her knee. She needed her hands. It was too dangerous for her to keep going like this. "We can still get to the motorcycle, can't we?"

"If he stays on the road, he'll cut us off or be waiting on us. Stop behind the hay bale for a sec. You need to be free." The shotgun dropped to his feet as he used both hands to untwist. "This thing is worse than a bread tie."

No DEBATE. JUST ACTION and keeping herself from inappropriately laughing at his analogy. Avery lifted her hands behind her as high as possible. It was a bit painful as Jesse twisted and then twisted some more. It was frightening to think of what might have happened if she'd moved before her feet had been snipped free.

Don't go there. Think about now. They were being surrounded in more light from the car. One wrist could now move.

"You have to hurry, Jesse."

"Just a couple more and we're...there. That's it."

She started to face him, but he held her in place. She felt him gathering the wire and shoving it down the back of her shirt.

"Done. Now you won't get caught. Let's go."

The wire still around her neck reminded her of the shock collar. The helplessness knowing that a sadistic monster had control of her fate. As they took the first steps, the car drew closer to them and Snake Eyes fired.

Jesse dropped to the ground, pulling her with him. He swung the shotgun around and fired the second barrel into the side of the car. Snake Eyes drove past and circled. They had seconds before he'd be able to fire at them again.

"You're going to listen to me for once, Avery. No questions."

"I'm not leaving you." She couldn't save herself while he stayed behind.

"I didn't think you would. But one of us has to get to the road and let the team know where we are." He gave her the shotgun and the phone. "Empty. But you can swing it, okay? First, climb the hay, babe. Up and over. Can you do that? Get clear on the other side and call Garrison. He's on his way. He just isn't in the right place yet."

She nodded. He was right. To a point. Snake Eyes wouldn't be looking above Jesse's head. She could take him by surprise. "Don't do anything stupid."

"Count on it. Now get out of here so I can stall him."

Jesse cupped his hands and gave her a boost high onto the bales. They were packed firmly and close together. She lay on her belly, getting ready to swing when Snake Eyes got close.

And he would get close. Even though he had the guns, he was fascinated and fixated on his knives. He was a sicko who would want to end Jesse with a blade.

"Here he comes," Jesse said below her. "Get ready to move. Please do this, Avery. For me."

Avery backed away from the edge so the headlights wouldn't shine on her. It was so dark out here that when you were out of the beam, you couldn't be seen. Snake Eyes pulled around wide.

The back of the car fishtailed across the pasture. He was going to ram Jesse and the stack of hay. The engine revved. The headlights blinded. She screamed Jesse's name, but he was already on his toes like someone playing chicken with a two-ton vehicle.

Snake Eyes didn't flinch. He shot forward. Jesse jumped out of the way at the last second. The car struck the bales, shaking her to one side. She clawed her way back to the top.

Jesse was already pulling the stunned Snake Eyes from the car. He quickly jerked away from a knife arcing toward his abdomen. Jesse continued backing away but took off his shirt and wrapped it around his forearm. It stopped the blade from slicing his skin to the bone and allowed him to get closer.

The headlights were buried in hay, creating an eerie effect. Avery jumped to the hood of the car, waiting for Snake Eyes to get closer. She had the stock of the shotgun raised and ready to hit the back of his hooded head.

Then the fight changed.

Snake Eyes locked his arms around Jesse's midsection and started moving the knife closer to his throat. He absorbed Jesse's elbow that repeatedly hit him in the side. The murderer ignored the pain he must have felt because of the shotgun blast. With his other hand, Jesse kept the knife inches away, holding it at bay.

The madman's grip around Jesse's middle had him pinned. Jesse threw his head backward, connecting with the man's nose. Then Snake Eyes spun him and shoved him into the car trunk, backing away. He pulled his mask off his head, sniffing at the blood coming from his nose.

"Avery, Avery, Avery," Snake Eyes chanted. "Here I am. Can you see me?"

She could barely make out the outline of his face. She didn't have to see his features to know the man had experienced a psychotic break. He spun around like a child watching snowflakes fall.

Jesse roared like a lion, shoving away from the car and throwing his shoulder into Snake Eyes's belly. He tackled him to the ground like a linebacker sacking a quarterback. Snake Eyes just wouldn't stay down. He fought like a crazy person who needed a straitjacket.

The glowing contacts made spotting Snake Eyes easier. A punch caught Jesse in the chin, momentarily shoot-ing him backward, but he returned with three quick jabs.

Get the guns! Avery jumped from the hood, deter-mined to find them inside the car. She could end this with a loaded weapon in her hand. Snake Eyes would be forced to stop. But when her feet hit the dirt, she caught the attention of their attacker.

He raised the knife with a maniacal cry and sliced into Jesse's uncovered arm. Jesse staggered. Snake Eyes was on her so fast she couldn't react. He shoved her back against the car, holding the knife to her throat.

"I wanted to play with you, Avery. We all did."

His rancid breath choked her after the sweet-smelling hay. The edge of the sharp blade held her where she was. She could see the dust floating in the buried lights. She would have been as crazy as Snake Eyes if she hadn't been frightened.

But she wasn't crazy. She had reason for hope. Jesse was slowly approaching.

"See the special eyes I have for you?" Snake Eyes took two rocks from his pocket and pushed her face to the hood. They were cool against her cheek where he set them.

As the blade moved from her neck to the corner of her eye, she asked, "What…what color did…did you choose for me?"

He seemed excited that she was curious. She didn't really want to know. Ever. She was trying to stall to give Jesse time. Still holding the shotgun, she wanted to club Snake Eyes with it but couldn't.

If she moved, the knife point might take out her eye. Jesse was close. She shoved the knife away from her face and kicked the shotgun to him. Snake Eyes turned to face Jesse. She rammed the crazy man in the back, causing him to stumble forward, away from her.

Jesse brought the butt of the gun straight up, hitting Snake Eyes's chin. The man lost his balance when his head snapped back. Jesse hit him again in the gut. The knife fell to the ground and Avery kicked it under the car.

Snake Eyes fell near the hay and stayed there. He didn't get up. Finally. She could no longer see the contacts that haunted her dreams.

"You didn't leave," Jesse panted between inhaling deep breaths. He shut off the car.

The world was strangely silent.

"You've got my back. I've got yours. That's the way it works." They walked toward each other.

"Next time—"

"There isn't going to be a next time."

"Point taken. But if we're ever in a...situation...try to remember I can handle the bad guy on my own." He tugged her close into the circle of his arms and kissed her quick, hard and possessive. "Your gun?"

"Should still be in the front seat."

"If he moves..."

She had the shotgun poised and ready to knock him for a loop again. "Got it covered."

Jesse found her Glock, picked up the cell from the ground and handed it to her. "Can you make sure those guys haven't missed the turn? Garrison should have been right behind me."

"Sure." With one hand she called Major Parker, who said they estimated that they were two minutes out. With the other she kept the crazy man they'd fought at gunpoint. Injured or not, she wasn't allowing him any freedom.

The Snake Eyes Killer's side was soaked red from the

buckshot, and the wound on his head had left a streak across his uncovered face. Jesse used the shirt he'd fended off the knives with to slow the man's bleeding.

She was proud of Jesse for being such a good man. She wasn't certain she would have helped the monster who had nearly killed them.

"There's more wire and tape in the trunk. Get it. We can't let him hurt anyone else."

Instead of going to the back of the car, Jesse pried the shotgun from her fingers. "Go sit down. I'll watch him."

"He deserves to be tied to where he can't move. We shouldn't have to think about him ever again." She wanted to secure him just as he'd tied her, but that wouldn't happen. Wire around his wrists should be enough. She'd make certain two rangers escorted him to the hospital and kept him handcuffed.

"He's not going to hurt anyone again. It'll be okay, Avery."

Even unconscious he was dangerous. Everyone needed to know that. "He's crazy treacherous. They need to be warned."

"Yeah, babe. We know. He's not going anywhere while I'm watching him. I promise, he's still out cold. Let me get this off of you." He twisted the knots of wire from her neck and dropped it on the ground. Then tipped his head toward the road.

Multiple vehicles were turning, and leading them all was a lone motorcycle. She had a few seconds at most. There was no telling how long it would be before they were alone again. There'd be statements and debriefings and whatever else the state needed for their case.

"Jesse, I just want to say that— Well, you know I'm

grateful. Thanks for finding me. I couldn't have gotten out of this one."

"Sure you would have, Avery. You were always smarter than him." He tucked her into the fold of his arm and kissed her forehead.

This man was everything she'd ever wanted. When was he going to realize they needed each other? More and more of the team arrived, shining headlights and flashlights on them and the scene. They suggested they sit in a car, offered them first aid and asked them to move away from Snake Eyes. But they didn't.

They stood with their arms around each other, sort of in a daze. She didn't know about Jesse, but she didn't really hear what they were saying. She took a bottle of water, and Garrison pried her free when the second ambulance arrived.

The guys said it was shock. The logical side of her agreed they were right. The emotional side of her watched Jesse from the gurney. There was no going back to the way things were before. They'd reached a turning point.

It was over. Everything was over.

Chapter Twenty-Five

The last time Avery had sat at a picnic table, both she and Jesse were barefoot. She'd had a shock collar around her neck. And she was wondering if they'd really get away from Thompson Grove alive.

No one had found her boots. Just an everyday pair she didn't mind replacing. Jesse's had been found on the feet of Scott Sutter. He didn't take them from the young dead man. Horrible to think no one took responsibility for him. They hadn't found any family yet.

"Enough about that." She checked her watch one more time. "He is late. So late."

She saw the white hat before anything else. Her heart literally skipped a beat in anticipation. But it wasn't Jesse. Her brother had been in the building and now was heading toward her.

"Clearly you don't need me coming to your rescue any longer. Looks like you can take care of yourself," Garrison admitted.

"Took you long enough to realize that *and* to find us in that field."

"I was sent for the cavalry. That takes time." He compressed his lips as if he wanted to say something.

"Where have they been hiding you?"

"I can't say, for obvious reasons. And they'll move Kenderly soon anyway. But it wasn't far from where they set up your sting. That's how I got there before they really knew I was gone."

"Makes sense."

Garrison pulled her close, squeezing her in a bear hug. "Avery," he whispered. "I'll always come to help whether you can fend for yourself or you find someone to help with that job. You're my sister. You'll always be my sister. I just came because I love you and would never forgive myself if something happened to you."

"I love you, too. And that's exactly how I felt when you were in trouble." She let him go and he stood protectively with his arm around her for a few seconds, gave her another squeeze and moved.

More men—rangers in white hats—walked to a car in the lot. "I've got to go."

"Sure."

"He's a good man." Garrison walked backward, pointing at her. "You need to give him a chance."

"What are you talking about?" But she knew. Jesse must have said something to him.

Blurting out that they'd slept together had put Jesse in an awkward position. And regarding her sex life, her brother treated her like an old-fashioned overprotective father would. Of course, he wanted them to get together.

Well, he'd get over it.

Now that she knew she was good enough to be a Texas Ranger—that she'd almost been one—it was a little awkward sitting in the park behind the headquarters for Company F. But she was over it. Dalhart might be on the edge of Texas—almost New Mexico, almost Oklahoma—but it was where she belonged.

Her home and friends were there. All but one of them...

Jesse walked up with a picnic basket. Officially in his white hat, his white shirt, jeans, new boots and his badge hanging over his heart.

"Thanks for having lunch with me before you head home to Dallam County."

"The least I could do for the man who saved my life. How's your arm?"

"Good. Stitches. They said there would be a scar."

He'd always have a reminder from that crazy night and crazy man.

"So I guess I'll see you again when it's time for Buster 'Snake Eyes' Hopkins to go on trial. It might be a long time. It seems he's gone pretty crazy." She tucked her bangs under a Stetson her mom had given her.

"Nice hat." He unpacked sandwiches in plastic bags, homemade potato salad.

Recognizing his mother's handiwork, her mouth watered a little for the picnic dessert... Yes, there they were—two individual servings. "It's been ages since I had your mom's banana pudding."

"She made a batch this morning. One of the reasons I'm late."

Avery helped him with the rest of his mother's basket supplies. An official picnic with cutlery, plates, wineglasses...and food.

"The hat was Dad's. It's a little big."

"Doesn't look like you'll have trouble fitting it. I think he'd be real proud of you, Deputy Travis."

"And of you, Ranger Ryder." She took a bite of the pimento-cheese sandwich...also her favorite. Then waited while he poured the fruity wine she liked. In fact, everything on the table was her favorite. "What's going on, Jesse?"

"Just trying to be nice."

"Are you forming words in your head? Looking for the right way to say something?"

"No. Why don't you go ahead and eat. You'll have plenty of time to get to the airport."

The situation made her a little tense. They could have stopped anywhere and grabbed a burger. He'd gone to a lot of trouble to make sure she had a pleasant picnic that included her favorite plain ruffled potato chips.

"I was about to say that I think my father would have been proud of you and Garrison."

"Are you still upset that you don't work here?" he asked.

"Not anymore."

"Still upset with me or am I forgiven?"

"We're friends for life, Jesse. I was mad for that long." She held her finger and thumb about an inch apart. "I was never going to stay that way. Eat. I'll need to get on the road soon."

His eyebrows rose, ready to ask her something. She responded with all her attention while raising a wineglass to her lips.

"Did you consider taking a later flight? I know your mom would like you to hang around awhile."

"Sorry, I have to get going. The guys have been covering for me long enough. I got a text from Bo that he needs a night out."

"Yeah. That makes sense. You need to work."

"Jesse, what is the matter with you?"

"I just thought we might have a stress-free evening together."

"No can do, my friend." She was really hoping that she'd pulled off the whole friendship thing. No matter what happened between them, she wanted to stay on good-enough terms to talk to each other.

After Garrison told her that he'd met *the one*, it looked as though she and Jesse would be standing up for them. Garrison said they'd be getting married as soon as the trial was over.

The first trial date for Tenoreno to face a jury was in September. So that meant she had to remain all friendly smiles and shoulder punches with Jesse through at least October or November.

The truth was, she didn't want to say goodbye to Jesse. Leaving before had been completely different... They weren't speaking. This time, would he call or text or message her? What would it be like to be his friend after sleeping with him?

Food finished, she put the last chip in her mouth and crunched to get Jesse's attention. He was staring off toward the football stadium. Working up his courage?

Talking himself out of something was more likely. She could see the cogs turning one by one.

"Avery, I wanted to ask... I mean, we never got a chance to hang out and catch up."

Brilliant man, but would he ever learn to just say what he was feeling? *Probably not.*

Hypocrite.

"There's no catching up necessary. Hey, that looks like my ride." She moved to his side of the table and awkwardly hugged him.

"I thought I was taking you."

"Sorry again. Mom and Aunt Brenda asked and I couldn't say no. Like you said, they hardly got to see me."

"But you didn't finish. What about your pudding?" He grabbed the bowl.

"Thanks. Tell your mom I'll return the container next trip home." She took hold of the container and he pulled her hand, forcing her to stumble a little toward him.

Jesse met her halfway, wrapping her in his arms, smashing his lips to hers. Their kiss sent shivers throughout her body to all the right exciting places. And the second, then the third did the same.

If he kept kissing her like this, he didn't have to say anything at all.

"I've got to go."

"I wish you wouldn't."

"It can't be helped." She backed away, tripping on an oak root but catching herself before landing a face-plant in the dirt. He tipped his hat, acknowledging that she was leaving. She couldn't stand the sadness that crept into her heart. So she ran to her mom's car.

"My goodness, Avery. My, my, my," her aunt said.

"How long has that been going on? I thought you were upset with Jesse before this little episode," her mom lectured a bit.

How her mother could categorize two attempted murders on her daughter as a *little episode* was probably how she dealt with both her children serving in law enforcement. Someday it would be a bump of excitement that happened way back when. When the trial was over, she might tell her mother everything that had happened.

"I was a little," she mumbled as the car pulled away and Jesse picked up their lunch. "And I wasn't upset very long."

"Why in the world did he kiss you like that?" the sisters said sort of together.

"Because I…I'm pretty sure he was about to ask me to marry him."

Chapter Twenty-Six

Three weeks later

The ring in Jesse's pocket had been on the tip of his finger so many times, it would have stretched if that had been physically possible. He fingered it constantly. Every time he'd spoken with Avery on the phone, he pulled it out to look at it.

Proposing had been on his mind for a long time. Now it seemed possible.

This was it. He pulled up in front of the tiny house, heart and hat in hand. Either a final chapter or the start of the rest of his life.

"Hey there." Avery sat on the porch. Cutoff jean shorts, black spaghetti straps across her shoulders, black hat on the crown of her head and a shotgun next to her hip. "You're late."

"Hit some construction north of Fort Worth."

"Everybody good at home?" she asked, extending him a beer.

He took it, nodded yes to her question and tapped the bottle neck against hers. "Nice shotgun."

"Saved my life once."

She'd taken him off guard again. All he could think

about were the long legs wrapped around him instead of resting on the top of those steps. And the top she had on had one of those built-in bra things, so it wasn't much of a challenge.

They'd been talking. For hours. They'd known each other their entire lives but still found something else to say. Standing here in front of her, with the most important question clearly ready to be asked, he couldn't figure out how.

"Bo called. Said you were speeding at the edge of town."

"That the reason you have the shotgun ready?"

"Just a reminder. I bring it out with me most days I'm here." Avery traced the initials they'd carved. "I feel Dad's comfort when it's by my side. And I can't help remembering the last time it was used."

Their years of history, their shared experiences—awkward, good, bad or frightening—were something he never wanted to give up. The first and last images of when he'd held the gun flashed in front of his eyes. "I've only been frightened like that one other time in my life. When you pretty much died in my arms."

"You haven't really talked about that or given me details."

Jesse pulled her to her feet. "Promise you won't do that again, Avery."

"I can't. If you're around I hope to die a little in your arms every night."

"That, I think I can live with." He caught a glimpse of the shotgun.

It was sort of like getting permission from Avery's dad. He pulled the ring from his pocket, keeping it in his fist. No box. No flowers. No bended knee. No prepared, memorized words. No special dinner at the closed diner that evening that he'd arranged.

They weren't anywhere special as their parents had advised.

"Avery, I love you. You're a smart woman and I'm sure you've figured that out by now. What you might not know is that there's never been anyone else for me. Life is just better with you in it. Might not have seemed that way when I came here before, but we're better as a team. Always have been."

"I—"

"Hold on. Before you tell me it's a logistical nightmare to have a relationship. I got a transfer to a special unit, so that won't be as much of a problem. I've told you this plenty of times in the last three weeks, but I wouldn't think of asking you to leave the sheriff's department. You're good at your job. They deserve you. No, I'm serious. As long as you like it here, you should stay."

"Jesse—"

"You gotta let me get this out, babe. Would you marry me and put me out of my misery?" He unfolded his fingers, producing the ring.

"If you'd stop talking long enough for me to say yes."

Hands shaking like a dog after a dip in a swimming hole, he slid the ring into place, staring at the smile in her eyes.

Kissing Avery was just about everything to him. Someday he might need more, like a kid or two, but he was whole with her. "You did say yes. Right?"

"I did."

His hands were still shaking. She took them into hers, steadying him. "I have this thing all planned for tonight.

You'll have to act surprised or something. Otherwise, you're going to disappoint the diner folks or your friends."

"I can do that. For such a smart man, it sure took you long enough to figure out I've been in love with you my whole life." She admired the simple ring. "Is this…? It can't be the same one. You went back and found the ring I saw at that antique shop in Austin?"

"I…um…I didn't have to go back."

"But that was— Jesse, that was two years ago."

"Close to it."

He could kiss on her all day. Right there on the porch, learning every possible way to hold her. But there were also more private holds he was ready to discover. He skimmed his hands up her arms, surrounding her delicate yet capable fingers with his, then moved a step toward the door.

Avery stopped him. "That was a beautiful speech. Did it take you the entire drive up here to think it all out?"

"Straight from the heart, babe. I saw your daddy's shotgun and forgot every word in my head."

"That's all I've ever wanted…words from your heart."

"I probably need to cancel the marching band, then."

She laughed, dabbing at her eyes. Then she glanced at his face, which must have let her know he wasn't joking. "You're not serious."

"Yeah, but I can call Julie. She'll cancel."

She flung herself into his arms, knocking their hats to the porch. "Oh no you don't. Words and a ring are great—don't get me wrong. But a marching band? All for me? I'll take it." She kissed him, smiling so bright he was certain she was happy. "I'll also take you."

* * * * *

MILLS & BOON®

INTRIGUE
Romantic Suspense

A SEDUCTIVE COMBINATION OF DANGER AND DESIRE

A sneak peek at next month's titles...

In stores from 10th March 2016:

Available at WHSmith, Tesco, Asda, Eason, Amazon and Apple

Just can't wait?
Buy our books online a month before they hit the shops!
visit www.millsandboon.co.uk

These books are also available in eBook format!

MILLS & BOON®

Why not subscribe?
Never miss a title and save money too!

Here's what's available to you if you join the exclusive **Mills & Boon® Book Club** today:

✦ *Titles up to a month ahead of the shops*
✦ *Amazing discounts*
✦ *Free P&P*
✦ *Earn Bonus Book points that can be redeemed against other titles and gifts*
✦ *Choose from monthly or pre-paid plans*

Still want more?
Well, if you join today, we'll even give you
50% OFF your first parcel!

So visit **www.millsandboon.co.uk/subs**
to be a part of this exclusive Book Club!

MILLS & BOON®

Why shop at millsandboon.co.uk?

Each year, thousands of romance readers find their perfect read at millsandboon.co.uk. That's because we're passionate about bringing you the very best romantic fiction. Here are some of the advantages of shopping at www.millsandboon.co.uk:

* **Get new books first**—you'll be able to buy your favourite books one month before they hit the shops

* **Get exclusive discounts**—you'll also be able to buy our specially created monthly collections, with up to 50% off the RRP

* **Find your favourite authors**—latest news, interviews and new releases for all your favourite authors and series on our website, plus ideas for what to try next

* **Join in**—once you've bought your favourite books, don't forget to register with us to rate, review and join in the discussions

Visit **www.millsandboon.co.uk**
for all this and more today!